Nicole Helm grew up [with] dream of one day becom[ing] failed career choices, she gets to follow that dream—writing down-to-earth contemporary romance and romantic suspense. From farmers to cowboys, Midwest to *the* West, Nicole writes stories about people finding themselves and finding love in the process. She lives in Missouri with her husband and two sons, and dreams of someday owning a barn.

Juno Rushdan is a veteran US Air Force intelligence officer and award-winning author. Her books are action-packed and fast-paced. Critics from *Kirkus Reviews* and *Library Journal* have called her work 'heart-pounding James Bond-ian adventure' that 'will captivate lovers of romantic thrillers.' For a free book, visit her website: junorushdan.com

CLANDESTINE BABY

NICOLE HELM

WYOMING COWBOY UNDERCOVER

JUNO RUSHDAN

MILLS & BOON

First Published in Great Britain 2023
by Mills & Boon, an imprint of HarperCollins*Publishers* Ltd
1 London Bridge Street, London, SE1 9GF

www.harpercollins.co.uk

HarperCollins*Publishers*
Macken House, 39/40 Mayor Street Upper,
Dublin 1, D01 C9W8, Ireland

Clandestine Baby © 2023 Nicole Helm
Wyoming Cowboy Undercover © 2023 Juno Rushdan

ISBN: 978-0-263-30737-5

0823

CLANDESTINE BABY

NICOLE HELM

For anyone who's ever found their family
outside of the one they were born into.

Chapter One

The dog wouldn't stop barking.

Cal Thompson frowned, walking closer and closer to the incessant yelps. Considering he didn't *have* a dog, his best guess was that a stray had maybe been hit on the old country road on the ranch border and no one had stopped to help the poor creature out.

Now it would be his problem. A common occurrence in his life. Cal Young's entire life had been cleaning up other people's messes…before he'd been declared dead, had left the military and moved to this out-of-the-way ranch in the middle of nowhere, Wyoming.

This version of himself, Cal *Thompson*, was supposed to be your everyday rancher, running the old Hart place with his brothers.

The men he ran the ranch with *were* his brothers, if not biologically. They'd fought together for years, had been a team that had taken down terrorist organizations all over the Middle East. Until a clerical error of all things had made their identities known, and they'd needed to be erased.

In Cal's estimation, not much had changed. Sure, he was a rancher now, and he had a different last name, but he still cleaned up problems. They just didn't tend to be in war zones. He still considered himself a sort of de facto leader of their group—which now wasn't just his five brothers, but their various significant others, and one twelve-year-old belonging to one such significant other.

Every group/family/whatever needed a leader, and everyone tended to look to him to be it. Habit or because he was just good at it? It didn't matter. When shots needed to be called, he was usually the one calling them.

He preferred it that way.

Cal finally saw the dog. It was over the fence and in the ditch next to the highway. But it appeared to be fine as it ran toward him, then back to the ditch, over and over, as if trying to signal Cal to come closer.

Cal got the very distinct feeling he wouldn't like what the dog wanted him to see. And while he always listened to his gut, he rarely worried about what he *wanted*. He tended to focus on what needed to be done.

So he moved forward and hopped the fence, watching the big, hairy beast warily. He liked dogs well enough, but there was no telling what kind of stray this was—especially when he was practically the size of one of their horses.

But then he forgot all about the dog, because the dog was leading him to a body.

Cal hurried forward. A woman's body was lying in the ditch, motionless. Dark hair matted with dirt and, potentially, blood draped around some kind of bundle. There was a slight rise and fall of the chest, so the woman wasn't dead.

He supposed that was something.

The dog pranced around the woman, still barking. But it didn't growl as Cal moved closer and carefully crouched next to the woman.

"Good dog," he murmured, then very carefully rolled the woman over. Her head lolled, she didn't open her eyes, but none of that mattered.

Everything stopped. The barking. The wind. His heart.

It couldn't be.

And then the little bundle the woman's body had been shielding began to wriggle. Then wail. The dog whimpered. The breeze picked up again, and Cal's long forgotten heart began to thud against his chest once again.

It was a baby.

My baby?

He pushed that thought away, because it didn't matter. Nothing mattered. Except getting them safe. And to do that he had to somehow shove all of the emotions whirling around in his head away—far away.

He pulled his cell out of his pocket and called Henry, who he knew was out in the truck. He ignored the fact that his hands shook. "Henry, I need the truck about a mile west of the east entrance. Near the ditch of the highway." Was that his voice? Tinny and weak?

"What's up?"

"I found someone in the ditch. She's hurt. I need your help. Get Dunne if he's close. Hurry." He pressed End on the call. He shoved his phone back into his pocket and then, struggling to keep his arms from shaking, reached out and picked up the crying baby.

The bundle was still warm, whether because they hadn't been here long or because… He looked at the woman.

Norah.

Maybe it was some kind of…twin situation. Like Jessie and Quinn, who'd grown up not knowing about each other despite being identical twins. Maybe…

But he knew… He knew it was Norah, and this baby…

He looked down as the baby wailed. "Shh," he murmured, holding the child close to his chest. He reached out and put his fingers at Norah's pulse. Steady, but she was completely unconscious. There was a bloody gash on her forehead, which didn't look as new as he might have liked. How long had she been out here? Bleeding and unconscious?

He looked at the dog and tried to make sense of any of this, but there was no sense to be had.

Norah was supposed to be dead. Not a mother. Not here.

There were so many emotions battering him—hope, fear, confusion and the desperate desire to understand how—that the time actually passed quickly and Henry's truck appeared on the rise.

Reluctantly, Cal stood to wave him down, baby in his arms. The child had quieted a little, but still made odd noises that made Cal's stomach feel like leaden knots.

Henry parked and both he and Dunne hopped out.

Henry swore, Dunne said nothing. Par for the course. "Someone dump a…"

Then they both looked down at Cal's feet. Dunne immediately went into combat medic mode to assess the situation, but he paused for a moment to look up at Cal. Eyes mirroring all the shock that had slammed into Cal.

"But…"

Cal shook his head. "I don't know."

Henry swore again. "Get her in the truck?"

Dunne nodded. They worked together to pick up Norah's limp body and move her.

"It'll be too much jostling to try to get her inside. Let's lay her out in the back. Cal?"

Cal was already moving to grab a blanket out of the back of the truck. He spread it out in the bed, doing his best work one handed, with a baby cradled in the other arm.

Dunne and Henry worked in silence to place Norah carefully in the bed of the truck.

"Should we take her to the hospital?" Henry asked as

Dunne crouched over her, taking her pulse, examining her the same way he'd examine any fallen soldier in a war zone.

"Someone tried to kill her," Cal said. He didn't know that for sure, but based on everything he'd seen, what other conclusion could he draw? There'd been blood. A struggle. Maybe not in that ditch, but somewhere.

Dunne looked over at him, knowing what that meant— keep her away from places she could be traced. "I can take care of the wounds at the ranch, but the lack of consciousness worries me, and I don't know a damn thing about babies, Cal."

"Jessie does."

Dunne sighed, but then nodded. "Quickly."

Henry hurried to the driver's seat. Cal didn't have to whistle for the dog. It seemed intent on following the woman and the baby, and hopped right in behind them.

Dunne kept Norah stable, and Cal sat in the bed of the truck, a whimpering baby in his arms and a similarly whimpering dog snuggling up next to him as Henry drove them back to the ranch house.

Norah made a noise. She didn't move. It was just a kind of groan. Dunne kept his hand on her shoulder, but looked up at Cal. "I guess it might not be her. We've got identical triplets and twins running around. It could be…"

But Cal shook his head. He wished he could believe it. A twin would make more sense, but he knew. "It's Norah." He stared down at the little baby in his arms. A girl, if the pink blanket and hat were anything to go by. *Mine?* he wondered again.

He didn't know.

"She's supposed to be dead," Cal said, not sure what else to say. Not sure…of anything in the moment.

"Yeah," Dunne agreed. "But so are we."

SHE AWOKE FROM the pain of black and fear to…peace. Warmth. Something smelled vaguely familiar but she couldn't place it. She blinked her eyes open, and the pain started creeping in. Everything hurt—her body, breathing, opening her eyes. Screaming agony everywhere, but she knew she needed to wake up because…

The baby. She had to… She had to protect the baby. She managed to look around. She was lying in a bed in a spacious room. Sunlight streamed through the windows. It was spartan, but not…scary.

Still, she didn't recognize anything. She couldn't… "My baby." Her throat hurt, and her words were garbled. She couldn't remember anything…anything…except her baby. Safe. Her baby…

Why couldn't she think of a name? Her baby's name? Her name? Anything that had happened?

A woman appeared in her vision, a little bundle tucked into her arm. The baby. *Her* baby. She tried to reach out, but couldn't get her arms to move enough. Everything hurt and she had to close her eyes again.

"Your baby is just fine," the woman said. "Why don't I hold on to her until you're feeling a little stronger?"

Stronger. She definitely didn't feel strong. She wasn't sure what she felt. She tried to open her eyes again. She had to figure something out.

"Where am…" Her gaze tracked the room and stopped on a man who stood at the doorway, and she felt…something. He looked grim and forbidding, but his eyes were… Were they familiar? Did she know him?

She thought she should know him. She thought… She couldn't come up with anything. Anything besides keeping the baby safe.

Was he the man who'd done this to her? Should she…

"Norah," he said, and his voice was dark and low and she thought dimly she should be scared, but she was desperate for him to say more.

She thought that must be the name of the woman holding the baby, but he was looking at her. Was that her name?

She couldn't remember.

"I don't understand." Anything. *Anything.*

The woman sat in a chair next to the bed, giving her a good view of the baby. "I'm Jessie," she said, calmly and soothingly. "What's your little one's name?"

She looked into the baby's blue eyes, and the baby smiled at her. Her heart filled with a joy she didn't understand. But no name came to mind. "I don't know," she whispered.

The Jessie woman flicked a glance to the man at the door. He nodded and disappeared.

"I don't know anything. Her name. My name." Tears began to fill her eyes. She didn't know…

"You've been hurt," Jessie said, laying a hand on her cheek. It didn't soothe out all the panic, but it settled her some. A warm, calm anchor.

"Very hurt," the woman continued. "But you're safe now. I can promise you that."

She swallowed. The pain was a raw, throbbing thing, but she had to speak. "That man… He called me Norah."

Jessie looked at the empty doorway, some indecision on her face. "He did. He thinks you're a woman he used to know."

"Used to?"

The woman shifted in the chair to give her a better look at the baby. "Why don't we call you Norah for now? What would you like us to call the baby? It doesn't have to be right."

Norah looked at the baby—hers, somehow she knew the

girl was hers—but no names, nicknames or otherwise would form in her head.

"I don't know. I just don't know." And then she began to cry.

Chapter Two

Cal had talked to a doctor whom Dunne had found through an old military contact they could trust to keep things confidential, and she was coming to the house later today with some equipment that could do the necessary scans. She'd check out the baby too, though there seemed to be no outward trauma there.

Norah didn't remember, and Cal didn't know what to feel. It was both a blessing and a curse. There was so much…emotion mixed up in remembering. But without her memory, it was hard to determine who was after her.

And why her father had lied to him about her untimely death last year.

He looked around at his brothers. They were situated in the living room, Landon at his computer, but the rest of them staring at Cal. Waiting on an explanation.

They knew some things, but not much. Certainly not that he and Norah had gotten secretly married before he'd shipped out with them on their last mission as Team Breaker. He'd never even fully admitted he'd had a relationship with Norah. She'd been their superior officer's daughter after all.

"I can't come up with any death records on her," Landon said, squinting at his computer screen.

"Her father told me she was dead." Cal knew it didn't matter what he told his brothers now. Eventually he'd have to tell them everything if that baby was his and…how could it not be? Jessie said she figured the baby was around four or five months old. The timing was *him*.

And still he said nothing about that to his brothers, to the closest thing he had to a family.

"There's absolutely no record of that being so. In fact, I can find records of her continuing to live a fairly normal life for the past year and a half. Bills and taxes paid. Doctor exams, hospital records for the baby being born. Well, this is something. I found the birth certificate, so we can get the baby's name."

Landon typed away and Cal stood there…saying nothing. He should say something. He should explain, but he couldn't get his body to do what he wanted. He felt frozen. Wound so tight it was a wonder he didn't shatter apart.

It was all too much and…

Landon looked up at him over the computer screen. "Cal."

He saw it in Landon's eyes, and still he couldn't… "What?"

The silence stretched out as Landon studied him. "So, you're reasonably aware of what's on that child's birth certificate?"

All his brother's gazes seemed to intensify on him. He found he had to clear his throat. "I didn't know, but you add it up, I figured…"

"You figured *what*?" Henry demanded.

When Cal said nothing, because his throat was too tight and because he still hadn't fully accepted or dealt with this himself, Landon shook his head.

"The kid is *his*." Landon looked back down at his screen. "Evelyn Marie Young. What the *hell*, Cal? This says Norah's last name is Young, too, and that you're married? Norah didn't seem like the type to lie or forge records."

Evelyn Marie. His mother's name and her mother's name. His real last name.

And yet, Norah had never had any contact with him after her father had told him she was dead. She hadn't called or written, and he hadn't been declared dead until the end of his mission, when there'd been a mistake…

He'd always taken all that at surface value, but now there were questions. Now he *wondered.*

"Cal."

Cal managed to look up at Brody, who was staring at him with that calm, direct way he had. They all wanted answers, and likely deserved them, but Cal still wanted to keep them wrapped up in all the ice he'd used to just…get through the day without mourning.

And now there wasn't anything to mourn because Norah was *here*, and he had a daughter. *Evelyn Marie.*

"We got married about a week before we shipped out." The words basically fell out of his mouth. Little bombs he didn't know how to disarm or detonate. So they just sat there, between them. Explosions punctuating all that quiet.

"And kept it a secret?" Jake asked, carefully. Oh so carefully. "From us?"

Cal felt wrapped up in a thick fog, so many competing emotions they just sat on his shoulders like a weight. "She didn't think her father would approve. Or I didn't. I don't know. I look back and it's…a blur." Which wasn't exactly a lie because he'd tried so hard to forget.

In a way, it made her amnesia almost ironic. He'd been told she was dead. Car accident. Head-on collision. The woman he'd loved, dead, while he was in the Middle East trying to infiltrate terrorist groups.

So he'd done everything to forget she'd ever existed. To get through the day, the mission. He hadn't cared then so much if he died, but he'd had brothers to keep safe and so he had.

And just like then, these were his brothers. His only family left, or so he'd thought. He owed them more than *I don't remember*.

"We just… We both wanted to keep it a secret until I could be done with the military. So her father couldn't… She wasn't afraid of him—she was afraid of what he'd do to my position. And I was afraid of how it would affect you all and our mission. So we didn't tell anyone. No one. She was going to get things settled while I was deployed. Ready for when we came back and then I'd retire from the military. Do something—anything—else, so we could tell everyone. So we could…" *Start a family*.

He sucked in a breath. There was a sharp, stabbing pain that caught in his chest. It threatened to take him out at the knees. "I didn't know about the baby. We'd only been gone a week when her father called and told me she was dead."

And that was the point. The jumble of things that didn't make sense started from that moment. "The point is, her father told me she was dead. And for the past year plus, she hasn't been. But someone *recently* tried to kill her. I may not be a doctor, but I know those injuries weren't accidents. And she's *here*, and that can't be one either. It has to connect, and we need to get to the bottom of it before someone tries to finish the job. She doesn't remember, so we have to figure it out."

"We will," Jake said calmly, but he looked down at his own wedding ring, twisted it around his finger. "But this is about more than figuring out danger, Cal. You're a husband and a father."

"And you didn't tell us," Henry added, his arms crossed

over his chest. "All this time. Even when we found out she'd died, you didn't tell us you'd been *married*."

"I wasn't going to compromise the mission." That had been the thing he'd held on to. He'd needed that. Something to focus on that wasn't the excruciating pain of losing the woman who'd…found a way under all his scars. Turned him inside out and somehow made him whole.

It was better to be pieces. Compartments. Easier. Stronger.

Henry muttered an oath. Landon made a snort of disgust. The rest of them rolled their eyes.

"We're done with missions," Brody said firmly.

"I'm not," Cal said distinctly, because how else was he going to get through this? "*This* is my mission. Someone wanted me to think she was dead, and now someone's trying to make that a reality. I won't let that happen."

"We won't," Brody agreed. "But if you don't take some time to deal with the fact your secret wife is *alive*, and you have a child…that mission is going to break you. So take a minute. Deal."

Deal. *Deal?* How was he ever supposed to deal with this lost year? With being a father to a baby who…

A knock on the door sounded and Dunne stood. "That should be the doctor."

Cal nodded, glad for the interruption. Because nothing about what he felt or was dealing with was important. Norah and Evelyn being okay and safe was what was important.

The end.

NORAH LAY IN bed while the doctor hooked up machines and asked her questions.

She was trying to think of herself as Norah, so when someone addressed her with that name she responded. She couldn't say it felt right, but what did?

She looked down at the baby dozing in her arms. Well, this did.

Norah was strong enough to hold the baby now while the doctor went through tests, and more questions. So many questions she didn't have any answers for. She didn't remember anything.

When the doctor was finished, she took a seat in the chair next to the bed. Like all the women who'd come in to help, she had a kind smile and a reassuring demeanor.

"For everything you've been through, you're in decent shape. You've had a nasty concussion, quite a few bumps, bruises, lacerations." There was a slight hesitation, then the doctor reached out and gently touched her neck. "Someone tried to strangle you."

She—*Norah*—reached up to touch her neck with her free hand. *Strangle.* "That's…"

"Scary, I know. And it explains why you're struggling to remember. Your body experienced trauma—physically and emotionally—and your brain is working hard to deal with that. While it does, it's either forgetting or blocking out information in your memory." The doctor smiled kindly. "I believe that as your body heals, your brain will too. There's no physical damage that caused the memory loss that I see. I'll get a few consults on the tests I ran, but whether you remember everything or not, you are going to be okay."

Norah nodded, even though her heart beat double time in her chest. Someone had tried to *strangle* her? Left her for dead in a ditch or…

"As for this sweetheart," the doctor said, stroking the baby's cheek, "she's in great shape. No signs of injury or malnutrition or anything that indicates she'd been left uncared for for long. Whatever happened, you protected your little girl."

Norah looked down at the baby. Whose name she also didn't know. "You really think… I'll remember?"

"I do. But be patient with yourself. Your body needs to heal. You need to rest. Once all that happens, the likelihood of your memory returning gets higher and higher."

"Thank you."

"I'll likely want to do a checkup in a few weeks, or if you have any symptoms crop up—headache, nausea, insomnia… anything out of the ordinary, you'll get in contact with me ASAP, okay?"

"I don't know what the ordinary is," Norah replied. The doctor's diagnosis didn't settle her any. If anything, she felt more adrift. There were no answers. Only time and rest.

"You've got quite the crew here taking care of you and your baby. It's going to be all right."

The door behind the doctor opened and one of the men stood there. Cal, she thought. He seemed to come more than anyone else aside from Jessie, who was almost always around to help with the baby.

This man never smiled. He rarely spoke. But he was so often *here*. Looking at her with the same dark, unreadable gaze.

"I'm going to consult with an expert on brain injuries, make sure I'm not far off," the doctor said. She looked at the man in the doorway. "Don't worry. It'll all be done anonymously, and I'll get back to you as soon as I can."

He nodded and said nothing, just ushered the doctor out of the room. Norah was surprised that he returned, and even came to sit down on the chair next to her bed.

She didn't know what to say to him. Clearly he knew her. He was the one who'd said her name. Every time he was in here, he looked at her…with some kind of expectation in his eyes he tried to hide. But she saw it.

"How are you doing?" he asked.

Norah took a deep breath and studied him—rather than try to remember who he was, she simply collected facts. He was objectively handsome, if a little severe. His eyes were dark, his jaw sharp. He was tall and broad and she thought maybe she should be afraid. He had big hands, certainly capable of strangling her.

But even as she searched his face, his eyes, and saw nothing but a grim kind of disconnect, she didn't feel scared of him.

"I just wish I remembered."

The man—Cal—nodded. She knew he was…something to her. Just in the way he acted around her. Jessie was kind and warm but didn't act like she knew her. The other men who came in and out were the same. But this man, he had pain in his eyes and she felt a soul-deep yearning to ease it.

"I think the important thing is to rest. Heal." He stared at the baby with an intensity Norah couldn't understand. And it gave her the courage to finally ask…

"How do we know each other?"

His dark eyes rose to meet hers, but he didn't hold her gaze. He looked back down. "Well…"

"Please, just tell me the truth. The doctor said someone tried to strangle me. I don't remember *anything*."

"You need to rest and—"

"I need to understand *something*," she insisted, trying not to cry. It felt imperative to just…be strong somehow. Deal with this somehow. But she had to know something—she had to have some fact to hold on to.

"We found the birth certificate for the baby. Her name is Evelyn."

Norah looked down at the baby, whose blue eyes were the same as what she'd seen in the mirror when Jessie had helped her clean up a little bit. But Norah had blond hair and the baby's hair was dark.

Like this man.

But if he didn't know the baby's name until he'd found the birth certificate… "You knew me before I had a baby? But not after?"

He looked up at her again. "Yes."

"Yes. Yes…? That's it? Just yes?" She knew she shouldn't start panicking, but she couldn't seem to help it. She tried to shift without waking the baby, without making her body throb with all the aches and pains the painkillers only moderately dulled. "I'm lying in this house I don't know with a baby I don't know. Random people walk in and out. That doctor… Maybe she wasn't a doctor." Her voice was getting more and more shrill with every word, but she'd held herself under control for so long and he…they all just patted her on the head and said it would be fine.

It wasn't fine. "I don't know anything! I don't know—"

The baby—Evelyn—scrunched up her face, and whimpers quickly turned to wails of distress.

"I'm sorry, baby. I'm so sorry." She rocked the baby, and the tears began to fall. She figured she had a good reason to cry, and still there was embarrassment with the tears. "How do I even know she's mine? How do I even know I'm safe? You could have strangled me. You could be the bad guy."

"She's yours." His jaw tensed, but he held her gaze for once. "I don't want to hurt you, Norah. I've never wanted to hurt you."

"Not knowing hurts me." She sniffled, but she held the baby to her chest rather than wipe away the tears. It was a bit like a pressure valve. A few tears and she felt less like exploding. More capable of taking this step-by-step.

But she needed somewhere to take that step from. "How do you know me?" she repeated.

He hesitated again, looked down at his big hands. She could tell, somehow, that he was deciding what to say. But it was better than nothing.

"We met a few years ago. I was in the military and your father was my superior officer."

Father. Military? None of it rang any bells.

"We…" He trailed off and his eyebrows drew together. Usually she couldn't read his expression beyond intensity, but she saw uncertainty there now.

"Just say it. *Say* it. How am I supposed to rest and relax when everyone around me knows more about me than I do?"

"We hit it off," he said, as if each word was some great admission. "You didn't think your father would approve, and I was in no rush to upset my superior officer—a man I looked up to. The first time I deployed, we both kind of accepted that was it."

She tried to imagine *hitting it* off with this man, but he was so serious. So aloof and cold. Of course, she couldn't even remember herself. Maybe she was serious too.

When he gave nothing else, she pressed. "But it wasn't it?" She kept…studying him. Trying to find truth in any of these words. This was clearly no happy, tearful reunion. He was so tense. So brittle. Every word was an admission he didn't want to make.

Somehow that made it seem like the truth.

"No, I came back. We ran into each other. Nothing…" He was staring at his hands, shaking his head. "Nothing had changed. We…were in love with each other."

She tried to imagine *loving* this man, loving anyone. But it all felt like a blank—not just the truth, but any feelings about the truth she was supposed to have.

"I still had some time left, a secret mission your father wanted me to lead up. It required another deployment, a particularly dangerous one. But… I don't know, I guess we were both foolish enough to think it didn't matter. A week before I shipped out, we got married. Secretly."

He took a deep breath and before she could even try to wrap her head around being *married* to him, he pressed on. The information seeming to pour out of him now. "Not a week later, I was informed you'd died. I never heard from you again and had no reason to doubt it. Then I found you in a ditch near my property. With this baby. And that giant dog. Far away from *everything* that was our life together. So, I don't have the answers we need, Norah. I only *know* the bare minimum more than you do."

She'd asked for one thing, and he'd certainly given it to her. "We're…married."

"I don't even know what we are. I was told you were dead. I don't know what you were told."

"The baby…"

"My name is on the birth certificate, but I wasn't… I don't know."

He seemed like the kind of man who desperately struggled with the phrase *I don't know*, which almost seemed humorous considering she was currently in a constant state of not knowing. Down to… "Am I the kind of person who'd have an affair? Because if not, this baby has to be yours, doesn't it?"

Cal shook his head. "Like I said, I don't know what you were told. You might not have thought we were married. You might have been told I was dead, too. But the timing…" He cleared his throat. He seemed to wrap himself in something… cold. Detached. What little break in all of that was gone. "It's likely she's mine," he said flatly.

Norah looked down at the baby, who'd snuggled into her

chest. There was a comfort in holding the warm body against her, feeling the rise and fall of her breathing. She was beautiful, and even when Norah hadn't known anything, she'd known her only job was to protect this little one.

"I don't remember... None of this sounds familiar, but nothing does. I don't know who'd want to strangle me. I don't understand any of this, but I know when I woke up...the only thing I remembered was that I had to keep her safe."

"I'm sure you're a wonderful mother," Cal said, but he was still distant, and he stood carefully. "I'll go get Jessie to come take her so you can get some rest. The doctor insisted that rest is imperative."

Norah looked from the baby to him. He was already backing toward the door, but no. Not after all that.

"If she's yours, shouldn't you take her?"

Chapter Three

Cal stood frozen. *Shouldn't you take her?* No doubt. But he knew nothing about babies. He was already too...ripped apart. He hadn't meant to tell Norah *everything*, but it had poured out of him. A dam break of words.

Now, he needed to find a way to build that dam back up. Take control of the situation.

And she wanted him to take this baby. This child.

Evelyn Marie. Yours.

All the while Norah's blue eyes studied him, still looking for the answers. Answers he didn't have.

But would.

Stiffly he moved back toward the bed. The baby was curled up on Norah's chest. He didn't have the first clue how to lift a baby. How to do anything with her.

If she's yours, shouldn't you take her?

He didn't have the first clue how to be a father. He'd never known his own. He and Norah had spoken of building a family as a fuzzy future. Not a real, living breathing certainty.

But how could he admit to Norah he didn't know what to do with a baby when she couldn't remember *anything*? He had to be the one in control. The one who handled things. She'd been hurt and she couldn't remember.

So, he had to step up.

Stiffly, he bent over the bed and managed to shift the baby into his arms. The baby let out an odd noise—a mix of displeasure and acceptance. Every time he picked her up—and he did everything in his power to do it as little as possible—he felt like the weight of the world was on his shoulders. He looked down at her now. Small, eyes open, staring up at him like she understood everything even though she was just a baby.

"There's something about her... She does look like you," Norah said softly.

He didn't see it. Or didn't let himself see it. But that ocean of blue... "She has your eyes," he managed, though the words felt choked in his throat.

Norah nodded. He looked at her then. Bruised but patched up. Pale with bags under her eyes. She'd been alive all this time. Then someone had tried to kill her.

"You need your rest," he said, because if he stood here for much longer, cataloging all the ways she was the same and different, he might lose it altogether.

She nodded again, her eyes drooping. "I guess so."

Cal didn't know what else to say. Didn't think he could get the words out even if he did. So, he left her to go back to sleep. He tried to get the dog to come with him, but it refused to leave her bedside unless Sarabeth urged him outside with a treat and to do his business.

Jessie's daughter who now lived with them had that kind of pull with all the animals around the ranch.

Cal tried not to think about how much he owed that dog.

The doctor had eased some of his concerns about Norah and Evelyn's well-being. He was grateful for Jessie's experience as a mother, because she'd immediately made a feeding, changing and sleeping schedule for the child and they all took turns helping take care of her.

Cal stepped into the kitchen, where Sarabeth was sitting at the table, kicking her heels against the legs of the chair. When she saw him, she jumped to her feet. "Can I hold her? I'll be so careful. The careful-est."

Cal looked around, desperate for an adult who knew what they were doing to swoop in and save him, but there was only Sarabeth's insistence and his own confusion.

"I guess," Cal muttered. But everything in the kitchen was hard surfaces and sharp edges. "In the living room. On the couch."

Sarabeth practically danced the whole way there, then settled herself on the couch and held out her arms. Cal carefully transferred the baby, hands clammy, heart beating a little too hard. How did people just…go about their business holding a squirming life?

The baby squealed and grabbed at Sarabeth's braid.

"What's her name?" Sarabeth asked, offering her finger instead of the braid. The girl's chubby fingers closed over Sarabeth's slender ones.

"Evelyn," he said, sounding strangled even to his own ears.

Sarabeth seemed to mull that over as she gazed down at the baby. "That's pretty. Just like you." She stroked the girl's cheek.

It was my mother's name. But he didn't say that to the twelve-year-old currently loving on…not the baby, *his* baby. *His* daughter.

Evelyn. His daughter.

The front door opened and Jessie stepped inside, carrying a few bags. "Oh, good, you've got the baby." Henry followed, looking a bit shell-shocked as he held even more bags. "I picked up a few things for her."

"A few things," Henry muttered. "I think she bought out the store."

Jessie gave him a disapproving look. "We had *nothing* for a baby, honestly, and I think she can roll over both ways. It won't be long before she's crawling. We've got to babyproof. Feed her properly. Dress her. Diapers. Et cetera. And I got a few things for the dog. He shouldn't only be eating scraps."

"Thank you," Cal said stiffly.

Jessie settled in next to Sarabeth, already murmuring sweet things at Evelyn. Sarabeth looked up at her mother.

"Can't you guys have one so I can be a big sister?"

Jessie turned the shade of a tomato but looked up at Henry with a little smile that had Cal looking at Henry too.

"Working on it," Henry muttered with a shrug. Jessie and Sarabeth settled Evelyn onto the ground and held a toy over her, causing her to babble and wriggle in happiness.

"How are you *working on it*?" Cal replied, not sure why that was…surprising.

Henry shrugged and gave Cal a nudge out of the room and into the kitchen. "Bought a ring anyway. We're going to talk the whole marriage thing over with Sarabeth, and adoption and all that jazz, but since she's subtle as a Mack truck, I figure she'll go for it."

"Yeah."

"You can stand there and act surprised, but here we all thought you were the last holdout. Instead, you beat us all to it."

"I don't know how to…" Cal had never been sure he'd know how to be a husband, but he'd trusted Norah to guide him. In that. In building a family, whatever that looked like. But he'd had no real time to worry about it. He'd shipped out and she'd been gone. Dead.

Except she wasn't, and that was the only thought he could hold in his head at the moment. "I need to go talk to Landon and see what he's found out about Colonel Elliot."

"We'll keep an eye on Evelyn."

Evelyn. His daughter. Maybe he should be taking care of her, but the only way he really knew how was to figure out who'd tried to kill her mother. And why he'd been told Norah was dead over a year ago. "Thanks."

He started moving for the back door. Landon was living with Hazeleigh in her little cabin across the way. He'd either be there or out working on the ranch.

"Listen, Cal…" Henry said, before Cal could go fully out the door. "There's no handbook for this. No mission plan. It's life. Not war."

But it felt a hell of a lot like a war inside of him, and war Cal knew what to do with.

A lot more than he knew what to do with life.

A COUPLE DAYS LATER, Norah was feeling strong enough to move around. Someone had to be with her as she still got a little lightheaded if she got tired, and she didn't dare hold Evelyn unless she was settled into bed or a chair, but she could tell her health was improving.

Her memory remained a frustrating blank, as blank as the expression forever on Cal's face as he worked to keep his distance from her and the baby. Though she'd catch him watching her intently from across the room.

Still, if she could set aside her memory loss, there was a certain coziness about the days. One of the women of the ranch was always around to help with Evelyn—mostly Jessie or Sarabeth or Kate. The men were kind, but careful. They tended to stop talking when she entered a room, looking at each other as if they weren't quite sure what to say.

That Norah didn't care for.

On this evening, she'd come into the kitchen to get a little after-dinner snack, the dog trailing behind her. Sarabeth had taken to calling him Brownie, though Norah knew he needed a more admirable name. He was her hero. He'd alerted someone she and Evelyn were there.

"Maybe we'll call you Hero," she said, patting the dog's head as they left her room.

She was hungry and she wanted something sweet and full of calories. Maybe some ice cream. Evelyn was asleep, and Norah was hoping to run into Cal and maybe grill him for more details on all she didn't remember.

He was her husband. Maybe. Sort of. He seemed to dance around the subject with the ease of… Well, she didn't know.

When she walked into the kitchen, all six brothers were there. They went immediately silent.

Norah frowned. "I just came to get a snack."

Cal moved out of the kitchen area and over to the table, giving her ample room to get what she wanted. The dog followed her like a shadow.

She decided to take her sweet time. Scooping ice cream. Adding some chocolate syrup. Whipped cream. Once she'd made herself a rather impressive sundae, she went straight to the table, took an open seat and settled herself down to eat.

And talk. "I think it's time we discussed who tried to kill me," she announced. Hero curled up at her feet.

All six men exchanged glances—and boy, was that annoying.

"Do you remember something?" Cal asked, studying her as if one look and he'd *know* what she remembered.

"No." She'd had a dream last night, something terrifying, but it was misty and confusing in the light of day—and as likely to be fictional as actual memory. "But someone tried to kill me. And you six seem to lurk around talking about it behind my back. I get the impression you're looking into it, and I want to know what you know."

"Don't—"

She pointed her spoon at Cal, fixed him with the sternest look she could manage. "Don't you dare tell me not to worry about it. Someone tried to *kill* me. I want to know what you know."

"It's only fair, Cal," Jake said. She remembered Jake's name because he was the most friendly. He smiled the easiest. And he was married to one of the sets of identical women running about. That *did* make things hard to figure, though Zara and Hazeleigh were so different she could usually distinguish them by clothes.

Jessie and her twin sister, Quinn, were harder, but they spoke a little differently and Quinn had no interest in fussing over the baby like Jessie did.

The men all looked different despite the fact they were brothers, but they acted so much the same she had a hard time remembering name to name. But Jake was speaking, urging Cal to give her some information.

Cal scowled, but when all the other brothers nodded along, he sighed heavily. Then he took a seat across from her.

"We've started from the beginning. When your father told me you were dead. There's no evidence anywhere anyone else thought you were dead." He kept his eyes on her face, like he was constantly looking for signs of distress. "So, I started looking into your father."

"You say that like you're worried about my reaction, but I don't *remember* my father."

"But I do, and you loved him. After your mother died, you took care of him. You were the light of his life."

"Okay. So, you think he found out about us? Tried to kill me?"

"Strangulation is a personal attack, typically. But he told me you were dead one week into my mission. The attack on you didn't happen until recently—which is over a year later. They might be related, but the time between suggests not so directly."

Norah rubbed her temple. Everything was starting to throb. "Does he always talk in circles like this?" she muttered to the men sitting around the table.

"Yes," they all replied emphatically, causing Cal to frown deeply.

"I have the skills to get any information that might be out there," one of the brothers said. The one that lived with Hazeleigh in the cabin across the yard. Landon. "I was able to find Evelyn's birth certificate, your bill payment history for the past year, but there's nothing about you actually being dead. So, I started digging into Colonel Elliot—your father. I didn't get far when I found a police report. You reported your father missing three weeks ago."

Norah didn't feel anything, because whether Colonel Elliot was her father or not, it was all a blank. She didn't *remember* him. She couldn't think of what he looked like or what he'd done for her.

Still, Cal had said she'd been the light of her father's life. "So, he went missing three weeks ago, and a few days ago someone tried to kill me. Is it connected? Or is he the attacker?"

If Cal was surprised by her lack of emotional connection, neither he nor his brothers showed it. "We don't know," Cal said grimly. "But we're going to find out."

Chapter Four

Eventually, Cal convinced Norah to go back to sleep with not much more information than that. Not that he had all that many more details, but he had the beginnings of a plan. By the morning, he had a fully formed one, if next to no sleep in the meantime.

Still, he went to do his morning ranch chores, and explained everything to his brothers.

"I should go to DC."

Cal knew the plan wouldn't go over well with anyone. He'd thought about just leaving—sneaking out in the dead of night, not giving them a chance to talk him out of it, but it was better if they worked together. They'd find answers sooner, and Norah and the baby might be safe here, but Cal still knew the sooner they had answers the better.

Maybe he'd be able to really breathe with a few answers.

"Sorry. Not happening," Brody replied, saddling one of the horses. As if *he* were in charge.

Cal opened his mouth to argue, to issue an *order*, but Henry shook his head from his spot pitching hay.

"We discussed it before you got out here. Sure, we need to do some groundwork in DC, get to the bottom of Elliot's disappearance, but it's not going to be you."

"Oh, really?" Cal replied coolly. "Because it's your wife and child on the line?"

"The wife and child you're avoiding like the plague?" Jake offered, just as coolly, which wasn't like him at all.

Cal scowled.

"We went through all the options," Henry said. "Including you, but you should be here with them. In case Norah remembers something. In case she takes a turn for the worse. She's—they're both—your responsibility. So, you stay put. Dunne will stay in case Norah or the baby need medical attention. Jake runs enough of the day-to-day at the ranch with Zara, it's not a great time for him to take off. Jessie's instrumental in taking care of Evelyn, so I'll stay put with her and Sarabeth. We were going to go with Brody, but apparently *everyone's* got secrets."

Cal turned to Brody, who had his hands shoved in his pockets. He rocked back on his heels. "Not a secret," Brody replied, and it was strange to watch him try to fight back a smile as he explained why he'd be staying put. "Kate was wanting to keep it on the down low a few more weeks, but she's pregnant. She doesn't really feel up to traveling, and we think going in couples would be good for optics."

Marriages. Babies. Things his brothers had chosen in this new life of theirs. Brody smiling. It caught him off guard enough that he couldn't mount an argument.

Henry continued the plan they'd formed without consulting him. "That leaves Landon."

"I'll take Hazeleigh," Landon said. "We'll tour the museums by day, lay a nice cover, then I'll do some investigating by night. I'm the least likely to be recognized, and it'll just look like a vacation to anyone who might be paying attention."

"You're going to take Hazeleigh straight into danger like that?" Cal demanded.

"Staying put is danger too," Landon replied with a shrug. "If someone tried to kill Norah, and they realize they failed, don't you think they'll come to finish the job? And when they do, don't you think they'll look into who helped her? And if it *does* connect to Colonel Elliot, then the chances of it connecting to us—the *before* us—are pretty high too."

Cal had thought of all that, so he shouldn't be surprised his brothers had as well. "It's an unnecessary risk."

"It isn't," Brody replied. "It's a necessary risk."

Cal could argue. He could demand everyone back off and let him handle it, but things had changed. He was no longer the commanding officer. Even if he was something like *a* leader, his word wasn't law.

Much as he'd like it to be.

Still… "I should be the one to go. I don't have—"

"You have a wife and kid, remember?" Dunne said in his quiet way. "If this does connect to Colonel Elliot—good or bad—we are *all* potentially connected. It's *all* our danger. So, we're all going to get to the bottom of it. Landon and Hazeleigh will leave tomorrow. They'll spend five days tops in DC. If Landon finds info, great. If not, we'll move to plan B."

"And in the interim, we'll make sure no one comes to finish the job on Norah," Jake said, leading his horse toward the stable doors. "I'm late to meet Zara in the east field. I'll be back at lunch."

"We've all got work to do," Brody said, leading his own horse outside. When Cal took a step toward his horse's pen, Henry stopped him.

"Not you, buddy. I don't know much about amnesia, and the doctor said rest will help, but I'm guessing being around a face she might actually remember—and fondly,

God knows why—is the next best thing. Stay put and deal with your family."

Everyone scattered to do their work around the ranch. Except Dunne and Cal himself, because he felt rooted to this spot in the stables. *Deal with your family.* He hadn't had one for so long, and the blip with Norah before felt like some other…person. A dream, maybe. Because she'd died, like everyone who loved him always did. Colonel Elliot had been so…

"Avoiding them doesn't do anything except put off the inevitable," Dunne said quietly.

Cal had forgotten he wasn't alone. He blinked once, trying to find that inner core of determination that had gotten him through everything. *Everything.*

Inevitable. Norah and the baby—*his* baby—were indeed inevitable, but he hadn't figured out how to make it…right.

He had to make it right, not worse, and that required a certain amount of space. He knew he couldn't explain that to Dunne.

"Is it secret whispering time?" a female voice asked from outside the stable. Quinn popped her head in. "Do you need a third?"

"Just giving Cal a bit of a pep talk."

Quinn's eyebrows rose as she marched toward them, her limp almost unnoticeable these days. "The dull giving the terminally tight-assed a pep talk?" Quinn clucked her tongue. "Sad state of affairs."

"Dull, huh?"

She flashed Dunne a grin, one that spoke of private things Cal had no doubt she'd start talking about right here in front of him if he didn't escape.

"All right," Cal muttered. "I'm out." Causing both Dunne and Quinn to laugh.

Quinn turned to him. "Hold tight. I'm heading into town with Hazeleigh. Norah said she didn't need anything, but she could use some clothes of her own, so we're going to pick out a few things. Plus get Hazeleigh some stuff for her trip. But I wanted to ask you if you've got any hints about her style, you know?"

At Cal's blank look, Quinn rolled her eyes. "Favorite colors? Does she run cold? Like big neon lions to decorate her clothes? Or did you not know anything about your *wife*?"

Cal scowled. "She likes…" He didn't want to remember what she liked. Who she was. It was too hard. Too painful. Even knowing she was alive and right here, it opened some door to a past self he'd tried to kill off.

But Quinn's usually sharp gaze softened with pity, and Cal…hated it. To get *pity* from someone who'd been through everything Quinn had gone through. No. Absolutely not.

"She likes darker colors. Nothing neon. But not dull. Soft, comfortable. She always looked…" *Perfect.* He curled one hand into a fist, trying to stay somehow in the here and now. Danger. Protection. Not memories. "Put together."

Quinn nodded. "That's good, thanks."

"I thought you hated shopping," Dunne said to her. Clearly helping to change the subject because they both *pitied* him.

Cal wanted to punch something.

"Don't worry, I'll only buy a few lethal weapons, sweetie." She waved and disappeared.

"How do you put up with her?" Cal muttered. Quinn did her level best to be outrageous, antagonistic or just plain shocking…the very opposite of Dunne. They made no sense, and yet.

Dunne laughed, a real one, which had always been rare. "Not really sure *how* we put up with each other, but we do."

Cal didn't have to ask if it made him happy. Dunne might

not be a light, demonstrative, smiley type guy like Landon was, but dating the irreverent Quinn, and dealing with his family's past, had loosened something inside of him. He was still decidedly his quiet self, but not so dark and brooding any longer.

"It isn't like you to shirk a responsibility," Dunne said after a few moments of watching Quinn walk away.

The commentary was quite unwelcome.

"I'm hardly shirking."

"You're avoiding them. And I get it, Cal. This isn't just a responsibility. You loved her or you wouldn't have married her. You thought she was dead for over a year. It's emotional upheaval, and well, that isn't a strong suit for any of us."

Cal said nothing because it was all too close to the truth.

"But she needs you. Not to know what to do, not to be perfect and have all the answers. Just to be there."

But who was he if he didn't have all the answers?

NORAH WOKE FEELING much stronger. She'd had dreams last night, but in the warm glow of morning couldn't quite put them together. Were they memories? Fictions her mind was playing tricks on her with?

She sighed and sat up carefully. Her body still ached, particularly her throat, but she wasn't dizzy or light-headed.

She got out of bed and padded over to the door, Hero on her heels. They'd come up with a kind of routine. Though Hero rarely left her side, in the morning she would let him out of the room and someone would let him out of the front or back door so he could do his business.

And no matter that they were in the middle of nowhere Wyoming, he never ran off. He always came back to her.

So, she opened the door and he trotted off. Norah walked over to the portable crib where Evelyn slept. She looked down at her daughter and was bowled over by a tide of love. It was so all-encompassing, so big, it very nearly hurt.

This was her baby. She couldn't remember anything, but she held on to the fact Evelyn was hers.

She heard something, thought it was Hero already back, but when she looked over her shoulder Cal stood there in the doorway, that inscrutable look on his face.

She felt…something for him. It wasn't like that wave of love she felt for her daughter. But it wasn't that blank nothingness when she tried to think of her father—whoever he was. There was just this twisting sensation in her chest she didn't know how to describe.

But sometimes she wanted to reach out and stroke his cheek and tell him it would be okay, just as she did to Evelyn when she fussed.

She looked back down at the baby. "It's so strange," she said conversationally, though she kept her voice near a whisper so as not to disturb Evelyn. "I love her so much. I don't remember anything. Not you. Not my father. But her?" Norah pressed a hand to her chest. "I'm bowled over by this."

"You protected her."

Norah looked up at him. He still stood by the door. She couldn't understand why he held himself so apart. Part of her was glad for it. What would she do if he wanted to act like they were married when he was a stranger to her? Still, she wished he'd…be more than a strange, quiet ghost. "And now you're protecting us."

His face somehow got *more* blank, and she realized it was the wrong thing to say to him. What would be the right thing? She didn't have a clue.

"I thought of something interesting." She turned from Evelyn, moved closer to Cal. Both because she wanted Evelyn to sleep as long as she would, and because she wondered if he'd back away.

He didn't, but he did look wary. Still, she held out her hands.

Cal looked down at them, but she could tell he didn't see what she saw.

"It's your hands."

She rolled her eyes. "Yes, but look at my ring finger." She wiggled it. "I've been laid up for a few days now, but there's still a tan line where rings would have been. It's my right hand, but if it was a secret marriage…"

Cal nodded. "You wore them on your right hand." Each word sounded like a scrape against the quiet.

She had to curl her hands to keep from reaching out. It seemed like a natural thing, to want to comfort him. But maybe that was who she was. Someone who wanted to comfort anyone hurting—and he was clearly hurting, no matter how many layers of stoicism he hid it under. Did she know that because she knew him, or because it was obvious?

She closed her eyes for a moment. The constant loop of questions was just exhausting, but she didn't know how to shut them off. So she tried to focus on what she was trying to tell Cal.

"But you weren't wearing them when I found you," he pointed out. "You don't have them."

"No, but if there's still a tan line, I was wearing them close enough to now that either *I* only took them off a few days before this happened, or they were taken off me. I think it proves that someone told me you were dead," she said. "Just like someone told you. Because if I thought you'd…just, like, gone off on a mission and never spoken to me, I'd be mad. Not still wearing your rings." She hoped, anyway. She didn't want to be the kind of woman who pined after someone who'd clearly left her behind—even if the leaving had been a lie. "I would have tried to tell you about Evelyn, and if I hadn't been able to reach you, knowing you were alive, I'd be furious. Not still wearing your rings."

"I suppose," he said, but his voice was rusty. Like some great emotion held him hostage there. He looked over at the crib but made no move to go see Evelyn sleeping inside.

"Evelyn was my mother's name," he murmured, almost like he hadn't meant to admit that. Maybe he hadn't.

Norah kept her gaze on Cal's face. So stoic. So *tense*. She wanted to reach out, but she didn't dare. "Did I know her?" she asked gently.

He shook his head. "She died when I was thirteen."

"I'm sorry."

He shrugged. "It was something we had in common. Marie was your mother's name."

Norah rubbed at her chest. It was so strange to know she should feel something, and not. "I don't remember. But…if I named her after your mother when you weren't there, again, I had to think you were dead."

Cal swallowed but nodded. "I suppose you're right, but your father told me you were dead. A week after I deployed, and that was over a year ago. If you reported him missing three weeks ago, if nothing documentation-wise proves you were dead, he's behind some part of this. Looking into it… it might not give you the answers you want."

"But if he's missing, doesn't that mean something happened to him? Maybe he did something bad, but maybe he's a victim."

"But him missing is recent. Him faking our deaths to each other is over a year old."

Norah sighed. "I wish I could feel something about that, but I don't. I can't feel what I don't remember."

"You will. When your memories return, and they will. And you might feel differently about…everything."

He said *everything*, but she had a feeling he meant she'd feel differently about him, when she didn't know how she felt about him in the moment. "Are you afraid I'll still love you, or afraid that I won't?"

He flinched, and it felt like some kind of win that she could affect him enough to make him do that.

"I'm not afraid of anything. The only thing I'm concerned about is your safety." Which did not answer her question.

"Such a soldier," she said, without fully thinking the words through, or what they meant. It just felt like the right thing to say.

This time he didn't flinch, he flat out paled.

"What?" she asked, taking a slight step back at the way he stared at her. It was…unnerving. More intense than usual.

He shook his head, and though he didn't get any of his color back, he spoke in that clipped, closed-off manner again. "Landon and Hazeleigh are going to go to DC and do some investigating."

She could press the previous question, but she got the feeling it would be like beating her head against a brick wall. So, she focused on what this new development meant. "Investigating my father?"

Cal nodded. "His disappearance, what he might have been doing leading up to it."

Before Norah could decide how to feel about that, Evelyn began to fuss. Norah crossed the room. "Good morning, baby," she cooed. She picked Evelyn up since she was feeling sturdy. The baby wriggled and made her hunger known.

"She needs a change and a bottle. I'll change her if you can go get a bottle ready."

He hesitated, but then nodded once and left the room. Hero

trotted back inside the room, someone having let him in. He circled the room, sniffed at the crib, then settled himself in a shaft of sunlight on the floor.

When Cal returned with the bottle, Norah turned to him. The morning feeding was her favorite time. Just her and Evelyn and she could keep some of her questions at bay and just enjoy the moment. But...

Cal was Evelyn's father, and as little as Norah understood about what that meant or how to move forward, she knew he needed to start interacting with her. "Why don't you feed her this morning?"

"I don't know how."

"Don't you think you should learn?"

There was something like anguish in his eyes, a brief flash of it, then gone. As his posture got straighter, somehow, and his jaw tighter.

"Norah, I need you to understand something. Whatever is going on, whoever is out to hurt you, I will find them. I'll solve this for you. But after that? I'm legally dead. I'm not Cal Young anymore. I'm not your husband. I'm not her father. I'm a completely different man, so terrorists don't come after me or anyone I'm connected to. I may not be able to be a part of either of your lives once we know you're safe."

Something that felt like anger stirred in her, though it wasn't fully formed enough to lean into. If he loved her, remembered her, and had married her, shouldn't he want them?

Maybe he did. She thought it sounded like he was trying to protect her, or her feelings. She'd have to think about it a little more, so for now she just nodded. "Then I guess you should spend as much time with her as you can while you can." And she handed him the bottle.

Chapter Five

Cal fed Evelyn, having no choice once Norah walked out of the room. The little girl in his arms, his responsibility and yet... He was a danger to anyone he loved, or who loved him back. He was a ticking time bomb, and the only reason he had his brothers was that they were too.

And look at the families they're building.

Cal wasn't sure how they could be so...optimistic. Sure, they'd been moved here in an attempt by the military to make up for the mistake that had put their lives in danger. "Killed" off and erased and given a fresh, out-of-the-way spot to live. To be.

But if one mistake could be made, more mistakes could. Cal figured it was only a matter of time...

His life had always been only a matter of time, and whenever he'd let himself be fooled into planning a future, the universe had rid him of his delusions real fast.

So, he didn't see how there could possibly be a future where he knew his daughter without putting her in danger.

He looked down at the baby. Her face was scrunched as she wriggled. He had no idea how to feed her, and Norah had sailed out of the room as if that would force him to handle it. He didn't have to. He could go find Jessie or someone who knew what they were doing.

But the dog sat there, looking at him expectantly. Like he should know how to do this. Like he should handle himself, because he was the adult in the situation.

Cal frowned. He'd seen it done before. He'd watched Norah feed her. You just put the bottle in the baby's mouth. *I hope.*

He looked around the room, but the only comfortable place to sit was Norah's bed. He frowned deeper but settled himself on the edge, resting a pillow under his elbow like he'd seen Jessie and Norah do.

Then he put the bottle to Evelyn's mouth, and she immediately took it. She even grabbed it with her tiny hands. Her eyes, less sleepy now, latched on to his. Norah's eyes. A dark blue, wide and seemingly holding all the multitudes of the ocean.

He'd been so arrogant once to think he could control the universe. Marry Norah in secret. Take down a terrorist organization. Come back home and start a family even though he didn't have the faintest clue how to be a father as he'd never had one himself.

He'd thought Colonel Elliot might be a good example, except now it seemed that the man he'd admired could be…

Cal didn't know what he might be, didn't even have any clues as to *why.* Why lie? Why disappear? Why leave Norah and Evelyn unprotected?

And wouldn't that be what Cal would be doing himself if he cut all ties with them after this? It was a terrible catch-22 of leading them to danger, no matter which way he looked.

Why hadn't he had the presence of mind to think with his head instead of his heart before he'd said *I do?*

But he'd loved Norah. Painfully. With so all-encompassing a passion that even he, of the famed self-restraint, hadn't been able to control how he felt, what he wanted from Norah. And now there was a child.

His child. And she was so perfect, and looked at him, *really* looked, like she knew what he was to her. Like she understood things in the universe he never could. As if holding her here in this moment would let him in on all the secrets.

Someone cleared their throat and Cal looked up to see Dunne in the doorway, Brody behind him.

Cal had to blink, at the odd moisture in his eyes, at the pull of too many things to sort through.

"Thought you should know I asked my father, in a roundabout way, if he knew anything about Colonel Elliot's disappearance," Dunne said. His father was a contemporary of the colonel, the other superior officer who had handled their military missions as Team Breaker, so would surely know if Colonel Elliot was missing. "Since I couldn't come out and ask without explaining why I might have heard that, I didn't get anything out of him. Either he doesn't know Elliot's missing, or he didn't want me to know."

Cal nodded, then had to clear his own throat to speak. "Hard to think of a reason he wouldn't want you to know."

Dunne shrugged. "I can't think of a reason he wouldn't know about a disappearance Norah reported to authorities."

Cal couldn't deny that.

"Landon's waiting for us in the kitchen to discuss his DC plans," Brody said.

Evelyn began making noises, and Cal realized the bottle was empty though she was still trying to suck down the last drops. He pulled the bottle from her mouth and stood. "Is Jessie around?"

"There's a little playpen thing in the living room. You can put her in there and we'll discuss Landon's plans," Brody replied.

Cal wanted to argue, but he sensed his brothers *expected*

an argument, so he simply walked out of the room, Evelyn in the crook of his arm.

"You've got to burp her after a bottle," Brody said as they trailed through the kitchen and waved Landon with them to the living room. The dog followed at Cal's heels.

"You're an expert?" Cal asked, irritably.

Brody shrugged. "I read a book. Just over your shoulder and pat, pat on the back till she burps."

"Look at him. *Mr. Dad*." Landon grinned, slapping Brody on the back.

Cal maneuvered Evelyn against his shoulder, then gave her back a few gentle pats.

"You've got to do it a little harder," Brody said when nothing happened.

"Harder? She's tiny." And so soft, so vulnerable. Where the hell had Norah gone?

Landon reached over, pushed Cal's hand out of the way, and rubbed Evelyn's back. "This is what I always saw my mother do."

Evelyn let out a barely audible pop of noise.

"Was that a burp?"

Brody shook his head, pushed Landon's hand out of the way, then gave her a few solid pats. Nothing too hard, but Cal still winced as she felt like nothing but a feather there against his shoulder.

But a surprisingly loud sound erupted from her mouth, and then she babbled happily, wriggling not in what he thought was discomfort but in a need to get moving.

"Four men and a baby," Landon said with a laugh. "We'll figure it out yet."

It was a strange sensation. The way his brothers just seemed to accept…everything. His secret marriage. This baby. When he still felt frozen in a block of ice. But Landon was joking, Brody was reading *baby* books because he was going to be a father too.

The pain in his chest was familiar. That old yearning for things he knew he couldn't have. Things that didn't belong to him. He'd always won in war, but when it came to people, he lost.

Always.

Henry put a hand on his shoulder. Gave it a squeeze. "She's a baby, not a bomb. She's yours. And she's not even a year old. You can't mess her up just yet, and you wouldn't, even if you could. But, brother, you're going to have to unclench. They're your family, just like we are."

"I know that."

"No, you want to find a way to put a wall between you and *that*, because you think it'll keep them safe. But did you think about why Norah was on that road? How she was *here*?"

"Of course I have." Not that he could explain it, but he'd had to wonder. How could he not?

"She knows. Her father knows—was one of the architects of the whole thing. Whoever put them in danger? It wasn't you. This is on them. Again."

"But I have to protect them."

"Yeah, we all will. And we'll protect each other. For the lives we're building." He pointed at Evelyn. "And I think I get it now, in a way I didn't. Why you resisted that so hard. Because you had a life before."

"It needs to stay in the before."

"Why? Because you're scared for their safety? Or because you're scared? Period."

I'm not afraid of anything. He'd said that to Norah, and he'd meant it, but he couldn't manage to say the words to Henry. Even if Henry was wrong. Of course he was scared for their safety. Why would he be scared of anything else?

He crossed to the playpen and set Evelyn down, just as Norah came down the stairs. The dog trotted over to her and she petted him, her eyes never leaving Cal's.

Her hair was wet, so she'd been upstairs taking a shower. She wore some of the new clothes Quinn and Hazeleigh had bought her. A turtleneck, likely to cover up the bruising on her neck he'd still seen so clearly this morning when he'd gone into her room.

She met his gaze, those blue eyes of hers like a window back in time. When he'd been so arrogant and sure he could make something of himself. Be a military hero, be her husband. Make everyone proud.

They said nothing—and neither did anyone else, though truth be told, Cal had forgotten about everyone else the minute she'd come down the stairs.

He itched to touch her. Press his mouth to her neck and revel in all the ways she was *alive*. Alive. And still, just the thought of any of it was a physical pain.

He'd said goodbye. Mourned…or pushed the mourning down as deep as it would go until it was almost like a dream he'd made up that she'd even existed at all.

Now she was here and she didn't remember and what was he supposed to do with that?

Because he was scared. For their safety. Of his feelings, and making all those old mistakes over and over again. Afraid she'd never remember, and he'd never know how to help her. Afraid, *petrified*, that he couldn't make this right— because he couldn't go back in time and fix the past year and a half.

"And what do we do when we're afraid, Callum?" his mother had asked him, dying there in her hospital bed. Wasting away. Him a gangly thirteen-year-old, already too well equipped to handle adult things like hospitals and medica-

tions and bills and phone calls to doctors. *"Put one foot in front of the other."* She'd said it so firmly when everything about her in the moment had been weak. *"You have so much life to live, whether I'm here or not."*

"But I want you to be here."

"I do too, but we don't always get what we want. We don't get to choose when we arrive, or when we leave, but we get to choose what we do while we're here. Never be afraid to choose."

Two days later she'd been gone. He'd been shuttled off to an aunt, then a cousin, then a group home. But he'd made his choices. He'd built himself into Cal Young, exceptional soldier. Above reproach. Phenomenal leader.

And maybe that was really what was eating away at him. It felt as though losing Norah—or thinking he had—had stripped away all those choices again. So he was a young man again, tossed from home to home, place to place, with no say in it.

Never be afraid to choose. "I fed her," he announced, into the quiet that had stretched out into discomfort. "Brody helped with the whole burping thing. I'm sure I made mistakes, but we'll get it right as we go." *One foot in front of the other.*

Norah's mouth curved ever so slightly, some of that gravity leaving her face. "I feel like it's a bit of a learning curve. Some things come instinctually, but I remember so little. Jessie's been a godsend." She moved a little closer, peered down at Evelyn in the playpen. The baby rolled and grabbed her feet, garbling happily.

Before Cal could figure out anything else to say, aside from the *I love you, I've always loved you* that wanted to escape when she didn't remember *anything*, even how to care for their daughter, there was a shout from outside. It sounded like Zara maybe, and she kept shouting. Not totally unusual.

Henry glanced out the window, then swore. "Jake's hurt."

The brothers moved immediately, pouring out the front door. Norah didn't venture outside, but stood in the doorway as they rushed to where Zara was helping Jake off a horse. The dog sat next to Norah as if watching too.

"Someone shot him," Zara said, her voice high-pitched. "We were walking the property line and he thought he heard someone and just *bang* he went down."

Jake was holding something rolled up at his side, and it was bloody. It took Landon and Henry to keep him upright once he was off the horse, Zara hovering close as they began to move him toward the house.

"Are you some kind of bullet magnet?" she said, clearly trying for humor but there were tears on her cheeks.

"Tell me what happened," Cal demanded.

Zara looked up at him and swallowed. Her hands had blood on them, and he wondered how she'd gotten Jake up on the horse, but they needed to know who before they rehashed how.

"Like I said. Soldier boy here thought he heard something, went for the tree line. Then out of nowhere, *boom*. I had my gun, but I didn't really see anyone. I heard something—saw a bit of a shadow, so I shot back," Zara said. "Maybe I hit someone, but maybe not. If I did, nothing serious, because the shooter ran. So I sure got a shot off that scared him into running."

"That's good. You did good, Zara." They'd been in the east field today. Tree line. "Brody?"

"Truck or horse?"

"I think truck, then foot. Dunne, you'll take care of Jake here. Get Quinn and or Jessie to help out. Landon and Henry, once he's settled, follow on horse. Bring the walkies." Everyone began to move. When it came to emergencies, his leadership was rarely questioned.

Until Norah trailed after him. "You're just going to…go after someone with a gun?" Norah asked, her mouth hanging open, shock radiating off her.

"I'll have one too," he replied. He grabbed the truck keys from the kitchen, then walked back through the living room. Dunne had Jake sitting down on the floor, probably because Norah and Evelyn had taken up residence in Dunne's room that also acted as medical center when necessary.

Dunne gave his verdict. "Passed through. Not as bad as the last one."

"That does not ease my concerns, Dunne," Zara said, still hovering, hands squeezed together. "Since the last one almost *killed* him."

"Almost doesn't count, Zaraleigh," Jake said, trying to smile, but he was gray and gritting his teeth.

"Don't call me that while you're bleeding out."

He reached up, winced, but took Zara's hand. "We're all right."

"We," she snorted, knuckling another tear off her cheek. She looked up at Dunne for confirmation.

"Not as bad. Promise."

Cal had to set aside the worry, because someone was out there. Someone threatened all their safety. But he knew if things were more serious, Dunne would give him *that* look. So, it was okay. It was going to be okay.

Dunne started issuing orders to Zara and Jessie, who'd just appeared, getting his supplies and creating a more sterile environment to stitch Jake up.

"I'll be back," Cal said to Norah, who was still standing

there looking at a complete loss. But he didn't have time to assure her anything was okay.

He slid his cowboy hat on and went out to find the shooter.

And the dog followed at his heels.

Chapter Six

It took Norah a few minutes to get over her shock. Cal had just...disappeared outside, grim and determined, looking like some sort of Wild West hero.

Or villain, she supposed, with the gun and the dark hat.

But Brody had accompanied him. Hero, who hadn't left her or Evelyn's side, had gone with them. Quickly, after getting Jake situated, Henry and Landon had followed out the front door. Guns and hats and grim expressions.

Jessie had gone and fetched Quinn, who was now acting as Dunne's assistant of sorts. While Dunne cleaned and sewed Jake's side up right here in the living room. Zara alternately held Jake's hand and paced.

Jessie, bless her, came over to Norah. It finally broke Norah out of the reverie of shock and confusion.

"I'll take her into the kitchen," Jessie said, pointing down to Evelyn in the playpen. It was only then that Norah realized her daughter had begun to fuss. "She really liked the peaches yesterday. We'll try those again. Sarabeth was begging me to let her try to feed her, if that's all right? I'll supervise, of course."

Norah nodded. "Thank you. Really. I don't know what I'd do..." Or what her baby would have done, without Jessie's help these past few days. But trying to articulate that made her throat feel tight.

Jessie waved her away. "I'm happy to help. I miss this stage," she said, reaching down and picking Evelyn up. She cuddled her to her chest. "I didn't quite get to enjoy it when Sarabeth was little. So, I should thank you."

Norah chewed on her lip, looking over at the door. "Aren't you...worried?"

"About Henry, you mean?"

Norah nodded.

Jessie inhaled, seemed to think the question over. "I do often worry. It's hardly the first time Henry's waded into danger, but...the thing I've come to understand is that this is who they are. They need to face down threats or trouble. Maybe it was ingrained in them in the military—and they're all more than capable of handling threats because of that—but I think that need to protect the little guy, fight wrong with right, is just a part of them. I think it's what bonded them together. So, yes, of course I worry. When you love, you worry. But I also know it's what they have to do. So I can't let that worry overwhelm my every waking moment."

Jessie looked down at where Dunne was finishing up the stitches. Jake looked more ashen than he had earlier. But it could have been so much worse. And it would have been her fault.

"Dunne was a combat medic," Jessie explained. "I can't tell you how many times Jake's been shot. Old hat for them."

Old hat. Without thinking the motion through, Norah raised her fingers to her throat. The turtleneck covered the bruises that still marred her neck, but it made her think maybe she was *old hat* too. At being hurt and victimized.

Something inside of her recoiled at the thought, but what did she know? A fat lot of nothing.

Jessie took Evelyn into the kitchen, and Norah thought she should follow, but all she could do was stare at the door. Worrying. Willing Cal and his brothers to return unscathed.

Which didn't even fully make sense. She didn't really remember anything, any connections she might have had to these men, to Cal, but the worry curled in her gut like its own weight.

Dunne, Zara and Quinn moved Jake up to his room, Jessie and Sarabeth came in and out, asking to do more things with Evelyn, and Norah just…nodded. Kate came and sat with her awhile, attempting to make conversation and get Norah to eat something, but Norah knew she didn't hold up her end of the bargain. And she couldn't stomach the thought of food when everything in her was leaden.

Because this was…connected to her. She didn't want to believe it was her fault, but it had to be, didn't it? She'd been found on their property, then someone had shown up and shot Jake. So, it was her fault. They'd been nothing but kind, generous and wonderful. And her repayment was danger and injury.

"Why don't you take this feeding, Mama?" Jessie said gently, entering the living room with Evelyn in her arms and a bottle in her hand. She transferred the baby to Norah's arms, handed her the bottle. "Then you're going to eat something."

Norah shook her head. "I can't." But she looked down at her daughter, that wave of love crashing over her as it always did. Evelyn sucked down the bottle, though her eyelids drooped more and more.

Norah realized she'd wasted a whole day sitting here worrying, while other people had taken care of her daughter, who was now just about ready to go down for the night. That much time had passed.

Jessie patted her shoulder gently. "If something had happened, we'd know by now. They're just searching for clues. For answers."

Because of me.

But Norah forced herself to smile at Jessie. "Thank you. I think it's strange to not remember anything. It's like... I can't distract myself. Because there's only the fact he—*they're* out there." *And it's because of me.*

Jessie nodded.

"But I'll feed her, put her down, then fix myself some dinner."

"There's a plate in the fridge for you. All you have to do is warm it up in the microwave. If you don't eat, we're going to have to have a long talk, missy." She waved a finger at Norah, but smiled kindly. "I've got to go wrangle my daughter into eating dinner instead of trying to dress up her cat." Jessie stood, traced her finger down Evelyn's cheek. "I'll admit, I don't know Cal very well. He keeps himself a bit apart, but I've come to think that's because a part of him was always with you."

Norah felt tears prick her eyes, though she blinked them back. She wished that were true, but he kept himself apart from her and Evelyn now that they were here. So how could what Jessie said be true? "I wish I could remember."

Jessie nodded. "You'll get there. I have faith."

"You don't even know me."

"I know you somehow fought off someone who tried to kill you, protected your baby and got to the people who could best protect you. That takes a lot of courage, and a lot of grit. You'll remember."

Norah didn't know why it steadied her. A stranger's opinion of a medical condition, when she wasn't any kind of medical professional, but Jessie's certain faith did seem to give her some strength. She fed Evelyn, burped her, then as the baby dozed, Norah got up and went to put her in the crib.

Norah turned on the baby monitor Jessie had bought for her the other day. She'd never be able to repay them all for their kindness. Never.

She went to the kitchen and warmed up the plate of food. She tried to eat. She really did. But it sat like a lump in her throat, and though she felt guilty for doing it, she scraped the food into the trash can and cleaned her dishes in the sink. All so Jessie would think she'd eaten.

You may have lost your memory, but you're still an adult who doesn't have to answer to anyone about your food intake, she lectured herself. And still felt guilty.

It wasn't late just yet, but still Cal and his brothers had been gone most of the day. What did that mean? They were out there searching for someone—and if she could only remember *something*, she could help.

She needed some air. She hooked the baby monitor receiver to her belt loop and stepped out onto the porch outside the kitchen. The sun was setting. A riot of vibrant colors against a beautiful landscape of green and pretty little ranch buildings. It was like a dream.

And someone had been out there shooting people. Because of her. What if someone had shot all four of them? And they were out there... But something in her couldn't panic at the idea. They just seemed so...strong and capable. Sure, one could get shot, hurt, when they weren't looking for trouble, but who could take down all four of them on alert?

If only she could remember. She could help. She could protect everyone. She was stronger, healing. Shouldn't she remember? The doctor had said she would.

"Worthless brain," she muttered.

"Hardly worthless."

She whirled around and saw Cal standing there inside the screen door. He opened it and Hero trotted out and over to her, stopping her from rushing to Cal. She crouched and petted the dog, then hugged him as he licked her face. How'd she get so lucky to have so many people and this dog protecting her?

She looked up at Cal, but whatever she'd been about to say died at the bleak look on his face. "You didn't find anyone." It wasn't a question. She could see it on his face.

"Some evidence someone had been walking around the property, but no. We didn't find the shooter or any clues to who it might have been, or why. Just one set of prints, so there's something positive in that."

Norah wrung her hands as she stood, and she said to Cal what she hadn't been able to say to Jessie. "This happened because of me."

"Were you out there with a gun?" Cal asked, raising an eyebrow—a very *sarcastic* eyebrow.

She didn't remember anything about this man, but she could tell he was tired. She wanted to reach out and touch his face. Run her palm down the line of his jaw, feel the scrape of the whiskers beginning to grow.

Was that a memory in and of itself? Or just basic…chemistry?

She sighed, her head beginning to pound. She wanted to rub her temples, but no doubt he'd start in on making sure she ate and rested and all that. "You know what I mean. Someone tried to kill me. Someone left me to die. Now your friend is getting shot. It's because of me. It has to be. And if I could remember any damn thing, we wouldn't be in this mess."

Cal was silent for a long moment. Because he knew she was right, *obviously*. But then he said something that made no sense. "I think we would be in this exact mess. Memory or no."

"How can you say that?" she demanded.

"I had a lot of time to think while we searched the property. About some things I'd been avoiding thinking about. But Henry pointed it out this morning and I couldn't ignore it. You were here, Norah. You shouldn't know I was here, but there's no reason you'd be here except for me. I think you fought off whoever tried to…kill you," he said, clearly struggling with the words *kill you*. "You were hurt, yes, but you fought them off and then tried to get to me. The strangulation bruises weren't fresh when I found you on the side of the road."

"So?"

"So. You fought whoever off. You got Evelyn and your dog here and got away. And you came here. I don't know how you knew to. But there's no way you were walking down a highway in Wilde, Wyoming, by happenstance. No one tried to kill you and then dumped you on the edge of my property—still alive with your baby and your dog. So, I think, whether you remember or not, you were coming here because you'd found out, because you thought I could help."

"But from everything you've told me, I had to have thought you were dead."

Cal nodded. "Three weeks ago you reported your father missing. It's possible that however that came to be, it included your father telling you I was alive. Where I was. Or you somehow finding it out on your own if he had records or something."

She suddenly felt like her legs couldn't keep her upright anymore. She sat down, right on the porch floor. Hero pressed his nose into her neck.

Cal stepped a little closer. "The bottom line is whatever this is, I think I'm connected. Not just because we were once married, but because of the old mission. Because of your father, maybe. We don't have all the pieces, but we're working on it. We'll get there."

"We'd already be there if I remembered."

He crouched next to her, and he gave Hero an absent pat, but he looked right at her. "Someone tried to kill you, Norah. Strangle you. Someone gave you that head wound. You got away. You protected your daughter and yourself. You got here. Maybe things would be simpler if you could remember, but you managed to handle all that? You don't get to give yourself a hard time for the ways your body needs to heal, okay?"

She felt that *thing* in her chest. An emotion she couldn't find the words for. One that cropped up whenever he was here. Close. Talking to her.

And he was close. Close as he'd ever allowed himself to be. Sure, he was petting Hero, but he was so near and she could just reach out. Run her palm across his jaw like she'd thought about doing. It felt...like something settled into place. The rough scrape against her palm. His dark eyes locked with hers.

He stilled. So still. While she absorbed the warmth of him, the strength of him.

A part of him was always with you. She so badly wanted that to be true in this moment. Needed to think that something about this man was connected to her more than just the daughter and history they had once shared.

He didn't pull away from her hand, and that need had built up so huge inside of her, she let whatever this feeling was propel her. Muscle memory. Real memory. Yearning. She leaned forward and pressed her mouth to his.

Maybe it was all wrong, but her entire life was *all* all wrong right now. People trying to kill her, and good people being shot. Not remembering anything, even this.

But kissing him felt right. His hand coming up to her shoulder, the gentle glide of his mouth against hers. Even the way he eased her back. It felt...safe.

She could see the hope in his eyes—the hope that she'd remembered something. Part of her wanted to lie and say she had, but honestly, she was too tired to muster the lie.

"I don't seem to remember things. Names. Events. Memories. But sometimes a feeling washes over me, and I think that might be its own kind of memory. I felt like I should kiss you, so I did."

"Ah." He was still crouching there in what could hardly be a comfortable position.

And it was all so bleak she desperately needed to lighten it. "I mean mostly I was hoping for a little Prince Charming magic, my memory magically restored."

He shook his head. "I've never been any kind of Prince Charming."

"Clearly," she said, *almost* tempted to smile. "I do feel something for you. I just don't understand it."

"You shouldn't."

"Feel it or understand it?" She shook her head and continued before he could—because she knew he'd probably say *both*. "I'm afraid you can't dictate what I feel. Even I can't do that. I know you think this is all hopeless between us, with your daughter, and maybe it is, but that doesn't change whatever feelings are here." She patted at her chest. "Even if I remembered, Callum."

He jerked, and for a moment she thought maybe *he'd* been shot.

"What did you say?" he said, his voice as raw as she'd ever heard it.

And she realized she hadn't called him Cal. That something had... She remembered this little sliver of something.

"Callum. Callum, that's your full name. Callum Daniel Young." She blinked. "I remember." It was a jumble. Not a rush of everything. Just a little…blip of him. She remembered pieces of him.

Then she laughed, because…well, maybe his kiss had unlocked something after all.

Chapter Seven

Cal still crouched, though his legs were starting to fall asleep. But he was very nearly afraid he'd shatter if he moved. Break into a million pieces he was barely keeping together.

Callum. He'd stopped going by that name after his mother had died, but Norah had wheedled the information out of him the first time they'd dated, when it was supposed to be a secret fling. Nothing more than fun. Back then, she'd teased him with it. And it hadn't been until that second time, when he'd come back from some long-ago deployment he barely remembered, and hadn't been able to pretend like he'd gotten over her, that he'd told her what the name meant. He'd asked her to marry him and he'd told her his mother always called him that.

Then it had become less teasing when she said it, and more...weighty. When it mattered, she called him that.

And she'd somehow remembered. She'd *kissed* him.

All while someone was out there, taking shots at people. At his brother.

And Norah laughed, like something could be funny in this whole mess. Except she was alive. Here. Maybe remembering...something. When he didn't want to remember any of it, because he'd learned his lesson that no good came of trying to be *happy*.

Because happiness and feelings and all this didn't matter, especially when they were sitting ducks here on this porch. Even with Landon's security measures, they didn't understand the threat against them. So sitting outside was a risk they didn't need to take. "We should go inside," he said, standing despite that pins-and-needles feelings in his legs.

Norah slowly rose. She was staring at him, but she didn't offer to say anything else.

"Landon has cameras set up all around the buildings," Cal explained. "But of course the ranch itself is too vast. So, we'll take turns keeping watch until we're sure there's no further threat."

She nodded, and when he opened the door, the dog trotted inside and Norah followed, but when he trailed behind her, she stopped. Practically boxing him in—his back to the now closed screen door, his front to her—unless he retreated back outside.

He thought about it. But in the end, he supposed he was too stubborn, too conditioned to stand up to a threat rather than retreat.

It wasn't a threat. All she did was put her hand on his chest, looking up at him like he had a million answers he knew damn well he didn't have.

Which maybe felt like a threat after all.

"Callum." She said it like she was testing the syllables on her lips. She put her palm on his jaw again, just like she used to do when she was trying to convince him he needed to relax. When she was trying to remind him there was life outside of the military and his duty.

Then she let her hand slide away, but she stepped into him, wrapping her arms around him. She leaned her head against his chest and he…

Froze. Had to. If he didn't, he'd…

"Hold me like you would if I remembered," she murmured into his chest.

Before he could stop himself, his arms came around her. It wasn't like any before time, because she felt fragile to him now. Not quite real. If he held on too tightly...

He couldn't do what needed to be done. Because there was no future here. The marriage they'd planned on died the moment a terrorist organization had his name. Norah Elliot connected to Cal Young, and so they could never, ever be connected again.

Except for this brief moment—for this period of time, to be protected against whatever was after her. He would always protect Norah and Evelyn.

But that meant, once it was safe, keeping her safe would include making her leave. Staying away from each other.

She sighed against his chest. "Is it that...you thought I was dead for so long that you had to...accept and move on? Stop loving me?" She looked up at him, and there was so much she didn't remember, but it felt like she knew more than he did.

Still, stop loving her?

Never.

He'd tried.

But in a strange way, it hadn't been all that different than losing his mother. His anchor had died, and he'd been left to drift away. But the love didn't stop. It couldn't.

He couldn't let her know that. It would make the eventuality harder. But there was heartbreak in her eyes, and she'd always been his Achilles' heel. The thing he couldn't deny. The person he couldn't lie to, no matter how hard he'd tried.

"I'll never stop," he said, the words torn from him even as he tried to push them down. But no, they came out, no matter how rusty. She didn't smile or relax, she just kept looking at him like there was more.

When he'd already told her everything he shouldn't.

"I guess I just don't understand why that hurts you," she said after a long moment that felt as though it might tear him in two.

Still, his whole life had been about putting duty ahead of pain. "Me loving you puts you in danger."

"It appears I'm already in danger," she said, pointing to the spot on her head where she had stitches, though her hair mostly covered it from the way she'd brushed it.

"You won't be in danger forever."

"But you will?"

"Yes, I will." He eased her away from him, forced himself to release her and move away. "I'm glad you remembered something. Hopefully continued rest and healing will give you back the rest of your memory, and then you'll understand."

She raised an eyebrow. "Will I?"

No, not by a long shot, but he liked the fantasy she would. "I need to go check on Jake."

She said nothing as he began to walk out of the kitchen, but the dog gave a little yip, which had Cal looking back. Her knees were giving out, and Cal managed to reach out and grab her before she fell.

"I'm okay, I'm okay," she muttered, trying to get her legs back under her. "I guess I'm a little light-headed."

"What did you eat for dinner?" he demanded.

"Well…"

"Lunch?"

"Um."

Cal swore and settled her into a chair at the table. "You're going to sit there and eat, and I'm going to watch you swallow every bite."

CAL MOVED AROUND the kitchen while Norah watched from her seat at the table. It was an interesting sight. He moved like he was angry, like he should be banging around, but he was nearly silent as he prepared her food.

She wanted to resist out of spite, but that was stupid. Now that she knew he was safe, she did feel a little hungry, or that vague nausea that would be quelled by eating anyway. The weight in her had lifted. Maybe Jake had been shot, but she'd remembered something. Cal thought maybe this wasn't her fault...but an inevitability instead.

Her head throbbed, and she was exhausted. Hungry, obviously, though she still worried about being able to stomach whatever he put in front of her. And still, she kept reliving the way he'd said *I'll never stop*. And it had echoed inside of her, even not remembering a thing about him.

Except his full name. She'd remembered that. It had fallen out of her like a habit. Maybe she was trying too hard to remember. Maybe she needed to just...feel. And the information would come back.

Cal put a plate in front of her. It was a peanut butter sandwich. Then he put a glass of milk on the table as well. "You have to take care of yourself," he said, eyebrows furrowed in irritation.

"I tried while you were gone." She looked at the sandwich and her stomach growled. "I couldn't stomach it. Knowing I was why your friend was shot."

Cal scowled. "You're not to blame. No matter what we find out, you're not to blame for what evil men decide to do."

She supposed she couldn't argue with that, though she considered as she took a bite of the sandwich under Cal's watchful eye. She had no doubt he was going to stand there and watch her until she'd swallow every last bite just as he'd said.

It went down easier, though if she'd been left to her own

devices she wouldn't have eaten the whole thing. But Cal watched, so she ate. She drank.

Then she asked him the thing she didn't really want the answer to. "Do you think my father's one of those evil men?" She'd remembered Cal's full name, some feelings even if she didn't understand them all, but when she tried to think about her father, she could only come up blank.

Cal's expression didn't change, but she watched him carefully enough to see a certain kind of tension take up residence in his shoulders. "I don't want to think that. Your father was my mentor. I honestly thought he was one of the best men I've ever known."

"*Thought. Was.* Those are past tense."

"He told me you died while I was deployed. You weren't dead. You were pregnant. I could have…" He trailed off, his hands flexing into and out of fists even as his words came out gently.

"But you wouldn't have," she finished for him. "Because of danger. If you'd known I was alive, pregnant, you wouldn't have come home, would you? You would have left us to think *you* were dead, because that would keep us safe."

He was silent for a long, long time. Eventually, he sighed and shook his head. "I guess we'll never know what I would have done."

"I guess not." She took her last sip of milk. Would it matter? She didn't remember much of anything, but she knew somehow that you couldn't linger in what-ifs. There was only now. "Do you have any pictures of my father? Maybe something that would jog my memory?"

"I can get you some."

She nodded, then stood to take her dishes to the sink, but Cal plucked them out of her hands and went to the sink and washed them himself. She thought about what Jessie had said, about Cal and his brothers…needing to help people. Needing to stand between right and wrong.

She supposed Jessie had meant in war and random gunfire, but Norah watched Cal hand-wash a dish and glass and felt like…this was him. A man who took on responsibilities that were not his own—and that could get downright annoying. A bit of a martyr, she supposed.

But there was also something deeply *good* about it. Heroic maybe, if you didn't take it too far.

Oh, I think he probably takes it too far, she thought wryly.

And still that *feeling* deep in her chest, that yearning to go to him, intensified. She wanted to kiss him again. To whisper things about love when she still didn't fully remember loving this man.

It was somehow inside of her, though. Or had been. Maybe she'd been angry with him at the time of her injury. Maybe she'd thought he'd left her. Maybe this was some echo of something she no longer felt. Maybe when she remembered, she'd remember nothing but anger and betrayal.

But the depth and breadth of the feeling made it hard to believe it was old. Gone. Either way, she didn't *know.* And that was a frustrating, constant dull ache at the base of her skull.

She sighed. She'd remembered something. Maybe she needed to consider it a win for today and hope tomorrow yielded more. "I feel much better, thank you," she said stiffly, because if she let herself relax she might be tempted to go to him.

"Make sure you eat. All your meals," he said in return, which made her frown. She understood he was a…caretaker type, and it came with this bossy, overbearing side. Instinctually, however, she didn't care for his tone.

"And rest. We'll handle everything else. Now I'm going to go check on Jake."

She reached out and grabbed his arm before he could move past her. She frowned up at him. "I'll let you handle a lot, but not *everything else*. I want pictures of my father. I have to *try* to remember. You can't just lock me and Evelyn away until you figure this out, then ship us out when you think we're safe. We're people. Not objects."

He didn't move out of her grasp. He was so still she wasn't sure he breathed—how did he *do* that?

She could *feel* the want inside of him. He *wanted* to reach out. Hug her, maybe. Touch her definitely. And yet he held himself back. So much self-control. So much…warped sense of duty.

For a moment, so fierce and sharp, she *hated* it. And it was a familiar feeling. Even if she didn't understand it, she knew she'd felt it before. So, she didn't let go of him and she didn't stop herself from saying *her* piece.

"My daughter deserves her father, and I like to think when I remember I'll still feel that I deserve my husband. Even if I don't, the first remains true. No evil men should stop that from happening. I won't let it."

"Nor—"

"No, I need you to listen. To think about this. You're letting outside forces win, and I don't think that's you. You're letting fear win, and I know that's not you. Somehow I know that. So, you go check on Jake because you care about your friend, your *brother*. Get me the pictures and any other information about my father when you get the chance, because I have to try to help. And *you* make sure to eat and rest, because you're not a robot even if you'd like to be."

"You have the wrong expectations, Norah," he said. Sadly. *Resignedly.*

"I may not remember much, but I know you're wrong

about that," she said, then turned on a heel and marched to her room. Because she wanted to cry in peace.

And then try to remember.

Chapter Eight

Cal didn't immediately go check on Jake. He was too...everything. Wound tight. Frustrated. Angry and sad. There was a thorny, desperate yearning inside of him he would damn well quash before he dealt with *anyone*.

He texted Henry he'd take over the patrol and didn't wait for Henry's response to set out. He walked around the property buildings, gun in hand, eyes on the dark, half wishing someone would jump out so he had something to fight.

But there was nothing. Nothing but the stars and his own frustration that he hadn't stopped two people he loved from getting hurt.

After an hour, Landon texted that it was his turn. Cal sighed. He didn't feel any better about the situation, but he supposed he'd walked off some of his overwhelming emotions.

When he finally got back to the main house, it was late and the house was quiet. He carefully tiptoed upstairs, and when he heard low voices coming from Jake's room he knocked on the door.

Zara opened the door and waved him in. "Come on. Revolving door."

"Sorry," Cal muttered. "Just wanted to make sure the patient is doing okay."

Jake sat in his bed, propped up on the headboard. He held a bowl and gestured with it. "Gunshot wounds equal ice cream night."

Zara leaned close to Cal and spoke in a soft whisper. "The painkillers make him a little loopy, but he's mostly fine."

Cal nodded and approached the bed.

"Here for a report, Captain?" Jake asked with a mock salute.

Cal looked back at Zara. "You sure he's all right?"

She smiled a little and nodded, then came to sit next to Jake on the bed. "Clear-headed, just goofy and thinks everything is way more funny than it is. We've been talking about what happened. What we each saw. What could have happened. Just trying to get a clear picture of it. I'm sure that's what you're here for."

It was, but something about the way she said it rankled. "And to see how he's doing."

Zara held his gaze. He wasn't sure her expression was skepticism as it was too soft, but he couldn't quite figure out what else it would be.

"Well, we both agree it certainly wasn't planned," Jake said between bites of ice cream.

"Why do you say that?"

"Everything the gunman did was...reactive, you know? I thought I saw something, so I went to investigate. *Then* he shot—or *she*, as my wife keeps pointing out. One shot. I went down. Zara shot back, and he or she bolted—hit or not, they bolted. This wasn't some planned attack, or if it was, it was really badly planned."

"We didn't find any evidence of the gunman being shot," Cal said, not sure if anyone else had transmitted the news to Jake or Zara.

"That's what Henry told me," Zara replied. "Which pisses me off."

Cal *almost* smiled. He did appreciate Zara's bloodthirsty demeanor at times.

"So, you've got someone acting alone, reacting," Jake continued. He shook his head. "I just don't think he was here to hurt anyone."

"Then why was he here?" Though Cal already had his suspicions.

"Had all the earmarking of a recon mission," Jake replied. "But you already know that."

Cal didn't respond, because yes, that was the conclusion he'd come to. And it was worse, somehow. Because recon meant an attack—a planned, careful attack, likely with more people—would come.

And they still didn't know *why*. Who? Was it about Norah? Or about Team Breaker?

"Can you sit with him for a few minutes?" Zara asked, sliding off the bed. "Dunne said not to leave him alone while he's taking the medication."

Cal nodded, but Jake grabbed Zara's hand—surprisingly quickly for a man on painkillers with a bowl of ice cream in his hands—before she could move away from the bed.

"Aren't you going to give me a goodbye kiss, wife?"

"I'm going to the bathroom, you loon," she replied, but she leaned down and pressed a kiss to his forehead. Then she rolled her eyes and disappeared.

But she was smiling. And so was Jake.

Cal couldn't help but stare at the door where Zara had disappeared. "Doesn't it…ever worry you?" He turned slowly to watch Jake's expression. Which didn't change as he ate his ice cream.

"What?" Jake replied.

Cal didn't know why he was asking such a serious question when Jake was hopped up on painkillers, but he couldn't seem to stop himself. "That we're sitting ducks. One mistake on a computer did this to us. Who's to say one mistake on a computer won't mark us again? And then Zara's marked too."

Jake seemed to consider this, as though he'd never thought of it before. "I don't worry about that."

"How can you not?"

He shrugged. "If I spent my life worrying about stuff like that, then I'd have to worry about…getting hit by a bus. Crashing my truck. Getting kicked in the head by a horse. I'd have to worry about her getting thrown and breaking her neck when she's off ranching alone. Or that one of the guys her cousin locked up over in Bent might try to target his family. You think like that, it never ends. What-ifs might not be deadly in real life like they are in war, but they sure can ruin the good parts of life you *should* enjoy." Jake sighed heavily, the spoon clattering against the now empty bowl before he set it down on the nightstand next to him—wincing a little bit, making Cal wince in return.

He'd been shot himself, once, a long time ago, but he still remembered the lingering, obnoxious pain of healing. And so much worse, he remembered when Jake had stepped in front of a bullet meant for him, almost a year ago. And watching Jake slowly heal from that, only to be here, injured again because of him.

Didn't you just lecture Norah that this isn't her fault, so it sure as hell can't be yours.

"You married her, Cal," Jake said simply. "You can't take it back."

"I'm not trying to take it back." He was thinking about her safety. Her and Evelyn's being *alive*. "There are some things in life you can't control, yes. Believe me, I'm intimately acquainted." He'd been thirteen and left with nothing, let alone any control over his life. "But there are some things you *can* and should. Norah and Evelyn need to be safe and away from any danger that might connect to me, and I can control that. I didn't understand that when I married her. Or I was too arrogant or something. But it's different now. You don't…" Cal trailed off, for a few reasons.

But Jake was Jake. "You were going to say I don't understand because Zara and I haven't jumped on the baby train yet." He laughed to himself, possibly at the term *baby train.* "Henry's there. Brody's there. Ask them, I guarantee their answers will sound like mine."

Cal looked out the window, into the dark night that surrounded the ranch. He hated that Jake was right. Hated that he felt mired in too many situations where he didn't know what to do.

"But more than that, Cal, if this is about your mom, that's not really fair to Norah *or* Evelyn."

Cal's jaw tightened. He should have known Jake would see what lay under that. He should have known he couldn't have this conversation and win.

So why did you come up here and start it?

Well, he wasn't going to stay in it. "We've got someone with a gun doing recon missions and shooting people. I don't think Landon and Hazeleigh should travel."

Jake snorted. "Good luck stopping them."

Cal sent Jake a look that would have once gotten a *yes, sir* out of him. But they weren't in the military anymore, and Jake wasn't his subordinate.

Jake's raised eyebrow and wry smile clearly said, *That doesn't work on me anymore.*

"We need more info on Colonel Elliot," Jake countered. "You know that. And if Dunne's dad wasn't giving any info, we've got to be careful. It could be pretty damn complicated. Landon and Hazeleigh will go find what they can, and we'll—or you guys, while I'm laid up—will safeguard the house and the people in it. You can brood about it, hyper focus on it, but it doesn't change anything."

Cal didn't respond. It *could* change something. If he thought of a perfect answer. If he figured out what was going on. How could he not try to change everything that was wrong? Fix it? Stop the pain and suffering and danger?

That was all he'd ever wanted to do since he was thirteen, and it had never weighed on him until…

Well, until it had all blown up in his face.

Zara returned, rolling her eyes at Jake's exuberant greeting.

"He thinks he's going to stop Landon and Hazeleigh from going to DC," Jake said, pointing in Cal's direction.

"Oh brother," Zara replied. "You're a piece of work, Cal."

"I don't understand why wanting everyone safe is me being a piece of work."

"Because you're like…trying to control everything. Like you're the smartest and best so you know what's right and no one else does."

"I do not think that," he replied, and started heading for the door. Because he wasn't in the mood for the regular programming of Cal bashing. They didn't understand—couldn't—the weight of it all.

"But you're making this about you," Zara offered, settling once again next to Jake on the bed.

Cal stopped, turned slowly. Gave Zara an icy stare that had melted stronger men than her. "Excuse me?"

She didn't melt. "And I don't just mean you. I mean all six of you."

"Hey," Jake said, frowning at her. "How's this about me?"

"Sorry, but it's true. And it's what you guys always do. I get it's a knee-jerk, because you guys were out there fighting the big bad and then you became a target. I get it. But right now, this is about Norah. Sure, you guys connect. Can't ignore that. But someone tried to *kill* Norah. So, whatever it is, even if it has to do with you, she either knows something someone doesn't want her to know—enough to kill her over. Or she pissed off the wrong imbalanced person."

"Thank you for that recap," Cal said, his words dry as dust. "I was unaware."

Zara rolled her eyes. "She thought you were dead. You thought she was dead. There's no way someone tried to kill *her* because of *you,* at least based on the information we have. So maybe you all should get your heads out of your military asses and start looking into *Norah.* Which means, Landon and Hazeleigh should go to DC and try to find out what's going on with her dad. And you, Cal, should be with Norah doing whatever you can to support her in remembering."

It wasn't new information. He understood someone had tried to kill Norah. He supposed he'd just assumed…it was about him. Which meant Zara was right on target. Which was damn annoying. "And how do you suggest I do that?" Cal returned irritably.

"I don't know Norah well enough to have specific suggestions, but you could, I don't know, *talk* to her. Be around her. Rehash your past. Not ignore her, hide from her, and otherwise act like the coward you're not."

"I am not a coward," Cal said through gritted teeth.

"I know. You're very brave and smart when it comes to men with guns and clear villains. Seen many a performance of you be all Mr. Military Man in the face of that. It's impressive. When it's the time for it. It's not the time for it now. It's time now to help Norah. And unfortunately for you both, you suck at people. You run away, because all the things you *can't* control beyond life and death scare the hell out of you." She smiled at him. Smugly. "And I can say that, because been there, done that."

Jake grinned at her. "Isn't she great?"

"Yeah, great. I'll leave you two to be great together," he muttered, and left to the sound of Jake and Zara's laughter.

Even in the midst of all *this*. He'd never understand it. Or them.

Or people.

NORAH WOKE UP to Evelyn's insistent crying. Morning light streamed in through the pretty curtains, and Norah struggled to remember what she'd been dreaming about. She sat up, massaged her forehead.

There'd been something. Something that felt important now that she couldn't access it. How frustrating.

Still, she got up and moved over to the crib. Picked up Evelyn. Instead of continuing to fuss, like she usually did, the baby cuddled into her chest and made a little, sighing sound. Then her eyes fluttered closed again.

Norah swayed back and forth as Evelyn went back to sleep, enjoying the weight and warmth of her little bundle. She returned to her bed, crawling in and enjoying the feel of her baby sleeping peacefully against her chest.

She sat there, watching the sunlight filter through the curtains, and just let herself enjoy the moment without trying to remember anything. More than sleep or even peanut butter sandwiches, this felt like the kind of rest she really needed.

She couldn't imagine anything as peaceful or wonderful as this right here.

Then she flashed back to Cal saying he'd never stop loving her.

Well, *that* wasn't peaceful. Nothing about Cal held any promise of relaxation or peace. But it still felt wonderful to know someone loved her. Particularly after thinking she'd been dead for over a year.

Someone knocked lightly on her door, and she gave a quiet *come in*. As if she'd conjured him, Cal stood there when the door opened.

"Oh… Sorry. I thought I heard her up."

"She was, but she fell back asleep, so we're just having some snuggle time."

He held a laptop under his arm, but just stood there and stared at them. Sort of like how someone might watch a train wreck. She didn't know whether to laugh or be irritated.

"Did you need something?"

That seemed to break him from his reverie. He cleared his throat and gestured to the laptop. "I have some pictures of your father and a few other things you might recognize, if you'd like to go through them."

"Yes, of course. Come in." She waved him in when he hesitated at the door. But after a few moments he stepped in and closed the door behind him. He walked slowly to her.

"She's asleep?"

Norah nodded. "She sleeps pretty soundly on me. Go ahead put the computer on my lap."

He hesitated again, this man who had absolutely *no* hesitation when leaving the house to chase down a gunman. What had life done to him to make him so afraid of or unsure of life over death? Would she remember and know, or had she never known?

He opened the laptop, brought up a picture, then set it on her lap carefully, eyeing Evelyn to make sure he didn't jostle her.

Then he stood, hands behind his back, all military stiffness. She frowned at him, not quite ready to look at the picture on the screen yet. "Are you just going to hover?"

"Would you rather I leave?" he asked, with a faint frown.

She rolled her eyes then patted the bed next to her. "Sit down, Callum."

Again, hesitation. "You don't have to keep using my full name."

Norah shrugged. "I like it."

He frowned. "I don't."

"Why not?"

His jaw tightened, and then he gingerly sat next to her on the bed, the mattress dipping with his weight. He left a healthy couple inches between them.

He did not answer her question.

Instead, he pointed to the computer screen. "This is the most recent picture of your father."

Norah turned her attention to the computer screen. A man in a military uniform filled it. He had salt-and-pepper hair, cropped short. It was hard to tell his height, but Norah didn't get the impression he was very tall. A little thick around the middle, like he'd once been fit but had maybe stopped holding himself to that high standard as middle age struck.

She felt nothing. A lump in her throat threatened to form—frustration and disappointment weaving through her hard enough to make her want to cry. But she swallowed it down. Forced away the feeling of failure. It was only the first try. "What's his name? His full name?" She'd remembered Cal's full name.

"Colonel Julian Elliot."

He may as well have said Colonel Peanut Butter Sandwich. It meant nothing to her. She sighed. "Are there others?"

"Yeah." He reached over, hit the arrow button and the picture changed. "This one is from about three years ago."

The man was still in his military uniform, but laughing, with a drink in his hand. A more candid shot, like it was at a party or something. And he looked a little bit younger, more black than gray in his hair.

Norah stared at it, trying not to let frustration take over. "I just don't know... When I remembered your name, it wasn't like a flash. It was just...there all of a sudden."

Cal nodded. "Well, maybe you just look and you don't remember or feel anything in the moment, but at some point it'll pop up."

There was something comforting about the idea that even if these pictures didn't yield results *now*, they might still later. She hit the arrow button to the next picture.

"This one is from before you were born," Cal explained. "It's your parents' wedding photo. Colonel had a copy on his desk, and you had a copy in your apartment, so I thought maybe you'd recognize it."

It was indeed a wedding portrait. The man from the first two pictures, much younger, still in uniform. A woman in white whose face had her catching her breath.

She didn't feel some gong of recognition, but the woman—her mother—looked so much like her own reflection. Norah reached out and touched the woman's face on the screen. "I look like her, don't I?" she whispered.

"Quite a bit," Cal agreed.

"And she died? When?"

"You were seventeen."

Norah swallowed at some unknown emotion that rolled through her. Memory? Loss? Just empathizing with a younger version of herself? "How?"

Cal hesitated, and in that hesitation, Norah's stomach trembled. It would not be something as simple as a disease, or an accident. She could tell from the troubled look in his expression.

"Just tell me."

"Ah, she was…" He cleared his throat. She didn't see him move—it was stealthy or careful, but suddenly his hand was very gently on her back. Not quite a hug or having his arm around her, but still some offer of support or comfort. "Your mother was murdered."

Murdered. It hit hard, and she didn't know if it was simply the shock of it, or an echo of knowing that. "How?" she managed to ask.

"Sort of an accident, from what I was always told. There was a shooting at a place she did volunteer work at, and she was caught in the crossfire."

Norah looked at the woman in the picture. Accidentally murdered. Wrong place. Wrong time. And yet Norah couldn't access a memory of the woman or the loss of her.

She wanted to cry, but she was tired of crying. Of feeling wrung out and used up. She needed something…something to hold on to.

Callum Daniel Young. She'd remembered his name. It was something. She had to hold on to it as a sign the rest would come.

"She's awake," Cal said, his voice rough.

Norah opened her eyes and looked down. Evelyn was squirming in her arms, but she'd reached out to Cal. Her little fingers brushing against his sleeve. Evelyn was looking at him. Her father. Not fussing to eat or be changed, just reaching out to her *father.*

Norah wouldn't let herself cry, but it was a near thing. Still, she shifted. "Here. Take her."

She knew he resisted the idea, but he didn't hesitate this time. He let Norah shift Evelyn into his arms. He looked down at her like she was some kind of alien, and Norah thought it was because the alien thing wasn't the baby, it was the feeling that washed over him. The same feeling that washed over her even when she remembered nothing.

Evelyn wrapped her little finger around Cal's, then began babbling to him.

Norah realized that for the first time, she was witnessing her child and her husband have a moment. And as much as she wanted to remember *everything*, this moment was worth all the memory loss in the world.

Chapter Nine

It was the babbling that did it. Or maybe the eye contact. The way this little girl just looked at him and spoke, even if it was gibberish to him, as if he mattered. As if he was hers.

Because he was. She had Norah's eyes, but there was something about her mouth that reminded him of his own mother. Bits and pieces of genetic material he could pick apart, but altogether she was just Evelyn.

His.

Her babbling began to get more intense, her little mouth turning into a scrunched frown, then she wriggled not from energy but from frustration.

"She needs a change and a bottle," Norah said absently, still staring at her parents' wedding photo. "Maybe some of the food Jessie bought. Could you take her to Jessie? I want to look through these again."

Cal hesitated. He'd never felt so unsure in his life, or at least not since he'd been a child. Because he knew he should keep his distance, but he couldn't seem to manage it. How did you keep someone safe and out of your personal orbit?

They were *here*. Just a few days and already knowing he'd have to send them away in the imminent future broke his heart. He'd have to give them up, *had* to, but would it really be any easier if he kept his distance? Or would he always know he'd missed this precious time with his daughter? What little there could be of it.

"I'll do it," he managed.

Norah looked up from the computer, eyebrows winging up. But she said nothing. Just watched him as he got up off the bed, Evelyn cradled in his arms. Then she turned her attention to the computer, chewing on her bottom lip, eyebrows furrowed and the echo of an old pain in her eyes.

He moved over to the makeshift changing station. He hadn't done this yet, and Evelyn wriggled and yelled her displeasure as Cal inexpertly changed her diaper. He adjusted the little self-fastener flaps once, twice, three times until it looked close to what Jessie and Norah managed.

"There are fresh clothes in that drawer," Norah said. He glanced at her and she was watching him carefully. Her expression was neutral, and that felt...painful almost.

She wasn't sure how to feel about him doing this. She wasn't sure what it meant. He should make it clear it didn't *mean* anything. Or maybe it meant everything, but it couldn't change the inevitable future.

Then she looked away, back down at the computer, and he could tell she was thinking about her mother. Her parents. Trying to remember, putting the pieces together of what he'd told her.

He hated being the one to tell her about her mother, but he would also hate for her to remember offhand, without anyone around. Something so traumatic, and awful. Something you never fully healed from.

It was what they'd first bonded over. The unfairness of it all, the uncertainty after. She'd had her father still, not been jockeyed between family and foster care, but she'd had the added complication of knowing someone else had ended her mother's life for no real reason.

For the first time, he admitted that this desperate ache inside of him wasn't just because he knew he couldn't have her, it was because he knew she didn't remember. He couldn't go and hold on to her like she remembered, like she wanted. It wasn't right when he was a stranger she only remembered vague, possibly long-gone feelings for.

Was he even the same man she'd loved? Did it matter?

He looked down at Evelyn. She wasn't crying, but she was still doing the scrunchy-faced frown like she might start any minute. He finished clumsily buttoning up her onesie—his large fingers far too big to easily snap all the tiny buttons. He lifted her to his shoulder, gave one last glance at Norah, who was still focused on the computer.

She wanted some alone time. To think. Probably beat herself up over not remembering. So, he slipped out of the room and into the kitchen.

Jessie was there, cleaning up the breakfast debris. She looked over her shoulder at him. "Oh." She said nothing else, but Cal could read the simple surprise in that one word.

He tried not to scowl. "Norah said she should eat and then have a bottle."

Jessie wiped her hands on a dishtowel then held them out. "Can do."

Cal didn't hand the baby over. "I've got it," he replied, trying to sound casual.

Jessie seemed surprised but mounted no defense and made no move to intervene, though she likely would accomplish all this better than he would.

But he was a father. As his brothers had so kindly pointed out, time and again. He couldn't undo it or run away from it. She was his duty. And as Norah had said, irritably, they weren't objects. They were people.

He settled Evelyn into the high chair, just as he'd watched Jessie and Norah and even Sarabeth do at meals. He got one of the jars of baby food. Maybe he'd kept himself apart, but he'd always been a careful observer.

And Jessie watched his every move—silently and pretending like she was finishing cleaning, but Cal had no doubt she was ready to jump in if he faltered.

But he wouldn't. He mimicked everything he'd watched the women do, and Evelyn seemed happy to give the terrible smelling apple-carrot mush a shot.

Sarabeth clattered inside, then came to an abrupt stop, shoving something behind her back when she saw her mother.

"Sarabeth, I swear to all that is holy," Jessie said, already pointing out the door Sarabeth had just come in. "That cat has caused enough damage in this house for nine lifetimes."

Sarabeth's chin fell, then she trudged right back outside, the cat climbing up her back as she did. Cal blinked, realizing with an odd poignancy that someday, Evelyn would be just like Sarabeth. Running around. Sneaking animals into the house. Saying things to make her mother blush.

But Sarabeth's childhood had been harsh, and Cal... He had to do everything to make sure Evelyn's wasn't. That she had everything. *Everything*.

Even him.

He looked back at her, her face covered in the orange mush. Smacking happily as he brought another small scoop to her mouth.

It would be impossible for him to be around as she got older. He knew that.

But as she stared at him with her blue eyes, she looked somehow both impossibly innocent and deeper than anyone who'd only been on this planet a few months had any right to be, and it reminded him of the argument he'd had with Norah right before he'd proposed.

The argument that had made marriage and a future seem possible.

He'd tried to break up with her. He'd told her, plainly, that he didn't know how to be what she wanted. How to do a relationship. He could tell she wanted more. Weddings and babies, and it had terrified him.

If only because he'd wanted them too.

She'd turned from the sink in her tiny kitchen in her tiny apartment and pinned him with that *you are a particularly superior brand of stupid* look.

He'd seen it a few times here, even if she didn't remember. She might not have her memory, but she was still *her*.

And back then, he hadn't been so afraid to tell her bluntly. To flat out say: *"Norah, I don't know how to do this."*

"So?"

"So...so. I can't."

The silence had stretched out, so long, so piercing, he thought he was bleeding out, but he couldn't find the wound.

"Who said you have to know how to do everything?" she'd asked when she'd finally spoken.

"I always have." Because he'd had to take over when Mom had gotten sick. He'd had to figure himself out when she'd died, because no one was all that interested in helping him get there.

"No one knows everything. No one knows how to get through life. Even my father. He's Mr. Military Man now, but I saw him fall apart when my mother died. You can't control the world. You can't know how to deal with what comes at you." She'd crossed to him, where he'd sat at her table, trying to end things.

For her own good.

She'd pulled a chair over, then covered his clenched hands with hers. *"Callum, you know how to do a lot of things and I know how to handle some things and what we don't know we'll learn together."*

He'd known he shouldn't believe her, but her blue eyes had been wet and sure, and he hadn't known how to disagree with *we could do it together*, when that was all he'd ever wanted.

He'd been a different man with her. Trying to learn how to do it together.

And then she'd been ripped from him, or so he'd thought. But unlike all the other loss in his life, this one had been a lie and here she was.

Here *they* were.

They couldn't stay. Norah might be alive, but the life they'd been determined to build was still gone. He didn't know how they could stay and be safe.

What we don't know we'll learn together.

And perhaps sensing his distraction, Evelyn chose that moment to slap her hand out against the container of food and send the spoon, container and food sailing.

Then she laughed, as if it was the funniest thing in the world.

And Cal did too.

NORAH HAD A terrible headache, and still she couldn't stop. She'd begun searching the internet for information about her mother's murder. She'd found newspaper articles, and even news segments on it. She'd seen her own face, younger, in grainy pictures of the funeral.

It had happened almost a decade ago, but something about the whole thing pulled at Norah in the here and now.

Was it memory? Was it something important? But how

could a ten-year-old murder, an accidental, wrong-place-at-the-wrong-time type of murder, have anything to do with…

Well, someone had tried to murder *her,* hadn't they?

But it was targeted. Probably connected to her father, and possibly connected to the military. It was desperate grasping at straws to think there'd be something here no one else had thought of.

The door eased open and Norah looked up. Cal stood there. His hair was wet and he was wearing different clothes. Instead of carrying Evelyn, he was carrying a tray.

"Evelyn decided to give us both a carrot-and-apple shower, so Jessie handled the bath because I wasn't quite sure how to manage that. I was going to have her teach me, but then I remembered you haven't eaten anything."

He set the tray down on the bed next to her—where she'd rather *he* be than a bowl of cereal, a little container of yogurt and a glass of orange juice. Still, it was a sweet gesture.

"You didn't need to wait on me."

He shrugged. "Don't mind."

He seemed different somehow. Less tense.

"I, um, hope you don't mind. I was using your computer to look up some things."

"Feel free. We've got plenty of tech around here. You can keep this one for the time being. Look up whatever you'd like. But right now, you need to eat." He reached over and took the laptop from her. He glanced at the screen before frowning and setting it down on the nightstand.

"I was looking into my mother's death. I guess that's silly. It happened so long ago."

He was still frowning, but he didn't agree with her. "It's not silly to want to understand something." He picked up the tray again, then pointedly set it on her lap. "Eat."

She tried to smile, pulled the flap back on the yogurt.

"There's just something…fresh about it? I don't know how to explain it. I just had this feeling that I… That I've done this before. Looked through these articles, looking for clues. Feeling…unsettled."

Cal frowned a little, looked at the screen again. "What about it feels unsettled?"

"I don't know." She ate a spoonful of the yogurt. "It's hard to filter through… I don't remember. Am I feeling something new? Old? Is it wrapped up in the not remembering? Is it based in reality? I can't sort through it all. I don't have enough baseline knowledge to."

Cal seemed to consider this, then carefully lowered himself onto the now empty side of the bed. He still kept inches between them, but she hadn't had to insist he sit.

"It's just, I don't remember you ever having any questions about it. Any uncertainty. It was a terrible tragedy, but not targeted or anything with questions, really."

"Exactly. Everything I read about it is so straightforward. It all makes sense. And those are facts. My feelings aren't." She really didn't want to eat, but she knew Cal would fuss if she didn't. So, she swallowed down the yogurt and moved to the cereal.

"Maybe relying on your feelings isn't the best option, but I don't think we should discount them out of hand," Cal said carefully, as if working through a very complex problem. "It's like Zara told me last night," he muttered, clearly more to himself as he pulled the laptop onto his lap and began typing away.

"What is?" she pressed.

He didn't look at her. Frowned at the article about her mother's death. "Zara said we—me and my brothers—were focusing too much on us, and I thought she meant personally, but even beyond that we're trying to tie it to the military."

"It makes sense. That's what you have in common with my father."

"But not with you. Someone tried to kill *you*." He looked at her, his gaze dropping to her neck. The bruises were almost gone now, but she would still likely put on a turtleneck once she finally got dressed. She hated that look in his eye, like somehow the marks on her were his fault.

When he'd thought she'd been *dead*.

"You think it's…separate?"

"No. I think it makes the most sense to connect to your father's disappearance. But maybe that had nothing to do with the military."

"But that doesn't explain how I got here."

"No. It's just another possibility more than an answer."

But it got her thinking about the other things that had cropped up when she'd read about her mother. "I was reading about…" She had no clear memories of her mother. Even the picture of her in the paper or the wedding photo was like looking at a stranger—sure, one that looked almost exactly like her—but a stranger nonetheless.

And still, there was this woman's voice. In her head. Norah wasn't sure, but she thought it was her mother's voice. *Good night, my darling.*

It was all so strange, so garbled and warped—memories and feelings and thoughts in the here and now.

Cal's hand came over hers. "Even if you don't remember, it's a hard thing to read about," he offered. Because this was him too. He had all the annoying ways he wanted to take care of people, but there were also the kind ways. Like other people's anguish made him want to soothe it.

She figured that was probably one of the things she loved most about him. Who wouldn't?

"It isn't just that it was hard. It's that… All those details added up. But mine don't. When you found me in the ditch, I just had Evelyn and Hero. No phone. No ID or wallet. Mom had those things on her. I had to have had those on me at one point. Something on me to get me here. How did I get here with no cash? No phone?"

Cal stared at her for the longest time. She got the impression he was calculating things in his head. She could remember him doing that. She could recall sitting in dining rooms and her apartment—which she could remember bits and pieces of: green curtains in the living room, a picture of mountains in her bedroom. Nothing concrete, no full images. But tiny fragments of memories. Cal at her kitchen table, looking grim.

Cal, outside some building. Cold outside. Warm inside. This same look on his face.

I'm being deployed.

I guess that's it then.

I guess so.

"Cal…" She didn't know how to explain to him that she both remembered and she didn't. Flashes of things that didn't fully make sense. He'd be able to make sense of him, but there was some…need to figure them out on her own. To have her own memory fill in the blanks first.

"I don't like what I'm about to say," Cal said gruffly. "And I can't believe I'm going to say it, but time is of the essence. I think we should take Landon and Hazeleigh's place. We should be the ones who go to DC. Together."

Chapter Ten

It was a terrible idea. Cal kept trying to talk himself out of it even as he prepared to take Norah to DC.

They were keeping the reservations under Landon and Hazeleigh's names, and Landon was just switching out the ID photos. Cal didn't want anyone knowing Norah was anywhere near DC.

But she was right. All her belongings had to be somewhere. Someone had tried to kill her somewhere.

And none of those somewheres was here.

He didn't think it was DC—how had she gotten all the way here without phone, money or things for Evelyn? Add in the man who'd shot Jake, and in all likelihood it had taken place closer.

But maybe not *that* close. Because otherwise someone could have finished her off in that ditch.

Cal fought off the shudder of horror at the thought as he packed a suitcase, trying to consider what a man on vacation might pack to go somewhere.

When he'd never been on a vacation in his life.

Norah was doing the same. She'd been eager to agree to Cal's plan, far more eager than he was to put it in motion, but he knew she still had some reservations about leaving Evelyn behind.

But it was bad enough taking Norah. He'd be damned if he waltzed into danger with their baby in tow.

Theirs.

He zipped the suitcase—borrowed from Jessie, who'd been the only one between the twelve of them who had real luggage—not just duffel bags and backpacks.

He could force Norah to stay, Cal knew that, but the bottom line was that the answers, at least some of them, were there in her brain. If he took her back to her old life, her apartment, her father's house, she might remember something. Or they might find something in any of those places.

He thought about the look on her face as she'd explained what she felt over her mother's murder. Her insistence that she felt unsettled didn't sit right with Cal, even as he tried to convince himself it was just her gaps in memory causing that feeling.

She said some things were coming back to her, but mostly in such small pieces they didn't make much sense. And she had no memories of the day someone had wrapped their fingers around her throat and tried to squeeze the life out of her.

Cal paused in his packing because the red haze of fury, and utter terror at thinking about what she must have done to survive, threatened to envelope him so he was nothing but revenge.

And as much as he might want revenge with every fiber of his being, he was soldier enough to lock it away. The mission came above revenge. The truth mattered more than inflicting damage on someone.

For now.

He looked around the tiny attic room he'd taken as his from the first. Knowing he'd never want more space, or to be more comfortable, because a life without the military, without Norah, had been bleak. Why would he need space for anything else?

But now there was a woman downstairs, a baby downstairs, and he wanted more. So much more than he'd ever have the courage to articulate. But to have that more, he'd be putting them in unknown danger.

He pushed that thought aside. Maybe it'd be better to hold on to it. A reminder. A talisman, so the end of all this didn't destroy him completely.

But what did it matter if it did destroy him? His brothers had wives and girlfriends, soon-to-be children and stepchildren. He could fall apart in this little attic room and no one would know the difference.

He could be hard-ass, annoying Cal. A gargoyle or ghost or whatever he pleased once Norah was ensconced somewhere safe, in a life where she'd raise Evelyn to be a young woman. Evelyn would grow up safe and loved.

Without a father. Just like you did.

What if we learned together?

He jerked the suitcase off the bed and moved for the door. *Enough.*

He had a mission to complete. No time for all the personal, painful merry-go-rounds of indecision and memory, yearning and knowing better.

Right now, the only thing he'd allow himself to think about was finding out what had happened to Norah and punish whoever had done it. Nothing else could possibly matter.

He carried the suitcase out of his room, down two flights of stairs, satisfied he'd have everything he needed.

Then he turned the corner of the bottom stairs and stopped cold. Because a few yards away, through the little doorway, he could see his family assembled in the living room. Jake sat on the armchair, Zara perched on the arm. Landon was at the little window nook, going through some papers, Dunne standing over his shoulder, while Hazeleigh sat next to him talking to Quinn.

Norah stood in the middle of the room with Evelyn in her arms. Jessie and Sarabeth were standing, making faces and noises at Evelyn, while Henry watched with a bemused expression. Brody and Kate shared secret little smiles curled up on the couch, heads together.

It stopped him cold. The whole tableau. The woman he'd once vowed to love forever, till death did them part, with his child in her arms. Like she belonged here, with the family he'd found, in this little patch of good in the middle of nowhere, Wyoming.

Right where he wanted her to be.

Then she turned a little, like she sensed him there. Her blue gaze met his, and she smiled.

They were going to find out who had tried to kill her, and still she turned to him and smiled.

Cal had never believed in miracles. Miracles would have saved his mother—or hers. It would have saved him from the hell of the ages of thirteen on. It would have stopped all the wars he'd put on a uniform to fight. Miracles didn't exist anywhere.

But she felt like one.

He didn't have the first damn clue what to do with miracles.

Norah smiling at him seemed to alert everyone else to his presence, and Landon waved him over.

"Here you go," Landon said, slapping a billfold to his chest. "ID, credit, everything you'll need. Address to Dunne's secret house."

"My father's," Dunne corrected, handing Cal a small key.

"I was careful, but my father's a suspicious man. So watch your back."

Cal knew Dunne had a complicated relationship with his father, but it certainly wasn't one of hate. If Dunne's father was mixed up in this...

"I don't think he's involved, but if he is, we'll deal with it," Dunne said, his voice low. "The most important thing is the truth."

Cal didn't miss the *we*. Because the men who'd become his brothers *were* his we. No matter how they went on from this moment, or the ones before, they were linked. Always. And it wasn't just by the threat posed by a terrorist organization that might know who they were.

"I'll drive you to the airport, drop you off," Henry said. "We can bring the baby if you'd like."

Norah shook her head. "It'll be easier to say goodbye here." But she clutched Evelyn like she'd never be able to say goodbye.

"We'll take good care of her," Jessie assured her.

Norah nodded, swallowing. "I know you will. You..." She looked down at Sarabeth fondly. "You've *both* been a godsend." She kissed Evelyn's cheek, squeezed her tight, whispered goodbyes and *I love yous* to her, then turned to Cal. There were tears in her eyes, but she still smiled.

Cal didn't hesitate when Norah held Evelyn out to him. Not anymore. He took her and whispered his own goodbyes. And promises.

He'd bring her mother back and give her all the answers she deserved. Justice would be served. For both of them.

Then he handed Evelyn off to Jessie, and it was like handing a part of himself. Some long-lost part of himself he'd only just gotten back.

But there was a mystery to solve, a mess to be cleaned up, a mission to complete. He turned to Norah. "Ready?"

IT WAS SURREAL, for so many reasons, to go through the airport with Cal. to sit next to him on a plane, switch planes in Denver. to land in DC knowing this was supposed to be her home, and she felt no sense of recognition or belonging.

Which was strange, because when she looked out the window in Wyoming, something had settled inside of her like she really was home.

Or maybe it was just that without Evelyn, nothing felt like home. Jessie had been a saint and sent multiple pictures and videos, so that as they got into a car Cal had rented, Norah could go through and see her baby, healthy and loved on, perfectly happy.

Evelyn would never remember her parents had left her in Wyoming to solve her mother's attempted murder. She'd remember none of it.

Norah hoped.

They drove through different areas, and Norah searched the streetlights in the dark for some blip of memory. But she only felt out of place. Unsettled. Overwhelmed not just by the fact that she didn't remember, but at the fact there were so many lights. So many buildings and people.

"You're frowning," Cal noted, which was one of the first things he'd said to her that didn't have to do with where they were going, or what the next leg of the trip was.

She shook her head. "I'm trying to remember something. Trying to feel some sense that this is home. But all I can think is there are too many cars, too many buildings and lights. It's hard to believe I actually lived here."

He was quiet a beat, then sighed. Like she was somehow dragging what he'd say next out of him. "You weren't the biggest fan of DC. You were here because your father was, and you didn't want to abandon him after your mother died. You had someone... A great-uncle or somebody who owned a ranch in Colorado. You always said that was your dream, but you didn't want to be that far away from your father. So, it had to wait until he retired and you could convince him to move."

Norah mulled that over. This devotion to a father she didn't remember. She could picture him now, because she'd seen pictures. But there were no snippets of memory of him like there was with Cal. Even her feelings were muted. She couldn't access whatever devotion had lived inside her.

Was it the memory loss, or was it that somehow she'd lost that feeling? Was her father the reason she was in this mess? She glanced at Cal. His face seemed harder in the cool lights that played over him as they drove.

"My father was the one who told you I was dead?" she asked. He'd told her that, more than once, but she kept hoping that rehashing would unlock something inside of her. Her bruises were almost completely healed now. Why wasn't her brain?

"Yes. I..." He didn't quite fidget—Cal wasn't a man who fidgeted—but it was almost like he was tensing as if to ward off a blow. "There's no getting around the fact he lied to me. Me and my brothers had arrived at our camp, but we hadn't moved in yet. You and I had minimal communication during that time, as much as was allowed, but we were getting ready to move in and I knew I wouldn't be able to communicate with you for a while. I wanted to talk to you one more time, so I called and your father answered. I know it was him, and he said you'd been in a terrible car accident. He wasn't sure you'd make it."

Norah's stomach twisted. "You went off on your mission

not knowing if I'd make it?" It seemed a terrible burden to ask of someone, even a soldier.

Cal shrugged, turning off on a more residential street. "Didn't have much of a choice."

But there was something in the way he said those words that had her pressing. "What about leave or whatever?"

Again, there was no outward response, but she could see he stiffened. "I requested it. Both then, and when I returned and got your father's message that you hadn't made it." His jaw worked, through a myriad of emotions that played out in his eyes but so quickly that she couldn't identify them all. "Both times I was denied," he said flatly.

"By my father," she clarified, though she supposed she didn't need to.

"Not directly, but I can only assume, now, that he had something to do with it."

Norah's fingers fluttered up to her neck. She had shied away from directly asking about this, because she'd been so focused on her memory. On Evelyn. On anything but… "Do you think my father could have been the one to…"

Cal flicked her a glance, not that she could read it in the dim light of the car's interior, but he reached over. Unerringly found her hand and squeezed. "First, you reported him missing three weeks ago, so the timeline wouldn't add up. Second, he loved you. I don't have any doubts about that, Norah. Maybe he's messed up in something beyond his control, but he loved you. And I can only assume he was lying to us because he was trying to protect you."

"From what? You?"

"A family-less soldier without a cent to his name or any sort of prospects aside from dying in war? Yeah. If I had to wager a guess, he found out about us and wanted to put an end to it. But only to protect you, Norah."

She wasn't sure she believed that. What a terrible, nasty kind of protection. Selfish. If her father truly loved her, she didn't know how to believe he would have told her Cal was *dead*. Or vice versa. That wasn't love. That was control.

She closed her eyes for a moment, trying to come up with any memory of her father. A smile. A hug. A warm word. A cold one. Anything.

But there was nothing.

"This is it."

Norah opened her eyes and Cal was squinting through the dark. She didn't see anything at first, but he pulled the car into an alley and a narrow, well-kept house came into view. It was mostly in shadow, but the streetlight gave her a little glimpse. Very unassuming. There were no numbers visible, so she wasn't sure how he knew, but he no doubt did.

"I want to take a look around before we walk in. Just make sure everything is on the up and up. I think you should stay here, but…"

"But?"

"We don't know what kind of danger we're wading into here." He reached forward, pulled open the glove compartment. Inside was a gun. Norah could only blink at it. He'd rented this car form the airport. Or so she'd thought.

"How is there a gun in here? How do you *know* there's a gun in here?"

"We've got our ways," he said. "But they are ways that also might put us on the wrong person's map. So, I want you to hold on to this." He picked the gun up, then took her hand. He curled her fingers around the heavy instrument—not just handing it to her, but putting her fingers where they needed to be to shoot it.

"I'm not going to shoot someone," she said, more reflexively than because she'd thought about it. She supposed if she had gotten away from someone strangling her, she just might have shot someone or worse.

"You won't have to use it," Cal said, a soothing note to his voice. "It's just a precaution."

"Doesn't 'precaution' mean I *might* have to use it?" she demanded, not liking the feel of it at all. So heavy and cold and deadly. She would start shaking any minute—she could feel it internally already.

"Just be on the lookout. Okay? I promise, Norah, nothing is going to happen to you under my watch. If on the very slim chance someone appears, and tries to hurt you, you flick this, point, then pull that. At the very least, I'll hear the shot and come take care of it."

"What if someone tries to hurt *you*?" Norah demanded, trying desperately to sound strong to quell her panic.

Cal's mouth curved, ever so slightly. Arrogance, maybe. Probably not misplaced since he'd gone on *missions* and fought in wars and come back alive. "Just let me take a quick look around the perimeter, okay?"

When she said nothing and he just *waited* for her okay, she realized he was actually waiting for her *permission*. He wasn't going to just leave her here with a gun. He needed her to be okay with it. Which hit her harder than maybe it should have. She looked down at the gun. "Did I know how to do this before I lost my memory?"

"Yes."

She looked up at him and something about the expression on his face prompted her to ask the next question. "Was I any good at it?"

"No."

She laughed, couldn't help it. "Comforting."

He leaned forward and did something so shocking she had no words. He pressed a sweet kiss to her forehead. "Just sit tight. I'll be right back." Then he got out of the car and slid into the shadows.

Norah could only watch him go. Then look down at the gun in her hands. She didn't like the feel of it. Cold and heavy. She remained unconvinced she'd ever really learned how to use a gun. It felt so *wrong*.

And it was dark around her. How would she know what to shoot? When?

Her heart pounded, thundering in her ears. How would she possibly hear someone approach when she could only hear her own body—heartbeats and heavy breathing. She didn't want to be in the dark alone. She didn't want a gun.

Norah? Where are you? I promise, sweetheart, let's talk this out and everything will be okay.

She remembered the words—the voice here in her head—but there was only dark in her memory. And she didn't recognize the voice. It wasn't Cal, she knew that for certain. There was almost a drawl to the man's voice in her memory.

Norah, you don't understand.

Something about the words had a fury erupting inside of her. Violent and dark. But the pounding in her chest, the breath coming in pants subsided. So she could hear the quiet of the car.

She was calm now. A kind of deadly calm, one that wanted to take a shot at something, just to feel the kick of the gun.

Maybe she *didn't* want to get her memory back.

A little swath of light to the left, Cal stepping into it. The light was from his phone. He walked to her door, then pulled it open. "Looks clear. We'll leave the suitcases but bring your purse or anything with the fake IDs on it."

Norah looked down at the gun, the way her fingers were curled around it. She didn't want to relinquish it now, which was so utterly ridiculous after not wanting to hold it in the first place.

But in a smooth, calming move, Cal took it from her. He held the car door open, waited for her to collect her things, then closed it behind her. They went up the walk with only the light of the phone.

"We'll eat. Get a good night's sleep. Start fresh in the morning," he murmured, his hand coming to rest on her back. A gentle pressure, leading her toward the door.

"We?" She asked looking up at him pointedly.

He glanced at her, the little quirk of a smile barely visible in the shadows. "I don't know what part of that 'we' you're questioning."

She didn't either. She'd meant it as…was *he* really going to rest and eat when she did? But then she started thinking about *resting* and *together.*

She probably shouldn't. What with her amnesia and all. Attempted murders and danger and being half a country away from her daughter.

But she'd kissed him, and now she wanted to know what else she was missing.

Or you want to pretend you aren't here to figure out who tried to kill *you. Pretend you didn't just remember somehow you were furious at an unnamed voice in the dark.*

Maybe, somehow, it was both. Pretend and yearning.

She stepped onto the little porch, but Cal stopped abruptly, his hand on her back turning into a fist in her coat, stopping her just as suddenly. He reached out with his other hand and took her arm and pulled her back to him.

"Someone's here." He said it so quietly she was almost convinced she'd imagined the words. But his grip on her arm was so tight she couldn't have moved forward if she'd wanted to. "Go back to the car, Norah. Now."

Chapter Eleven

Cal didn't watch to see if she went back to the car, but maybe he should have. There were no lights on inside the house, but he'd seen movement in the sidelight. Just a shadow, but movement was movement.

"I'm not going back to the car without you," Norah whispered behind him.

He should have known she wouldn't listen, memory or no. Not her forte.

Cal had to pretend she wasn't there and think this through. It could be innocent enough. Dunne's father kept this as a kind of safe house when he needed to put someone up. Secretly. It could just be that, although Dunne had asked his father if they could use it for a day or two. Maybe a major general didn't keep the clearest tabs on secret guests to his secret houses.

Of course a major general knows who's coming and going.

If Cal was alone, he'd sneak in and handle it. Without a second thought.

He looked back at Norah. Secreting her away in the car didn't do much if he actually had to go in—she'd be out of sight, too far away to protect completely. He'd done a full sweep of the outside of the house and seen no signs of anyone, but that didn't mean someone couldn't arrive and attempt to hurt her.

"What if we called the police?"

He spared her a look. "This isn't quite a get-the-police-involved situation, what with fake identities and potential murderers."

Norah sighed. "Okay, it's not ideal. But I mean, we *do* have the fake identities. Couldn't we pretend like this is our rental house or whatever, and we're afraid to go in because someone's in there?"

Cal contemplated. He didn't want to get the cops involved, but the plan had some merit. It just needed a little finesse. "Here's the deal. We're going to go in. Just like this is *our* rental, like you said. You stay behind me. We'll make a lot of noise—key jiggling in the lock, chatting loudly, give whoever is in there lots of warning."

"What if whoever it is just *shoots* with all that warning?" she demanded, her whisper cracking into a bit of a shriek.

"Highly unlikely," Cal replied, though he couldn't say it was impossible. "Shooting people attracts attention. Particularly if they think we're just some lost tourists or something. Just stay behind me."

"You want me to stay behind you because they think you might shoot!"

Cal tried to bite back a sigh and tried not to wish he'd left her back in Wyoming. Where she'd be safe. Where she'd be out of the way so he could get this *done*.

But she was here, and he supposed that it should be comforting she was worried about him. Of course, she didn't remember *him*. It was very possible that at any moment she could remember everything and want to stay right here in DC. Well, not without Evelyn...

Hell, he needed to concentrate. He took her hand in his. "Trust me. Okay?"

He couldn't see in the dark, but he had no doubt she was frowning. "I mostly do. Except the part where I don't trust you not to martyr yourself to a cause, particularly when the cause is *me*."

She sounded so much like herself then. Not that she'd sounded different in the days she'd been back in his life, but the way she cut right to the heart of things, without seeming uncertain.

Yet another thing he didn't have the time to think about. "No martyrs. Just answers." He shoved the key into the lock, making as much noise as possible. "Good size," he said, putting a lot of volume and over-joviality in his voice. "I suppose we could have rented something a little smaller."

Norah sighed, but she held his hand in a death grip. "Oh, but it's nice to have the space to stretch out. Especially if we do all the sightseeing you have on your list."

He smiled in approval, then turned the key, making sure to roughly turn the knob so it made as much noise as it could. He swung the door open, let it hit the opposite wall with a thud.

"Whoops," he muttered with a chuckle. "Guess I'm a little too excited."

He stepped over the threshold, a tight grip on Norah's hand so he could keep her safely behind him. When she stepped over the threshold, she tripped loudly.

"Yikes," she said, with an overloud chuckle of her own. "It's awfully dark. I can't see a thing."

"Should be a light switch around here," Cal replied, but he took a moment to still, to listen. He watched the dark for another movement of shadow. He didn't reach for a switch, he was too busy analyzing the threat, and determining all the ways he'd keep Norah safe from it.

"Are you sure this is the right place?" Norah asked, sounding cheerful with just a touch of hesitation that suited their little charade perfectly.

"The key worked, Cheryl," Cal returned, with just enough edge to his voice to sound like some weak-willed husband.

"No need to get snippy, *Tom*," she replied, a matching edge to her own voice.

Cal nearly laughed. He slowly started to feel along the wall for the switch. He had his gun in his other hand, and though he couldn't see in the dark he knew Norah held hers as well. She was playing along just right. His only complaint was he kept having to move her behind him.

His fingers brushed the switch, but before he could flip it on, he heard the movement. It was almost a surprise, as the movement wasn't that far away and he hadn't sensed anything in his room, but Cal was ready.

Always.

He expected the swish of an arm moving a gun to aim, but it wasn't a gun or a shot, but an arm moving through the air in an attempt to land a blow. So, he didn't use his own gun in return, too risky.

Cal managed to push Norah back closer to the door they'd just entered. He ducked and narrowly dodged the blow, at the same time sweeping out a leg to kick at the attacker's leg.

The body didn't go down, but he heard the low grunt of his foot coming into contact with the attacker's shin. Now that he had a better idea of where the attacker stood and how, Cal quickly stepped forward and landed a hard blow to the man's throat.

There was a gasping, gurgling sound, then the *thunk* of the man folding, his knees hitting the ground. Cal immediately moved around to the back of the man, grabbing his arms and pulling them sharply back.

It wasn't much of a fight, which concerned Cal. Either he'd bested someone who had nothing to do with anything, or he was *meant* to best whoever this was. Still, he held the man's arms tight and did a quick sweep of the man's pockets and body to make sure he had no weapons on him.

"Get the lights," Cal said to Norah, being careful not to use her name.

He heard her moving around, likely pawing the walls for some kind of switch. When the light finally popped on, Cal had to wince as his eyes adjusted from light to dark. He could only see the back of the man's head from his angle, but still Cal knew...

He knew this man. And so did Norah.

"Colonel Elliot," he breathed out.

What the hell was Norah's *father* doing here?

NORAH STARED. It *was* the man from the pictures, though he looked older than he had in any of the photos she'd studied, looking for resemblances, memories, feelings.

He stared at her like she was a ghost. She supposed she was staring back the same way. *And* she was pointing a gun at him. She lowered it immediately.

Slowly, and with a very unreadable expression on his face, Cal dropped her father's hands. Her father got to his feet carefully, like his body hurt. He took a halting step toward her, then as if he thought better of it, looked over his shoulder at the man who'd restrained him.

The color seemed to leech out of his face. "Cal." His head whipped back to her, then to Cal again. "You..."

Cal didn't make it, Norah. I'm so sorry.

But...

It was a freak accident. No fault of his own, of course. But they're all gone. A shame. A loss for all of us.

He'd told her that. She could remember it now. Something about his voice, that look in his eyes. It brought back the scene in her mind. Her father, holding her hands, looking her right in the eye.

Lying.

"What's going on here?" Cal said, in an authoritative tone that brooked no argument.

But it clearly ruffled her father's superior military officer feathers, because some of his color returned and he straightened, smoothing out the sweater he was wearing. "I don't answer to you, Young." He turned his eyes to Norah. "Where's…"

"Where's who?" Cal returned, crossing his arms over his chest, a carefully raised eyebrow.

He was going to ask about Evelyn, but he didn't. Her father—her *father*—said nothing, wouldn't look Cal or Norah in the eye.

"I need some ice," he muttered, moving his jaw tenderly and then striding down the hallway. He flipped on lights as he went. Cal frowned after him, but didn't follow until Norah came to stand next to him.

"Any ideas?" he muttered.

Norah shook her head. She was still unsteady from the memory of her father telling her Cal was dead. Or was it a dream? Old or new. Maybe she'd made it up in the aftermath of everything that had happened as some sort of answer.

But it seemed so clear. So real. She gripped Cal's hand, needing something to hold on to. Some steady force. "Cal…"

"Let's see what he has to say before we say anything he might overhear," he said quietly. He took her gun, and shoved it into the holster under his shirt. He kept his in his hand. Then he moved forward, pulling her along.

In the kitchen, her father stood by the freezer holding a

bag of frozen vegetables to his face. When Cal and Norah entered, his eyes dropped to their hands.

He didn't sneer—in fact, nothing on his face moved at all—but there was still something about the moment that *felt* like a sneer. Like she should drop Cal's hand and step away.

But why on earth would she do that? When Cal was the one who'd found her and saved her, and she'd reported her father missing but he was *here*. Alive and well.

"I suppose Wilks gave you a key."

"Did he give *you* one?" Cal countered.

Her father said nothing to that, his mouth going into a firm line.

Norah didn't know what to think—she didn't know enough, remember enough—but she had to believe that however her father was here, Dunne's father didn't know or he would have mentioned it.

Right?

She wanted to rub her temples. None of this made sense. But Cal held on to her hand and kept with his calm but direct questioning.

"You're alive and well. Aren't you surprised to find Norah the same way?"

Her father's eyebrows drew together and he dropped the bag from his face for a minute. "What do you mean?"

Did he not know someone had tried to kill her? Or was he pretending?

Norah looked up at Cal and got the sense he had the same questions, but he didn't voice them. He didn't say anything.

Her father sighed, shoulders slumping. "Why don't we sit?" he said, gesturing to the table. Norah watched him as he lowered himself into the seat at the head of the little table. He held the bag to his cheek, but somehow...made it seem like he was in charge. While he sat there, patiently waiting for them to sit. Waiting for them to sit down and take whatever lecture he was about to give.

She recognized this man. The mantle of authority he wore as if he'd been born with it. *We'll sit. We'll talk. Because I said so. I'll sit here patiently until you're adult enough to join the conversation.*

Had he said that to her once? Surely the voices in her head were real, were memories, but it was still such a jumble. But the jumble seemed to be unraveling faster with every passing hour, with every person she connected to who she'd once known.

She remembered this man. She could picture him in a cozy little kitchen with sunlight streaming through the windows. A cold fury on his face, carefully packed away and smoothed out with a smile.

It didn't make sense, but the thing that struck her as the most concerning was that no warm feelings rushed to the surface like the days back in Wyoming with Cal. Or when she held Evelyn. There was no wave of love or yearning she didn't understand. There was no sense of safety or trust.

Only questions. Only worry.

She took a deep breath and was the first to move, first to sit. Cal followed, but she could tell it was reluctantly. He put his gun on the table in front of him, his hand resting on it. A warning, or threat, or maybe somehow both.

"All right, Elliot," Cal said, and somehow Norah knew leaving off his rank was purposeful *and* made her father mad. Though he made no attempt to express his displeasure, it was there in his shoulders. In the icy expression on his face.

For a blinding second, all Norah could think was *I have to run*. But that was… Cal had told her her father loved her. That she'd wanted to stick around DC until he retired. Her faulty memory, even as it came back to her in bits and pieces, really couldn't be fully trusted.

But haven't your feelings been on point so far?

She stared at her father, trying to get some grip on something she could trust. A fact. A full memory. A feeling that felt good instead of uneasy. He didn't look at either of them as he sat across the table. He was organizing his thoughts, Norah figured.

She glanced at Cal. His gaze was icy as well. Everything about him was tense and coiled, ready to react. But only *react*. Not act.

And in between these two cold forces of men there was her. Uncertain. Tired. Scared.

She looked back at her father and when he finally met her gaze, she saw questions in his eyes. Uncertainties. She *knew* Cal wanted to give nothing away. But something told her...

"I don't remember anything," she said, and bit back the urge to add *or not very much*. "Cal found me, unconscious, bleeding. Someone had tried to kill me." She didn't tell him where. She didn't mention Evelyn.

She wanted to see his reaction. She wanted... No, she desperately needed to see some flare of surprise. Even if she'd question if it was good acting, she needed him to at least *act*.

His gaze turned to Cal, all accusing. "Why are you trying to lie? What is this?" He pushed back from the table, standing. "I told you to let it lie," he said, pointing at her. "What did you do?"

But Norah had no idea what she was supposed to let lie.

"What was she supposed to let lie?" Cal demanded, as if he could read her own questions, but had the strength to voice them.

She didn't feel strong. She felt weak. And like she wanted

to run away and hide. Which didn't make *sense*—not with the information Cal had given her.

But maybe there was information that even Cal didn't know. "What?" Cal demanded, his voice laced with steel but none of the edgy energy pumping off her father.

"*You*, you lousy son of a bitch."

Chapter Twelve

It took Cal a full minute for those words to coalesce in his brain with any kind of understanding. "I don't know what you're talking about," he said, trying to keep his voice even. Trying to keep the crazy, wild beating of his heart under control. "You told me she was dead, and I did your bidding—in the Middle East, and when we were brought home with our fake deaths and new identities."

Colonel Elliot didn't say anymore. Cal could see a cold fury behind his gaze, but he held it under control.

Cal figured it was for Norah's sake. Not his.

"You married my daughter in secret, bad enough, but then you went ahead and left on that suicide mission."

Cal's blood ran cold. He didn't breathe for too long, and when he finally did the only thing that saved him from a gasp of pain was all the damn training he'd gone through to be prepared for the missions Colonel Elliot had sent him on.

When he spoke, it was through gritted teeth because no matter how he tried he couldn't get his jaw to relax. "We were told it was an imperative mission, and while it came with the same dangers as any other mission, it was hardly *suicide*."

Elliot scoffed. "Yes, that's why we found a bunch of soldiers who didn't have a family," he replied, as if Cal should have known all along.

And he had. He hadn't wanted to. He'd convinced himself in a million different ways they were chosen because they were good. Damn good.

But they were expendable. He'd wondered that, as his brothers had shared their childhoods and lives and what had led them there. He'd wondered if it wasn't just that no one would miss them if they were gone.

In the end, even Dunne's own father viewed them as expendable pieces to a far more important venture. Cal wished he could believe it was peace, but even now he wondered.

"But you ruined it."

"By coming back alive?" Cal returned, the bitterness leaking into his tone like acid.

"You married her," Elliot said, jerking his chin at Norah. "Left her pregnant and alone. The fact that you came back was just another step in the betrayal."

Cal shook his head. The fact Colonel Elliot could sit there, talking about suicide missions and Cal's survival like it was a *betrayal*... He didn't know how to navigate this. He wanted to cover his face with his hands, find someplace private to absorb all this.

But there was no quarter, only the pain and confusion and doing everything he could to keep it buried deep under the surface.

Elliot turned to Norah. Cal found he couldn't. He wouldn't survive whatever look was on her face.

"I did what was best, and I thought you understood that," he said to her. Earnestly. Cal had always thought Colonel Elliot doted on her. He'd loved his daughter, but there was something about the way Elliot said those words that didn't *sound* like love.

Now that Cal knew what love really was. It was what he'd felt when he thought he'd lost Norah. It was what made Jake step in front of a bullet for him last year. It was Evelyn, locking eyes with him.

It wasn't twisting things so Norah would agree with him.

Cal turned, even knowing it would hurt to look at her. She'd paled, and underneath the table her hand trembled, but she didn't let her father see that. Her chin came up. "I don't know what you're talking about. I don't remember anything."

He snorted. "Yet here you are. With him." Elliot blew out a breath, clenched his hands into fists, then relaxed them. "This isn't what's important," he said, evenly enough. "Why are you here?"

Cal could not trust this man. Ever. He never should have in the first place. Never should have idolized him or believed in him, but he had.

That was the betrayal. One he'd have to deal with later, when there weren't bigger issues at hand. He considered not telling Elliot the real reason for being here. There was no way to know what Elliot was doing, or how much he'd had to do with…anything. Maybe he was acting like he didn't know someone had tried to kill Norah.

But surely he'd figure out why they'd come all this way. Together. Without Evelyn. And if he truly didn't know about the murder attempt, maybe no matter how many betrayals there were, he could help find out who'd done it.

Can you trust this man's help?

Cal looked Elliot in the eye, icing away all the emotions that swirled deep inside of him. Focusing on the reality of this situation. The fact fury and blame were plain as day on the face of the man he'd once idolized. The fact there was an empty bottle of Jack near the sink, and the flush on Elliot's face wasn't only from exertion and anger.

This wasn't the Colonel Elliot he'd once known, so he needed to treat him like a stranger. Maybe the colonel wasn't drunk, but he'd been drinking heavily since coming here. Enough to lose some of a veneer that had always been there.

If the man was drunk enough, would he get violent? Had he? With Norah? Because of Cal. It didn't matter why. It only mattered who. So, Cal told the bare-bones truth. "Someone tried to kill Norah, and we're going to find out who."

Colonel Elliot frowned at that, eyebrows drawing together. "I don't understand why anyone would want to kill Norah," he said, rubbing at his temple with his free hand, his other occupied with the bag of frozen vegetables.

"Neither do I," Cal returned. Pointedly.

Elliot slowly lowered the bag from his face. "You think *I* had something to do with it?" he demanded.

"Someone strangled her. That's not random. That's not strangers passing. That's personal. She reported you missing over three weeks ago, and then someone tried to kill her and as far as *I* can tell, no one has reported her or Evelyn missing."

"So you know about…"

"My child? Yeah, I do." Cal had known fury before. Blinding rage and anger, but it had nothing on the full-blown realization that Elliot hadn't just caused the emotional trauma of telling them each other had died, he'd meant to deprive Cal of *ever* knowing his own child. Ever.

Norah's hand found his under the table. He couldn't unclench his fist, but it was something. An anchor, he supposed, to help remind him that his anger did nothing. His fury didn't get him back to Wyoming. Didn't keep Norah safe. Only a calm, clear mind would do that.

Elliot looked from Norah to Cal. "I don't understand any of this, but I can be certain neither do the two of you. I had to go into hiding, yes. But for military reasons that have nothing to do with Norah."

"Do they have something to do with me?"

Elliot shot him a look, and there was fury there. Hate. "You're dead, Cal. Remember?"

Which didn't answer the question, and Cal decided in this moment not to push. It would be better to have Landon poke into things without Elliot being too aware of their suspicions. Of what they knew or would know.

"Listen," Colonel Elliot said, and there was a calm now in the way he spoke that Cal remembered. It wasn't harsh or angry. It was almost kind.

Almost.

"This is a complicated and clearly confusing situation, and it's the middle of the night. No doubt you two are tired, and I need to unearth some painkillers for my jaw." He looked at Cal archly, but not with the same daggers he'd been aiming his way. "There are three bedrooms here. I suggest we all lie down for the night. Rest. In the morning, clearheaded, we can tackle this."

"Tackle *what*?" Norah asked, evidently baffled by this change in demeanor.

Cal wasn't baffled. He understood it for what it was. A tactical retreat. Not necessarily nefarious, but obviously to get a hold of his emotions. Maybe check in with anyone else involved in whatever this was. Soldiers didn't let their feelings get the better of them, and they didn't move forward without the necessary information.

Colonel Elliot had taught that to Cal himself.

"We'll tackle finding out who hurt you. Trust me, Norah. I won't rest until they're brought to justice." He said it with just the right amount of fervor.

Except…

He didn't move to touch her. Not a hug. Not a shoulder squeeze. Not even the careful separation Cal had first employed, so sure if he touched her for anything other than basic medical care he might dissolve on the spot.

Cal had watched Colonel Elliot around Norah for *years* before this moment. He'd seen him beam at his daughter. Hug her. Carelessly sling his arm around her shoulders and talk about her as though she alone lit up the earth.

This…was different. Something had changed between them.

Yeah, she secretly married you, remember?

"*If* you're telling the truth," Colonel Elliot said, or muttered more like.

"You think I'd lie? About someone trying to *kill* me?" Norah replied, her voice raising an octave. Her outrage turned her cheeks a faint pink.

Elliot sighed. "I think he would," he said, pointing to Cal. "And I think he'd take advantage of your memory loss to make me the villain."

"You'd be wrong. Dead wrong," Norah returned, her own fury serving to level his out some.

As much as he wanted to demand answers from Colonel Elliot, Cal knew that there was no sense in fighting it here and now. It made more sense to wait. To check in with Landon and all of them back in Wyoming and figure out what was really going on.

Cal couldn't believe even now that Colonel Elliot was the one who had tried to kill Norah, but that didn't mean he hadn't done something wrong. And they needed to figure out what it was.

Soon.

"Elliot is right," Cal said, turning his hand to envelope Norah's. "We're all tired and…emotional," he said, aiming a pointed look at the man across the table. "We'll get some rest. Reconvene in the morning and try to talk this out." He held Elliot's cold gaze. *"Rationally,"* he said, with an unnecessary emphasis that had Elliot's calm demeanor tightening into something closer to rage.

"My thoughts exactly," the older man agreed icily.

NORAH WAS FROZEN. Or that was what it felt like. Ice all the way through.

Everything Cal had told her about her father did not match the man who sat across from her, at times calm and authoritative and at times seething with rage.

But at no point reaching out and touching her. At no point looking at her the way Cal had looked at her in those first days after waking up—intense, as if he was memorizing every line, shocked and surprised but *grateful* she was alive.

She trusted Cal, but none of the things he'd told her about her father made sense in this moment. Had it ever made sense? Or had something…changed?

It dawned on her then. It was Cal that had changed it. She couldn't picture it, but she remembered her father telling her Cal was dead. He'd told her that because he'd known—about the marriage, about Evelyn.

It was wrong, but that was how angry he'd been. *That* was what had changed everything.

But she didn't remember the person her father had been in the aftermath. Was it someone capable of trying to kill her?

"Norah."

It was Cal's voice. Gentle. His hand on her arm. He'd stood and she still sat at the table, staring at her father. Her father wasn't looking at her, or Cal. His gaze was kind of blank, like he wasn't staring at anything at all while he remained at the table, holding the frozen vegetables to his face.

She looked up at Cal. His expression was patient, as gentle

as the hand on her arm. She sucked in a breath and let it out and then allowed Cal to draw her to her feet.

"Take your pick of rooms," her father said with a careless wave of his hand. "There are three. Everyone can have one."

It was pointed enough, Norah bristled. But Cal shook his head vaguely as if trying to impart there was no point arguing. He led her out of the kitchen, and she couldn't help the look over her shoulder.

Her father still sat at the table, drumming his fingers along the surface. His other hand held the frozen vegetables to his jaw. He was clearly lost in thought.

And not all that excited to find her alive and well. But then, maybe he hadn't known she'd been missing or hurt. Maybe he thought she or Cal was lying or exaggerating. Maybe...

But she was making excuses for a man whose behavior didn't make sense to her, and why should she do that?

She remembered him telling her Cal was dead. She remembered that. It was real. It had happened. And her father had told her a lie.

Cal led her upstairs. He poked his head into every room. There was one clearly being used—rumpled bed, clothes on a chair in the corner, one window with curtains open, one closed. A few bottles on the nightstand. Cal hesitated, then shook his head, drawing her to an empty bedroom. It reminded her of some sort of display home. Everything overmatched, in aggressively neutral shades.

Cal led her in, closed the door behind her. He gave an exaggerated yawn. "I know we don't have our things, but we can make do till morning."

"Oh. Well, I could—"

He turned abruptly, practically spinning, and he reached

out and took her by the arms. Gently, yes, but then with no warning his mouth covered hers before she could say anything.

She stood there, rigid for far too long, trying to get her reeling head to make sense of any of this. She wanted to lean into it. To forget everything except the way he held her, kissed her...

But there was so much wrong, so much confusion. Then he moved his mouth to her ear.

"Don't speak. Room is bugged," he whispered, so softly it barely fluttered the strands of hair.

Bugged. Another wrench thrown into any attempt to have a clear handle on the situation. Her heart *pounded.* He thought someone was listening. Maybe even watching, by the way he fake-smiled at her.

She knew, somehow she knew, that was not Cal's real smile.

"Why?" she managed, but then shook her head. He could hardly answer.

He slowly released her, keeping that weird smile on his face. Then turned as if to survey the room, but she watched him very carefully pull his phone out of his pocket, keeping it at his side. With his other hand, he purposefully and exaggeratedly put the gun he'd still been carrying on the nightstand.

He still had the one he'd given her in the car strapped to his body and made no move to take it out of its holster.

Cal opened the closet, peered around, then moved to another door. While he moved, one hand moved over his phone without him even looking at it. He was texting, maybe one of his brothers, but didn't want to look like he was texting.

Norah started to look around the room as if maybe she could see these cameras or listening devices or whatever was supposed to be here, but Cal said her name.

"This is a bathroom," he said, gesturing at the door he'd just opened. "Why don't you clean up a little bit? Get ready for bed."

She opened her mouth to argue with him—or demand to know why he was acting so weird—but the whole someone watching or listening was reason enough, wasn't it?

So, she smiled, nodded and moved into the bathroom. She closed the door behind her. She wanted to sink into the ground and cry, but she stared straight ahead. At her reflection. At whoever Norah... Elliot or Young or whatever her last name was.

Did anything about her life make sense? Even when she remembered, would she have answers?

She closed her eyes and breathed. Maybe she didn't need answers. Being here felt like a mistake. She wanted to be back in Wyoming with her daughter. With Cal and the little family that had been built around him.

A knock sounded on the door. Then Cal's voice. "Can I come in?"

"Of course."

The door squeaked open and Cal stepped in, still smiling all *wrongly*. He left the door open. "You're exhausted, honey. Come on to bed," he said, in that overloud, fake voice. But he made hand motions toward the bath, and as confused as she felt, she finally understood.

"I just want to take a shower."

"Well, I'll join you. Saves water." He closed the door.

She sent him a baleful look, and for a moment there was almost some humor on his face.

He moved around the bathroom, looking everywhere. He turned the water on in the shower. Then pulled the curtain closed. When he spoke this time, he was dead serious, his voice just barely an audible whisper.

"No cameras in here. Bug right outside door might pick up normal voices, but whispers should be okay with the water going. Could be nothing—part and parcel with the safe house—something Dunne's father monitors if he needs to. I don't know, but I'm not about to trust it."

Or Dunne's father, Norah thought sadly. She wasn't sure if it was knowledge or just understanding that both her father and Dunne's had been Cal's heroes and now he had to suspect them, convinced they were bad men, and what a blow that would be.

Norah ran her hands over her face. "What would they be listening for?" But she knew the answer. It was the same answer for everything. *I don't know. I don't know.*

No one knew anything. Her father included.

As if he sensed her frustration, and her exhaustion, Cal reached over and gave her shoulder a squeeze. "I know that was…weird. And gave us more questions than answers, but that's an answer in of itself."

"How?"

"He's involved in something he wants to keep secret. He *hates* me. He treated you…" Cal trailed off, shook his head. "I've never seen him treat you quite like that."

"He didn't touch me," she whispered. "Shouldn't he have… hugged me? Looked at me? Assured himself I was okay?" She could still see the marks of her attack in the mirror. Shouldn't that have caused *some* reaction from her father?

Cal looked at her and she could tell he'd wondered that too, but he hesitated on agreeing with her, for whatever reason. "He was drunk," Cal mused. "Or on his way to it."

"Drunk?"

"Maybe not falling over drunk, but he's relying heavily on alcohol. There were empty bottles in the kitchen, in his room… It was on his breath, in his bloodshot eyes. Stress?

Guilt? A problem no one knew about? Not sure. Too many things I don't understand."

"And I don't remember. Except…"

He looked at her expectantly. She shouldn't have said anything. It would only hurt. Didn't everything hurt enough?

"Norah."

"I just had this…flash. Not even a visual memory. All talking."

"Of?"

"Him telling me you'd died."

Chapter Thirteen

Cal had his own memory of Colonel Elliot informing him of Norah's accident and then death, so he had no doubt the man had lied to his daughter. But her remembering it was like another layer of betrayal when he was already reeling from the way his mentor had turned on him.

"In the memory, he sounds…regretful, I guess," Norah continued. "A lot of 'I'm sorries', and 'what a loss.' But I can't see it, and in a strange way it's like how he was in the kitchen just now. Like… There was an emotional reaction he should have had, but didn't."

"He knew I was alive. Which means he knew…"

Norah let her hands fall from her face and looked at him. "Knew what?"

"At that point, he knew we'd gotten married."

She nodded sadly, as if she'd already come to that realization as well. "I just don't understand why that would… If I wanted to marry you, why should it bother him?"

"I can think of quite a few reasons."

"That's your martyr complex talking," she returned, irritation simmering under all that exhaustion she was trying to battle. "But think of it from a father's perspective. I loved you."

"I had nothing when I entered the military. I was less than

no one. Who would want that for their daughter? I was a soldier, with no education or experience doing something else."

"Isn't he?"

"And he probably wished he hadn't sentenced your mother to that kind of life."

"What male nonsense." She threw up her arms in disgust. "Like women don't make a choice. Like we're just purposeless beings until a man comes along to marry us and ruin us with their manly enterprises."

Cal wanted to smile because it reminded him of *her*. The *her* he'd fallen in love with. So sure of herself, the world and her place in it. Never afraid to call him out on what she'd always termed his *male* nonsense. But this was not the time or place to have this conversation, to remember old arguments. It didn't matter if it *was* nonsense, because clearly her father had felt that way enough to lie. "We'll take turns sleeping," he said, ignoring the subject altogether. "We go nowhere alone."

"Maybe if I spoke to him alone…"

"No," Cal replied, too harshly, he knew, but the thought of Norah being alone with Elliot… "We can't be sure he didn't try to kill you."

"You said he loved me. Doted on me."

"He did. But something has changed, or he's changed. I don't trust the man who spoke to us tonight. Not with anything, including however he treated you before all this went down."

She nodded, and there was something sad in her eyes, but it wasn't disappointment at the betrayal. It was just that she understood. But she held his gaze, purposefully. "Then you have to promise not to be alone with him either."

"I promise," he agreed, if only because getting Elliot alone would mean leaving Norah alone. He wasn't about to let that happen. "What bothers me isn't just the way he spoke to you, it was the things he said too. *I did what was best, and I thought you understood that.* As though you'd had a conversation about it. As if you'd discussed it."

"If we did, I don't remember."

He rubbed her shoulder, wishing he could take that guilt away from her. She was putting too much pressure on herself. It wasn't like it was her fault she couldn't remember, but she blamed herself. "I know, but it wouldn't change anything if you did."

She clearly didn't agree with him, but she didn't argue.

"What bothered me was the *I did what was best*. Like he alone knows what's best. Better than I do. And I think he does believe that. As much as I hate to admit it, I believe he thought he did what was best. That's who he is." She said it without thinking, but something about the way she spoke made it seem like she remembered. Just like the male nonsense comment.

Cal kept still, kept silent, willing her to keep talking, hoping against hope she'd talk herself into another memory.

"He does try to do what's best, it's just… He wants what's best for *him*. It's never about me. It's my safety. My future. But isn't that just about him?" Norah frowned. "It was Evelyn."

When she fell silent, Cal tried to bite his tongue, but he couldn't manage it.

"What was Evelyn?"

"It was… I started to see him differently. The way he treated me. It wasn't love. It was control." Her frown deepened, lines digging across her forehead. "Before Evelyn, I didn't see it. He didn't want me to go out of state for college, take a job outside his office. He didn't want me talking to you or your friends. And I grew up thinking that because of how Mom died, he wanted to protect me."

Cal nodded. "That's what you always told me. That's what I always saw."

She shook her head. "But I was wrong. Naive. Blinded by love or something. And you were too, because you looked up to him. Because he said all the right things. But don't you see, he didn't *do* the right things."

Cal didn't particularly like to think back and believe he'd been wrong about everything, but he supposed it eased some of the burden that Norah had been too. They'd been young and maybe he could admit they'd been manipulated by someone who *seemed* good, because they knew how to play the role.

She sucked in a breath. "I remember… Cal, when I told him I was pregnant, he was mad."

Cal felt a new wave of fury try to spark to life, but there was already so much and he needed a cool head. "Because she was mine."

"No." She shook her head vigorously, reaching out to hold on to him. "Because pregnancy and having a child would interfere with my *duties*." She looked up at him, and her eyes were starting to get suspiciously shiny.

"Maybe—" He wanted her to take a break. To rest. To not remember if it was going to hurt. But she pressed on.

"It took me a while to untangle that. While I was pregnant, everything…soured. He had competition now—he wasn't my world. He didn't want to be a grandpa. He wanted me to do what I'd always done even when I wasn't up to it or had a doctor's appointment."

Cal should have been there. By her side. Instead, he'd gone off to fight one more mission. Needing some kind of validation that he was good enough to be her husband.

But it had been a suicide mission, and he'd been stupid enough to fall for it.

"He wanted the perfect hostess. Someone to blindly take care of all the parts of his life he didn't want to take care of. And I started to wonder if that was his objection to you too. Maybe it wasn't you, though he could certainly blame you— it was anyone who took me away from him." She sucked in a breath. "Yes, because he didn't want me to have my own place. And it was all reaching this point... I didn't want to be around him. I started... I started pulling away. Reading about toxic narcissists. He fit the bill. I just had been too young and naive to see it."

"Or he's that good at the facade. Because I would tell you that no one could ever fool me, Norah. But I thought he was...a hero. A mentor. A good man and a good father."

"My whole life. But then..." She pushed her palm to her temple. Clearly she was in pain. Pushing too hard.

"Let's go to sleep. Rest. We'll figure it all out—"

"But I want to remember it all. I want it to all come back."

"It will. With rest. Remember? The doctor said your brain is healing too. You can't push it."

She looked at him, and one of her tears escaped. "We're running out of time."

He reached out and brushed it away. "We've got time. We've got time for you not to hurt."

But there was that stubborn set to her jaw he remembered so well. He'd seen glimpses of this Norah back at the ranch, but this was full-fledged back to the woman he'd fallen in love with. Because when she wanted something, she dug in. She never gave up. And she refused to let anyone stop her. Even him.

"Here is the timeline, as I remember it," she said. Firmly. "You left... You left." She repeated it, not because she needed to but like saying it unlocked new memories. "I remember saying goodbye."

She'd cried. He'd promised her everything would work out. But it hadn't. Had it? Every promise he'd made, he'd broken—or someone had broken for him. But it didn't matter who was to blame. The result was the same.

She reached out and put her hand on his chest. "I hope you know, I understood. Even when my father told me you'd died, I understood why you'd gone. You needed to. I understood you felt like you needed to make your mark, and there was nothing else that would make you feel that." Her eyes lifted to his, a few more tears had fallen over, but he couldn't wipe them away.

He was frozen, transported to a time he'd shoved away for over a year now. "It really worked out for the best, didn't it?"

She shook her head a little. "Someone did this to us, Cal. Not you. Not me. Maybe my father, but not *only* my father. Someone went out of their way to hurt us. I want to find out who… I think…" She swallowed. "I don't have a clear memory. Maybe this is all wanting it to be true, but I think I knew. I think I'd found out something. Something someone wanted silenced."

EVEN AS NEW memories seemed to cascade inside of her, Norah struggled to think rationally. Just because something felt real, it didn't necessarily mean it was real. And some things were still fuzzy. Vague. She didn't remember marrying Cal, but she remembered saying goodbye.

Then there were feelings. Ones she couldn't articulate or maybe rationalize. And she just had this *feeling* that she'd discovered something.

But what? What could she have discovered? And why wouldn't her father mention whatever she knew. Did he not know? He'd said he thought she understood that—

"You need some sleep, Norah," Cal said gently. "Plus, we can't stay in this bathroom forever."

She looked at the shower. Steam didn't fill the small room, so clearly he hadn't put it on hot. But that did cause a problem. "If we go out with dry hair and the same rumpled clothes and someone is watching the video, they'll know we didn't take a shower."

He pulled a face, clearly irritated with the hole he'd dug himself into. "Well, we didn't bring any extra clothes, so we'll just have to get our hair wet." He took a step toward the shower, flicked the knob, then ducked his head in.

Norah rolled her eyes and looked under the sink for towels. She found a couple of folded hand towels. She handed him one before he got out of the water.

He took it and ran it through his hair. She, on the other hand, draped one towel over her shoulders, then delicately moved her hair into the spray of the shower. She did everything she could to keep the water off her clothes.

She supposed she could have taken them off, but there was a reason they were both dancing around that subject. And it wasn't just her memory; it had to do with danger too. Besides, it was bad enough he could see the cuts and bumps and bruises on her face. The rest of her was still healing and she knew, somehow she knew, it would bury that guilt and responsibility he felt even deeper.

She pulled away, turned off the water, then worked on drying her hair enough not to drip. When she was satisfied and stood up straight, Cal smiled at her.

"See? Fresh as daisies."

She rolled her eyes, but she smiled too. He was trying to take her mind off everything, and she appreciated it. But she couldn't hold the smile for long. "Cal—"

"You're going to rest. Maybe you wake up and remember everything. Maybe it takes a while longer, but every day you're remembering more. Don't push it."

"We might be walking into something dangerous here."

"Someone tried to kill you. Someone shot Jake. At my home. It was always going to be dangerous."

"Is Wyoming really your home?"

His expression was inscrutable. But he held her gaze when he responded. "Yeah, it is."

She nodded. She knew it—didn't need her memory to see how he fit there. How, even with all his many issues, it had become his home base. The family he so sorely needed.

She didn't know what it would mean for her future if—no *when* she remembered everything, but it was good to know that he belonged there.

"Check your phone," Cal said, heading for the door. "Jessie sent you some more pictures and a video of Evelyn sleeping soundly. I don't know what those cameras can pick up, so do it in here. Call her if you need to. I'll go out and see if I can inspect the bugs a little more closely without tipping the camera off."

Norah took in a deep breath and then let it out. "Okay." But...she couldn't just let their earlier conversation go. "I need you to understand something. A parent should always want what's best for their child, and sometimes that's hard because it isn't what's best for the parent. But you loved me, Cal. And I loved you. You have always been a good man. There was no reason for him to treat you or me the way he did—no matter the reason. Don't let him make you think it was right, even if he thinks it was."

He stood very still, almost as if it took him time to fully absorb those words. His mouth curved ever so slightly. "I married you, didn't I?"

She wished she could remember that. But she knew... "I

know you said because of the whole military-faked-your-death thing we're not technically married, but I consider us technically married. You'll have to do a lot more than die on paper to get rid of me."

He looked pained, but she understood somewhere deep in her consciousness that was struggling to reassert itself that it was only because he was trying to protect her.

And possibly himself.

But whether or not she remembered the exact moment the vows were said, they had made vows to one another, and she intended to keep hers…and make him keep his.

Chapter Fourteen

Cal went into the room. He saw three bugs and suspected two camera points, but there was no real way to inspect any of them without being caught on the possible camera.

When Norah emerged from the bathroom, her hair still damp, he could tell she missed Evelyn but also was more re-laxed because she'd had a chance to check on her.

Cal felt the separation himself, though he didn't understand how or why. Sure, Evelyn was his daughter, but it wasn't like he'd spent any significant time with her, and still he missed the weight of her in his arms. The way she looked at him with her mother's eyes, as though she understood far more than a baby could.

Cal sighed but forced himself to smile at Norah. "Let's hit the hay, huh?" He pulled back the covers and gestured her toward the bed. She crawled in, her eyes darting around the room. Cal killed the lights, hoping the camera didn't pick out her clearly *looking* for them.

He slid into bed next to her. She stiffened a little, but he needed to be close enough that she could hear him if he whispered. So, gingerly, he wrapped his arms around her and pulled her to him so he could settle his mouth at her ear.

It was…awkward, unlike any of the other times they'd

shared a bed before. But this wasn't about…them. "I'm going to stay awake," he whispered.

"You need rest too."

"I'll get it. We'll switch. You first."

She sighed but nodded against his head. He started to release her, though some old muscle memory definitely didn't want to, but she wrapped her arms around him and held him there.

So…he didn't pull away. He kept his arms around her, his head rested on hers. They never would have slept like this before. She was a light sleeper. Fidgety. But she fell into even breathing quickly, likely exhausted from *everything*.

He held her there in the dark, and for the first time in over a year, let himself remember. As much as he still wondered how they came out of this in one piece, how they could move forward with a future together, he remembered why they'd risked it in the first place.

No matter how he'd tried to hold himself back, break it off after that first *fling* when he'd fallen for her, he hadn't been able to. Because she made him feel whole the way no one else did. It wasn't like she thought he was some paragon of virtue—which was what he'd thought she wanted—but she treated him like…someone of value. Sure, he made mistakes, and he had quirks she made fun of, or thoughts she wanted to argue with, but she listened. She cared. Sometimes, she put his needs above hers.

He didn't *want* her to, but he supposed that was love. Not wanting the other person to give things up, but wanting to do that for them, and valuing it when they did it for you.

Which made him think about what she'd said about Colonel Elliot as a father, and all the things she'd once taken at face value but had to question once she'd become a mother.

And how they all landed with harsh truths he wasn't sure he was ready to face.

Because there had been something familiar about Colonel Elliot. Like some of the more problematic foster families he'd been a part of. But Colonel Elliot wore a uniform. He was a war hero. So, Cal had only sensed a familiarity, but seen the facade Colonel Elliot wanted people to see.

But underneath it all, Elliot was a man who'd always gotten his way. Who'd manipulated not just Cal, but his brothers, into going on what he now dubbed a suicide mission.

There was no thinking Cal was…well, as much as he hated to admit it, special. That was what Colonel Elliot had made him feel—special, chosen, important. It was why he'd resisted Norah as much as he could. He felt like he owed Captain Elliot for giving him the chance to be better than what he'd come from. For thinking he could be a war hero too.

But that hadn't been the hope at all. There was only hoping Cal was collateral damage. And that…that was even before Elliot had found out about him and Norah.

Cal didn't care for any of those realizations, but he had to face them. Maybe Norah would wake up remembering, but more than likely they were still in the dark. And they had to navigate whatever Colonel Elliot would bring down.

Cal knew the colonel hadn't suggested getting "rest" this evening for fun or even out of the goodness of his heart. It had been to plan, to line whatever he needed up to accomplish whatever his end goal was.

Cal watched Norah sleep and knew sleep would be impossible for him even if he tried. Later, as the sun began to rise, he slid out of bed and went into the bathroom. He checked his text messages.

From Dunne:

I checked with my father. He's being incredibly cagey—knows something. But confirmed Elliot has a key to safe house.

Cal closed his eyes, and for the briefest moment let himself...grieve, he supposed, the loss of everything he'd thought Colonel Elliot was. Maybe even Major General Wilks. If he held on to those feelings of loyalty and awe and *owing* it would cloud his thinking, and he couldn't allow that with Norah's safety in the balance.

So, he let himself accept that the men he'd idolized weren't idols. Now, it was time to figure out what to do about it.

He texted Henry, because he was afraid anyone else would beat around the bush. Any more sightings?

The response came back quickly. None. Still keeping an eye out, but seems to have left when you did.

Cal didn't think they'd been followed, but maybe it hadn't been a direct following. The fact Norah had somehow ended up at the ranch still bothered him. How had she found him? Why had she come for him?

But Zara's point kept rattling around in his head. This wasn't about *him*, even if he'd been brought into it. It wasn't even about Colonel Elliot necessarily. It was about Norah— she'd even said something about feeling as though she knew something she wasn't supposed to. She was the target, and there was no getting around it.

Which meant he knew what they had to do today.

He tucked his phone back in his pocket and was about to leave the bathroom when Norah entered. She still had bags under her eyes, but she'd gotten rest and that was what mattered.

"It's morning," she said, accusingly.

"Yeah."

"Cal, you need to—"

"I'm good. I promise." He flipped on the sink water at full blast to hopefully drown out what he was about to say. "Listen, I know what we need to do today, and I'd like to try to sneak out of here before your father wakes up. Hopefully the amount of alcohol he consumed last night means we've got a chance."

He watched her struggle with wanting to argue with him about rest, but she sighed. "What do we need to do?"

"We're going to your place."

She didn't say anything at first, but her grip on the doorknob she still held tightened. "That sounds smart." But she sounded...

"Do you not want to?"

She swallowed. "Just one of those feelings. Like it's a terrible idea. Which means it's probably our best bet."

THEY SNUCK OUT of the house like rebellious teenagers, except there was no joy in it. No freedom. Only a churning, roiling dread in Norah's gut.

Cal drove through the streets of DC, then out to the suburb where she'd been renting an apartment for a few years.

Information she didn't quite remember. She didn't even remember her address, and she thought about pointing out she didn't have keys or any way of getting in, but that was probably silly to point out to a man with Cal's skills.

He pulled into the parking lot of an apartment complex and Norah felt...nothing. The dread in her stomach remained the same as it had since Cal had told her this was the plan. It didn't dissipate, but it didn't worsen. She just felt...wrong.

Cal parked then looked at her. She knew he was searching her face not just for signs of recognition but signs of distress. He didn't want to hurt her. Didn't want her to *hurt*.

Because he loved her, and though her memories on the matter remained fuzzy in places, she knew she loved him too. Then. Now. It was who they were. Somehow.

But love didn't matter until they figured this out, because she understood this was somehow all about her, even if she didn't remember why. So, she had to put on a brave front. Act like she was perfectly happy to dive in.

Blank all that terror and dread away so Cal didn't see it. She turned to face him, tried to smile reassuringly. "Cal, I can do this."

"I know you *can*, but—"

"No. No buts. I can do it. I have to do it. If it hurts… It's only because someone tried to hurt me. At some point, that hurts whether I remember or not."

He frowned at that but nodded. They both got out of the car, and he walked over to her. He put his arm around her, guiding her to the buildings.

Nothing looked familiar, and that had her heart pounding with a different kind of nerves, but she let Cal lead her. And she tried not to lean on him too much.

"You're on the third floor," he said, nodding to a stairwell. "Apartment C."

She looked up the stairs and found herself stopping without really thinking it through. She did *not* want to go up those stairs.

But you have to. Before Cal told her they didn't have to do this—and she had no doubt that was what he was about to say—she forced herself to take the first step. Maybe it required a death grip on the railing, and a supreme amount of effort and energy, but she wasn't going to turn away.

Because, yes, the truth was going to hurt no matter what.

Cal seemed to sense she needed to lead the way, or maybe

he was hoping she'd find a memory in walking there herself. But he followed, close behind as they climbed the stairs.

She looked in every corner, every shadow for some pop of memory, but there was nothing except a slight headache and vague, churning nausea. When they reached the third floor landing, Cal stopped somewhat abruptly.

She looked back at him and he glanced around, his frown deepening. "There used to be security cameras in all the outdoor hallways. I made sure of it before you took out the lease on this place. They're still on the first and second floor like before, but none here."

Dread intensified, like a heavy weight pressing against her lungs. "Well, it suits our purposes now," Norah managed to say.

"Unfortunately, it means we can't get any footage there might have been of people coming and going." He looked at her, no doubt seeing all the swirling emotions on her face. His expression softened. "Since I don't think you've got your keys, I'll pick the lock." He bent over the knob, pulling some little tool out of his pocket and making quick work of picking the lock.

He nudged the door open slightly, peeking in. He swore. Then swung the door open the rest of the way, his gun out in his hand.

It wasn't that there was someone in there, it was that he was looking for someones in any potential corner of her trashed apartment. Because it was utterly *destroyed*. Shards of glass across the floor, things ripped off walls leaving gaping holes in the plaster. Even the TV had been knocked off its stand and lay crookedly on the floor.

Norah sucked in a breath. "Why..."

Cal crept forward. She followed, though with space between them. She doubted anyone was here. Why would they be? Was this where someone had tried to kill her? Had she made it all the way to Wyoming with her injuries?

"Stay right there," Cal ordered, then slunk into the darkened hallway.

She looked around the living room and recognized nothing. Because there was nothing *to* recognize. The couch and chair had been slashed to ribbons. Even what had been either an end table or coffee table lay in splintered pieces next to the couch.

Cal returned from the hallway, holstering his weapon. "It's clear, but every room is in the same shape." He studied her face, no doubt looking for signs of recognition, but she had none.

"Who would do this?"

Cal shook his head. "Landon didn't find any police reports. Any missing persons. Someone should have heard something, reported you missing—friends, coworkers, your father. *Someone*."

"Maybe I didn't have any of those things. And Dad was already supposedly missing."

"You had friends. You had a job."

"You don't know. You weren't there."

He stiffened at that and said nothing. She sighed. She wasn't blaming him, but she couldn't manage his feelings right now. She couldn't...

Her eye caught on something in the corner of the room. A little splotch of something brown. Her stomach pitched, but she felt drawn to it. Dimly, she heard Cal say her name, but something inside of her was roaring too loud to fully comprehend it.

She moved for it like she was in some sort of heavy fog. Her heart beat rapidly and her head suddenly felt too...full.

There was pressure all around her. But she knew what that splotch was. She knew…

She had impressions, more than a full memory. Terror. Shadows. Crashing.

"Blood," Cal said flatly, staring down at the stain in the carpet.

Norah tried to swallow, but she couldn't… Cal's hands were on her, squeezing gently. "Norah."

But her breath was trapped in her lungs. She couldn't seem to look away from the stain. She couldn't. She couldn't…

"Breathe. Baby, you gotta breathe." He gave her a little shake. "Norah. Come on now. Breathe *in*."

He said the last so sharply it cut through some of the fog, and she managed to suck in a rattling breath. Then let it out. She focused on his hands, curled around her arms. Slowly and painfully she managed to look away from the blood, and up into Cal's face.

The memory didn't present itself in some sort of chronological, sensible fashion, but she remembered things. Bits. Pieces. They were coming together.

"It's not mine."

"What?"

"It's not my blood. Someone…" She was shaking, she realized, as Cal pulled her into him, murmuring calming things, and it helped, but no amount of reassurances took the terror away.

Someone had been in her apartment. She'd been terrified. But…not surprised. Not surprised because… "I…was looking for you."

He pulled her back enough to look at her face and she knew this would hurt him, but she couldn't not tell him. Not in the moment.

"Like, researching your death. Something… For some

reason I can't remember I was suspicious. Your death. My mother's death. I started…asking questions. Researching. And then weird things started happening."

"Okay. Okay. Don't push. Just breathe and—"

But Cal didn't finish his sentence. He dropped her and whirled in one fluid motion, gun somehow drawn without her even seeing him pull it out. But she heard the click of something, from over by the door.

"Put it down."

It wasn't Cal's voice.

Chapter Fifteen

Cal didn't drop it right away. He assessed the situation.

But the gun wasn't pointed at *him*. It was pointed at Norah. Which Cal could have handled... It was the two other men with guns behind the first that made this tricky.

"Now," the man said. He was big—dressed all in black, short military haircut. Cal didn't recognize him, and when he glanced at Norah he didn't get the feeling she did either.

All three men cocked their guns and Cal had no choice but to lower his, even as he considered all the ways he could take out all three men without Norah getting hurt.

But first he had to make sure she didn't get hurt. His best bet was to keep the men at the doorway, and his body between them and Norah.

"Drop it," the man ordered.

Cal moved a step so his body blocked Norah's. He had lowered the gun, but he hadn't let it go yet.

"We can shoot through you," the man said.

"Yeah." That they could, but if it bought him some time to set this up...

"So drop your gun now," the one in the doorway ordered. "Last warning."

Cal nodded, though he didn't immediately drop it. He bent his knees a little, giving Norah a tiny wave behind his back with his free hand that he hoped she interpreted as crouching when he did. But as he moved, and saw she was indeed crouching too, he felt something press to his back.

The gun he'd given her.

He glanced at the three men. If he shoved Norah down at the same time he whirled, he could maybe get two shots off before he got shot himself. And if he moved while he did it, he could keep it down to a nick. The third guy was the biggest problem. There'd have to be some way aside from a shot to get him to either aim poorly or not shoot at all.

He placed his gun on the floor, even as he curled his other hand around the gun Norah had given him. She was crouched behind him, so he had to act quickly before the men came closer. The minute he released the one gun, he swung the other out and shot three quick times, at the same time he gave Norah a push to the left and he swung his body to keep shielding hers.

Two men went down, and the return bullets crashed into a lamp and the window. Norah screamed, but Cal shot again, barely nicking the man still on his feet.

Then something went sailing through the air from behind him, hitting the door so it slammed shut. Cal looked at Norah. She'd thrown a bronze vase. Perfectly.

"Good move. Out the sliding glass," he said, already pushing her toward the door that would lead them out to a little patio.

She dove for the door, scrambling to get it open, but as she stepped outside, she stopped abruptly. "We're on the third—"

He eyed the distance, then reached across to the rail of the neighbor's balcony.

"Cal."

He eyed the front door—it hadn't opened immediately. So the shots he'd got off had slowed them down. Still, it wouldn't stop them. This was the best way. The best chance to get away. He wanted to get her over first, but he could already tell she wouldn't go. He swung his leg over, held on and made the little leap, then crawled over that railing. He heard the door inside crash open.

He held out his hand. "Now."

She swallowed, and he could tell she was terrified and wanted to argue, but she took his hand.

"There's a fire escape right there." He held his hand across the small expanse between the balconies, and he didn't tell her not to look down, since no doubt she'd do it the minute he pointed it out.

"Brace yourself," he muttered, aiming his gun at the man about to come through the doorway. He shot. He didn't think he got the man—instead the man dove back inside. Norah's whole body jerked at the sound, but he kept his grip steady on her arm. "No time, Norah."

He shot at the doorway again, hoping to ward them off— but there was still the possibility one of them ran downstairs and would be waiting at the bottom of that fire escape.

Norah was shaking, but she managed to take the jump and quickly scramble over the rail. She was still shaking even on the other side, but Cal knew they didn't have time to wait for her to calm.

He shot once more, this time through the shattered glass, and managed to take the one man down. But Cal knew one man just meant the others were either going to the front— even with their injuries—or backup would.

He looked down the fire escape. So far no sign of anything, but it would be harder and take longer for them to get down than it would be for a man to run down the stairs. Backup might be far enough away they had a chance to escape. He didn't have time to weigh his options about who was better to go first. He started climbing down himself.

He could fight anyone who met them. He could help Norah if she struggled. But the man from the apartment could also follow them this way and…

He was already halfway down. Norah not far behind. He knew she was struggling—both with fear and the fact she hated heights—but she hadn't said a word. She knew this was life-and-death.

Good God, why was it life-and-death?

He hopped onto the ground and surveyed the parking lot. More out of instinct than seeing anything, he hit the ground—a bullet narrowly whizzing by his head. "Stay right there," he yelled at Norah.

From his prone position on the ground, he got his own shot off, then rolled, so that he was hidden behind the building. "Jump off this way. Then run that way," he said pointing in the opposite direction of the shooter. "Keep the building between you and the guy."

She hesitated, but he shook his head. "Has to be this way."

She didn't like it, but she jumped off the fire escape, wincing enough to worry him, but he had to deal with the gunman before he could check how much she'd been hurt.

"Cal, we should stick together."

Cal army-crawled forward to see if the assailant had made any progress. Only a few yards away, but using cars as cover. "Just go hide behind that side of the building, okay? Please, Norah."

It must have been the *please* that did it because she nodded sharply and then ran down the length of the building.

Carefully, Cal got to his feet. He needed to get closer to the man. He needed to get some answers. Maybe they should just run, but whoever this was would only follow.

He got two quick shots off, then ran full tilt toward the car the man was hiding behind. When the man's gun came into view, Cal dove behind his own cover car.

The shot went off, the sound of it hitting the car echoing through the quiet neighborhood. This wouldn't go on much longer without interference. From other people, or the police.

Cal needed to get Norah out of here. Enough of this hiding around. He jumped the car and lunged at the shooter— who was so surprised by the brazen attack he didn't manage to turn and shoot. He just took the full weight of Cal's force.

He landed hard on the cement, and the gun came loose, clattering a few inches away from his hand. Cal managed to get a good choke hold.

"Who do you work for?" he demanded.

"The same people you do," the man gritted out. He'd been shot. Blood was seeping down a slash on his neck. It was just a graze, but it would need medical attention, and the blood loss was likely helping Cal in this fight.

He tightened his grip. "I don't work for anyone."

"That's what you think."

Cal didn't know what *any* of this meant, but he could hear sirens now. Too close. Too much potential for every kind of complication. So, Cal did the only thing he could. He took the man's gun…and ran.

Back to where Norah was hopefully waiting. Hiding. He rounded the corner. She was there, but she was not alone. She stood just a few yards from a man standing in front of a car.

Cal stopped short.

It was Major General Wilks.

Dunne's father.

And Cal didn't have the slightest idea if he could trust him or not.

The imposing man nodded toward the car. "Get in. Now."

And much to Cal's utter shock, Norah did just that of her own volition.

WHEN NORAH REALIZED Cal hadn't followed into the car at the man's command, she realized…she'd just followed a stranger's orders.

Except he wasn't a stranger. She knew him. Somehow.

She couldn't remember the details. And as she looked around the car and realized all the windows were tinted black, she had some serious reservations about whether or not she'd made the right choice. She didn't *remember,* so maybe this feeling of knowing the man was bad.

But before she could try to scramble back out of the car, Cal slid into the back with her and the man got into the driver's seat.

Cal was looking at her with a hint of disapproval, but his eyes also tracked over her like he was looking for injuries. Trauma.

"I'm all right," she said, reaching out to take his hand. She turned to the man in the driver's seat. He'd already pulled out into traffic. She could only see the back of his head and his eyes in the rearview mirror now, but she knew somehow…

"You helped me."

His eyes met hers in the mirror. "Of course I helped you."

"No, I don't… I don't think you understand." There was something at the edge of her memory, something she couldn't quite access, but she knew it was there. "I don't remember things."

His mouth pressed together. Then he gave a short nod. "We'll get somewhere safe and discuss it."

"Will we be alone in this somewhere safe?" Cal asked, distrust and disapproval dripping from his tone.

This time the man in the driver's seat turned his gaze in the mirror to Cal, briefly. "I don't know what you know, Cal, but I can see you don't trust me."

"Such a strange turn of events, Major General," Cal retorted dryly.

Major General. Another military person? She couldn't understand for the life of her why she'd been mixed up in some military thing, so that someone had tried to *kill* her. But as the man drove in silence, she realized there was something about the man's jawline, and the things she'd heard about Dunne's father being involved in Cal's military service that she put it fully together.

"You're Dunne's father."

The man sighed. "Might as well call me Owen for the foreseeable future." He flicked a glance in the mirror at Cal again. "You're not a soldier anymore, Cal. And 'Major General' or 'Dunne's father' is a mouthful."

He pulled the car into what seemed like an abandoned industrial area. Warehouses and empty parking lots and long, concrete roads leading to what appeared to be nowhere. Logically, Norah knew this should seem bad. Shady. Dangerous. But she couldn't work up the anxiety she *should* feel.

Though Cal clearly felt it enough for the both of them. He kept his hand curled around his gun, and his eyes tracked over every building they passed. When the man—*Owen*—pulled the car to a stop, he turned in his seat to face them. "Stay put. I don't want to risk anyone seeing you. I'm going to open the doors, then drive us in." He nodded to the gun Cal had. "You can keep that. I don't expect you to believe me out of hand, Cal, but I do want to help you. Sit tight."

Then he slid out of the car and walked for the door. He put a key in the lock and began the process of pulling the warehouse door back.

Norah looked at Cal. His face was stone. "Cal, I know...
I know my memory is faulty, and I don't remember him...
specifically. But I knew he was safe. I had the feeling I could
trust him, and while I don't know if I really *can* trust my
feelings, so far they haven't led me in the wrong direction."

Cal nodded. "I want to believe you. I don't think you can
understand how much, but he was your father's partner in
recruiting, training and sending us on our secret missions. If
your father thought they were suicide missions—didn't he?"

Norah's heart sank. "It would be hard to believe otherwise." She looked out the windshield again. Owen was
walking back toward the car. She shouldn't trust him. She
shouldn't trust herself. But...

"I think, no matter what he might have done or not done,
he wants to help now. I have to believe that."

Cal nodded sharply. "And I have to be suspicious."

She squeezed his hand. "I guess we make a good team
then."

He didn't smile, but some of that tense blankness softened.
Then Owen got back in the car and without a word drove it
into the warehouse.

Which was when Norah realized it wasn't a warehouse.
It was an airplane hangar. A small plane was parked inside.

Cal eyed it warily as Owen pulled to a stop once again.

"Private," Owen said, gesturing at the plane. "It'll get you
back to Wyoming without anyone being aware you're back."

"Why would we go back to Wyoming?" Cal demanded.
"A group of men just attacked us. Who claim to work for the
same people *I* do, when I don't work for anyone. I'm dead."

Owen sighed. "I'll be the first to admit I don't know everything that's going on. When it comes to who attacked Norah,
I'm in the dark. But I've been watching Colonel Elliot for
the past month. From when Norah first came to see me, to

his fake disappearance, to the moment you two showed up at my safe house—his hideout. He wants you gone, Cal. Not just fake gone. Really gone. And he's convinced a few other soldiers you're a military mission."

"Isn't that a bit extreme?" Cal returned.

"He wants them all gone," Norah said, and it was a memory. "I remember…talking with you in a room." It wasn't the whole picture. Just bits and pieces. A leather chair. Crying. A handkerchief. She looked at Owen, whose face was as impassive as Cal's. "I went to you with my suspicions. You confirmed them. We started…looking into things. His plans to erase all of you. Not fake this time. But for good." Norah felt nauseous, and her head was pounding, but she remembered it. Really remembered it. The knowledge her father was ready to kill…not just Cal, for whatever imagined betrayal was there, but all six of them.

She looked over at Cal. The color had drained from his face. Still he sat with military posture and rigid composure. He said nothing.

So, Norah said it for him. "But why?" she asked Owen.

"Let's get on the plane. We'll talk details in the air."

Chapter Sixteen

Cal had been through all manner of hells. From losing his mother, foster care, boot camp, actual war. His life had been a series of disappointments, losses and horrors.

And still he had no idea what to do with this. It was one thing for Colonel Elliot to want him dead. Insane, sure, but it at least followed some semblance of a thought process he could follow.

But all of them? His brothers. Men who'd risked their lives time and again to do good in the world.

Norah's "But why?" echoed in his head like a terrible earworm he couldn't get rid of. No matter how he thought of it, he couldn't work out a reason Colonel Elliot would want to erase *all* of them.

"Cal, open those doors," Owen instructed, pointing at the hangar doors that presumably led to a runway. "Norah, go ahead and climb in the plane."

"No," Cal said. He held on to Norah's hand, knowing that she'd follow orders. For whatever reason, she trusted Dunne's father, and while Cal couldn't argue with her feelings—not when they'd been right so far—he couldn't fully get on board either. "We're not separating."

Owen sighed, clearly irritated, but he didn't argue. "You were trained how to fly, right?"

Cal studied the plane. "Not one of those, but I can figure it out enough to taxi the plane to the runway."

Owen nodded. "Then you can both get in. I'll open the doors to the runway. Get the plane clear of the doorways, then I'll close up, climb in and take us up."

Cal knew they didn't have time to hesitate. If his brothers were in danger, he wanted to be boots on the ground in Wyoming, not dodging bullets in DC. But this was a gamble, and the life he was risking was Norah's.

But what other options were there? They'd been ambushed back at Norah's apartment. It had to have been at Elliot's behest. His death was some other soldier's mission now.

He pulled Norah to the plane, speaking in low tones under his breath that Owen wouldn't be able to hear as he strode in the opposite direction.

"Text Jessie. Ask about Evelyn, then say we won't be back for a few days, but we're sending a package. And say that it'll be addressed to Dunne."

"But we aren't…" Norah looked up at him. "Is that some kind of code?"

Cal nodded. "Not the sneakiest, but I think we have to be careful. I think with all this…we can't be too careful." Of course, he wasn't being careful putting all this trust in Dunne's father. Dunne had never considered his father a *bad* man, but Cal knew there was a tension there. An uncertainty. After all, his father *had* sent him into danger. Put him on their team of people without families.

Had Owen knowingly sent his son into a suicide mission? The thought filled Cal with dread and distrust.

But Norah trusted, and her feelings hadn't steered them wrong until now. She remembered Owen Wilks helping her, in a way. Surely…this was the best course of action?

Cal helped Norah into the plane while Owen walked to the

back of the hangar. He began to pull back the large doors that would give the plane enough room to taxi outside.

Cal sat in the pilot's seat and studied the dash. He'd had all sorts of education in piloting the kind of transportation that could get him and his brothers out of any situation they might find themselves in.

He tested a few knobs, thought he had a handle on it enough to move the plane forward, then started the engine. He did just as Owen had instructed, taxiing the plane out of the hangar and into the sunny afternoon.

Owen closed the hangar doors, then climbed in. Cal slid out of the pilot's seat and let Owen take it. He wanted answers now, but Norah was sitting in one of the two seats in the back looking pale and worried, so he stepped back to her and took the seat next to her.

"Are we doing the right thing?" she whispered.

"We're doing the best thing," Cal replied firmly. Maybe it was the wrong choice, but he didn't have any other options. If it turned out wrong…he'd find a way to make it right.

For her.

He sat with Norah the entire long flight. When Owen brought them in for a landing, Cal could tell they were in Wyoming. Which was good. He'd at least brought them where he'd said he would.

Cal looked out the window. The runway was grass, and the small building at the end of it looked only large enough to house this one small plane.

The plane came to a stop, and then Owen slid out of his seat. "Same process. I'll open. You bring the plane in. There's a car inside."

Which all felt far too…planned. Ready.

But Cal still had his gun, and they were on his territory now. He had to trust that whatever came at them, he could handle it. He leaned toward Norah as he got up. "Text Jessie. Set your phone so she can trace your location."

Norah nodded and Cal headed for the front of the plane. He did just as before, pulling the plane into the hangar. Owen pulled the doors closed behind them and Cal turned off the plane and they got off.

There was indeed a car waiting. Cal had expected another slick, tinted-window affair—but quickly realized he should have given a major general in the military a little more credit. The windows were in fact tinted, but the vehicle was a heavy-duty truck similar to ones possessed by many landowners in the area, capable of navigating ranch work, hauling trailers and dealing with tough Wyoming winters. It would also fit right in with any other vehicles on the road, down to the Wyoming plates.

Owen held his phone in one hand, keys in the other. "Elliot's on the move, but I've got a guy following him. He took a flight to Chicago, but that might be a fake. So, we need to get to the ranch as soon as possible. It's about a forty-five-minute drive."

Owen opened the driver's door, then turned to face him and Norah. Neither one of them had made a move for the truck.

Owen was clearly at the end of his patience, but he still didn't snap, or demand compliance. He took a deep breath and explained.

"Look, when Jake got himself involved in that murder case last year, and shot in the process, I thought perhaps there needed to be a little oversight to make sure the six of you didn't end up bringing enough attention on yourselves to tie it back to your military service. But, for obvious reasons, it had to be careful, unmonitored oversight. Not on paper. Not traceable. Personal."

"Was Elliot part of this oversight?"

"At first, in the planning stages" Owen said. "But he wasn't particularly interested. I always found it odd. Until I realized…"

"Being vague doesn't help your position, Owen."

The man sighed. "I think you can understand, if you let yourself, how delicate this situation is. Elliot is a high-ranking military official. He has a lot of people working for him, doing the dirty work. In order to catch him, really catch him and have him pay, I have to have irrefutable evidence of his wrongdoing. Some of it he hasn't actually *done* yet, is just planning. Norah was helping, though, feeding me information."

Which explained why Elliot had thought she had been on his own side. Norah had been pretending.

"Helping you seems to have almost gotten her killed."

But Owen shook his head. "No, at least, not that I can prove. After Elliot disappeared, but before Norah did, Norah felt like she was in danger, which is why I was monitoring her father's every move. He did send the men who trashed her apartment, but they didn't hurt her. She wasn't there."

"What about the blood on the carpet?"

Owen sighed again. "We assumed one of the intruders injured himself with all the destruction. Norah wasn't there when it happened. She arrived home, called me and I went and investigated. I later learned it was Elliot's men, but they didn't hurt Norah. Didn't even try."

He turned to face Norah, and either he was the best actor in the world, or he was dead serious. "Whoever tried to kill you, Norah, it wasn't your father. Not unless he planned it long before I was monitoring him."

"Then who was it?" Cal demanded.

Owen shook his head, looking both resigned and tired— two things one was *never* supposed to show in their line of work. "I don't know."

NORAH WONDERED WHAT she was supposed to feel. She supposed it should be relief her father hadn't tried to kill her... but that just meant some unknown person had put their hands around her neck and tried to squeeze the life out of her.

And she couldn't remember. She had bits and pieces now of other events from the past. But trying to bring back the moment of someone hurting her...? Nothing. Absolutely nothing.

It felt like she was floating. Untethered.

Until Cal touched her back. His hand a gentle pressure, an anchor amid all this...confusion.

"You're telling me you honestly believe Elliot wants six men he once trained dead, but he has nothing to do with the attempted murder of his daughter who was helping you investigate him of wrongdoing?"

Cal's voice was scathing, and Norah could sense Owen's impatience. Two men used to calling the shots arguing with each other when...

"It doesn't matter what he believes, or you do," Norah said, surprised at how calm her voice sounded when she wasn't even sure how she was still standing. "I want to be with my daughter now." She turned to Cal. "And you should be with your brothers. All six of you are a target, so you need to be together."

Cal looked at her in that disapproving way he had that she figured most people would read as a firm disagreement. But Norah knew, for her, he'd disapprove and do it her way anyway. It made her want to smile, lean into him. And it made her want to go home—or at least what felt like home in the midst of her fuzzy memories not all coming back—Wyoming and their daughter.

Those probably weren't the right reasons to want to go back. She should probably think about this strategically. Or lock herself in a room until she remembered everything. But

Cal had been right back there—there were no *right* answers. Only next steps until they had more information.

Until she remembered. And the only thing that seemed to help her remember was to keep moving forward.

"We'll get in the car," Norah said, looking at both men, chin raised and just daring them to argue. "Owen will drive and take us through this whole mess from the beginning— leaving nothing out no matter how delicate the situation is from a military perspective. Maybe it'll jog my memory. Maybe whatever you know will help Cal connect the dots. Maybe we arrive at the ranch as in the dark as ever, but standing here disagreeing does nothing for anyone."

She looked at Owen, then Cal. She knew neither one wanted be the one to agree first. Some alpha standoff, but when she looked at Cal and gave him a significant look, he sighed. "All right," he muttered.

"Fine," Owen added.

They all got into the car together. Owen driving, Cal sliding into the back with her. They held hands, and she got the feeling he wasn't just her anchor—she was his. She remembered pieces of their life together now, and it put love into context more deeply than it had before. She *was* his anchor. They were…two pieces of a puzzle. Not perfect for one another, not without their disagreements or their jagged edges, but still the right fit.

They paused driving only for Owen to get out and close the hangar doors behind them as they left. Norah wasn't familiar enough with the area to get a good sense of where they were going or where they'd come from, so she concentrated on trying to remember the parts of what Owen told them that she'd been involved in.

"I'm not even sure what the beginning is," Owen said, and

he was starting to sound tired. Like a man who'd exhausted all options.

"Was it always a suicide mission?" Cal asked.

Owen shook his head. "I know Elliot said that to you at the house. I listened to everything he said to you at the house last night. I think he even believes that, now. In a warped way, he's rewritten his own history. Because, no Cal. I didn't send you, let alone my son, on suicide missions. We definitely targeted soldiers who didn't have families, so they wouldn't have to *lie* to said families, so there wasn't an inadvertent leak. These were highly classified, intense missions and we needed men who...could give their all. Not because the six of you were expendable. You were some of the most promising soldiers across all branches we had."

Norah felt something in Cal relax. Like he'd been prepared for the worst, and she supposed he probably had been. His life had been a series of blows and worsts. When her father had called it a suicide mission...she understood how easy it probably was for Cal to believe it.

She leaned her head on his shoulder.

"There was something...off about the last mission," Owen said as he easily navigated the deserted Wyoming highway. "We'd been planning it for a few months, but suddenly Elliot wanted some changes, and to move up the timetable. I suggested caution. He threatened to go over my head."

Owen tapped his fingers against the steering wheel, but Norah kept her head on Cal's shoulder. She knew there was a thread here she needed to find, pull.

"When did you find out Cal and I had gotten married?"

Owen flicked a glance into the rearview mirror. "Not until you told me last month. Your father had never mentioned your child. He'd in fact stopped inviting me to social occasions where you might have been present. You told me that he'd encouraged you to isolate. That grieving Cal was better done in private since the missions were so secretive. So, I probably hadn't seen you in over a year when you came to my house, so early in the morning it was still dark."

Norah tried to search her memory. Heart racing. Dark house. Nocturnal animals rustling. The sound of a dog barking somewhere in the neighborhood. Evelyn fussing in the little carrier she'd wrapped her in.

"You demanded to know where Cal was. The baby threw me at first, but I kept up with the story. He'd died in a mission last year. But then you started hammering me on dates. Exact dates. And they did not add up to what your father had told you."

"You thought I was having some sort of...grief-imposed crack with reality." She remembered the disapproval. The disbelief. But he'd also invited her in, had her take a seat on a leather chair in his living room, and handed her a handkerchief.

Owen had the good sense to look shamed. "Until you presented me with your box of evidence."

Norah couldn't remember that part.

"And a lot of your evidence matched up with when Elliot had started...acting strangely."

"Strange how?" Cal demanded.

"It wasn't in the military setting. It was more...personally. Dressed a little more, shall we say, youthful than we are. He wouldn't invite me to his home, didn't have dinners anymore, but he wanted to go out to clubs. I'd find him talking to some of the younger women at the offices in ways...well, if they'd been my daughter *I* wouldn't have been comfortable with. But it was none of my business. Look, I'm almost sixty years old. Plenty of my friends have gone through a midlife crisis. I know the signs. It wasn't any of my business."

The world around them was starting to look familiar, but Norah couldn't remember anything about a midlife crisis.

"I kept my nose out of it. But some of Norah's evidence, some of her theories, didn't connect to a midlife crisis, but they coincided with a change in behavior."

And they coincided with when Evelyn was born, Norah realized or remembered. Not just the narcissism that had come screaming back to her at the safe house, but the fact he hadn't wanted to be called *grandpa*. He hadn't wanted the reminder that he was an older man.

"The problem was, once Norah pointed some things out to me, I realized it wasn't the first time I'd seen Elliot exhibit signs of wanting to be young again."

"When was the first time?" Cal asked.

"When my mother died," Norah whispered, as a terrible thought—or memory—slammed into her. "No, *before* my mother died."

Chapter Seventeen

They were getting close to the ranch, but Cal took his eyes off the world around them to look at Norah. She'd gone pale. Her hands shook.

"He killed my mother."

Cal could only stare at her. There were denials on the tip of his tongue. Maybe Elliot was a bastard. Maybe he wanted *Cal* and his brothers dead, but surely...

"I thought she was reaching," Owen said, and again the emotion they'd both been trained to hide and push away leaked through. A sadness. A betrayal. "But the timelines all added up too perfectly. The shooter was killed by police, so no one ever got his side of the story, but the police officer who shot had a connection to Elliot. Once Norah handed me some details, I started digging into some of his confidential military files. Still, we didn't have enough evidence to go to authorities and guarantee Norah and Evelyn's safety," Owen said. "We tried, Norah and I, to find something concrete we could take to police, but we were getting nowhere. Still, in the process of this whole thing I couldn't keep lying to Norah. I finally had to tell the truth about you. It went against everything I promised myself when I set you all up in Wyoming, but... You deserved to know you were a father, Cal. And I knew I could trust Norah to handle the situation delicately, since she wanted even less than I did for you to be dead or a terrorist target."

"So, that's how she knew to find me in Wyoming, but it doesn't explain someone trying to kill her and her somehow making it here."

"No, it doesn't." Owen shook his head. "I've been trying to track down Norah for the past week. When Dunne called me about the safe house, I had hope. But this whole attempted murder thing? Sure, it makes sense to look at Elliot, but I've had tabs on his every move. His phone, his computer, his leaving the house. If he planned it, he planned it before he knew she suspected him of something, and I just don't see how that could be the case."

"What about…" Norah frowned, and a faraway look crossed her face. Cal recognized it as the one she had when she was close to a memory but couldn't quite put the pieces together to make sense of them. "There's someone else. I can… I just know…" She rubbed her temple and Cal held her closer.

"Pushing won't change it."

"Maybe it will," she replied, but she relaxed into him. "If we have all the information, we can keep everyone safe."

Cal exchanged a look with Owen in the rearview mirror. They'd both been soldiers enough to know that sometimes even having all the information didn't keep innocent people safe.

Neither of them seemed to have the words or heart to break it to Norah.

"We could drop off Cal at the ranch," Norah began, and Cal didn't even need her to say another word to know where she was going.

"No."

"Callum."

But neither his name on her lips nor the pleading look in her eye would change his mind on this. "No. We're not separating. Whatever you don't remember, it'll come back to you when your brain is ready to deal with it."

She pressed her lips together and studied him with disapproval, but he wasn't moving on that. It wasn't even ego, or the conviction that he and only he could keep her safe. It was something…far more elemental.

They'd been apart too long. Completely lost to each other—thinking the other was dead. *Dead.* They weren't going to separate and let that become a reality—for either of them.

"Let's focus on what happened here after Norah arrived," Owen said. "Dunne mentioned there was a lone shooter?"

"Yes, and no retaliation, no return since that random shot."

Owen tapped his fingers on the steering wheel as he drove. Cal studied his profile from his spot in the back.

"But you've been watching him. You said you know his plans." Still Owen said nothing as he drove. Cal wanted to snap, but Norah's hand in his kept him dialing it back. "What aren't you telling us?" he asked.

Owen pulled his car onto the road that would lead them to the ranch. Cal was wound too tight to settle, but still it was strange how this place had come to mean *home*. It wasn't safe—Jake had been shot and Elliot knew where they were—but there was an emotional safety here. A belonging.

"Elliot was planning some kind of diversion. That would draw the six of you out of the house, so there wouldn't be… collateral damage. He hadn't worked it out yet. I don't know for sure the man who shot Jake worked for Elliot, but I do know he was trying to get a sense of the terrain, the layout, to enact his plan."

Cal had to carefully breathe through the white-hot rage that spread through him. That his wife, his daughter, his friends could be considered *collateral damage*...

"I suppose it's something," Owen offered. "The women and children will be safe, and—"

"No. Only *some* of the women and children. Someone still tried to kill Norah. They tried to *strangle* her. If this doesn't connect to Elliot, we have *two* threats."

Owen pulled to a stop in front of the house that had become home. "Yes, we do. But on the bright side, we have seven military minds to put together and figure out how to protect all of you." Owen looked back at them. "I promise you, this will be over. Whatever it takes, we'll put an end to it. I'm sorry it went on this long. And I'm sorry, Norah, that I didn't react as quickly as I should have. Sometimes feelings get in the way of what's right."

Norah leaned forward and touched Owen's shoulder. "Owen, I don't remember everything, but I know you've gone above and beyond in trying to help Evelyn and me. You're the reason I know Cal's alive. I understand now, probably in a way I didn't when you told me, how much that must have cost you to tell me, and how much trust you put in me by telling me. Not just Cal's life, but your son's. So, no matter what, I owe you."

Cal still held Norah's hand and watched her and the way her words loosened the tenseness in Owen's shoulders.

It was one of the many reasons he'd fallen in love with her. Not just her kindness, but the way she wielded it. He'd never known anyone who could just tap into an endless well of *goodness*.

"Let's get you inside," Owen said gruffly, clearly as moved as Cal was. His gaze moved to Cal. "And figure out how to stop this."

NORAH HAD TO hold herself back from running into the house. She wanted to hold her baby, except a sharp bark was their first greeting as Hero raced over to them. But, to Norah's surprise, he ran right to Owen.

He jumped and whined, his tail wagging as he pranced in a circle around Owen, whose face broke out into what was clearly an uncharacteristic grin. "There's a buddy," he said, kneeling down and petting the dog, accepting exuberant face licks.

"You know the dog?" Cal asked, coming around the side of the car and immediately sliding his arm around Norah's waist. She leaned into him, grateful for the connection. She knew she had to come to some place of strength, but she was struggling.

"Hero is my dog. I gave him to Norah for protection."

Cal's grip tightened a little bit. "He did a hell of a job," he said gruffly.

But Norah was more than a little taken aback. "Hero. That's his name?"

Owen nodded as he stood.

She looked up at Cal. "That's what I've been calling him. I thought I made it up, but I remembered."

"You're remembering lots of things," he said reassuringly.

But she wasn't remembering the important ones. Her father, the villain. Whoever had attempted to kill her. All the important information was still stubbornly behind some fog.

The front door opened and Jessie stepped out, Evelyn in her arms. Unable to stop herself now, Norah rushed forward. Jessie smiled warmly and easily handed Evelyn over. "She's been very good, but she missed her mama."

Norah held her close and was rewarded with a big smile. She felt as though her heart might break into a million pieces.

"Oh, baby. Mama missed you." She held the wriggling baby tight and breathed.

Here was her center. No matter what happened, no matter what was true, the only thing that mattered was keeping her baby safe.

She felt Cal come up behind her and turned to face him, and adjusted Evelyn so she could see him too. "Daddy too," she murmured, then looked up at Cal.

No matter what happened to her, she didn't think she'd ever forget the way Cal's expression changed. Like he felt exactly what she did. Evelyn was their anchor, their center, and the reason they'd keep fighting whatever all *this* was.

People wanted them dead for whatever insane reasons, but they would keep fighting it. For their daughter.

He touched Evelyn's cheek and said nothing, but Norah felt everything he was feeling. He tried to hide it behind that tough, stoic military act, but she saw all the longing and worry and love reflected in his eyes.

"Let's get inside," he said brusquely, his gaze moving away from Evelyn and to the world around them. So many threats and who knew where they were all coming from.

But finally, *finally* she had her husband back. She knew he had reservations about that.

But she didn't. Couldn't.

They all moved inside, and as if some signal had been sent around, everyone came to congregate in the living room. There were attempts at smiles, but most of the expressions were grim—especially from the men when they saw Owen.

They all held the exact same kind of tension in their shoulders—not exactly a bad tension, just a watchful one. Then Dunne and Quinn stepped in from the kitchen, grinning at each other as if they'd just been sharing some joke.

But when Dunne looked into the room and saw his father, the smile on his face slowly faded. His posture notably changed, somehow going straighter. Quinn gave him a puzzled look.

"Dad," Dunne finally said. Quinn's eyes widened.

Owen stood military-straight, as if inspecting his son. And the woman who'd just dropped his hand like it was on fire. "Dunne."

"This is a...surprise," Dunne managed.

"Well, I have some information, and it seemed like we were at the point in this whole mess it made more sense for me to come and sit down with you all and come up with a plan."

Dunne nodded, wordlessly. The he cleared his throat. "Ah, this is..."

"Quinn Peterson. I know." Owen stepped forward and held out his hand.

Quinn studied it like it was a snake that might bite. "Why does he know my name?" she asked Dunne in a low voice.

"I know lots of things," Owen said, smiling genially, which seemed like an odd change from how he usually acted. But maybe Norah just couldn't remember his affable side. "For now, let's focus on what I know about figuring out how to keep the men safe. Where can we all sit comfortably? In here?" Owen walked into the kitchen.

Henry and Jessie followed, Landon and Hazeleigh not far behind. Zara and Kate ducked into the kitchen. Brody gave Dunne's shoulder a slap as he passed, but Dunne and Quinn still just stood there, as if they were frozen.

Quinn was the first to come out of it. She looked at the people still in the room. "Well, keeping the men safe. That's a nice change of events," she said brightly, then turned and strode into the kitchen as if she was marching into battle herself.

Dunne followed her and Cal stepped forward, but Norah stopped him. "Cal…"

He looked down at her. Then melted her heart by touching her cheek, just the way he'd touched Evelyn's. "You're tired."

"I know I should help, and remember, and—"

"You're tired, and still healing. Why don't you go lie down? I'll fill you in on everything, I promise."

Maybe it was the coward's way out, but that was exactly what Norah did. Not just because she was tired, but because she didn't know how to face everyone and still not remember. To face all these people knowing she had the key to this whole thing somewhere locked inside of her—but she couldn't get it out.

She took Evelyn to the room she'd been staying in, curled up with her in the little bed, and tried to relax. Rest.

But her mind whirled, and even when Evelyn dozed off, Norah didn't. She watched her daughter sleep, and desperately tried to remember anything. *Anything.*

She must have finally dozed, because she woke with a start. Evelyn was still fast asleep, but when she looked behind her, Cal stood in the doorway. Watching them.

"How long did I sleep?"

"Probably not long enough," he replied, stepping inside. His gaze traced over her and Evelyn. She patted the mattress so he'd take a seat next to her.

She shifted, being careful not to disturb the bed too much, so she could curl next to Cal, and look at their daughter. *Theirs.*

Finally. Finally. This was everything she'd ever wanted. Right here. And yes, danger existed, but life was never going to be *easy.* They'd lost, they'd fought. Those things left scars.

But the love they shared, their daughter…these were the things scars healed for.

Norah looked up at her husband. She'd thought he was gone. Dead. But here he was. "What do you want, Cal?"

He stiffened and kept his gaze firmly on Evelyn. "You to be safe."

"No, I mean out of your life. What do you *want*?"

He looked up at the ceiling, looking as helpless as she'd ever seen him. "It doesn't matter. What matters is keeping you safe."

"More than that matters. We matter. You're my husband."

He shook his head. "Callum Young was your husband, Norah. I'm not him anymore." But he didn't meet her gaze, and she saw that for what it was worth.

God, she hoped she saw that for what it was. "Is that what you want?" she asked, meaning to sound demanding, but her voice only came out in a pained whisper.

"It's what *is*."

"I'm not asking what *is*. I'm asking what *you* want. Not what you should want. Not what's best for me or for Evelyn. I want to know what you want."

His jaw tightened, and for the longest time she didn't think he'd look at her. But eventually his gaze moved. Met hers.

"I want you. Both of you. I want my family under this roof. Without danger, without questions. I want the life I promised you, Norah."

"You know that's what I want too."

"You don't remem—"

She moved up, cut off his words by pressing her mouth to his. The only man she'd ever loved. And no matter what she remembered or didn't, she knew that love was the core of everything that mattered. "I love you, Callum," she said against his mouth. "Whether you're Cal Young or Cal Thompson or someone else altogether."

She cupped his face with her hand, and he stared at her.

Because she knew he was fighting his internal wars. And that was okay because she always won them for him. Always. "No matter what happens, you'll never get rid of us. No matter what I remember or don't, I'll always love you. No matter what's changed, or what will, you are my home, and I'm yours. We have already lost enough. I refuse to lose more."

He dropped his forehead to hers. "You never would let me go."

She shook her head. "Never."

"I love you, Norah." This time, he pressed his mouth to hers. And for a few moments, her fears and worries evaporated, because she'd thought she'd lost him, in so many ways, but here they were.

He sighed against her mouth, adjusted their position so they could hold on to each other and watch Evelyn sleep. She relaxed against his chest, and into his arms, and was so full of love she thought she might burst.

Until Cal spoke. "You were dreaming when I walked in. Talking in your sleep."

She snuggled in closer. "Oh yeah? About what?"

"Someone named Tara."

And all that warmth, and joy, disappeared in an instant and turned bitterly cold in her chest.

Chapter Eighteen

Cal felt the way she stiffened, but she didn't speak. He didn't know whether to push, or to wait. He'd never heard her speak of a Tara before, and she hadn't sounded…distressed in her sleep, so he hadn't really thought it would unlock some terrible memory.

But her breath was coming in short little pants, and she didn't answer him.

"Norah."

"I don't…" She sucked in a deep breath, then looked up at him. All the worry and confusion and *hurt* of the past few days was back on her face, and he was sorry to have put it there. "I don't remember. I don't know a Tara that I can think of, but when you said that name I just feel…cold."

He rubbed his hands up and down her arms, trying to give her some semblance of warmth. "Maybe Owen knows."

She nodded, but she was clearly distracted.

"I'll go ask."

Norah shook her head, and it was like she was shaking herself. "No. I'll ask him." Then she shook her head once more. "I'll see if I can get Evelyn down in her crib, and *we'll* go ask him." She looked up at him, blue eyes big and sad. But she still had hope, and it was that hope that had always snuck under all his defenses. Because he had none, and hers was irresistible.

"I'll put her down," he said, not sure why his voice came out so hoarse. Or why, when he'd handled guns and bombs and dying men, sliding his hands under his child felt like the most dangerous thing he'd ever done.

But Norah was here, and his child was here, and she was right, of course. She'd always been right. When he saw the complications, she held on to all that hope and found solutions.

Whatever happened, whatever came for them, they'd fight it together. Come out on the other side together. They'd already lost enough. He gently maneuvered Evelyn from the bed to her little crib.

She scrunched up her little face, wriggled a little bit, but then slowly settled back into a sound sleep. Norah turned on the baby monitor and attached the receiver to her belt.

For a moment, they stood side by side, watching their daughter sleep.

Cal hadn't cared about more than surviving in a very long time. But now, it was *all* he cared about. He pressed a kiss to Norah's temple and then they walked out into the kitchen where Owen, Landon, Henry, Dunne and Quinn had congregated around the table.

"Owen, do you know a Tara who might connect to all of this?" Norah asked, and he could feel her apprehension, but her voice was controlled and calm.

Owen lifted his gaze to Norah, but his expression was blank. There was no visible reaction to the name—carefully so. Which was reaction enough.

"You do," Cal said flatly. It seemed so unfair Owen knew all these things, and Norah couldn't remember them.

"I know a few," Owen hedged.

"I said the name in my sleep. I have this…awful physical reaction when I hear her name. But I don't know who she is. Owen, who is she?"

Owen scraped a hand over his face. "Tara Angelo was a young woman who worked in your father's office years ago."

"And?"

"I don't know for sure that it was true, but the rumor was they had an…affair."

"How many years ago?" Norah demanded, her hand finding Cal's.

Owen hesitated, but then seemed to realize there was no way out of this conversation. "Ten."

"Ten years ago. *Ten* years ago?"

Owen looked at Norah, then Cal apologetically. "Yes."

"An affair. When my mother died. You… We've been looking into this all this time and you never said…" She put a hand to her temple, anger clearly warring with her pockets of memory loss. "Or did you?"

Owen shook his head. "I didn't mention it. I didn't see the point. When I was looking into everything you brought to me, her name came up. Some old office gossip. But there's no connection there. Maybe it's a motive for your father's… potential involvement in your mother's death, but it doesn't have anything to do with now. I don't think this is quite the breakthrough you're hoping for, Norah. I'm sorry."

"Then why do *I* have a reaction to the name?" Norah demanded before Cal could demand for her. "Why do *I* seem to know who she is?"

"Tara Angelo. Age thirty-one. Currently living in Philadelphia, working in a dentist's office as an office manager," Landon read, clearly having looked her up on his computer. But his eyebrows drew together. "She was reported missing three weeks ago." Landon looked up at Cal. "Two days before Norah reported her father missing."

"I'd call that a damn connection," Cal said, glaring at Owen.

"My father had an affair around the time he may have killed my mother. Now this woman disappears around the same time my father supposedly did?" Norah shook her head, her hands curling into fists. "But it doesn't make *sense*."

She sounded so lost, and Cal wished he had any kind of comfort to give her, but none of this made sense, and the more they found, the more confused he felt.

"However odd that may seem, she hasn't shown up in any of our surveillance of your father," Owen said. "If this connects, it's not to him."

"That you know of. Clearly you don't know everything or we wouldn't be in this mess."

Norah sighed. "It isn't his fault."

Cal didn't want to agree with her because it felt good to have someone to blame. Someone to lash out at. But he saw an opportunity to point something out. "Then it isn't yours," Cal reminded her, holding her close to his side.

She frowned a little at that, but Cal figured he'd scored a point in favor of her not being so damn hard on herself.

"Let's try none of this is anyone's fault except the people trying to murder," Owen said, and clearly he felt like he was in charge of the situation. He was the superior officer, after all.

But weren't his brothers always telling him they weren't in the military any longer, so there were no leaders, no superiors? Just a team. Just brothers.

Owen was still in the military. Still used to calling the shots. Being the one in charge, and occasionally keeping pertinent details to himself. It had taken Cal a *long* time to get over that, so he thought he understood where Owen was coming from.

"You didn't find a connection between Tara and my father *now*, but what about a connection between Tara and me?"

Owen shook his head. "Not on paper."

All eyes turned to Norah, and Cal wished he could hide her from everyone's intent gaze. She already blamed herself for so much, and for not remembering. The pressure certainly wasn't helping her brain heal.

"I've never had amnesia," Quinn offered. "But I've been terrorized a time or two. You feel that creepy cold feeling when you hear her name? My bet is she has something to do with those bruises on your neck."

Norah brought her fingers up to her collar, but she said nothing.

"Bruises that didn't happen in DC," Cal muttered to himself, trying to tie all the pieces together so Norah didn't feel pressured to remember. "They happened *after* you knew I was alive, knew where I was. When you were on your way here."

Cal considered the possibility Elliot had tried to kill her because she knew Cal was alive, but Elliot hadn't left DC. He could have sent one of his men after her. It was all possible. But the more they looked into this, the more it seemed like two separate events that just were happening on a similar timeline. Did they connect at all?

Quinn choked on the sip of water she'd just taken. She coughed, pointing at Landon's computer screen. "Holy—" she croaked. "That's this Tara woman?" At Landon's nod, she looked up and met Cal's gaze. "I *know* her."

NORAH WAS GRATEFUL for Quinn, and probably not for any of the reasons she should be. But the attention wasn't on her anymore.

Because she didn't remember. No matter how hard she tried, she could not find facts in her foggy memories. She could not manage to find all the information that would stop this.

Information she had, somewhere deep inside her.

"What do you mean you know her?" So many voices demanded Norah couldn't even keep them all straight. She wanted to put her hands over her ears and go back to the little room with Evelyn and block this all out.

But it was her life, her mess, and she was so incredibly lucky she had all these people who wanted to untangle it for her, but that didn't mean she could just…let them. Not when so much was at stake.

Quinn looked over at Dunne. "Remember the pushy contractor I've been telling you about?" She looked at the group at the table. "Jessie and I are trying to make the Peterson ranch house livable, right? We have a contractor, and I've been dealing with him and he's fine enough. Work is about to start. But this lady shows up and starts saying she can do a better job, give me a better deal. Real pushy. I can't stand pushy."

Landon snorted. "Pot. Kettle."

Quinn gave him a dirty look, but she pointed to the screen again. "That's *her*. Her hair is dark now, and she told me her name was Marie, but that's her. I'm like ninety-nine percent sure."

"Marie," Norah said, and it was hard to stay tethered to this moment, with a buzzing kind of panic taking up space in her brain and her knees threatening to give out.

She heard Cal swear next to her, and she knew he wanted to leap into action. But he stayed put and held her upright.

"Can you get in contact with her?" Owen demanded.

Quinn nodded. "She gave me her card, multiple times. I

didn't keep it, but I think I just crumpled it up and tossed it in the truck. If I don't have her number, I'm sure she'll show up again."

"I'll go find it," Henry said, moving quickly outside. Then it was a flurry of action. All the men were *talking*, moving. Typing on computers and discussing plans and… Norah knew she should be part of it. She should demand a place at the table.

She wanted to run and hide. Instead, she took a deep breath and disentangled herself from Cal. He was distracted enough to let her, since he was arguing with Owen. Norah went over to where Quinn stood in the corner, biting her thumbnail.

"Hey, I'm sorry—"

"Sorry that you've given us a lead?" Norah replied before Quinn could finish the apology.

Quinn smiled ruefully. "Not much of one."

"More than I had," Norah replied. "If Cal hadn't heard me talking in my sleep, we'd still be in the dark." She looked at the table. They were all so intent on *acting*, when she felt mired in…something else.

They needed more information. They needed her to remember. She looked over Landon's shoulder at the picture on his screen, but no magical memory of who Tara was to her popped up into her brain. Just a soul-deep need to look away. To *get* away.

But it was that feeling, time and again, that led her to remembering. Not plans. Not moving forward. But information. Pictures. Being reminded of things.

"Quinn, can you tell me… Whatever she said to you the times you spoke? Whatever you remember. Even if it seemed boring."

Quinn nodded. "Yeah. Yeah, look… I'll admit I haven't paid attention too closely. I already hired a contractor for the house. But she just shows up one day, said she's had her eye on the house for a while—I doubt it, it's in the middle of nowhere. Tried to hard sell me and upsell me. But I hired this old guy who tells the worst jokes and has like fifty grandkids he lets work for him. Who's going to fire that guy for some pushy lady? Then she gives me some speech about women sticking together, like *I* haven't been personally victimized by more men than I care to count."

Quinn scowled. "It was just all manipulation, you know? Maybe some folks fall for it, and look, it's a big job. Total money pit. Definitely going to earn anybody a lot of money. I figured it had something to do with all that publicity about Jessie and me getting the gold."

Norah nodded. For a wild minute she just wanted to laugh. She was in the middle of Wyoming, with people who had inherited hidden gold treasure, and had long-lost identical twin sisters, six military men who were living under assumed names, and whatever else strange, bizarre backstories.

Her husband was alive. She had some warped form of amnesia.

Quinn patted her shoulder awkwardly. "Hey, this is a lot. You don't have to hold it all together, you know? You must be tired."

Norah shook her head, even though she probably *was* tired somewhere underneath the wired feeling of being so close to a memory she couldn't seem to get her hands on. "Is that all? That she wanted the job?"

Quinn considered, but the silence stretched out. Whatever interactions she'd had with the woman were through her own lens, so of course there wouldn't be any connection. Besides, the men were looking into her. They'd think of some plan to talk to her. They had a name, confirmation she was here. They'd find her and deal with her, this woman Norah couldn't remember. Who had once had an affair with her father but otherwise didn't connect.

Norah sighed. "Well, thank you. You've given us something to go on." She tried to smile at Quinn.

The baby monitor hooked to her belt loop gave a little blip of static as it did sometimes, and when no cry came through Norah knew it was just Evelyn moving in her sleep.

"Wait a sec," Quinn said, staring at the baby monitor. "One weird thing. She asked if I had kids. Big house, right? She asked if I had a lot of kids to fill it up. I told her no. She asked if I ever babysat. And I was like, no, I'm an adult woman who grew up in a cult, leave me be, lady, you know?"

Norah definitely did not know, but she tried to smile at Quinn.

"But it was like… The question itself wasn't weird, but it was the intensity and the way she wouldn't let it go. Dunne was there with me that day, and she was like he's a handsome guy, don't you want his babies? Kinda flirty, but mostly *weird*."

Babies. Baby. That cold feeling spread, and she kept listening to Quinn talk about the moment, but she stared at the picture on the computer screen. Focused on the woman's face. It was a driver's license picture, so it was small, head-on, but this woman…this woman and babies…

"And I was like, whoa, lady, we are *dating*, and I am a mess who didn't have a mother. I'm hardly ready to *become* one. And I bet Dunne remembers this part, she got all…weird. Like weirder. Wide-eyed and almost like she was in some kind of trance. Right, Dunne?"

Norah was only half listening, staring at the pictures so hard dots started to form in her vision, but Dunne's voice pierced through.

"Yeah, it was definitely off. Quinn and I wrote it off as

some ploy. Like Quinn said, do whatever it took to manipulate Quinn into giving her the gold money. It was strange, but we just figured it was that. She said something about being a mother, didn't she?"

"Yeah, I asked if she had kids since she was so obsessed with them," Quinn said.

"And she said *not yet, but soon*."

"Oh, right. *Right*." Quinn snapped her fingers and Norah startled. Her head pounded and she felt that untethered feeling again, but Cal was too busy arguing with Owen to be her anchor. The baby monitor crackled again, just static.

The cold trickled down her spine. She remembered something. Something fuzzy and confusing, but terrifying. "She wants Evelyn."

"Wait. What?"

"I don't know. But I…" It was still hazy. The memory. The images jumbled together without much sense. But it was coming back. It had to come back. *She's mine. You don't deserve her. She's going to be mine.* "That's what she wanted. Not me dead. She wanted my baby."

And when the static came through the monitor this time, followed by Hero getting to his feet and letting out a bark, Norah didn't hesitate. She sprinted for the bedroom, knocking over a chair on her way.

Chapter Nineteen

"We are absolutely not using Norah as *bait*," Cal said to Owen, growing more and more frustrated with Owen's plans that *all* seemed to put Norah in the middle of danger.

"If we're going to create the element of surprise—"

"Screw surprise," Cal muttered. He glanced back at Norah, who stood talking with Quinn and Dunne. She looked too pale. Too...fragile.

He knew she wasn't. Somehow she'd survived all this, gotten here without any help from him or anyone, really. But knowing how strong she could be didn't make it any easier to let her stand on her own two feet. He didn't want her to have to *be* strong.

Cal sighed. He didn't know how to fix this, but he supposed this Tara woman was a step in the right dire—

Norah darted out of the kitchen, knocking over one of the empty chairs as she rushed toward the bedroom. Cal didn't think, he followed, though Dunne and Quinn were on Norah's heels as well.

They all crowded into the room, even though Cal had no idea why. He only knew something was wrong, and he needed to fix it.

But the window was open. The curtains fluttered in the breeze.

And the crib was empty.

Cal felt his entire life end, right there. But then a little cry sounded, and Norah turned around, Evelyn cradled close to her chest. Still, she was pale and shaking. "I didn't leave that window open. I did not." She said it so defiantly. Like they'd try to argue with her when he was just as sure as she was that the window hadn't been left open.

"I'll go outside and check the window," Landon said.

"Henry's out there," Dunne reminded him. "Stick together."

"Hero jumped out," Norah said, her voice creaky. "He just jumped right out that window."

"I'll check on—"

A gunshot echoed through the slowly falling evening. And then another. It was another race of bodies—those behind him turning out of the room, but Cal figured it was just as easy to pretzel himself out the window.

Henry was leaning against the house, holding his side. "I'm good. Thanks to the dog barking, I think. Nicked me, but I'm good," he said. "It was a woman. Holding a bundle. She ran off. She had… She didn't have the baby?"

Cal surveyed the yard. Dusk had fallen, and he saw no sign of whoever had been at the window. "No."

"She made it look like she did. Or I would have shot."

Landon and Brody came around the side of the house. "No sign of anyone out front," they said. Dunne followed, his pace severely slowed by his limp.

"I thought you had cameras?" Cal demanded of Landon.

"I do," Landon said grimly. "Nothing changed on my end. Which means she had to have tampered with them."

"Explains why she was quiet for a few days. Figuring out how to get around the security," Henry said. "We've got to move before she can regroup and get around them again."

Cal nodded. "We'll fan out. Find her."

"The dog ran after her," Henry said.

Cal nodded. "Good. This ends now." He strode back to the open window and poked his head in. Norah stood with Quinn, holding Evelyn tightly to her chest. He handed Norah his gun. "Stay here."

She tried to reach out with her free hand and grab him, but he backed away. "Callum."

"Listen to me. She wants Evelyn, so you need to stay here where it's safe and protect her. We're going after her."

Quinn gave Norah's shoulder a pat and took the gun Cal still held out. "We'll handle the home front." She gave Norah a tight smile. "That's what women do," she said with a wink.

He knew Norah wasn't happy with the situation, but he couldn't wait for her to be. They needed to stop this. Now.

Norah moved forward and handed the gun back to him. "You take this. There are more in this house, right Quinn?"

Quinn nodded.

"You take the gun. Quinn will get me another one. You protect yourself. Be careful. Be... Please."

Cal took the gun and nodded. "I'll be back," he said. A promise. A vow.

He turned back to the men. He didn't want to leave Norah and Evelyn, but they couldn't keep holding close and tight and hoping for this to be over.

He wasn't leaving her alone. She had all the women, plus Jake, and...

He turned to Owen, who had come around back after Dunne. Cal wasn't 100 percent certain he trusted the man, but he didn't know the ranch like the rest of them did. He looked at Dunne, and they'd been brothers long enough to know...

Dunne shrugged, a clear sign he didn't know whether to trust his father either. Damn.

"All right. Owen, you're with me," Cal said. "Henry and Dunne—"

"I'm not staying back," Henry said grimly. "She shot me. I'm going after her."

Again, Cal turned to Dunne. Dunne gave a short nod, that Henry was okay and would be without immediate medical attention. "We'll take the front," he said. "In case she doubles back."

Cal nodded. "Brody and Landon, you're team three. Owen and I will head west. You'll head east. This ends tonight."

All the men around him nodded, and then set about to follow his orders.

Cal gave one last look at the window. It was now closed, but Norah stood behind the glass, Evelyn snuggled to her chest.

His family. His heart.

Yeah, this was going to end tonight.

NORAH STOOD IN the little bedroom while Quinn went to fetch her a gun. She felt...stupid and helpless. A pointless fixture in all this danger, and it infuriated her. Probably more than it should, because her role in this was just as important, if not the most important.

Take care of her baby.

"I'm so sorry, Ev," she whispered, rubbing her cheek against the baby's temple. "I don't know how we got into this mess." She sighed. She expected Quinn to return quickly, but when she didn't a little trickle of fear began to cause her heartbeat to race again.

"It's okay," she whispered, trying to convince herself she was talking to Evelyn and not herself. "It's going to be okay."

She surveyed the room and looked for something that could be a weapon. But before she could find anything, the door squeaked open. Thank goodness, Quinn was back and— Norah stopped and turned around, speechless, at the appearance of a strange woman in the room.

No, not a strange woman. Tara, just like the picture, but with dark hair.

"How…"

Tara rolled her eyes. "Do you know how *predictable* people can be? Military men always want to be tactical. Fan out. Blah, blah, blah. The dog gave me a start, but I was ready for him." She smirked.

Hero. "You hurt my dog?"

Tara shrugged. "Your *dog* almost killed me before. Kept me from finishing my job. He deserved everything he got out in those woods. And while the men were blabbing about *plans*, I could sneak into the stables, scare that little girl and distract everyone here."

Sarabeth.

"She'll be fine. I don't hurt kids." Tara smiled as Evelyn fussed in Norah's arms. "I'm an excellent mother. Or I'm going to be."

Norah felt that same cold from before. When she heard the name *Tara.* She still had no memory of why. The woman stepped forward and held out her arms. "Now, don't be stupid this time. Give me my baby."

This time.

She'd tried before. She'd tried to take Evelyn before. "You know I won't give her up." She would fight tooth and nail. Just like last time. *Last* time. When she'd been on her way to Cal, and gotten a ride from this woman, thinking she was just a harmless ride service driver.

But she'd tried to take Evelyn. Tried to kill Norah with

her bare hands. Instead, Hero had attacked and Norah had somehow managed to run. Run toward Cal.

"The dog is gone. Your little heroes are gone. It's so easy to manipulate these military men. Shoot one. Shoot another. Pit them against each other. A little tit for tat. Because no, your hero won't be coming to save you. Let's just say they're all otherwise occupied. For good."

"What?"

The woman moved around the room. "Your father wanted the men? I handed them over. Told him I wouldn't hurt you." She laughed. "So predictable. As long as he got what he wanted, he didn't worry about what happened to anyone else. But now, it's time to get what *I* want." Tara stepped closer, still aiming her gun at Norah's head. "Hand her over."

"Never. She is mine. My daughter."

"No, she's mine. Your father promised me a baby. He *promised*. But he's a liar. So. Now I'll have her. You don't have to worry. I'll take good care of her."

Norah wanted to cry. As much as she'd started to remember about her father being a terrible person, there was still a part of her that remembered the mask. Or the man he'd been before. Whatever it was, it hurt that he'd...he'd hurt so many women.

"I'm sorry my father hurt you," Norah managed to say, keeping her voice calm for Evelyn's sake. "But you can't take that out on me."

"Of course I can. You're an obstacle. I'm taking care of it. Just like I took care of your mother."

Norah's body went weak. "What?" she managed to rasp.

"She was the only thing between us, he said. So, I took care of it. I took care of it and her and we were supposed to be together. Then it was *you*. And his job. He was supposed to be *mine*, but he lied. He lied and he lied and he lied. All to get what he wanted. It's my turn." The woman lifted the gun. "Now, I'll get what I deserve."

Norah curled herself around Evelyn, who was starting to cry. She squeezed her eyes shut, desperate to think. She needed that weapon. She needed to fight. She'd survived this woman once, and she would damn well survive her again.

Which was when she realized she still wore the baby monitor receiver on her belt. It wouldn't stop a gun, but it could do some damage if she wielded it right. And if it was really true, that this woman wouldn't hurt Evelyn…

Well, it was worth a shot. Norah would use her body to shield Evelyn no matter what, and she wouldn't be alone forever. Even if the men were out looking for Tara, even if they got caught by her father—she tried not to think about what her father wanted to do to them—there were still people here who would come to help. Once Sarabeth was settled. Eventually.

"Please don't hurt her," Norah said, keeping her voice shaky and weak as she huddled in the corner, hoping her body shielded her hand trying to unhook the monitor from her belt loop.

"Hurt her? I'm going to be her mother now. And she'll never know the difference. And everything will finally be okay. Your father will lose, and I will win."

The gun cocked.

Norah took a deep, steadying breath. She whispered a little assurance to Evelyn, who was wailing now. Then she whirled, flinging the baby monitor as hard as she could at the gun.

It didn't hit the gun, but it caught Tara by enough surprise it did one better. It slammed into her face. Tara let out a howl of pain as the baby monitor clattered to the ground. Evelyn's increasing cries drowned out the sound.

And Norah darted for the door. She thought she'd made

it. Thought she could run—just like she had last time—but a sharp pain in her scalp jerked her back.

"You will pay for that," Tara said, giving Norah's hair another jerk.

She cried out in pain, but she wasn't going down that easy. Not with her daughter in her arms. But before she could decide what to do, something creaked.

"Stop." It was a cold demand from the now open window. Quinn stood there, aiming a gun right at Tara.

Echoed by Jessie at the door, also pointing a gun at the woman.

Tara stood there, hand still in Norah's hair, her nose bleeding. She seethed. "They won't come to save you! They're all going to die. And then so will you."

"Then we'll have to go save them. Drop Norah. Drop the gun."

"Make me," she spat.

Norah made eye contact with Jessie. She looked so cool and calm, and Norah did everything she could to match that look even as Tara's grip tightened in her hair. As she began pulling her closer by her hair, Norah jerked her chin down toward the wriggling Evelyn.

"Now, give her to her new mommy," Tara said, in a creepy singsong voice.

"Make me," Norah replied, mimicking her. She jerked once, hard, and though the grip in her hair didn't loosen, and the pain in her scalp was excruciating, Norah held Evelyn out and Jessie rushed to take her.

The second Evelyn was out of her arms, Norah rammed into Tara. Jessie ran with Evelyn, and Tara screamed in frustrated anger. But they were so close now that she couldn't move her arm to get the gun pointed at Norah easily. Norah grabbed her wrist, and they grappled.

Norah didn't think about Quinn at the window. She didn't think about Jessie running off with Evelyn.

She only thought about doing some damage.

Chapter Twenty

The dark was an obstacle. Cal hadn't brought a flashlight, though Owen had turned his phone's flashlight feature on.

Owen. Cal surveyed him every so often, trying to determine if this would be his downfall. Trusting the man who'd once sent him to war. A man even his own son wasn't sure he could trust.

At least in war he'd always known who'd had his back.

They still did, Cal reminded himself. He still had five brothers right here who were fighting to protect his daughter, his wife and him. Not because he'd ordered them to, but because that was what family did.

"Why are you really here, Owen?" Cal muttered as they moved through the dark otherwise silently. Cal supposed it wasn't the time to be having the conversation, but there was no sign of anyone out here.

Owen turned off his flashlight. "Up there. Two o'clock. You see that?"

Cal looked to where Owen instructed and did see a little flash of light. It was still a good ways off, but it was something to move toward. "Why are you here, Owen?"

Owen sighed next to him. He didn't turn on his light and they didn't move forward. "Sometimes, it takes a long time to realize the mistakes you made. And that the things you did thinking you were a good friend, a good man, were really just cowardly, because you didn't want to make waves."

"Elaborate."

Owen laughed, a little bitterly. "You were a great soldier, Cal. I could probably use you again, if you wanted, but I doubt you do."

"No, I don't." And it was a strange thing to realize. Because being a soldier had been…everything to him once. Until Norah. Maybe even until Evelyn.

"I had no idea Elliot planned to kill his wife, if that's what happened. I'd heard rumors about the affair way back when. And I'd noticed a change in his demeanor. But I figured those were his issues. His problems. Family, not work. So, I ignored it. And when the pattern started again recently, I would have gone right on ignoring it, but Norah came to me. With all these fears and what should have been crazy accusations, but they weren't. I couldn't even muster up surprise. I should have been horrified. But it just felt…grim."

Cal didn't know what to say to that.

"I'm here because I should have said something then. Before things got so out of hand my own son was somehow in the crosshairs of it all."

"I'm not sure any of that was your responsibility."

"Then whose was it?"

That was the eternal question, wasn't it? How involved to get. How much to stand up and say your piece. When to lie to keep the peace. Still, at some point, you couldn't hold yourself responsible for other people's issues. "Elliot's mostly."

Owen sighed again. "Then once we stop this Tara woman, let's stop him."

They moved toward the light. A team, and sure Owen could have been lying still, but it didn't add up. And though

Cal knew Owen and Dunne had a complicated relationship, it wasn't *bad*.

So, he took a leap of faith—because it was what Norah would have done. She'd put her trust in Owen before, and now Cal had to do the same.

They walked, focusing on the light, and Cal didn't doubt Brody and Landon would be doing the same on the east side of the property. It was quite possible that whoever had tried to take Evelyn—whether it was Tara or someone else—hadn't acted alone. They'd only ever seen evidence of one person lurking around the ranch.

The problem was that even with Landon's cameras and all their perimeter checks and work on the ranch, the land was vast, and the property adjacent to the ranch was just as vast and isolated. It was so easy to hide.

Then Cal heard it, just the tiniest *snick* of something in the dark. Just a shade too loud to be animal. Just a shade too close to ignore. "Behind," Cal called.

He couldn't see in the dark, not really more than shadows, but he had his instincts and his hearing and the training of years and years of combat. He punched out—and hit somebody. Not Owen.

He heard a thud, and Owen's quiet swear. So, there were at least two assailants. There was nothing else to do but fight. It was too dark to shoot when Owen was by his side, also fighting someone, so Cal punched, kicked, elbowed and used his gun as a weapon of blunt force trauma rather than to shoot.

He heard another person—so at least three. One of the ones fighting Cal managed to kick him so hard he lost his grip on the gun. Still, Cal kicked out, rolled and managed to get the attacker on the ground. He just needed to wrestle the gun from him and—

A gunshot pierced through the quiet night around them,

and Cal was grateful he didn't feel the familiar pain of bullet ripping through flesh, but he didn't know who had shot or potentially been shot.

And then a voice rang out, loud and commanding as a flashlight popped on. "That'll be enough." It was Elliot's voice. A military command that had the third man backing off, and the two injured men crawling over to where he stood. "You've always been an excellent fighter, Cal. Too bad you're such a lying piece of scum too. But I knew I'd need more than just these three." He looked at his men with disgust. Then at the man with Cal.

"Owen." Elliot seemed genuinely surprised. "You... This doesn't involve you."

"You want my son dead. I think it does."

"It isn't personal."

"Oh, well, then. Please kill my only child," Owen returned caustically. "What happened to you?"

Elliot straightened, his chest puffing out. "Nothing happened to me. I'm making things right. Making sure that everyone who lied to me pays."

"What about the people you lied to?"

"I'm not a liar. I do what's right."

"You had your wife killed."

"I did no such thing. That stupid woman misconstrued everything I said. She did everything wrong and made a mess. That's her fault and her problem, not mine."

That stupid woman... "You mean Tara?" Cal asked, desperate to connect the dots.

Elliot scoffed. "Tara." He shook his head. "I don't have anything to do with that nutcase anymore. She was a means to an end."

"An end that tried to steal my child from her mother," Cal returned, trying to keep his fury contained enough that he didn't make a grave mistake. "It's one thing to want to kill me, but you want your own granddaughter—"

"Your bastard. Your *lie. Not* my granddaughter," Elliot said, with such venom Cal couldn't even find words. Who could be so vile when talking about their own flesh and blood? A *baby.* "I don't care about that abomination. Tara can do whatever she wants with her. I want *you*, and your brothers. You tried to make a fool out of me. Well, we'll see who gets the last laugh."

A light clicked on, bright and directly in Cal's eyes. He squinted against it, determined not to close his eyes completely even as it blinded him.

The illuminated space was a hole that clearly had been recently dug. Deep and wide enough to bury a few people, as Cal figured that was the point. Because down inside the hole were explosives.

"Once your *brothers* arrive, they'll join you here. And they'll arrive. All of them, to save their leader. So honorable, so upstanding. Defiling my daughter and forcing her to lie to me."

"You're delusional if you think that's what happened."

"I know it's what happened. My daughter would never lie to me, leave me, betray me. You made her. *You.*"

"You had her mother killed. You told her I was dead. You told me she was dead. You're the liar. The one who betrayed—"

Elliot raised a gun, pointed it at Cal's head. "I was going to blow you all up, but this is fine. I'll shoot you and save the explosives for your bothers. No one lies to me. No one."

Before Cal could jump out of the way or grab one of the guns from the men behind him, an odd growl sounded in the dark, followed by a bark and a flurry of movement.

Elliot went down, even as a gunshot went off. Cal heard

it buzz by him, freezing him for a second before he realized how close it had been to his head and threw himself onto the ground. Owen ran forward and Landon and Brody appeared as Cal got back to his feet. Brody and Landon helped Owen detain the men who'd been fighting them, getting rid of their guns and tying them up. Cal went over to Hero, picked up the gun the dog had wrestled out of Elliot's grasp.

Elliot thrashed, his arm bloody and Hero standing on his chest, snarling menacingly. Red and blue lights flashed in the distance. Cops.

Never in his life had he been so *glad* to see law enforcement, and as much as identities were at stake, Elliot needed to be arrested and tried for *all* his crimes.

Hero growled at the approaching officers, but Cal petted his head. "It's all right, boy. It's all right. You really are a hero."

Hero had blood on him, and Cal realized he'd been injured. Elliot or one of his men had shot him. "Jesus. We need a vet." He pulled the dog off Elliot as law enforcement came with guns and handcuffs and backup.

Backup. Help.

One of the cops came over, and then spoke into his walkie-talkie, asking for a veterinarian. "Looks shallow, but we'll get him taken care of."

Cal nodded, then pressed his face into the dog's fur for one second, trying to collect himself. "You deserve a medal, champ." He looked up at the cop. "The house? The woman who tried to take the baby?"

"We've got officers at the house as well." But he didn't give any more information as the team of officers began dragging men to their truck.

"Text from Jake," Landon said, jogging over and out of breath. "They've got Tara. Zara called Thomas the minute gunshots started back at the house," he said, referring to Zara's cousin who was a police officer with the county. "Once the cops got to the house and found out what was going on, they sent a team out here. So, it's okay. Everyone's okay."

Okay. Cal didn't know how to believe it until he held his family in his arms.

NORAH WAS STILL SHAKING. Her arms burned where Tara had scratched her, and her eye was swelling where the woman had managed to elbow her.

But Tara had fared much worse. Norah wasn't exactly proud of it—okay, maybe she was. She'd taken care of herself. She'd protected her daughter. And now Tara was in police custody and *they* could deal with the woman who'd wanted to steal her child. The woman who'd conspired to kill her mother.

Norah held Evelyn close to her chest as the kind police officer finished questioning her. He was soft and gentle and paused anytime Evelyn fussed so Norah could calm her. But no matter how calm everyone was, Norah couldn't relax. Not until—

Cal burst through the doors. He'd been through a fight too, she could tell. But he was whole. And alive. That was all that mattered. Before she could even stand, he was at her side, pulling her and Evelyn close.

"You're all right," they said in unison, holding each other so tightly Evelyn began to squirm in protest. They both loosened their hold and looked at each other.

His face was bruised, and his lip and nose were bleeding. But he was okay. He was okay and…

Cal's hands framed her face—his were bruised and bloodied too. "Who did you fight? My father?"

"His men," Cal replied. He touched the edge of her swollen eye in a featherlight caress. "You fought too."

"She gave her hell," Jake offered. "They had to transport Tara to the hospital in police custody."

Norah thought she maybe should feel bad about that. But she didn't. Because they had certainly been through enough hell at the hands of other people. Maybe she could feel some sympathy for Tara, who'd clearly been used by her father, and hadn't been mentally stable to begin with, but that didn't mean she'd ever feel bad for protecting herself and her daughter with her own hands.

"My...father?" she asked tentatively, not sure what outcome she was hoping for. The man had betrayed her. So many times over. Maybe he hadn't been directly behind her mother's death, but he certainly hadn't handled the situation correctly.

"Hero saved the day again," Owen said—he'd clearly fought too, as he had a bloody lip and torn clothes and was leaning more on one foot than another. "Elliot was about to shoot Cal when Hero jumped in. Your father's injured, but he'll survive."

Norah couldn't take her hands off Evelyn, but she looked at Cal. "I'm sorry. I wish—"

"It's all over now. No apologies on our end necessary. They tried to hurt us. They failed. Now they're going to have every legal repercussion possible stop them from ever hurting us again."

He said it so fiercely, and with such confidence, she thought maybe she really could relax. They'd handled all the threats, and now they were someone else's problem.

"My deputies collected him and his men. They'll need to be checked out by a medic as well, but they're in custody and will stay that way," the police officer said. "We'll call in a federal agency to handle everything and the information Mr. Wilks gave us," he said, nodding at Owen. "I'm sure they'll want to talk to you all, ask a lot of the same questions I already have, but for the time being you can clean up and get some rest. We just ask that you stay put." He offered them a kind smile. "You're safe now."

Safe. *Safe.* Norah leaned into Cal, and for the first time that day let herself cry. In relief. Even if there were some things she never remembered, they were safe.

They were home.

"I love you," she whispered, as Cal held her tight.

"I love you too," he murmured.

And even in all this pain, she knew that it was going to be okay. Because they finally had each other again. And they had this found family who'd helped protect and save them.

So, no matter what happened in the future, they'd always have this. They'd always have love.

Epilogue

The puppy wouldn't stop barking.

Cal stared at him balefully. "You need some lessons, buddy."

The dog kept yipping, the pink bow around its neck hanging loose because the animal had spent ten minutes this morning trying to tear it off before giving up.

Cal was still waiting for the signal out here on the back porch. It was a beautiful day to celebrate his daughter's first birthday. At home. With his family. All things that even all these months later filled him with a gratitude so big it threatened to take him out at the knees.

But Cal Thompson was stronger than that.

Sarabeth clattered into the kitchen, then flung the screen door open. "It's time," she said, practically jumping with excitement.

Cal grinned at her. She'd always been a resilient thing, but she'd come a long way. She was going to school, caring for the animals on the ranch, so thrilled about becoming a big sister in a few months.

Cal followed Sarabeth into the living room that was decorated to the nines with pink and purple balloons, streamers and all manner of first-birthday decorations. Evelyn stood holding on to Norah's knees, and they both turned and grinned at him when he entered.

"Dog! Dog!" Evelyn babbled, because *dog* was her favorite word and favorite thing in the world. She toddled over to him as he knelt to the ground and held out the dog. Evelyn squealed in delight when the dog started licking her face.

Cal met Norah's gaze over delighted one-year-old and ecstatic puppy. Her eyes were shiny, with happy tears, he knew, their own version of delighted and ecstatic.

Eventually Evelyn opened the rest of her presents, while they all piled around the kitchen table and sang "Happy Birthday." New babies and wives and fiancées and his five brothers. Who had proven to him time and again that they'd never let him be that scared, lonely teenager again.

It was not what Cal could have ever imagined when they'd first stepped foot onto the ranch. That had been survival:

This was life. For all of them. Ever-growing families, hope for the future, and most of all love.

He looked over at Norah, who was trying to hold the squirming puppy still for a picture. She was grinning while Sarabeth talked a mile a minute, trying to get Hero in the frame so he didn't feel left out. Everyone was shouting suggestions for how to get the picture while Jessie tried to line it up.

Cal just watched, just enjoyed, twisting the wedding ring on his finger. A constant reminder that he'd somehow put one foot in front of the other, just like his mother had told him to do all those years ago.

And her namesake was right here, squealing in glee. His. Growing like a weed, just like all babies should.

Dunne bumped his shoulder to Cal's. "You did all right, Cal."

Cal smiled as Norah grinned over at him when she finally got the picture.

"*We* did great, brother."

Because the Thompson brothers were who they were now, and this was their life. Their family. Their future. Bonded together with love and sacrifice. And the hope Norah had somehow taught him.

Because it turned out, hope was the greatest weapon of all.

* * * * *

WYOMING COWBOY UNDERCOVER

JUNO RUSHDAN

For JBR, KIR and ABR.
Everything I do is for you guys.

Chapter One

A gunshot fractured the quiet night.

ATF agent Rocco Sharp stiffened behind the wheel of his parked Ford Bronco, where he was waiting to meet his informant. Darkness wrapped around him on the overlook of the mountain, surrounded by trees. Which was the point. To pick a location where prying eyes wouldn't see them.

A cool August breeze washed over him through the rolled-down window. His skin prickled. He climbed out of the SUV and listened, hoping it wasn't another bad sign. The first had been that his contact was late.

In nine months, Dr. Percival Tiggs had never once been late.

Pop! Pop!

More gunfire ripped through the night. To the west. Far in the distance, but it sounded closer than the first shot. He reached into his vehicle, tapped open the glove box and grabbed the binoculars that were beside a flashlight. From this catbird seat, he had a view of the road below, as well as the mountainside and the river bathed in moonlight. He could easily see an approaching vehicle.

Peering through the binoculars, he focused all his attention on the twisting road that cut through the canyon and mountains. He picked up the soft purr of a finely tuned engine along with the rumble of low gears and the growl of a powerful V-6. Possibly V-8. Getting closer.

Sure enough, headlights pierced the darkness. A light-colored vehicle raced down the narrow, treacherous road. Rocco recognized the make and model. Old school. Vintage-style Land Cruiser.

Percival.

Was he blown?

Right behind him was a black heavy-duty hauler truck with two rear wheels on each side—a dually. Orange muzzle flashes burst in tandem with gunshots fired from the passenger's side of the truck at the sedan. Metal pinged. Sparks flared. The sedan zipped past the turn for the overlook.

Had Percival missed it deliberately to keep from leading anyone to Rocco? Or had he simply been going too fast to take the turn?

Either way, it wasn't good for Percival.

Before he lost sight of them, Rocco tried to home in on the rear bumper of the truck to get the license plate. He rotated the focusing ring on the binoculars, sharpening the image. There was a tinted film and splattered mud over the plate, making it impossible to read. But he glimpsed two bumper stickers. One with an iridescent silver tree on a white background. The other was red and scratched. A white bolt of lightning ran through it.

The vehicles disappeared around the curve of the road. Swearing to himself, he hopped in his Bronco and took off down the path that would converge with the road. They were a good thirty-minute drive from the outskirts of town, but still within the sheriff's jurisdiction. The special task force he worked on had a good relationship with the department. He called Dispatch and relayed the details of the truck in case they had a deputy in the vicinity who might be able to intercept. Wyoming Highway 130 crossed twenty-nine miles through the Medicine Bow Mountain Range. If they stayed on it, they'd be near Laramie.

"Headed east on WYO 130," he said, taking a hard right turn onto the road, kicking up dirt, "but they haven't passed Wayward Bluffs yet." That was the first town on the outskirts of the mountain range before Laramie.

"Agent Sharp, we don't have any deputies in the area," the dispatcher said. "But Deputy Russo was checking out a disturbance at the Wild Horse Ecosanctuary—"

"That'll have to do." He knew the location. About twelve miles from Wayward Bluffs.

Rocco clicked off the call and put the phone in his pocket.

No guarantees that Angela Russo would make it in time, but it was worth a try.

Red taillights came into view. Rocco pressed down on the accelerator, desperate to catch up. To give Percival a chance to lose whoever was chasing him. But with the winding road he could only risk going so fast.

A hairpin turn was coming up, but a thicket of tall pines would obstruct his view. Both vehicles took the acute bend. Through tree branches, he barely made out their lights.

Rocco slapped the steering wheel. Despite the air whipping over him, sweat rolled down his spine.

Recruiting an asset like Percy was a tricky game. Endangering the life of another. Trying to balance it with protecting them while pushing them to get the information needed. Someone was selling ghost guns—untraceable firearms—along with machine guns, military-grade explosive devices and specially marked armor-piercing bullets. Almost anything was legal in the Wild West of Wyoming, except the explosives, but the supplier was trafficking the deadly weapons and ammunition across state lines, putting them in the hands of criminals and gangs.

Innocent lives were being lost. Just last week, two fellow ATF agents out of the Denver office had been critically wounded in a raid. Armor-piercing rounds had punched through their Kevlar vests. Bullets from the same supplier that he'd been after for a year.

One of those agents had been a close friend. This was now personal for him. Still, he didn't want to jeopardize Percy's safety.

The ends didn't always justify the means.

Rocco whipped around the hairpin bend, his tires squealing against the asphalt. The scent of burned rubber stung his nose. On the straightaway, he could see them clearly headed downhill. He hit the accelerator harder, eating up the distance between them.

Pop!

The sedan's back windshield exploded.

Pop! Pop!

Percy's car swerved, fishtailing, like a tire had been blown out, and he lost control. The sedan went into a spin, crashing into the guardrail. Metal screamed. Brakes whined in the night. Sparks flew. With an agonizing shriek, steel sheared.

Rocco's gut clenched.

Lay off the brakes, Percy. Straighten out the wheel. Come on.

The groan of metal rending filled the air as the car broke through the guardrail. The sedan flipped over the side, bounced, and rolled toward the vast, deep maw of the ravine.

No. His stomach tightened even harder, his heart hammering in shock.

The truck slowed a moment, passing the gaping hole in the guardrail and then raced off down the road.

Rocco jammed his foot on the gas until he reached the site of the crash. He noted the mile marker and threw the SUV in Park. Slapped the button for the hazard lights. Snatched his flashlight. Tossed his cowboy hat on the seat. Dashed from the vehicle.

Adrenaline surged through him. He ran to the torn guardrail and shone the flashlight over the side. The wrecked car was upside down. Nothing more than a hunk of battered, twisted metal. A tree had stopped its descent toward the river.

Be alive, Percival.

Rocco jumped, catapulting down the hill. He landed hard and unevenly, turning his left ankle. A stabbing pain shot up his leg as he teetered off balance. He righted himself and hurried onward over the steep, rocky terrain. Stumbled. Fell. Gasping, he was up on his feet. He was running at an angle down the slope now, trying not to slip again. His heart pumped furiously. Sweat dripped from his brow.

One thought drove him. *Get to Percival.*

The man was a fifty-year-old veterinarian. Had a wife. A son. Had done nothing wrong besides having the right type of access at a time when Rocco's task force was in dire need of answers.

He slid down to the car. Shattered glass glittered in the moonlight. A bloody arm hung out the window.

Kneeling, he shone the flashlight up inside the car. The airbag had deflated. Blood covered Percival's face. Rocco pressed his fingers to the man's carotid artery, checking for a pulse. He found one. Thready. Barely there. But his informant was still breathing.

Rocco unsheathed his tactical blade from the holster clipped on his hip. He sliced the seat belt—the one thing that had saved Percival's life—and hauled him free of the wreckage over to a somewhat level spot.

Percival coughed. His head rocked side to side.

Rocco cradled the man's head in his lap, whipped out his phone from his pocket and dialed the sheriff's department once more. "Agent Sharp again. I need an ambulance." He relayed the mile marker. "The shooter got away in the black pickup truck still headed east on 130." Percival reached for him, mumbling something, but he couldn't hear what it was over the dispatcher's response. He glanced down. The injured man was clutching his abdomen. His shirt was soaked with blood. But he hadn't been impaled by anything in the car. Had he been shot? "There are at least two individuals in the truck. Hurry with that ambulance."

He dropped the phone, not bothering with hanging up, and pressed a palm to Percival's abdominal wound to slow the bleeding.

"He kn-kn-knew…" Percival coughed up blood. "I was a CI…" Another cough. More blood.

"Shush, don't talk. The ambulance is on the way." But at the rate he was bleeding out it wouldn't reach him in time.

"No time," Percival said on a pained groan, echoing Rocco's thought. *"Wrong."* With a trembling hand, he dug in the pocket of his jeans and pulled out something. "We had it wrong."

Rocco took the balled-up wad and lowered it into the light. The bloodstained paper had a date written on it.

September 19.

Six days from now. "What happens on the nineteenth?"

Percy shook his head. "Something big." His voice was faint. "S-s-something horrible." His eyelids fluttered, his breath growing shallow. He mumbled more words, too low for Rocco to make out. "…planned it all."

"Who?" Rocco patted his cheek. Worry clawed at him as

he watched the life draining from this poor man. "What's going to happen? Who planned it?"

Percy's lips moved, but the whisper was lost in the wind.

"Say it again." Rocco brought his ear closer to his face.

"Mc-C-Coy. Ma…" The syllable slipped from Percival's mouth in his dying breath. His head lolled to the side in Rocco's arms, his eyes frozen open at the moment his life slipped away.

No! Rocco tightened his arms around Percy as if by doing so he could change his fate. "God, no."

He thought of Percy's wife—his widow—and the reason for his senseless murder.

McCoy. Marshall McCoy.

Guilt seized his heart and squeezed. Followed by a wave of white-hot rage.

"I'll find out who did this to you," he vowed. He'd track down those men in the truck one way or another. "And I'll make them pay."

Rocco knew precisely where to start.

With Mercy McCoy.

Chapter Two

Mercy McCoy padded through the entryway of polished steel and ten-foot-high windows that spanned the walls, beneath a gleaming chandelier and across a veined marble floor. At the door, she pulled on her canvas shoes and stepped outside. She descended the steps of Light House. It was her home, with private family quarters upstairs, but it also operated as the main building for the entire commune. On the first floor, meals were prepped and served where they ate together in the dining hall. This was the place where they gathered in celebration as well as mourning.

She slipped into the back seat of the SUV. She abhorred being chauffeured around and would've preferred to sit up front, but her father had forbidden it.

As I am your father, I cannot also be your friend. Not if I'm to do right by you. We are both leaders of the Light. You must know your place as everyone in the flock must know theirs.

She gritted her teeth against the rule.

Alex, the head of security, pulled off from the circular drive, taking the path downhill. "This is your last time going into town for personal reasons."

Mercy swallowed around the cold lump in her throat. "What? I don't understand. Why?"

"Empyrean's orders," he said, referring to her father, the great leader of the Shining Light.

"But he didn't say anything to me." She had seen him a few minutes ago. He'd simply smiled and waved. Not a word about any changes in protocol.

"I believe he wants to speak with you about it when you return," Alex said.

Her chest tightened. "Is this a temporary thing? Or permanent?"

Alex met her questioning gaze in the rearview mirror. He didn't respond, which was an answer in itself.

She scrubbed her palms down her thighs, her fingers suddenly aching. Mercy glanced over her shoulder back at Light House. At the luminous glass-and-metal cage.

Whenever she left to go to town—for herself and not as an acolyte bringing the word of their religious movement to others—she was usually filled with a pure joy that was as bright and warm as the sun. Mainly because it had absolutely nothing to do with her father.

Tonight, nausea roiled through her. The wrought-iron gates of the compound opened. They drove through, passing the guardhouse. Towering trees obscured a brick wall that surrounded the property's one hundred acres. She faced forward as they headed to town.

For six months, she'd had it good, able to leave the compound twice a week. At first, it was for a hot yoga class. Then she'd passed the Underground Self-Defense school. She'd watched Charlie Sharp teaching a class to other women. Showing them how to be strong, capable. Fearless.

That was what she wanted to be.

Inside the compound, she was sheltered. Lived in a bubble of strict rules. The price of being afforded a constant sense of safety and peace. But always under the umbrella of being Empyrean's daughter.

Out here, in the world, she often felt like a newborn foal running for the first time. Unsteady. Unsure. Uneasy.

But when she was at USD, throwing punches and kicks, she was on fire. She was *free*. To discover herself and all the possibilities that existed beyond the walls of the compound. To see what she might be without the Shining Light.

Now she was forced to do the one thing in the world that she did *not* want to do.

Give it up.

Alex stopped on the corner of Garfield and Third Street since he knew she didn't want anyone from USD to see her being dropped off like a child.

She was twenty-four years old. But she didn't have a license. Had never lived anywhere other than on the compound. Never gone to a regular school. Never eaten a meal that hadn't been prepared by the hands of those she called family. Never been to a movie. Never had a job that paid money. Never had a Christmas tree. Or a birthday cake.

Never donned any color but white. Leaders wore no hue, reflecting and scattering visible wavelengths of light.

All per her father's edicts.

A restlessness bubbled inside her, spreading and seeping through every cell.

Her father meant well. She suspected his overprotectiveness came from the loss of her mother when she was too young to remember her. He never talked about her, and she'd learned not to ask questions to avoid causing him pain. But the rules and restrictions everyone else in her community appreciated she now found stifling.

"I'll be back to pick you up at six forty-five." Alex flashed her a smile in the rearview mirror.

Her lungs squeezed. "That's okay. I'll walk back."

He turned in his seat and stared at her, his hazel eyes trying to peel away her layers, see what she was hiding. Alex had learned that look from her father. He'd gotten very good at it. At twenty-nine, he'd been with the movement from the beginning, before she was born. With each passing day he emulated the Empyrean more and more. His title might be head of security, but he was one of their top missionaries, guiding and counseling, ever expanding his role. As much as he longed to someday take over as leader, she would never see him as a shepherd.

Only as a big brother.

"Your father expects you home by seven," Alex said. "In time for dinner."

She curled her fingers in fists, her nails biting into her palms, and nodded. As if she'd ever forget her father's schedule or his expectations. "I'll be there. On time."

Alex glanced at his watch. "Then you won't be able to take the full class and walk back. You'll have to choose."

Why did her choices always involve her sacrificing something?

"I'll drive you," Alex said, giving her another grin that made her skin crawl. "Make it easy on you."

But she didn't want easy. To be kept in a gilded cage, being told what to do from sunrise to sunset.

Mercy swallowed the bile rising in her throat. "My father gave no order that I had to be driven back. Did he?"

Alex's gaze fell. "No. He did not."

"Then I'll figure it out and make my own way back." She was twenty minutes early for her class. If her trainer, Rocco, was already there, then she could have both.

No sacrifice required.

"This isn't the best time to be doing things on your own," Alex said.

"Why not?" It occurred to Mercy that the change in protocol might not be about her. "Did something happen? Was a threat made against us?"

Not all the folks in town accepted the Shining Light's presence. A few were curious. Others feared them, for being different, for following a path that seemed odd. She saw how people looked at her, dressed in all white. The way they whispered as she passed.

On occasion, during the select new moons that Empyrean dictated, they went to town en masse. Fifty strong, wearing T-shirts that advertised their message. Handed out flyers at the bus station and other chosen spots in town, offering food and shelter for those in need. It wasn't uncommon for someone to throw a tomato or an egg at them. Sometimes even rocks.

She had never experienced any problems while by herself. Maybe it was the large group that was hard to ignore and easy to fear.

Once they had received a death threat at the compound. A terrifying time. But her father had put the compound on lockdown and had beefed up security. None of which had happened today.

Mercy might've been questioning which path was right for her to follow because her father had never given her a choice. Unlike everyone else in his flock. But she believed in the callings. Witnessed how those who came to them broken, in need, had found healing and purpose. Regardless of what she ultimately decided for herself, she was willing to protect that sanctuary for those who wanted it, as well as her father's legacy.

"No, nothing like that. No threats," Alex said. "Empyrean

wants us to tighten our ranks. Focus more on the Light and less on the secular. He wants you to focus more."

There it is.

This was about her. It was just as personal as she'd suspected. What irked Mercy more was that her father had confided in Alex about *her* before speaking to her himself.

Mercy never should've let it show how empowered and happy she felt after a training session. Should've hidden her feelings better. She'd been well-trained and had let her guard falter.

You idiot. Stupid fool.

She'd brought this onto herself. It had always been a matter of time before Empyrean would take away the one thing that she had which was untouched by the movement.

"I'm certain my father will discuss it with me later. Thank you for the ride." Even though she didn't mean it, there was no reason to be rude.

She got out and closed the door.

A passerby looked at her from head to toe, taking in her Shining Light pendant that dangled from her neck—a crescent moon with a sun—plain white T-shirt, matching leggings and canvas shoes. The woman's mouth pressed into a thin line before she crossed the street like she didn't want to get too close to her.

Lowering her head, Mercy hurried down the street to USD, hating that this would be her last session. She pushed through the front door and shoved aside the creeping sensation of doom.

"MY APOLOGIES FOR being late. It couldn't be helped," said FBI Supervisory Special Agent Nash Garner, taking a seat at the head of the conference room table, where the rest of the team had been waiting for him. "I'm sorry you lost your CI last night."

Nash oversaw the special task force. Their mission was to investigate the Shining Light cult and determine their threat level as possible domestic terrorists. Throughout their investigation, an arms dealer had come onto their radar, one who was supplying the cult with their cache of weapons.

Rocco slapped his hand down on the evidence bag that contained the bloodstained piece of paper with a date. "Percy died trying to tell me something. Whatever it is will happen in five days. I need permission to implement plan C." Alpha and Bravo had failed, leaving them with no other recourse.

Wary glances were exchanged around the room.

Special Agent Becca Hammond rested a hand on her pregnant stomach and rubbed what looked like a basketball under her shirt. She was only six months along and already all belly, but he'd never seen her more content to be working a desk instead of out in the field. "There has to be another way," she said.

It wasn't how he wanted to proceed either. Rushed. Haphazardly. But now that a CI had been discovered—murdered—his task force was out of time.

Figuratively and literally.

Taking a breath, Rocco glanced at his watch. Mercy was at USD by now, waiting on him. To be early was to be on time for her. A trait he admired. He'd texted his cousin and asked Charlie not to let her leave. "They killed Percy because they're aware the authorities are looking into them. Any steps we take will be more dangerous now than ever before. The one informant you had embedded in that cult went quiet because they got scared," Rocco said to Becca.

She lowered her gaze. Whoever her CI was—she had never

revealed their identity—had abruptly cut off communication last month. Now with Percy gone they were dead in the water.

"We need to find that arms dealer," Rocco said. "The same one supplying the Shining Light. And we've only got five days to figure out whatever is supposed to happen and stop it." *Something important. Something horrible.* "Mercy McCoy is the key."

Brian Bradshaw, a detective with the LPD, leaned forward. "Are you sure that's the only move?" The question coming from his best friend—who was also close to becoming family as he was in a serious relationship with his cousin, Charlie—gave him a moment of pause.

But only one. Rocco was aware that everyone at the table was wondering the same thing. "I'm sure. Unless someone else has a better idea."

Silence.

The only sound in the room came from Becca opening a bag of pretzels. It was the only thing he'd seen her tolerate while she had morning sickness, which for her, lasted all day and throughout the pregnancy so far.

He did not envy women.

"I need an answer. Now." He needed it ten minutes ago.

"How close is Mercy to being recruited as an asset?" Becca asked. "I got the impression from your reports that she wasn't ready yet."

Her impression was spot-on. Mercy had shown signs of discontentment with the movement, but that didn't mean she'd be disloyal. Rocco didn't know if she would ever be prepared to spy on her father. "I want to approach it from a different angle. I already threw one person into the fire and got them killed." The weight of that rested heavy on his shoulders. He couldn't even give his condolences to Mrs. Tiggs and take responsibility for what had happened because it would expose his identity.

"It wasn't your fault that Percival was murdered," Nash said.

But the words rang hollow to Rocco. Sure, he hadn't been the one to pull the trigger. All the same, he'd made Percy a target.

"I won't endanger Mercy like that." She was young and kind. And beautiful. Had her whole life ahead of her. She hadn't asked to be born into a cult. But the day she'd walked into his cousin's school, asking about self-defense classes, looking like a lost lamb, he'd seen a golden opportunity to cultivate the best asset. Over the months, he'd gotten to know her. First through group training sessions. Then later, one-on-one with him. He'd grown quite fond of her. If he was being honest, it was more than that. Every time they were alone together it was getting harder to resist the fierce attraction between them, but he forced himself to tamp the feeling down. Way down deep into oblivion. The last thing he could afford was any kind of attachment to a potential asset. "I don't know what her father would do to her if he found out."

Becca opened a bottle of water and took a sip. "From what I know of Marshall McCoy based on his psych profile, he wouldn't kill his daughter." She was the resident expert on the Shining Light.

"There are some punishments worse than death," Rocco said. "Are you positive that he wouldn't hurt her?"

"No." She shook her head. "'Through pain comes atonement. Only through the crucible can one find enlightenment.' Those are a couple of their tenets. He'd feel justified in hurting her if necessary."

Rocco clenched his jaw right along with his fist under the table. "Because of that and the fact that Becca's right that

Mercy isn't ready to turn on her father, I want to use her to gain access to the compound instead."

Becca choked on her water as the other two men stared at him in disbelief.

"You want to go undercover?" Nash asked. "Inside the Shining Light?"

Rocco shrugged. "I do it all the time." It came with the territory of working for the Bureau of Alcohol, Tobacco, Firearms and Explosives. There was even a term for their elite undercover agents—Rat Snakes.

In the pioneer days, rat snakes were kept in jars and unleashed to kill the enemy—eliminating rodents—and then retrieved and put out of sight until the next infestation. The bureau used their covert operatives in the same way to rid the world of the worst criminals.

Only those clever and strong enough got inside and survived. Rocco was still standing. But he'd had to do things that most couldn't and wouldn't stomach.

"My cover is solid," Rocco said. Constantly changing every time that he relocated for a new assignment, this one he'd built around his cousin Charlie. The best cover had elements of truth. So, he was using his mother's maiden name, Sharp, and kept his military record with some alterations that hinted at a walk on the dark side. Threw in civilian gigs that wouldn't raise any eyebrows, including a stint at a private security firm that a friend of his owned up north. He'd made sure any check run on him wouldn't break his cover.

"You've infiltrated every kind of scumbag group out there from organized crime to notorious outlaw motorcycle gangs," Brian said. "But not a cult."

"I thought tapping Mercy as an asset was the worst idea," Becca said. "Until you suggested going inside the compound." She shook her head, not liking the idea.

"What if you two sat down with Mercy together?" Brian suggested. "Impressed upon her the urgency, that lives are on the line. Is it possible you two might be able to persuade her?"

"Possible," Becca said, hitching up a shoulder. "Not probable. She doesn't see the Shining Light movement as a potential threat and may never. But I prefer the idea of talking to her, trying to work her as an informant, instead of you jumping into the lion's den, Rocco."

The image of Percy's car going through the guardrail came back to him. His bloody face, his abdomen bleeding, his life slipping away in Rocco's arms. All because Rocco had pushed him to be an informant when he'd learned Percy's son was part of the cult.

This was a cold, hard business that required them to make ruthless decisions in order to catch the bad guys. But this was the first time he'd been rattled to the core.

Usually, his informants were criminals who'd been coerced. People who had already put their own lives at risk, and he was merely making it count for something good.

Percy had been an affable vet, healing animals and keeping them alive.

Mercy was even more innocent.

"And if you're wrong?" Rocco asked. "Then not only have I lost an asset but also my one way inside the compound." He turned to Nash. This was the head honcho's call to make and no one else's. "We have five days. I don't want any more blood on my hands." And the one life he was willing to risk this time was his own. "Give me the green light on this."

If Nash didn't, Rocco would go forward with the plan anyway. Even if it meant he had to surrender his badge when it was all said and done. Saving his career didn't matter.

Only doing everything in his power to stop whatever was in the works for the nineteenth.

"When's the next time you see Mercy?" Nash asked.

"I'm supposed to be with her right now." They had training sessions every Tuesday and Thursday. This was their last class for the week. The next time he saw her would be too late.

"Do you really think you can convince her that you want to join her father's religious movement after months of planting the seeds of all the things that might be amiss with the Shining Light?" Nash asked.

There was no denying that it would be a gigantic stretch. Like leaping across the Grand Canyon.

"Maybe if you had a week, a couple of opportunities to warm her up to the idea," Becca said before he responded. "But out of the blue? Blindsiding her?" She shook her head.

Frustration welled in Rocco's chest. Becca was usually the impulsive one, willing to take long-shot chances. He thought he'd have her support on this. "We don't have a week," he snapped. "I don't even have two more minutes to spare discussing this. I need to leave."

Becca sighed. "Broach the subject tonight carefully. You'll have to ease her into the idea. Their movement only accepts novices during the new moon. I don't think that's for a couple of weeks." She picked up her phone and swiped through a screen. "One angle you might want to try is that by letting you into her community she would be helping you in some way on a personal level. One of their core beliefs centers around selflessly aiding those in need. That might work with her father."

The clock was ticking. He'd try anything.

Becca swore and looked up from her phone. "The nineteenth, this Tuesday, falls on a full moon...during an eclipse.

I don't know what that means. If it's better or worse. Everything that they do is based on the lunar cycle."

"What does a regular full moon mean for them?" Nash asked.

"It's a significant time for transformation." She shrugged. "I know more about the new moon when novices who choose to stay are inducted. Marriages are blessed."

Playing this safe wasn't an option. "I've been the one working Mercy's recruitment," Rocco said to Nash. "I know her best. I think I can persuade her." His gut told him to use the rapport he'd built—the natural connection they had. "I just need a thumbs-up from you." Flicking another impatient glance at his watch, he clenched his jaw and stood. "What do you say?"

Was this going to be a sanctioned op or was he going rogue?

Nash's stone-cold gaze slid to Becca for a second of deliberation coming back to him. "You're a go. Find their arms supplier and figure out what's planned for the nineteenth. You've only got one chance at this with her. Do whatever it takes."

Chapter Three

Anxiety wormed through Mercy. She paced around the private training room, like a hamster on a wheel.

"Can I get you anything before my class starts?" Charlie asked, popping her head inside, yet again. "A bottle of water? A cup of tea?"

"No, thank you." Mercy chewed the inside of her bottom lip and fiddled with her pendant.

"Want to join us until he gets here?"

Mercy shook her head once. She'd started out with group classes, but that wasn't how she wanted to end her last day.

"Okay. Sit tight." Charlie was lean and athletic. Not one pushover bone in her body. A real spitfire.

Mercy admired her spunk and independence. She would've traded every drop of her quiet resilience for a glimmer of Charlie's fire.

"He's on his way," Charlie said, her smile soft, her green eyes pleading. "I promise." She strutted away with that fearless air about her.

Mercy had already warmed up, stretched, and her muscles were loose, raring to go. Still, no Rocco. She didn't know how much longer she'd be able to wait despite the assurances that he'd be there.

The thought of not being able to see him and say goodbye gnawed at the pit of her stomach.

Maybe him not showing up was a sign that she should submit to her father's will. Be grateful for what she'd been given. If not for his generosity in granting her such leeway to begin with and paying for her classes, she never would've enjoyed the luxury of training at USD.

Releasing a sharp sigh, Mercy turned, headed for the door. But Rocco stepped across the threshold, entering the room, his strides confident, strong, hurried.

His gaze locked on her, setting off an unmistakable flutter deep in her belly.

She suspected he had that effect on most women.

Tall and powerfully built. Skin the color of teak. Everything about him was strong and formidable like the dense hardwood tree. He was handsome, too, in an almost painful way. The kind that stabbed her in the chest, reminding her that someone like him would never be with someone like her.

Whenever she saw him, her palms would sweat as two words sprang to mind…good *god*. Not as in an actual deity. No man was a god. Not even her father, no matter how hard he tried to ascend to such unreachable heights. But Rocco was straight from the pages of an old-world myth.

He took off his cowboy hat and speared his fingers through his longish brown hair. The strands fell to the neckline of his snug T-shirt that did nothing to hide the wide-shouldered, narrow-hipped rock-hard body beneath.

To think, she'd once been intimidated by him. The sheer size of him. The tribal tattoos running down one arm. The rough-and-tumble look. The scorching magnetism he exuded.

Then she'd seen how gentle and kind he was to all the women. After that she only wanted to train with him. One-on-one. In the private room.

A harried smile stretched across his kissable mouth, and she moistened her lips.

"Thanks for waiting, Mercy."

Even the way he said her name made her pulse leap.

Throat too tight to answer, all she could do was nod.

"I know how precious and limited your time is here," Rocco said.

He had no idea. But she shoved the thought from her mind, not wanting to dwell on it.

"It's okay," she muttered, finding her voice. "I'm just glad you made it." She smiled. "I was afraid that you'd cancel."

"I hate missing a session with you. I look forward to our hour together."

The feeling was mutual. "Me, too. The highlight of my week." The one thing in her life that had been all hers.

"I didn't get a chance to change," he said, gesturing to his jeans before he dropped his duffel bag on the floor. "But I figured we could start with some speed drills. It'll sharpen your technique. Improve footwork. Helps prepare you for real-world situations. Then we'll move on to slow sparring so you can work on seeing the incoming movements. Retrain those panic reflexes into functional ones, for proper evasive movements and counters."

Everything he'd said blurred together in her ears. "Can we just jump to the slow sparring?"

"I know you want to get to the good stuff." He clasped her shoulder, and a spark of something she couldn't name ignited within her—so intense, so raw that her body lit up, every nerve ending coming alive with awareness. "For some reason you seem to enjoy it when I fling you to the ground and pin you."

Pushing her to writhe beneath him until she executed a contortionist maneuver to break free.

Who wouldn't enjoy it?

Clearing her throat, she lowered her gaze. "I'm not sure I have time to do everything. I've got to be back at the compound by seven."

His grip on her shoulder tightened. Her pulse pounded as he leaned in close. He smelled sinfully good. The yummy, woodsy scent of him had her thinking of the multitude of rules she wanted to break.

"I can give you a lift," he said, low in her ear. "Drop you off close without anyone seeing. Like last time. Our little secret." His smooth warm smile deepened.

Now all she could think about were the big, dirty kinds of secrets she wanted to share with him. "Sounds good." That would give her more time. With him.

He moved his hand, and her skin felt chilled.

She realized the hardest part of saying goodbye to USD would be knowing there wouldn't be any more moments such as these with Rocco.

He took off his shirt and stretched. Long, sinewy muscles flexed across his back and abdomen. Her gaze went over the intricate lines of ink that wound over one shoulder and inched across his sexy collarbone.

She swallowed hard, wondering what it would be like to touch him. Not as a result of a self-defense move. Purely for the sake of pleasure.

"Now that's settled," he said, "I trust you're ready for me."

In more ways than one.

Mercy had to suppress the thought, the urges that came over her whenever she was near him. She was only grateful her father didn't have a window into her soul. He would be so disappointed.

"Yep." She hopped side to side on the balls of her feet and stretched her arms. "I'm all warmed up."

Rocco put padded shin guards on her and then he slipped on a pair of padded gloves. He held up his protected palms and directed her through drills. A series of rapid-fire punches, kicks and other strikes he'd taught her. She listened and responded with the appropriate blows. They got into a quick, demanding rhythm. But her heart was racing too hard. Too fast.

Working up a sweat, she struggled to suck in enough air. The room started to spin. Her pulse throbbed against her temples, her chest growing tighter and tighter. A chill sliced through her. She stumbled back.

The strangest noise filled her ears—a sharp, keening wheeze.

To her shock, the sound was coming from her.

"Mercy?" Rocco asked, worry coming over his face. "Are you okay?"

She nodded, but she couldn't breathe. Couldn't talk. Was she having a heart attack? Was she dying? "Ambulance. I think I need an ambulance."

He ripped off the gloves and clasped her arms. She was shaking.

"Sit down." He guided her down to a mat. "Tell me what you're feeling."

She muttered off as much as she could through strained breaths.

"Close your eyes," he said, and she did. "Listen to the sound of my voice. I want you to inhale for a count of two. That's right. Exhale. One. Two." He repeated the instructions over and over, rubbing his warm hands up and down her arms until she was doing it. "Now I want you to inhale for a count of four." A pause. "Exhale the same. One. Two. Three. Four."

She didn't know how long it took, but eventually the shaking subsided and her lungs loosened.

"Open your eyes, Mercy."

When she did, he was crouched close in front of her. She met his gentle, concerned gaze. "I'm sorry."

"Don't you dare apologize."

She pressed a hand to her clammy forehead. "I don't know what happened."

"I think I do." He studied her face, frowning at whatever he saw there. "You had a panic attack. Have there been any big changes in your life? Anything different going on to cause you anxiety?"

Panic attack?

Sometimes her life behind the gates of the compound felt so small. Sometimes it was hard to breathe because her very existence was shrinking, withering, under her father's thumb. But this was the first time she had manifested any physical symptoms.

"This is my last training session." Dread bubbled inside her, the thought of not having any future sessions with *him* unbearable. She warred with her self-preservation instincts. "My father won't allow me to come back."

"Why not?"

"It doesn't matter." Tears that she refused to shed pricked her eyes. She wasn't a spoiled brat. She never whined. Never complained. Only complied. Like a dutiful daughter. "The point is I won't be able to see you anymore." She caught herself, at how that must have sounded to him. Embarrassment creeped through her. This was about Rocco more than anything else, but she didn't want him to know that. "I mean come back to USD for training."

Rocco cupped her face in his big hand. Something shifted between them, the air charging with latent electricity. There was no denying her attraction to him. Every time she saw him it got harder and harder to hide it.

But now she wondered if it was one-sided.

"Why do you stay with the movement?" He caressed her cheek, sending tingles through her. "You don't seem happy there."

Such a small question, but the answer was huge, layered with years of habit and doctrine and love. Love for her community. Love for her father, as overbearing as he was.

The Light can illuminate. But it can also blind.

She dismissed that little voice in her head that crept up in her moments of doubt. "It's complicated. I don't really have a choice."

He grimaced. "Are people forced to stay against their will? I thought anyone could leave at any time."

Anyone but her. "The others aren't forced."

"But you are?"

She bit her lip. "It's getting late. There isn't time to explain it all to you."

"Then let me come with you to your community."

Reeling back, she stared at him in disbelief. "Into the compound?"

"Yes."

"Why? To be reborn in the movement? I didn't think it was for you." It was part of the reason she found him so alluring, so appealing. He never judged and never showed any interest in joining.

"I'm worried about you. So often you talk about your family behind that wall, but not once have I ever heard you mention any friends. It must be lonely."

He saw right through her. Was she that obvious to everyone? Or had she simply overshared with him?

"We could continue our training classes on the compound," he said. "Where I can watch over you. Be the friend you need."

Their time together had become a sort of therapy. She talked to Rocco in a way that she couldn't with anyone else. Asked him any question. No subject off-limits. No topic inappropriate. No fear of him reporting back what was discussed.

She had an affinity with him that she wasn't ready to lose.

Her mind whirled toward a black void. Bringing people inside on a whim didn't happen. That wasn't how things were done. Not how the Shining Light operated.

But she wanted a solution that didn't involve yet another sacrifice on her part. "I don't see how that's possible."

He took her hands in his. Her fingers instinctively clung to him, afraid to let go. To lose *this* forever. A chance at something different. A tether to the outside.

"You once told me that through the Light all things were possible. Do you remember?" he asked.

Of course she did. "I'm surprised you do."

"I listen to everything you say, Mercy." As his gaze slid over her, she sensed that he not only cataloged her every word, but also observed her every reaction. "You are Empyrean's daughter. You don't realize the power you have."

Power? She almost laughed at the absurdity of such a thing. Her father didn't even want her to succeed him when the time came for him to choose their next shepherd. He'd told her that she was unfit to assume the position.

She shook her head, wishing she could explain it to him, but ultimately, she was too ashamed.

"How many Starlights are in your commune?"

That was the new surname acolytes took once they were reborn in the sacred ceremony, shedding their former selves. Then they chose a new forename as well and were anointed with a tattoo of the Shining Light. The same design as her pendant, but on the tattoo in the center of the sun was an eye.

"Five hundred and twelve," she said.

"How many of them get to come to town twice a week to take classes?"

None.

"I'm betting it's only you. Because you have your father's ear." Rocco squeezed her fingers, his gaze boring into her. "Why do you wear white?"

The question was rhetorical. She had explained the color system to him. At the Shining Light everyone had a function and wore a color that represented it. Security donned gray. Essential workers, green. The creatives—artists, musicians— wore orange. Yellow was reserved for counselors and educators. New recruits, novices considering whether to join were denoted by the color blue. "No hue for leaders," she said.

"Be a leader. Usher me into the Light. Where all things are possible."

His crazy logic made complete sense.

"The council of elders will question it," she said. "They can make things difficult." Unless her father condoned it, which wasn't likely.

Rocco shrugged. "Do any of them wear white?"

A calmness settled over her. "No." Her father had given the council a voice. But that was all. The elders could be loud and irritating, but they had no power. "But there's still my father to deal with. You don't know how he can be."

Unyielding.

Harsh.

The mountain that could not be moved.

"I don't want anything to happen to you." He searched her face for something. "Would he punish you? Beat you if you brought me inside?"

For this type of infraction? "No, but he'll fight me on it."

"Fight back. I've knocked you down countless times. And you always get up swinging. I've never seen you surrender. Not only are you strong, but you're a smart fighter. You think quickly on your feet. All you need to do is decide what you want. Then set your mind to it."

For months, he seemed to be luring her away from the Shining Light, daring her to question the teachings, tempting her to dream of a different life. Now he was inverting everything. A total flip. "Why would you do this for me? Put your life on hold to live among us?"

He looked at her with pity.

I am not fragile, on the verge of falling to pieces, she wanted to tell him. "I don't need you to save me." Mercy already had one man in her life dead set on doing that already. She didn't need another.

His features grew pained. He stroked his thumb over her cheek. The gesture was so tender and sweet, a tear rolled from her eye. Before she could whisk it away, he did it for her.

"It wouldn't be entirely selfless. I've been going through a rough time lately. Caught up with the wrong crowd. People who entice me to revert to unhealthy habits."

"Do you mean with drugs or alcohol?"

"Your questions are always so direct."

That was the way her father had raised her. Emotional transparency. Complete honesty. "I'm sorry."

"It's not an easy thing to talk about. But I need a break without the temptation. You'd be helping me out in a big way by sharing your community with me."

The principle of giving help when asked for was branded on her soul.

At the compound, the counselors were good at assisting people through rough patches. In their treatment sessions, they would get him to talk about everything. Unburdening was an essential part of the process. "You might find the movement difficult to accept."

"I want to understand it. Your world. Your way of life on the compound. I want to see why so many choose to stay.

Why you stay." His warm brown gaze fixed on her face. His expression was sympathetic. "Give me time to get to know you better. And you me." His voice was soft and comforting. "What do you want, Mercy?"

Change.

To have things on her terms for once. To step out of Empyrean's shadow.

Defiance prickled across her skin. She wanted to keep something for herself that her father held no dominion over. And this man she'd come to know and bonded with would not fall to his knees in blind worship of the Shining Light.

At least, she hoped not. Her father could be mighty persuasive.

But Rocco was tough and would not be easily swayed.

Embracing the rebellious idea, she tilted her head to one side, watching him as he did her, studying his ruggedly beautiful face. He was younger than he appeared. It was the threads of silver in his neatly trimmed goatee and around the edges of his hairline that made him look older than thirty-two. She remembered everything he told her also.

He stared at her with an intensity that left her trembling, but strength seeped through her as determination to take a chance set in.

Although Rocco only offered friendship, which was no small thing, to have a steady shoulder that was all hers to lean on—something she'd never had—she knew exactly what she wanted, even if it was only for a little while because he would never choose the Light.

And she could never truly leave it.

She wanted more moments with him. Private and special and hers alone.

She wanted Rocco.

Chapter Four

In preparation for dinner, Marshall McCoy changed from his white suit and button-down shirt into a simple white tunic with matching linen slacks. As he strode barefoot down the front staircase of Light House, a vehicle he didn't recognize pulled up the circular drive.

A Ford Bronco.

They didn't use that make and model at the commune.

Even more surprising, Mercy alighted from the passenger's side. He continued down the staircase, staring through the floor-to-ceiling windows to catch a glimpse of the driver. Wearing a cowboy hat, the man strode around the front of the vehicle into the amber light. Marshall stopped, frozen in curiosity as to who he was. The guy stood a head taller than the security guards gathering out front, or even Alex. His shoulders were broader than average. Dark hair fell, brushing his collar and obscuring his face.

The armed guards parted for him like the Red Sea to Moses.

Whoever this cowboy was, one thing was certain. He was trouble with a capital T.

Quietly, Marshall watched them enter the house from his position on the staircase. Mercy guided the stranger to remove his shoes, putting her hand on his arm as she whispered something to him. The man had interesting features. His body looked as if it had been sculpted from stone, every muscle defined. Striking tattoos ran down his arm.

His little girl was now a grown woman. Although she had never shown the slightest romantic interest in anyone at the commune, Marshall could see what she might find appealing about this one.

In five seconds, he could tell the attraction was mutual. This man stood close to her. Closer than any of their guards had ever dared. They kept sharing little glances as if their gazes were drawn back to one another.

Marshall had to resist the urge to crack his knuckles.

Alex hung back behind them, looking uncertain. As though he was the interloper.

A sense of trepidation whispered through Marshall. The stranger did not belong here and yet he stood as if ready to conquer the compound.

"My daughter returns with a stranger." The warmth in his voice surprised even him. Extending his arms in welcome, he glided down the rest of the steps. "Who have you brought to us, my child?"

"Father, this is Rocco Sharp. He's my instructor at the Underground Self-Defense school. Rocco, this is Empyrean."

"The man my daughter has been grappling and getting sweaty with for six long months."

There was a deep, ugly silence like a festering wound.

Mercy's cheeks flushed. Alex lowered his head.

But Rocco flashed pearly whites in a wide grin, removed his worn cowboy hat and proffered a hand. "Pleased to meet you, sir." Not an ounce of shame. No rush to dismiss the suggestive insinuation.

Gutsy.

"Forgive me for not shaking," Marshall said, pulling on

his stock smile that telegraphed grace. "I prefer to read a person's energy when they first enter my home." He raised both palms. "May I?"

Without glancing at Mercy with uncertainty, he stepped forward. "Certainly."

This was a strong one, not only of body, but also of spirit. He would not be easy to break.

But would he be willing to bend?

Marshall took Rocco's head between his hands, brought his brow down to touch his, and then put a hand over his heart. Rocco didn't shutter his eyes as they looked at one another. This might have been a staring competition for the younger man, but Marshall was on a mission.

Closing his eyes, he breathed deeply, opening himself to the energy within this other soul. Letting it flow through him.

There was darkness in him, as well as a powerful light. A blaze burning inside Rocco. An unmistakable sense of violence. Yet also control. But his heart, beating powerful and steady as a metronome, was out of reach. Guarded.

This man was not lost. But he was searching. For something.

As many who came here were.

Dropping his hands, Marshall said, "Come and let us speak." Bringing his daughter to his side, he led them deeper into Light House, down the hall. He glanced at Rocco as they passed the mural of the Shining Light symbol on the wall. The cowboy's eyes were drawn to it, as were all newcomers. They reached his office. "Thank you, Alex," he said once inside. "Could you wait in the hall and close the door?"

A flustered look came over his face, but Alex bowed his head. "Yes, Empyrean."

Marshall stood in front of his desk and clasped his hands. "What brings you here to us, Rocco?"

"I brought him," Mercy said, quickly, "because—"

Marshall held up a finger, silencing her. "I will get to you in a moment, my dear," he said while keeping his gaze focused on the stranger, his voice soft. "Rocco, please answer for yourself."

"We've become friends. After she told me tonight would be her last training session and that she didn't know whether we'd see each other again, I asked if I could come here. I've been going through a difficult time. Struggling with some things. I thought it might be healthy to get away from negative influences. Come here to better understand your ways. And Mercy. She's always talking about her faith."

"You've had six months to satisfy your curiosity." Marshall stepped closer to him. "Why all of a sudden?"

"I took for granted that we'd have more time together. The idea of not seeing her again and going back to some dark habits made this feel urgent, sir. Like this was my chance, and I shouldn't blow it."

Marshall didn't detect a lie, but he also wasn't getting the whole truth. "We only accept novices during certain new moons. If your interest remains in six weeks' time, you may return to see if our beliefs and lifestyle would suit you. Thank you for bringing Mercy home." He gestured toward the door.

"You misunderstand, Father. I've brought him here as my *guest*," Mercy said. "Not as a potential novice."

Another whisper of unease—a faint sixth sense of warning that this cowboy would be more than he could control.

This Rocco had already gotten his daughter to ignore custom and flout his basic edicts. What would be next?

To his credit, and as a result of five decades of faking it, Marshall didn't show the slightest hint of surprise or anger, even though both were brewing inside him. He tightened his smile. "You know the rules, sweetheart," he said gently. "We do not bring in guests."

"We haven't, in the past," she said. "Exceptions can always be made."

"If I allowed this with you, every member of the flock might seek to do the same. We can't have anarchy, with our gates open wide."

The flash of disappointment in her eyes was undeniable. As was the glimmer of determination. "You allow exceptions with me whenever you see fit because I'm not like the rest of the flock. I'm a McCoy. Not a *Starlight*," she said. A powerful distinction. "He asked for my help, and I was called to bring him here. That inner voice you commanded me never to ignore spoke. I have listened. You can't ask me to turn him away."

Was it the voice of a higher power?

Or that of Rocco's, flowing from poisoned lips into her ear?

"I will reconsider our current timeline," Marshall said, his voice light, his tone easygoing. "Instead of waiting six weeks, we will open our gates to potential novices, *guests*, at the next new moon." That should appease her. What was she thinking, bringing a stranger here so close to the full moon eclipse? Particularly this stranger.

Her blue eyes gleamed with a spark of rebellion that threatened to set him off, but he kept his facade affable. "You don't care about my calling, do you?" she asked. "Or that I'm trying to help someone in need. I have no place here. Not in the flock. Not as a leader. I'm nothing more than a shiny fixture on your shelf."

The tighter he clung to her, the more determined she seemed to slip free from his grasp. With each passing year, the restlessness in her continued to grow to the point where he could no longer ignore it. At first, he had tried to pacify her by letting her run their quarterly farmers' market. Then he put her in charge of the novices.

Still, it wasn't enough.

The glint for more never left her eyes. So, when she asked to take classes at USD, he'd thought, *what could be the harm?*

But those classes only poured gasoline on the burning embers of doubt kindling inside her.

"We'll discuss this privately." Marshall would find some way to get her to see reason once she was outside this man's sphere of influence. He was going to be the only one to pull his daughter's strings. Marshall turned to the cowboy. "Excuse us."

Rocco cast a questioning glance at Mercy, waiting for *her* to give him the okay.

His gaze slid back to his daughter. "Have your friend wait in the hall or I will have security escort him there."

Straightening, Mercy shook her head. "No, you won't."

Laughter devoid of humor rolled from his chest. While he found her refusal to back down, and pointedly so, surprising, he didn't find it the least bit funny. "Give me one good reason why not."

"Because I need something to change. We're too insulated and I'm suffocating." She clasped her hands behind her back, her chin jutting up, making her look every bit the warrior that he had forged, though he never expected her to turn on him. "For seven years, you've denied me the right of *penumbroyage*. If you don't let him stay as a guest where he can learn about the Light and our ways, I'll claim it before the elders tonight. And leave with him to do what I can to help him out there beyond the walls of the compound."

Her sharp sword cut deeply.

Marshall clenched his jaw against the bitter taste that

flooded his mouth. When she was a teenager, she had grown proficient at guerilla warfare with him, but he had learned to defend against her tactics. It was so rare for Mercy to stand up to him in a full-frontal attack like this that it completely blindsided him.

Turning, he strode to a window and stared out at the darkness.

"What is that? *Penumbroyage?*" Rocco asked.

Mercy looked at him. "Have you heard of rumspringa?"

"It's like a rite of passage for Amish teens, where they get to leave their community, live on the outside for a while before deciding to commit to their religion."

"*Penumbroyage* is the same for us," she said. "If you were born here or came in as a child, you can take a year away between the ages of seventeen and twenty-four. My father has insisted that I've been needed here to help him. He keeps demanding that I delay it."

A request. Not a demand.

As Empyrean he couldn't strip her of the right that he himself created to safeguard the purity of the hearts in his flock. He had stressed to Mercy the importance of her staying as a demonstration of faith. How would it look to their community for her to have doubts about their way? How poorly it would reflect on him as their shepherd if his blood needed distance to see the right path to follow. The stain it would leave, tarnishing his legacy.

Aside from appearances and the shame that would follow if she chose the secular world, he feared far more than a blow to his ego. He would do anything to avoid losing his only daughter.

Absolutely anything.

He never imagined that she would ever claim the right, taking a year away. With no money, no job, no place to stay, most didn't. The few young people who did leave had family on the outside that they could turn to.

Part of Mercy had agreed to delay her sojourn because she was a good, devoted child. But the other part of her simply had nobody on the outside to rely on for assistance.

Until now.

He stared at Rocco's reflection in the windowpane. Watched him put a comforting hand to the small of her back. Witnessed his daughter's response. The sharp intake of breath, the flush to her cheeks, the way she looked at him. He saw every unnerving, nauseating detail.

The sexual tension between them was nuclear.

Marshall spun on his heel, facing them. "Have you lain with this man?" he asked, pouring all his concern rather than reproach into his voice.

Is that what was really going on during her one-on-one sessions?

"Wh-what?" she stuttered, the color in her cheeks deepening.

The cowboy didn't flinch. Didn't even bat a lash.

"No." Mercy crossed the space separating them. "Father, I swear it. Not that it would be any of your business if I had. You conveniently didn't make any rules about chastity."

Rocco arched an eyebrow and gave a pleased-looking nod, which Marshall also caught. Maybe it was time he made such a rule.

He didn't want his people acting like free-loving hippies with no sense of self-control or decorum. Still, he didn't preach celibacy. Only celebrated monogamy. He permitted unions, often arranging them himself, formed matches and blessed marriages. Seldom was he without a carefully picked partner himself. Currently he was sleeping with the nubile

Sophia, who worked in the garden, and things had become serious between them despite his daughter's reservations.

"You were raised to treat your body as a temple." Marshall cupped her arms. "Not to violate my trust by sullying yourself with someone who is unworthy because he has not accepted the Light."

She narrowed her eyes. "I've done no such thing. I promise you."

Exhaling a soft breath of relief, Marshall forced a smile. "I needed to be sure of the purity of your intention in bringing him here." He had no choice but to take her word for it. Even if she was telling the truth, her attraction to him, her desire to lie with him was obvious. "I love you," he said, hugging her, "and only want the best for you." Which didn't include her new friend.

This man, who wrestled between the darkness and the light, would take her from him as surely as the sun rose in the east and set in the west. Unless he put a stop to it.

"I know you do," she said, pulling away and stepping back.

"You are welcome here," he said to Rocco. "To stay. To learn. To grow in the Light."

The corner of Rocco's mouth inched up in a grin just shy of cocky. Marshall wanted to slap it off his face.

"Thank you, sir."

"You'll need to hand over your cell phone," Marshall said. "Most here are not allowed to have them, not even Mercy. It is a distraction from growth."

"Your daughter told me. I left mine in the car. Along with the keys."

"Good." Marshall nodded and turned back to his daughter. "Mercy, I will only ask one small thing in return for my generosity."

She stiffened. "What is it?"

"We'll discuss it at dinner." If he could not get her alone, then he would continue this discussion in front of the entire flock where she would not dare cause a scene. "Why don't you go get cleaned up and changed? I'll show Rocco into the dining hall and introduce him to the community, where we'll wait for you."

"Thank you." She rose on the balls of her feet and kissed his cheek. On her way out, she grazed Rocco's arm and gave him a reassuring smile.

The sweetness of it sickened him.

Marshall needed to act quickly. "Would you like to wash up before dinner?" he asked Rocco.

"Yes, thank you."

"We passed the restroom in the hall. It'll be the first on your left."

With a nod, he exited the office. Once Rocco was out of earshot, Marshall snapped his fingers and beckoned Alex.

His right-hand man, his son though not of his blood but by choice, hustled into the room.

"I want you to run a background check on him," Marshall said.

"I already did after it looked like Mercy would be taking classes at USD regularly."

Marshall motioned for him to continue. "And? What did you find out? Criminal background? Deadbeat dad looking to duck out on making child support payments?" *Give me something to work with.*

They had all sorts show up seeking *refuge.* Even a couple of fugitives from the law. All could be put to good use in some capacity while he worked on healing their souls and mending their hearts.

Alex took out his cell phone, one of the few permitted inside the compound, and scrolled through the screens. "Charlotte Sharp has owned the place for about three years. She's his cousin. Goes by Charlie. They grew up together. His mother is her aunt, and his parents became her legal guardians. Rocco moved here last year and started working at USD."

"What was he doing before that?"

"Military for a few years." Alex swiped through to another screen. "His record was sealed."

"What does that mean?"

"He probably did special ops for them. But he did get a dishonorable discharge. I couldn't find out what for. He floated around for a bit, worked as a bouncer, bartender and for a private security company before settling here as a self-defense instructor. No criminal record. No marriages. No kids. But a couple of DUIs."

Clean. Except for that dishonorable discharge and the DUIs. "You mentioned that Charlie is his maternal cousin?"

"Yes."

Then why did he go by Sharp if his parents were together? "What's his father's name?"

Alex glanced back at his phone. "Joseph Kekoa."

"What kind of surname is that?"

"Hawaiian. I looked it up. It means warrior," Alex said, sounding impressed.

"Do a search on Rocco Kekoa. See if anything comes up. I need it fast."

"Will do," Alex said, making a note. "What's the rush?"

"I've agreed to let him stay here with us for a while."

Alex paled. "But why?"

"Listen to me." Marshall put a hand on his shoulder. "The only thing you need to know is that tonight I'm going to give you the opportunity you've long waited for. The one thing standing in your way is that cowboy. I'm going to give him enough rope to hang himself and you're going to help me do it."

At the sound of approaching footsteps, Marshall schooled his features.

Rocco waltzed back into the office. "My ears were burning. Was I the topic of discussion?"

"As a matter of fact, you were." Marshall headed out of the office, gesturing for Rocco to walk with him. "We were trying to decide what work detail might best suit you while you're here. Do you know anything about horses or farming?"

They headed toward the dining hall down the corridor lined with art made by his followers.

"I grew up on a ranch. Love horses. But I've got some military experience. I'm better with every weapon under the sun than I am with animals. Or plants."

"Is that so?" Marshall nodded. "What did you do in the military?"

"I'd tell you, but then I'd have to kill you." Rocco flashed a smile that probably made women swoon and nudged him with his elbow like they were pals.

"Why not put him on security under me?" Alex said, following them closely. "I could show him the ropes."

Translation: keep an eye on him.

"I like the idea." Marshall gave a nod of approval. "But let's hold off on assigning him a firearm just yet."

"What are your reservations?" Rocco asked. "I assure you I know how to handle myself and a weapon."

"I have no doubt about that," Marshall said, stopping at the entrance of the dining room. "But I see you for precisely what you are."

"And what is that, sir?"

"You're an agent."

Chapter Five

Rocco's heart skipped a beat, but he didn't let it show, keeping his features relaxed, his eye contact steady. "Come again?"

"You're an agent of chaos, Mr. Sharp. Sent to test me and the faith of my family. But my house is not built on sand and will weather any storm." Smiling, he put a hand on Rocco's shoulder and ushered him forward.

They entered a massive open space, large enough to be a ballroom, filled with wooden tables and chairs.

The dining hall was packed with a rainbow of Starlights. Green, gray, orange, yellow and blue sprinkled throughout the room. Everyone was seated. Plates filled with food in front of them, but no one was eating. From what he could see, no one wore shoes either. Mercy had explained that it wasn't allowed due to cleanliness.

A tense silence fell as all eyes turned to focus on them.

"My dear family," Marshall said, his voice bouncing off the walls of the hushed hall, "I want for you all to welcome Rocco. He will be our guest. Brought to us by your sister Mercy."

Murmurs flowed through the room like a current of air.

"I know this is unusual," Marshall said. "But your sister was called to help this man. We must support her as she blooms as a leader in answering what the Light has asked her to do. I trust I can count on you. What say you all?"

In unison the group bowed their heads and said, "So shall it be."

Marshall glanced at Rocco. "Let's get some food," he said, indicating a long table set against the wall.

There were large aluminum tins of rice, rolls, an array of vegetables, beans and lentils. But no meat. "Looks like you all are vegetarians," he said, pretending to be surprised since he'd never discussed it with Mercy and didn't want to appear to know too much. He took a tray and put food on his plate.

"We believe in sustainable living," Alex said. "We grow all our own produce. A plant-based diet lowers greenhouse gas emissions, reduces environmental degradation and promotes a healthy lifestyle. We strive to make the world better."

That was quite a mouthful. "Well, this looks delicious." Rocco was going to need a juicy double burger once he got out of there.

"You should try a piece of pie," Marshall said, getting a slice for himself. "There's strawberry rhubarb and pear. Baked fresh today by caring hands."

Rocco wouldn't turn his nose up at pie and went for the strawberry rhubarb.

They grabbed forks, cups of water, and proceeded to a table that had a few guys from the security team already there.

A young, attractive woman dressed in green made a beeline for them, juggling a dinner tray.

With a shake of his head and subtle wave of his hand, Marshall said, "It would be best if you sat with the others tonight, Sophia."

She faltered in her tracks, a disappointed look falling across her face. "Of course, Empyrean."

"But I would like to chat with you privately later in my quarters."

A huge smile broke out on Sophia's angular face. "I look forward to our discussion." She turned and walked back to the table where she had been previously.

Marshall took a chair at the head of the table, made introductions, and launched into a spiel. "Many get mired in the muck of the world beyond our gates, but we are excellent at helping all unburden themselves. You should be aware that you'll be expected to follow our rules. Transgressions are frowned upon."

But Rocco's focus drifted when Mercy walked into the dining hall.

A white cotton dress clung to slender curves, cupping breasts that were the perfect size for a lover's hands. Sunny blond hair, no longer up in a bun, hung past her shoulders in long waves, framing a face that was too angelic. Too pretty. She had an ethereal beauty. Radiated light.

She was… Wow.

Her eyes—a fierce electric blue that rivaled the color of a summer sky—found his for a moment that didn't last nearly long enough before she looked away.

She stopped at a table filled with children and briefly said something that made them giggle. Others rose, who'd been seated nearby, and flocked to her. They congregated around Mercy, speaking hurriedly as they touched her shoulder or arm with warm, sympathetic smiles. They all seemed captivated by her, which was no surprise to Rocco.

Finally given a break, Mercy approached their table with a plate of food. Rocco stood, shifting his plate down one seat, and pulled out the chair for her next to her father.

"Thank you," she said and then lowered her voice so only he could hear. "But please don't do that again."

He followed her gaze around the room. Everyone was staring at them.

Was being a gentleman frowned on, too?

After she sat, Marshall raised his palms.

As a collective, they said, "Thank you for the gift of this meal to sustain us. May it nourish our bodies and fuel our ability to make this a better world, so we may grow in the Light. We are grateful to embrace the movement in the pursuit of truth."

Once their prayer was done, the community began eating and conversations resumed.

Marshall stood. "I have a glorious announcement. One I have long hoped to make. The Light has finally spoken to me on the matter, and the time has come for Mercy and Alex to open their hearts to one another and begin a courtship."

Mercy's expression fell, like a building razed to the ground by an implosion. She stared at her father, jaw unhinged, and then looked at Alex, who gave her a smile that was quite charming. If one was partial to rats.

Based on her grimace, she wasn't.

This was the one *small* thing her father wanted in return for allowing Rocco to stay. He had to bite his tongue against a sudden surge of fury. He hated that he was being used as a tool to coerce her.

"This is not my will," Marshall said. "But that of the Light. What say you, Alex?"

The rat's grin spread wider, his eyes glittering. "So shall it be."

"What say you, Mercy?" When she hesitated, her father added, "We do not get to pick and choose. All is done for the greater good. What say you?"

Somehow Mercy appeared furious and torn at the same time. Straightening her shoulders, she glanced around the dining hall, at all the members of her commune waiting for her answer. The tension in the room was thick as smog, but far more toxic.

The tight hold this community had on her was evident.

"So shall it be," she said, lowering her head.

Raucous applause broke out in the hall along with cheers.

Marshall sat and clamped a hand on her forearm. "Have faith in the process. Many happy, successful unions have been made this way."

"You mean by forcing people together," Rocco said.

Marshall pulled on a pleasant expression that looked practiced. "In the US, the divorce rate is 50 percent. While over half the marriages worldwide are arranged and have a divorce rate of only four percent. In thirty years, out of all the unions I've put together, ninety-nine percent have thrived."

Regardless of his statistics, her father neglected to mention that sometimes "arranged" was merely a veneer, hiding abuse in the name of tradition. Oftentimes in developing countries access to divorce was limited and many women found themselves trapped.

The truth behind the impressive percentages didn't discourage Marshall from giving his daughter a gentle smile. "Sometimes the heart requires a nudge of encouragement to open to the right person. It's easy to be tempted by the devil." He threw a furtive glance at Rocco. "But we are stewards of a higher power."

"Yes," she said, nodding. "I understand."

A litany of questions flew through Rocco's mind about how this courtship process worked and whether it implied there'd be an engagement, but he'd have to wait until he could speak with Mercy alone. Not that she was anything more to him than an asset. Still, no one deserved to be ramrodded into dating someone, much less marrying them, especially if it was with slimy-looking Alex.

"After dinner, Rocco," Marshall said, "Shawn will take you to one of the bunkhouses for novices to get you settled in." He gestured to a security guard at the table he'd been introduced to earlier.

Mercy stiffened. "I'd like to show him around the compound and take him over."

"You'll be busy after supper, sweetheart." Marshall patted her arm again. "Spending time alone with Alex. You have to make an effort for it to work."

She pinched her lips while Alex beamed like a kid who was about to be unsupervised in a candy shop.

Gritting his teeth, Rocco wanted to hold her hand, give her the slightest touch of reassurance, but there were far too many eyes on them. "I promised to continue Mercy's self-defense classes. It's the least I can do. We should squeeze in one a day starting tomorrow."

Mercy perked in her seat, her eyes growing bright. "That's a great idea."

"I never really got why you needed those classes to begin with," Alex said. "I taught you how to shoot." He glared at Rocco. "You know, I'm a deadeye. No better shot here than me. Bet I can teach her how to throw a punch and a kick just fine."

Rocco cleared his throat to hide his chuckle. "There's a lot more to it than that. I'm trained in jujitsu and Krav Maga. I'm teaching her how to survive and to handle herself in close-range combat. Not a backwoods brawl."

Anger flashed over Alex's face as he clenched a fist.

Rubbing everyone the wrong way, regardless of whether he was provoked, wasn't going to do Rocco any good. He needed to make friends, but was well on his way to only making enemies. "I'd be happy to teach you a few things," he said to Alex, trying to clean up the mess he'd made. "And anyone else interested in learning."

"We'll see if there's time," Marshall said. "You're going to have full days, Rocco, starting at sunrise. Morning meditation. Our daily gathering, where I and others deliver homilies to the community. You'll need to get acquainted with the security team. And of course, there's the most important part, your unburdening session."

Alex glared at Rocco, but the others at the table nodded and chimed in, including Mercy, as though it were vital.

Unburdening was their version of a *share-fest* with one of their counselors, where you talked about your woes that brought you to the Shining Light.

He'd have to fake his way through it, which shouldn't be too hard. His life was full of wounds and emotional shrapnel that had taken him to dark places. Not that he wanted any cult disciples digging around in his head. It would be far better if he could figure out how to stave off any unburdening altogether.

Whatever he did, he had to work quickly.

TWO DAYS.
Almost.

Rocco had been on the compound for forty hours, almost two days, and had discovered nothing.

He spun in mind-numbing circles to the beat of music from a snare drum. He was with a group of novices in the middle of the quad. A large square meadow. On one side was their church, which they called the sanctum. There was the schoolhouse on another. Adjacent to that was a playground. The fourth side was the wellness building. A series of trailers where the counselors and Mercy worked. But he hadn't laid eyes on her since lunch.

These people were experts at stonewalling and deflection. He thought his time in basic training in the army had been hell. Nope. The Shining Light redefined the meaning of the word.

Up before sunrise for morning meditation. Followed by prayer. Then yoga. A cleansing with crystals. Sermons or rather homilies from the great Empyrean and others. Climbing a tree as a metaphor for ascending to a higher plane. But really, it was just climbing trees for over an hour. Then someone needed an extra hand in the barn, where he had cleaned out stalls and shoveled hay. Of course, there was learning to connect with his soul through singing and movement, better known as dance. Next was balancing and unblocking his chakras through Reiki—an energy healing technique where Harvey, one of the elders, had to lay hands on him. A creepy, older dude with sagging skin who seemed to be touching him for all the wrong reasons.

And that was the word that kept springing to the forefront of his mind about this place.

Wrong, wrong, wrong. Down to how every activity had to be done barefoot, even climbing a tree. Like they were worried a novice would make a break for it, but couldn't because they weren't wearing shoes.

The one good thing was that he had avoided unburdening. All he'd had to say was that he wasn't ready to share. They pushed, altering their techniques, and he kept repeating the single phrase until they stopped.

Sneaking out of the bunkhouse to investigate in the middle of the night had been impossible with guards posted at the front and back. A change in protocol that had started with his arrival according to the novices. Then there had been an emergency drill at two in the morning. A wailing siren had sounded. Everyone got up and gathered behind Light House. For a lecture, about safety and how during a real event that was the meeting point.

He had wondered if the drill was a sleep deprivation tactic directed at him.

Even though he learned nothing weighed on him, his frustration ticked through him like a time bomb counting down to when this mission blew up in his face. The worst part was seeing Mercy and not being able to talk to her. To touch her. To engage in any manner other than a shared glance because of her father's perpetual interference.

There were eyes and ears everywhere. Guards constantly on patrol.

He looked around for any sign of Alex or Shawn. One or the other had been consistently keeping close tabs on him. Shawn was easier to talk to and had let it slip he thought the compound got their weapons from the Devil's Warriors, an outlaw motorcycle club. He didn't come across as an unreliable source, since he used to be in the MC, but Shawn didn't seem the most informed either.

As Rocco whirled in the quad, pretending to empty his mind to the beat of the drum, he looked past the wellness building, not letting his thoughts divert to Mercy. Though she was a tempting diversion from this new kind of hell.

Tamping down his annoyance, he focused past the quad on the security building.

He'd only been inside once, to meet others on the team, and for a brief tour that included passing by a restricted area, where Rocco needed to venture. Then he'd been hurried out and handed over to Harvey.

Speak of the devil. Dressed in yellow, Harvey left his

trailer and set a course straight toward him. For a man in his senior years, he had quite the spring in his step.

Rocco groaned as Harvey stopped beside the drummer and swayed to the beat with his gaze transfixed on him, a wide gap-toothed grin melting over his leathery face.

The music finally stopped.

Eden, the counselor who had led the session, raised her palms. "You did a glorious job. I am so privileged to help you on this journey. I hope our time together has not only grounded you, but also freed you. May you feel more connected with your soul and one another. Go and walk with the Light today."

Everyone clapped.

Harvey rushed over to him.

Tipping his head back to hide the roll of his eyes, Rocco raked a hand through his loose hair and sucked in a deep breath.

"You were beautiful in motion," Harvey said.

"Thanks, man." Rocco picked up his Stetson, socks and shoes and started walking to Mr. Touchy-Feely's trailer.

Harvey put a hand on his shoulder and kneaded the muscle. "You're so big and strong. But also, very tight. Your musculature is exquisite. The tension in the fibers, not so much. It's quite disconcerting. I'm getting the sense you must be feeling a great deal of stress, and this is how it's manifesting. As though you were under immense pressure. Your burdens don't have to be carried alone. Our family is here for you, my brother. I was thinking that we could incorporate some massage into our Reiki session today. Help loosen you up."

"Nope." Rocco removed the counselor's hand that was wandering around his trapezius muscle and put on his cowboy hat. "Massage isn't necessary. I just need to go for a run."

"Open yourself to the process. You should try it. Everyone says I have magic hands. The commune raves about my Reiki massage therapy. Five stars." Harvey held up his hand, fingers spread wide. "I kid you not." He pressed his palm to Rocco's back and rubbed.

"I'm not ready for all the touching. It makes me feel too…" He searched for the right word. "Vulnerable."

Harvey's eyes brightened and he pushed his glasses up his nose. "But it is through sharing our vulnerability that we grow."

"Yeah, man, I'm not ready."

Mercy's trailer door swung open, and she stepped out. Lovely as ever in a white sundress and her hair pinned up in a loose bun.

Please, save me. But he had no idea how that could happen.

Smiling, she waved as she approached them. "Harvey, there's a change in the schedule for today. You're going to do a Reiki session with Louisa." She made eye contact with one of the novices on the quad and beckoned to her. "And I'm going to work with Rocco," she said. Harvey's mouth opened, the protest clear in his eyes. "This is the only break in my schedule where I can fit in a training session. You're such a generous soul, I know you understand."

Rocco put on his socks and shoes.

"Um, yeah, I guess so." Harvey gave an uncertain nod.

"I appreciate your cooperation," she said, patting his arm.

This was a side of her he rarely saw. Soft but firm, unapologetic and direct, confident yet kind. Everything a leader should be. No wonder he was enamored with her.

"Please tell our guest here," Harvey said, gesturing to Rocco, "how healing my Reiki massages can be."

"On a scale of one to five?" Mercy lifted her hand. "Five stars. He can correct any energy blockages in your life force if you give him a chance. The tension will melt from your body."

Harvey beamed. "See. I told you. Tomorrow, we'll try it." He put an arm around Louisa and guided her to his trailer.

Mercy started walking and he followed.

"Thank you," Rocco said, his voice low. "He makes me uncomfortable."

"Reiki isn't for everyone." She quickened her step. "Harvey can be effusive and affectionate. Expresses himself through touch. I think my father assigned him to you to get under your skin."

Mission accomplished. "Where are we going?"

"To my second favorite spot on the compound."

He was about to ask what was her first when she grabbed his hand, and they took off running. The moment was light and carefree, and he just wanted to go with it.

They ran past huts and tiny houses where couples and families lived, passing the infirmary, and darted into a grove. The trees were fifty feet tall and had clusters of green fruit. The air was spicy and fragrant.

"What grows here?"

"Black walnuts. My father had this grove planted when I was a child because I'm deathly allergic to peanuts, which he banned from the compound." She stared up at the nuts in the trees. "They'll be ready to harvest in a couple of weeks. We'll do it during the waxing moon, then we'll make black walnut butter for the year, which is delicious, especially with a little lavender honey."

"I thought if you were allergic to one nut you were allergic to all."

"That is a common fallacy. I was tested for allergies." She took his hands, interlacing their fingers. "Did you know peanuts aren't actually a tree nut? Their legumes."

Learn something new every day. "Had no idea."

She stared at him with patient, tender gravity that had devastated him from the first. He couldn't bear the thought of anything ever hurting her, much less killing her. The world was a better place because she was in it.

A breeze blew wisps of hair that had fallen loose from her bun. The golden strands brushed her face and he ached to touch her cheek and tuck them behind her ear. Why did she have to be so beautiful? There was something ethereal about the delicacy of her porcelain skin, and the arresting mix of her electric blue eyes and sunny blond hair. And her heart was so open, so strong and full of light. Why did she have to be everything he never knew he wanted and couldn't have?

Focus. You've got a job to do.

Rocco tore his gaze from hers and glanced up at the sky. "I've heard people talking about the upcoming full moon. But I don't get what the lunar cycle signifies to you all," he said, looking back at her.

"Well, new moons are a time to initiate beginnings. That's when we accept novices. We plant seeds for the future and set clear intentions for the month ahead. Full moons are about transformation when the seeds of the new moon come into bloom. We hold shedding ceremonies and people are reborn as Starlights. But this one, on Tuesday, is different."

Rocco drew her closer, bringing her flush to his body, and he heard her breath catch. The sexy sound quickened his blood, awakening every cell in his body "Different how?"

"Because of the eclipse."

He'd spent so much time during their training sessions learning about her, what made her tick, what made her smile and laugh, made her uneasy or blush, for the sake of digging deeper into her cult that he was at a disadvantage.

"How does a lunar eclipse change things?" he asked.

"It'll be a full eclipse. A supercharged version. Like a wild card, bringing volatility and exposing secrets. A time for one thing to end and something else to begin. The moon will be directly opposite the sun. There could be friction, intensified emotion, polarity. My father wants us to be cautious."

"Are you worried about something bad happening?"

"No." She shook her head. "We'll do a cleansing ritual that night and have a shedding ceremony. Things will be revealed, but whatever happens is meant to."

She amazed him. She had so much faith in how things would work out. "Don't you ever worry?" Unable to stop himself, he brushed her hair back behind her ear, caressing her skin. Keeping her close, he watched the flush creep up on her cheeks.

Mercy pressed closer. One small hand curled over his shoulder, up his neck, her fingers diving into his hair. Her other hand moved up his back, her fingers dancing over each vertebra, leaving a trail of sensation in their wake.

He could lose himself in her. Even scarier, he wanted to.

"You saw me have a panic attack," she said. "That's proof I worry."

She stared up at him, and he was aware of every inch of her that made contact with his body. The roundness of her hips. The softness of her curves. Her smile. Her smell—she smelled so good, vanilla and sunshine. Everything about her triggered a visceral response.

There was something here, between them, electric and charged, that neither of them could probably afford to explore. But that didn't curb his desire, no, his need to hold her. To kiss her.

A low, husky hum came from her, as though she were giving consent, the sound shooting down low in his belly. She rose on her toes, angling her mouth toward his, giving him a clear green light.

He lowered his head to hers, aching to taste her.

A horse whinnied, a rider approaching, and they jumped apart, separating like teenagers.

Chapter Six

Mercy's heart hammered in her chest as Shawn rode up on horseback.

What had she been thinking to get so close to Rocco? What if her father had seen them together, her body pressed up against his, lost in the feel of him, that manly musky scent of his curled around her right along with his arms?

She hadn't been thinking at all. Just feeling.

Feeling reckless and sensual. Hungry for his touch.

Well, she had been thinking a little, enough to assume this was a good spot where they wouldn't be seen. Someone must have watched them come here after they left the quad. She couldn't even get ten minutes alone with him in a black walnut grove when she wanted a solid hour behind a locked door in a bedroom. Which would never happen here on the compound.

But this was more than lust or hormones or chemistry, whatever she called it. He was able to soothe her. She could take care of herself, so used to hiding her unhappiness and unease. It was nice not to have to with him. Nice to have strong arms around her when she was shaken. To have someone to really talk to. They'd shared so much. Talked about their childhoods, their disappointments, their dreams. She wanted the Shining Light to branch out. To open a store in town that she'd manage, selling their honey, soaps, artwork. She wanted to make candles, too.

That was what was so powerful about what she had with Rocco. She trusted him with her story, with her pain, with her hopes, and he trusted her enough to do the same.

She'd thought being on the compound with him would bring them closer together, but everyone was conspiring to keep them apart.

Shawn was almost within earshot.

"I haven't had a minute to myself," Rocco whispered, with his back to the inbound rider. "I could really use some time to process all the lessons, try to open my chakras."

She wanted to respond, but Shawn was already on top of them.

He reined in his horse and slid off his mount. "They need some help at the barn, Rocco, cleaning out stalls."

"I can go to the barn," Mercy said. "I've already asked him to take care of something else."

"No," Shawn said, shaking his head. "That won't be necessary. I don't think Empyrean would want you to do that."

"Could you go handle that issue for me?" Mercy tipped her head to the side, giving Rocco the go-ahead to get out of there, and he didn't hesitate to leave. "Since I have you here, Shawn, I'd like to go over some security concerns that I have."

"With me?" His horse neighed. "Shouldn't you talk to Alex or your father?"

"I see such promise in you." Mercy smiled. "I'd rather talk to you." She shifted her gaze, watching Rocco hurrying away. She loved the way he moved—the long, impatient strides tempered by a sort of sauntering grace. She appreciated everything about him, down to the way he wore his jeans, low on his hips, the faded fabric washed to a softness that outlined the sinewy muscles of his legs. "Unless you don't think you're up for the task," she said to Shawn, unable to take her eyes off Rocco, excitement still rippling over her skin from touching him and being touched by him.

"Of course I am. Whatever I can do to be of service," Shawn said.

Smiling, Mercy refocused on the man in front of her to give the man she was completely falling for a chance to catch his breath alone.

ROCCO SLIPPED INSIDE the security building.

His timing was perfect. The others were patrolling the grounds and practicing at the firing range on the far end of the compound. That was probably why they either had him on lockdown with Harvey or out at the barn shoveling manure around now.

He darted through the building, passing the offices, lounge and bay of computers, heading straight for the restricted area. Reaching the locked door, he pulled out his kit that was strapped to his ankle.

Rocco opened the set of lock-picking tools and attacked the pin tumbler. He slipped the L-shaped part into the cylinder to keep pressure on the pins. Next, he slid the straight piece into place and searched for the right angle to access the locking mechanism. He had tackled this kind of lock before and estimated it would take him thirty seconds tops.

One tumbler clicked into place, then a second and third. He worked on the next two. Finally, the last pin gave way and the tumbler fell into place.

He opened the door and ducked inside, closing it behind him.

The breath whooshed out of him at what he saw. Racks of assault rifles—M16s, HK416s, SIG 550s, semiautomatic sniper rifles with scopes, a variety of pistols, cases of ammo, bulletproof vests. Hundreds upon hundreds of weapons.

He hurried through the space, mentally cataloging what he could. His primary focus was on the type of ammo they had beyond caliber: full metal jacket, hollow point, soft point.

No armor-piercing. At least not here.

No sign of any destructive devices. No grenades, no RPGs, no explosives.

There was one unopened wooden case in the back with a lightning bolt burned into the wood. He thought of the stickers on the bumper of the truck that had run Dr. Tiggs off the road. A white lightning bolt on a red background. This mark was black.

He'd seen the white bolt while thumbing through their books in the sanctum as he listened to Empyrean's homily.

Was this yet another case of weapons for them when they already had enough to arm every man, woman and child here twice over? Or was this case meant to be shipped?

Percy had told him that they'd gotten it wrong. Maybe the Shining Light didn't have a weapons supplier. Maybe they were the arms dealers.

He got up and hurried through the rows of weapons to the door. But when he opened it, Alex was standing on the other side, grinning, with three more guards for backup.

MARSHALL LAY IN BED, his need thoroughly sated, his body agreeably tumbled and lazy from his afternoon delight with Sophia.

The shower stopped in the en suite. Once she dressed and he sent Sophia on her way, he'd clean up. Go for a long ride on his stallion, Zeppelin.

There was a light rap on the door.

He groaned, hating to be disturbed when he was in his private quarters. "One minute."

Rolling out of bed, he grabbed his white silk robe and slipped it on, tying it closed. He checked his face in the mirror, brushed his hair in place. His gaze fell to his tattoo of the Shining Light on his chest.

All he had to do was stay the course and his empire would keep growing, expanding. Twenty novices would be reborn during the next ceremony. The most they've ever had at one time.

Nothing—and no one—was going to get in his way.

He went to the door and opened it.

"Empyrean." Alex bowed his head. "I'm sorry to disturb you."

Better now than twenty minutes ago. "What is it?"

His gaze lifted and a smile spread across his face. "You were right. Rocco broke into the restricted area in the security building. I found this on him." Alex held up a lock-picking kit.

The cowboy came prepared. "That didn't take long. I would've given him a week. Did anything turn up on him under the name Kekoa?"

"Nothing."

"No matter. This transgression will be enough. Where is he now?"

"Handcuffed in one of the unburdening rooms."

"Perfect. Dose his dinner with ayahuasca. Once it kicks in, we'll get to the bottom of whatever he's up to." He wouldn't be able to hide anything while he was drugged.

"Then what?" Alex asked.

Marshall needed to get rid of that agent of chaos. This was his chance, but it had to be done right. "Depends on what he says." His thoughts careened to his daughter. "Tonight, you and Mercy should try bundling," he said, referring to the practice of sleeping fully clothed with another person during courtship. The point was to create a strong, intimate bond before marriage. "She needs more encouragement to see you as her future husband. To take this process seriously."

"Yes, sir. I look forward to it."

"Of course you do." Marshall closed the door and turned around.

Sophia came out of the bathroom dressed, and a thought occurred to him.

"Were you listening?" he asked, striding toward her, already knowing the answer. He merely wanted to see if she'd lie.

She hesitated, debating. "Yes. I didn't mean to. I wasn't trying to eavesdrop."

Not this time. He slid a hand around the nape of her neck and tugged her to him. "Do you remember the lesson I taught you about discretion and loyalty?"

Sophia stiffened, her face flushing.

He'd taken a riding crop to her bare bottom. He made certain all his lessons were unforgettable.

"Yes." She trembled. "I won't say anything."

Oh, but she would. "I need you to be of service. To do what you're so good at."

Confusion swept across her face. She lowered to her knees and reached for his robe.

"No, not that." Sighing, he snatched her up by the arms. "The reason I had to teach you a lesson to begin with."

"I don't understand."

"Sit and I'll explain."

Chapter Seven

Finished with her updates to the lesson plans for the children who were homeschooled on the compound, Mercy was pleased with all she had accomplished in a couple of days. She'd integrated weekly art, music and movement/dance classes after weeks of coordinating with the creatives, as well as finding someone to start a soccer program. Her father had opposed organized sports for years, claiming it led to unhealthy competition and division. She'd been advocating for it to no avail until now.

Of course, she couldn't help but wonder if her speech about focusing on development, working together and exercise rather than winning, as well as her detailed plan to ensure the children rotated on teams had finally persuaded him.

Or if it had been Rocco's presence on the compound that had pushed him to give her what she wanted. Another tether tying her to the Shining Light.

She closed her eyes and fantasized what it would be like to be free of her autocratic father and obligations to her community. To her family.

Guilt seeped to the surface. Then she saw Rocco. His sexy smile. His kind eyes. And a warmth, a sense of serenity, washed away her shame.

Urgent pounding rattled the office door, startling Mercy. Before she could get a word out, Sophia burst inside the room.

"Thank the Light I found you." Sophia shut the door and hurried over to the desk.

"What's wrong?" Mercy jumped to her feet. "Is it my father? Is he okay?" Ever since she was a little girl when someone had taken a shot at him, she'd always worried about his safety and well-being. After that day, they built a wall around the compound. But it didn't stop her from fretting that a novice would infiltrate under false pretenses and hurt him. Or as their numbers skyrocketed that the responsibility of caring for so many would give him a heart attack.

"No, it's not about your dad," Sophia said, and relief seeped through Mercy. "It's Rocco. He's been locked up in one of the unburdening rooms."

Mercy's thoughts stalled along with her breath for a moment. "Why? What happened?"

Shaking her head, Sophia shrugged. "I don't exactly know. I think Alex caught him nosing around where he didn't belong. But I overheard your father saying that they're going to dose him later, then find out what he's up to."

Dose him?

The movement's use of ayahuasca, a powerful drug, was only for their religious ritual during the rebirth of a novice. The person would willingly consume it before unburdening to Empyrean in private. Then in a ceremony in front of the entire community that person would claim their new first name and become a Starlight.

Mercy had never been under the influence of the drug, but her father had explained that there was no way for a person to hide anything while on it.

But sacred tonic was never forced on someone. That violated what they believed in.

"Maybe you misheard my father," Mercy said, not wanting it to be true.

"I'm certain of what I heard. After they force Rocco to unburden, your dad plans to punish him for whatever he did wrong. Flagellation."

Bile rose in the back of Mercy's throat.

Their practices might seem antiquated, even harsh, to those on the outside, but as a result, they had a peaceful commune. A collective that loved and helped each other. This was a utopia to so many. No murder. No rape. No theft. No community beyond their gates could say the same, and for that reason their numbers grew each year.

But Rocco was a guest. Not a member of their community bound by their rules and subject to their punishments. This was wrong. "I've got to speak with my father."

"And once you do, what do you think will happen?" Sophia asked.

Her father would patronize and stonewall her. Might even lock her inside her room until he was finished with Rocco. Which would be too late to help him.

"You need to get him out of there and off the compound," Sophia said as though reading her mind. "Right now."

Mercy turned to the top drawer of her desk and entered her code in the digital lock. The drawer opened. She grabbed her set of keys that gave her access to most areas and doors, except for any that belonged to her father.

But something terrible occurred to her. She looked at Sophia, who was watching her expectantly. "Why did you come here to tell me all this?"

The notion that this could be a setup, contrived to get Mercy in trouble and drive a wedge between her and her father, couldn't be dismissed.

"You've never liked me, have you?" Sophia asked.

There was no regard or even shared interests between them. That was a truth Mercy had not bothered to hide. Sophia came to them as Enid Stracke, aka Candy, a junkie and a stripper. Mercy was not one to judge her previous profession or her addiction, but she hadn't taken kindly to how the woman, only two years her senior, had ingratiated herself with Empyrean. Climbing into his bed as soon as she had been reborn.

And Mercy hadn't been blind to the fact that her father had taken advantage of this woman, lost and susceptible, empty and longing for something to fill that void, replacing what she had left behind in the outside world.

The reality of Sophia and her father being together repulsed her.

"It's not that I don't like you," Mercy said. "It's that I don't trust you. What's your angle? What do you get out of helping me?"

Sophia came around the desk and stepped in front of her. "We're going to be family, and I don't mean in the sense of the commune family." She took Mercy's hand and placed it on her stomach. "I'm pregnant."

The words hit Mercy like a physical blow. She reeled back, pulling her hand away.

"I know you'll never look at me as a stepmom, but maybe we can be sisters." Tears glistened in Sophia's eyes. "Or at least friends. I'm telling you all this to show you that you can trust me. I can be Empyrean's wife and be on your side."

Mercy's stomach roiled and it was all she could do not to roll her eyes. She might not remember her dead mother, but she did know that Sophia was no substitute. This was not the time to think about her father marrying this woman, so she shoved the image aside. "Prove I can trust you."

The woman's eyes brightened as her tears dried up. "How?"

"Create a distraction for me. Something to draw the attention of security." If Sophia agreed, then they'd be in this together, both culpable of helping Rocco escape.

"Okay." Sophia took her hand again. "But if I do it, promise me that we'll be sisters."

Not all sisters had a harmonious relationship. From the stories the novices had shared with her, some families barely tolerated one another. But she understood what Sophia was asking—to be Empyrean's queen and have the princess fall into line with the new world order.

Mercy never imagined she'd be the type to sell her soul for anyone's favor or help, but the one thing she wanted even less than playing nice with Sophia was for her father to hurt Rocco. He'd overstepped and made a mistake, perhaps out of curiosity. She knew he was a good man, and she refused to believe he'd done anything maliciously wrong. This was probably more about her father wanting to demonstrate to her who was in charge, teaching her a lesson about standing up to him, using Rocco as a pawn. No matter what he was guilty of, she wouldn't stand by and allow him to be drugged and beaten.

"I can promise to be your friend and a sister to your baby," Mercy said, for Rocco and the sake of the unborn child. She'd grit her teeth, swallow her displeasure and embrace this. No matter how much it sickened her.

Sophia nodded, a smile tugging at her mouth. "Good enough for me. Get ready for my signal. I'll need twenty minutes. But that will still leave the guards at the front and back gates."

"They won't matter."

"Once you get to Rocco, how will you sneak him out of the compound?"

They weren't friends yet, and clearly her father hadn't entrusted Sophia with all their secrets.

"Don't worry about that," Mercy said. "Leave it to me. Just hold up your end of this deal."

"I will." Sophia opened the office door and bolted from the room.

Mercy hauled in steadying breaths, trying to ground herself. Regardless of her reservations about going against her father's orders, she had to do the right thing and put a stop to this.

Not wanting to appear as if she was rushing, she took her time locking up the office. Her keys jangled in her trembling hands. She crossed the quad toward the sanctum where they worshipped. Behind the building were the unburdening rooms that were little more than modified shipping containers on cinder blocks with climate control, stairs leading up to the door and bars on the windows. Each one had a desk, two chairs, a toilet and bed. Sometimes unburdening took hours, but it always took a toll on the body, requiring undisturbed rest afterward.

Forcing herself to stroll rather than run, she mentally kept track of every minute that ticked by. The air was cool and clammy. There would be rain. On the horizon, dark gray clouds rolled through the sky over the town, moving toward the compound. A bad storm was brewing.

With each step, her pulse quickened. The chance she was taking, the risk—reputation, retribution, her father's wrath— was immense.

Out of the corner of her eye, she spotted Alex. He was on a trajectory headed straight for her like a mayfly drawn to light. Any second he'd be a nuisance, buzzing in her ear.

Best just to get it over with. The faster the better.

Slowing her pace, she allowed him to intercept her.

"Hey, Mercy," Alex said, catching up. "Hold on a minute."

Sighing, she stopped and faced him. He'd always been attractive—in an unmemorable way—overzealous and not quite right for her.

"What is it?" she asked, wondering if he'd have the decency to mention the incident with Rocco.

"I'm looking forward to spending time with you later tonight," he said, and she gritted her teeth at his ability to disappoint her. "Especially since you got sick last night, and it cut our evening short."

Too bad for him she had planned to get a sudden case of uncontrollable nausea yet again. "Let's play it by ear. I've been queasy off and on throughout the day." Seeing him triggered it.

She turned to leave, but he caught her by the arm.

"Empyrean thinks we should try bundling tonight."

Mercy had heard whispers of some who had done more than talk or cuddle in the night, engaging in non-penetrative sex.

Every couple who had bundled, that she was aware of, had been quick to marry.

She flashed a tight-lipped smile around the foul taste coating her tongue. "I'll consider it."

"Your father wasn't making a suggestion. He doesn't believe that you're taking this courtship seriously and I agree with him. Would you prefer your room or mine?"

The audacity of him.

Seething, she let the fake grin slip from her face and with her fingertips, grazed his Shining Light tattoo at the base of his throat. "When I was younger, I was so scared of you. Remember how you'd sneak into my room and crawl into my bed?" His was right down the hall from hers. Empyrean wanted his daughter by blood and his son by choice under one roof. Always together. "Your hands were like fire as you held mine, your fingers clinging so tight to me. Back then I used to think that you could never really love someone. A dalliance, sure. But not for a lifetime. You needed too much. Approval. Admiration. Validation." It was always: *look at me, am I good enough, am I special, am I worthy?* "Because you're weak. And I was right." It felt good to speak this truth after being pushed so far, and she considered how she'd share the same thoughts with her father soon.

He clenched his jaw. "My problem has always been that I love too much. Too deeply," he said through gritted teeth. "This is going to happen. You and I were always meant to be. The sooner you realize that, the better."

His self-assuredness knew no bounds.

She glanced down at his hand on her arm. "Let me go," she said, meaning it in more ways than one.

Something predatory sparked in his eyes like he'd picked up on her implication. "And if I don't?"

Then she would make him. A quick punch to the throat should do the trick.

He squeezed tighter, even more possessive, before his hand fell, releasing her. "On the full moon, your father plans to announce my transformation from gray to white. He also expects us to seal our union by the end of the year."

Alex would be her father's successor instead of her. She felt like she'd been the one punched in the throat.

But why him? There were others on the council of elders who were better qualified.

She should have seen her father's plan all along. Alex's ascendance from gray to white, elevating his position. Making him her equal before his inevitable succession. The desire for them to be married, despite the fact she considered Alex an overbearing brother.

Not a potential husband.

"I guess I'll cross that borderline incestuous bridge when I come to it." Or burn it to the ground. Either way, there wasn't going to be any union between them. "As for bundling, we did quite enough of that years ago."

Even though it had been innocent then, she would never share a bed with him again. In any manner. Under any circumstances.

He narrowed his dark eyes. "We were kids. It was different—"

Gunshots rang out, making her jump. People screamed, dispersing and running for cover.

Her head snapped to the side out in the direction the reports had come from—on the east end of the compound near the farm.

Sophia. Perfect timing with this distraction.

"We'll finish our discussion later." Alex took off as three more shots resounded.

Whirling, Mercy bolted for the backside of the sanctum, passing two more guards who were in a flat-out sprint toward the gunfire.

She hustled to the bank of Conex trailers, where Shawn stood, posted by room number two.

"You have to hurry!" Mercy raced up to him. "Alex needs as many guys as he can get to help him."

Shawn glanced back at the door of the unburdening room, as though questioning the order.

Another gunshot pierced the air.

"You better go!" she said.

Giving a curt nod, Shawn put a hand on the hilt of the gun holstered on his hip and dashed off to assist.

She waited until he was out of sight. Then she fumbled through her keys, found the right one and unlocked the door.

Her gaze collided with Rocco's angry stare, and it was as if he stole the air from her lungs with that one look.

He never failed to take her breath away.

Seated on the cot, Rocco was shackled to the bolted down frame. She hadn't factored in the possibility that he might be handcuffed.

"Nice to see you," he said, his brown eyes warming.

She shut the door. "I didn't bring a handcuff key."

"Give me one of your hairpins," he said, holding out a hand.

She plucked a bobby pin from the messy bun she wore, dropped it in his palm and he got to work. "Can you really unlock it that easily?"

"Sure can. Just have to get it between the ratchet and the ball, the catch mechanism. Disengage the teeth and—" The cuff popped open, releasing him. He held up his free wrist. "I've had practice." He stood and clutched her shoulders. "What are you doing in here? It's a risky move on your part. I don't want to get you into any trouble."

"We don't have much time. I need to get you out of here, off the compound."

"Why?"

"I don't know what you did, but my father plans to dose you tonight with ayahuasca. It's a powerful drug we use for rituals."

"I know what it is."

"If you've got anything to hide, it will come out while you're under the influence."

His gaze shifted to the floor. His whole body tensed.

He *was* hiding something. But what? If only she had a chance to find out, but they didn't have minutes to spare for that discussion.

"Afterward, for your transgression," she said, "you'll be beaten."

He rocked back on his heels. "Like hell I will."

While drugged and weakened, they'd restrain him. "There won't be anything you could do to stop it." But she could intervene now before it got to that point. "You didn't take any vows, agreeing to follow our ways. You're here to learn and understand. The only way to prevent this from happening is to get you off the compound."

"I can't leave."

"Why not?"

A muscle twitched in his jaw, and he looked away from her again.

Her heart squeezed. What wasn't he telling her?

"If you stay, whatever secrets you have will come to light. And you will be beaten," she repeated. She pressed a palm to his warm cheek, not wanting anything bad to happen to him. "I can't say how severely." But whatever anger Mercy's father had toward her for her recent acts of rebellion he would take out on Rocco. Of that she had no doubt. "We're out of time. Decide. Stay or go."

She wanted him to choose to be here. With her. But deep down, she knew that was no longer a possibility because of whatever secret he was harboring.

He raked his hair back and slipped on his cowboy hat. "How can you get me out of here?" he asked, and something inside of her deflated. "I won't make it to the gate unseen and earlier your father increased security."

"I have a way. We have a bunker beneath Light House. There's a tunnel that leads to the woods. I can get you out there. But we have to be quick."

IN THE STABLE back from his ride, Marshall put Zeppelin in his stall. Years ago, his daughter had asked him why he'd chosen such an odd name. He'd told her about a type of rigid airship named after the German inventor Count Ferdinand von Zeppelin instead of telling her the truth. That he called his horse after his favorite rock band. Led Zeppelin.

There were other truths he kept from her.

Sometimes he thought about letting Mercy have her year away in *penumbroyage*, to experience things such as the music he loved, like "Stairway to Heaven," to eat whatever she wanted, to explore and make mistakes. To feel the pain that would inevitably come from that wicked world.

But he loved her too much to let her stray, even for a little while, and wanted to spare her that darkness. If only she could see that he was protecting her.

The vast majority of children who had been raised on the compound, like Alex, never sought to wander or question as adults. In fact, they became his most die-hard disciples.

Why hadn't Mercy followed suit? How had he failed her?

The handheld radio he carried while riding squawked.

"Empyrean, this is Alex. Come in."

He took it from his satchel and pressed the button. "What is it?"

"I have Sophia with me at the farm. I had to restrain her."

Horror streaked through him. "Why on earth would you do such a thing?"

"She managed to take a gun from one of the guys on the security team and started shooting apples in a tree and talking nonsense."

That didn't sound like Sophia. "Untie her and put her on the radio."

"But, sir—"

"You have the weapon, don't you?"

"Yes, but—"

"Then put her on."

"As you wish."

Marshall left the stable and headed back toward Light

House while he waited. The path would take him close to the farm.

Gun safety was a top priority on the compound. They trained everyone how to properly handle, shoot, clean and store a firearm. For the life of him, he couldn't understand what could've possessed her to do such a thing.

"Empyrean," Sophia said.

"Is what Alex told me true?"

"Yes."

"You could've hurt someone by accident." The act was beyond ludicrous, complete madness. And dangerous. "Why would you take a gun and shoot apples?"

"Because Mercy asked me to create a diversion."

He stilled. "Did you do as I commanded?" Did she bait Mercy by telling her about Rocco, getting her emotional over the thought of flagellation, setting his plan in motion?

"Yes, my love. Exactly the way you wanted."

"Good girl." Marshall smiled. When the sun set, he would be rid of that man once and for all. "Did she tell you how she plans to get him out?" he asked.

"She wouldn't say, but she wasn't concerned about the gates."

This was worse than he feared. His daughter was willing to reveal one of their most precious secrets to help a stranger escape. "Put Alex back on."

A moment later, his son said, "Sir, is there something going on that I should know about?"

"Mercy is headed for the bunker with Rocco to sneak him out through the tunnel. You have my permission to use lethal force." He wanted Rocco dead. It was the only way to end Mercy's infatuation with him.

"Yes, sir," Alex said, and Marshall could hear the grin in his voice.

Alex had been aching to take a shot at Rocco since he'd arrived. Now he'd have his chance. He better not blow it.

"Make sure Mercy doesn't get hurt, and, Alex, don't miss."

"I never do."

Chapter Eight

Lightning lit the sky as they made their way to Light House. The clouds were almost black. Rocco fretted about what would happen to Mercy for breaking the rules by helping him.

He should have been worried about the mission. About failing. Getting caught as he tried to get off the compound.

At that moment, his sole concern was for her.

If he could've stayed, he would have. Not only to meet his objective, but to spare her from suffering any consequences. He'd never once rattled under fire. Whatever the dangers might be, Rocco was ready for them, but being forced to ingest a drug—legal for religious purposes and illegal under all other conditions—spill his guts and take a beating was not a possibility he could entertain.

In the end, he'd break his cover and have nothing to show for it besides bruises.

What her father had planned for him was brutal and inhumane. To think, the entire commune accepted such practices as normal.

This was supposedly the safest place on the planet for her, but his protective instincts had been in high gear since he drove through the front gate. Her father's stunt with that forced courtship only made the knot in his gut tighten. Despite her assurances that he need not worry, that was all he did.

Keeping his head lowered, he scanned the area and glanced over his shoulder.

"Stop looking around," she said. "It's suspicious."

"Where are all the security guards?"

Mercy flashed him a smile. "Preoccupied at the farm with a little distraction."

She was full of surprises.

Instead of entering through the back, they went around the main building. At a side door, Mercy stepped inside first, made sure it was clear and waved him in.

"Is your dad here?" Avoiding a run-in with her father would be ideal. Not that he wouldn't like the chance to punch that man in the face.

"He likes to ride his horse before dinner, but since you've been on the compound, he's varied his schedule. There's no telling where he is now."

She closed the door behind them and locked it.

In the hall, she led the way past a mudroom that had racks lined across the walls for people to set their shoes on after they entered. He'd seen an even larger one near the rear entrance.

Up ahead was the staircase to the second story.

She put her hand to his chest, stopping him. "Wait here," she whispered, steering him into a dim alcove beneath the stairs.

"Where are you going?"

"I need to get something from my room." Her blue eyes looked more panicked and desperate than he felt. "It'll only take me a minute."

No distraction was going to keep the security team preoccupied indefinitely.

Before he could ask her if they had the time to waste, she was gone, disappearing around the corner like a ghost.

THIS WAS THE first time Mercy had kept her footwear on inside the main building. Rather than it being an act of defiance, it was one of desperation that felt entirely disrespectful. But they had to move quickly and quietly and couldn't spare precious seconds taking off their shoes.

Mercy raced up the steps on the balls on her feet, holding tight to her keys, not making a sound. She raced down the hall to her room. Slipped inside. Grabbed what she needed from the top of her dresser. She spun around and stopped. Her heart flew into her throat as she came face-to-face with Daisy.

The middle-aged woman kept the private living quarters meticulously clean, as well as her father's office.

Daisy smiled. "Hello. I was just finishing up. I got a late start today because…" Her gaze dropped to the shoes Mercy was wearing and her smile fell, too.

Mercy couldn't help looking down at her sneakers—a blatant sign of rudeness. "Oh, I forgot to take them off. How silly of me."

Daisy cocked her head to the side. "You never forget."

That was true. Great care was taken to keep the house clean. It required little effort or thought to remove filthy shoes and avoid tracking in any unnecessary dirt.

"First time for everything. I was rushing." Then she wondered if that would lead to more questions. For starters, why was she in such a hurry? "I'm sorry." She removed the canvas shoes and held them to her chest, along with the other item that she hoped wouldn't be needed. "Please don't tell Empyrean."

"Transparency is the way to the Light. Are you asking me to obfuscate?"

Yes. Yes, I am. "No. Of course, not. I want to be the one to tell him about my transgression." Wearing shoes in the house would be the least of them today.

Daisy nodded. "All right."

"I'll get out of your way." She went to the door and squeezed by her. "I really am sorry. I know how hard everyone works to keep things clean. I appreciate your efforts." Mercy hugged her, sincerely grateful for her diligence and years of service.

Daisy returned the affection. "Thank you. It's so nice to hear."

"May the Light be with you."

"And also, with you."

Mercy rushed down the steps with her heart pounding a frantic rhythm against her sternum. She hustled back to the alcove. "Let's go."

Rocco glanced at her bare feet, but thankfully didn't ask questions.

They crept through the hall, passing the great library, a vaulted two-story room, where she had spent thousands of hours as a child, reading and playing hide-and-go-seek. It was her favorite space in the whole house. One she would never get a chance to share with Rocco, like so many other things. She had so hoped this would be an opportunity to let someone she had formed a powerful connection with into her life and world. To build on it. Explore where that bond might lead.

As always, her father was two steps ahead of her, doing what he could to sabotage any of her efforts that contradicted his wishes.

Disappointment sliced through her, but dwelling on it wasn't a luxury she could afford. She had to get Rocco out of there. That was all that mattered.

Voices, the clatter of dishes and aroma of food being prepared came from the kitchen.

Before reaching the dining hall, she whispered, "They'll begin setting up for supper soon. This way."

She cut down a short corridor that led to the basement, where they kept everyday supplies, and opened the door. After she slipped on her shoes, they hurried down the stairs. Those who worked in the kitchen regularly came to the basement, which appeared to be no more than six hundred square feet, but they didn't know what else was hidden down there.

At the bottom of the steps, she took his hand in the pitch-black darkness. Not only because she longed to touch him, but also for a more practical reason. "I'm not going to turn on the light. Not until we reach the bunker. Just in case anyone passes by upstairs, I don't want them to get suspicious."

He drew closer and the scent of him curled around her. Sweaty, pine-laden musk.

"I trust you," he said, his warm, strong fingers tightening around the edge of her hand.

She was aware he hadn't missed the sound of her sharp intake of breath, but hoped he couldn't hear the way her heart thudded in response to his touch, to his proximity.

Whenever they got close, he turned her into a messy bundle of sensual frustration. No one else did that. Ever. Alex had never even come close.

"Lead the way," he said, his voice low and deep.

Mercy guided him through the dark depths of the basement, with the heat of his body tickling, teasing, almost pressed against her back. Having him so close, unable to see and only feel, made her dizzy.

She knew every inch of this house and could make her way through blindfolded, if necessary, but Rocco was a distraction.

Forcing herself to focus, she extended her other arm. They'd reach the far wall soon.

Her fingers grazed cool cement. She turned left. "Not much farther."

A few feet ahead and they came to the last shelving unit that was always kept empty.

She placed his hand on one of the steel racks. Then she grabbed onto it as well. "Help me pull it."

Together, they gave it a hard tug. There was a faint click and the fake wall attached to the shelving unit slid open with barely a whisper.

She felt her way around to the lever. Yanked down on it and pulled open the door to the bunker. She stepped inside, ran her palm along the wall, fumbling for the switch and flipped on the lights. Fluorescent strobes flickered and buzzed as they came alive. Everything inside Light House drew power from the solar panels. Her father believed in being prepared in the event of a worst-case scenario.

Rocco entered the bunker.

Quickly, she tugged the faux wall back in place, but didn't bother closing the heavy steel door to the bunker. Unfortunately, she couldn't lock it. Her father had never entrusted her with a code to do so. It was possible he was indeed a prophet, a spiritual seer who'd foreseen that she'd one day betray him like this.

But Rocco made her feel—impulsive, reckless, selfish— in a good way. He brought out the most intense version of herself.

Rocco wandered deeper inside and glanced around, peering at the long gun rack filled with rifles and automatic weapons. He took a 9 mm from the wall, pulled back the slide and peeked inside the chamber.

"Empty," he said.

"They're all unloaded. We store the ammo separately." She went to the cabinet beside the rack of weapons and used one of her keys to unlock it.

Rocco grabbed a loaded magazine from one of the many stacks. "I can't believe you have a full armory down here as well as in the security building." He inserted the loaded clip into the gun, working the slide to chamber the first round.

"The tunnel is this way."

They ran by shelves stocked with nonperishable food: dried beans, rice, jars of preserved fruits, vegetables, crackers, jams and black walnut butter. In another part of the bunker, they had cases of Meals, Ready-to-Eat—not enough to feed five hundred for weeks—a stockpile of toilet paper, and other essentials. They passed the small kitchen, toilets, shower rooms and an infirmary that was fully supplied with medicine.

"What's with the bunker?" he asked. "Are you preparing for Armageddon?"

No, they were prepared for a siege. Everyone in the commune believed that if they ever faced any danger, it would come from the outside.

"Better safe than sorry. At least that's what my father says. He wants to prevent another Waco from happening here in Wyoming." He'd protect his people at all costs. This was only one measure. "Come on."

She led the way through a large open bay of three-tier high bunk beds that they'd made on the compound. It was the same kind they used in the bunkhouses for novices.

Whenever someone asked what they did with the unaccounted-for extras, her father had told the carpenters that they'd sold them, like their other products that brought in a profit. And some had.

After a couple of turns through an area that was designated

as restricted for most of the commune, in the event that they had to use the bunker, they entered the private quarters—another open space for Empyrean, her, Alex, the council of elders and their loved ones.

They reached the door that led to the tunnel.

She slid back the heavy barrel bolt. There was no lock or code on this door in case of an emergency and they needed to evacuate. She pushed it out, opening it. The first set of motion-sensor lights flicked on.

"Follow the tunnel. It goes for less than a mile and will let you out in the woods, closer to town. There are three different paths you can take, depending on where you want to go, but I'd recommend staying off them. If you hurry, they won't be able to intercept you once they realize you're gone." She gave him the wooden wedge she'd taken from her dresser. "It's a doorstop."

On her fourteenth birthday, when her father had declared her a *woman* to the community because she had gotten her first menses, she asked the carpenters to make one for her to keep Alex from slipping into her room. There were no locks on the bedroom door handles to stop someone from getting in. But there were padlock hasps fitted to the outside in case her father wanted to lock either of them in. Something she had never questioned. That was simply the way things were done and she'd never known anything different.

"Use it, just in case," she said. That way they wouldn't be able to follow him through the tunnel.

He stared down at her with such intensity, his eyes burning into hers, and moved closer. A little step that didn't feel little at all. She looked at the pulse beating along the line of his throat, at his chest rising and falling with quickened breaths.

"Mercy," he said, her whispered name sounding like a question on his lips, and an echo in her heart.

He caressed her face, his fingertips diving into her hair that was still pinned up, and bent his head, setting his mouth to hers.

She dissolved on the spot as she kissed him back.

Would she end up in the fiery hell her father preached about for this intimacy with a nonbeliever?

All she knew for certain was that it felt like heaven.

So she silenced the conflicted voice in her head and sank into Rocco. When he parted her lips with his own and slid his tongue inside her mouth, she made a quiet noise of pleasure that was just shy of a moan.

He tugged her even closer, putting a hand at the small of her back. No longer waiting for this delicious moment that seemed as though it would never happen, she put her arms around his neck and pressed her whole body against the muscular landscape of his. All at once, hunger and heat rushed through her. She fisted the back of his T-shirt, pushing up onto her toes, welcoming the sweet slide of his tongue, the heady taste of him filling her senses. He tasted like mint and coffee. He tasted like happiness, and she could not get enough of it. Couldn't get over how he kissed her, as if he were consuming her in such desperate, frantic urgency.

Nipping at his lower lip, she rolled her hips against the hardness bulging between his thighs, unable to stop herself. As though she had been untethered and set free. She didn't want to stop there, at a kiss, and if circumstances were different, she'd get her hands and mouth all over him.

On a groan, he clutched the mass of her hair bundled at her nape and tipped her head back, making her gasp.

"God," she muttered, excitement running in wild molten rivulets through her.

His head whipped to the side as if he'd heard something.

Then she caught it—the sound of approaching footfalls in the bunker. Dangerously close. Almost on top of them.

"Go." She shoved him toward the tunnel and her heart cracked like glass splintering in her chest.

"Come with me."

Her breath hitched, blood roaring in her ears. Had she misheard him? "What'd you say?"

"Come with me," he repeated, this time taking her hand and pulling her close.

The footsteps grew louder. At least three or four men. Any second they'd enter the restricted area and see them.

If she stayed on the compound, there'd be horrendous consequences. And if she left with Rocco, there would be uncharted terrain and obstacles and cliffs ahead.

She'd never been so conflicted, so torn in her life.

Alex and three others charged into the enclosed space.

Pop! Pop!

Gunshots boomed, bullets biting into the concrete wall near her head. Rocco moved her out of the line of fire.

"Don't shoot!" Alex ordered. "Mercy's not to be hurt."

Time was up. Her gaze flew to Rocco's hard stare, and she knew that taking this leap of faith would be worth it.

That he was worth it.

All hesitation evaporated, and she gave him her wordless answer. Mercy shielded Rocco with her body—Alex could hit a melon the size of a human head with a single shot from fifteen yards day or night—and scurried backward, getting them both across the threshold into the tunnel.

Alex stopped running and took aim, but Rocco returned fire, forcing the men to take cover.

She met Alex's eyes for a split second, saw the horror and anger contort across his face right before she slammed the door closed.

Rocco shoved the wooden wedge under the lip of the door. Using his foot, he rammed it tight.

He grabbed her hand, and they took off down the tunnel. Along the way, he shot out each light that flashed on, shattering the bulb. Once Alex and the others eventually got the door open, they wouldn't be able to open fire into the darkness without risking hitting her.

A loud banging resounded on the door behind them.

Clutching Rocco, she ran faster. As fast as possible.

With each panicked step she took, three things filled her ears—the frenzied beat of her heart in time with the pounding of fists on the door, and Alex's screams.

"Mercy!"

Bang. Bang.

"Mercy!"

Chapter Nine

It was nightfall by the time they made it to the outskirts of town. A downpour had started while they were racing through the woods. Rocco had been impressed with Mercy. Not only had she broken him out of the unburdening room, saving him from being drugged and beaten, but in the bunker, she'd stayed calm, even while Alex's men shot at them. In the woods, she had kept up with the grueling pace he'd set over rough terrain. He'd only had to help her once or twice after the ground had turned muddy and slick. Most surprising of all, she had left with him when it would have been so much easier for her to stay.

The wind and rain continued to buffet them, soaking them through when they reached a small service station—the Dogbane Express. Panting, weary and wet, she had to be physically nearing the end of her endurance. Even though he was already blown away by her fortitude, he hoped she could wring a little more out of herself.

He marched up to the door and pulled it open, ushering her inside first.

"Wow, you two are drenched," the attendant said. She gazed out toward the empty gas pumps. "Were you out walking in that storm?" The stocky woman came from behind the register.

"We were already far out and got caught in it." Rocco glanced around and spotted a pay phone. One of the few still in the state. "Is that pay phone in service?"

"Yep. Sure is."

He took out his wallet from his back pocket. The one item that security hadn't confiscated. Cursing the fact that his vehicle was still on the compound, he whipped out a dollar bill and slapped it down on the counter. "Can I get change in quarters?"

The attendant hit a button on the register. The cash drawer opened with a beep. She set four quarters on the counter. "It's on me." She pushed the dollar back toward him.

"Thanks." He slipped the bill in his pocket and grabbed the quarters. "I'll be right back," he said to Mercy.

Keeping an eye on her, he went to the pay phone and picked up the receiver. There was a dial tone, like the attendant had said, but he exhaled in relief, nonetheless.

The older woman looked over Mercy from head to toe. "Are you one of those Starlights from that compound?"

Rocco suspected it was her necklace that gave her away. He'd never seen her without it.

Shivering, Mercy nodded. "Yes, ma'am."

He put fifty cents in the slot and dialed a taxi company.

"Make a break for it, did you?" the attendant asked with a curious smile.

"Sort of."

"I'll get you a towel. Feel free to help yourself to some coffee. That's on me, too. It's fresh and it'll warm you up."

"Thank you," Mercy said. She grabbed two cups and filled them with piping hot coffee. "That's very kind of you."

"I'll go get a couple of towels from the back."

He ordered a cab and then called Charlie. "Hey, it's Rocco."

"I haven't heard from you since you took off with Mercy McCoy. It's been days. Are you all right?"

"Yeah. I'm working."

"With Mercy?" Shock rang in Charlie's voice. "Is she an asset?"

Rocco never discussed work with his cousin. All this time, she had no idea that he had been cultivating Mercy McCoy as a potential asset. Only that she was the sole client he was willing to work with one-on-one.

Mercy headed toward him, trembling like a leaf, and handed him a cup of coffee.

He mouthed, *thank you.* "I can't get into specifics right now. Listen, we're about to take a taxi to a motel." He rattled off the name and vicinity in which it was located. From what he could tell from the outside, the place wasn't a fleabag dump, but it wasn't the Ritz either.

"Why are you going to a hotel? And why are you taking a taxi instead of driving your car?"

"It's a long story. Short version is that folks from the compound might come looking for her at my place. Maybe even at yours, too. You should stay with Brian for the next few days." He took a long sip of coffee, grateful for the warm liquid sliding down his throat.

"I'm at his house almost every night as it is anyway. I won't say we're living together because I've still got my house, but he's given me two drawers and closet space."

Not only had Charlie's relationship with Brian caught him completely off guard, but the two had gone from zero to serious at lightning speed. He wasn't complaining. In fact, he was thrilled that his cousin had finally let someone in behind that steel wall she'd put up around her heart, and for it to be a great, solid guy like Brian made it even better.

"It might be a good idea to have Brian hang out at USD as

well. Some Starlights might try to harass you there to find out where Mercy is." Nash should approve it. They didn't hem and haw when it came to the safety of their loved ones.

The service station attendant came out from the back and handed them both towels.

"Can you bring me some things from my place and pick up stuff for Mercy?" he asked his cousin. "We both look like a couple of drowned cats. I could also use a car."

Charlie sighed. "We've got you covered. I'll let you use my Hellcat and ride with Brian. See you in a few." She disconnected.

Rocco went to the ATM and withdrew his daily limit so he could pay for a room in cash. To be sure they couldn't be tracked down, he'd get the room under an alias. Beside the ATM was a rack of prepaid cell phones. Grabbing one, he wished the attendant had mentioned that the store carried them earlier.

He went to the register, paid for it and used the activation card as the taxi pulled up.

AT THE MOTEL, Rocco unlocked the door to the room and let Mercy in. There were two double beds, a microwave, mini fridge and a dank, musty smell. "Sorry it isn't nicer."

He took off his sopping wet Stetson and fired off a quick text to Charlie.

It's Rocco. This is a temp number. We'll be in room 12.

THE ROOM WAS FREEZING. He turned down the air-conditioning. In the closet, he found an extra blanket and put it around Mercy's shoulders.

She edged deeper inside with her arms wrapped around herself. "I thought I'd get a chance to see where you lived."

He would've liked nothing more than to welcome her into his home. Show her how he lived and all the things about himself that he'd hidden. "I'm sure your father knows where my house is. He'd only send Alex and others to come get you."

"I don't think so. You didn't kidnap me. It was my choice to leave the compound."

Things happened quickly with bullets flying. No telling what version of the story her father had been told. Regardless, Alex was the type to retaliate. If he thought he knew where to find Mercy, nothing was going to stop him from going after her.

The man was either obsessed or in love with her. Either way, Alex wasn't going to simply let her go.

"You left without permission or claiming *penumbroyage.* Which means there'll be consequences for you, right?"

Looking lost, she pressed a palm to her forehead. "I didn't really think about that when I decided to go with you."

"Regrets?" he asked.

If she had any, rather than letting her have a good night's sleep, he'd have to get straight to questioning her about what she might know. Any innocent detail could lead to something fruitful. Then he'd drop her at the gates to the compound. Reluctantly say goodbye.

But he hoped she didn't have any remorse about taking his hand and getting away from the commune. Even if it was only for a few days.

She turned to him, her mouth opening to answer when headlights shone in front of the window, drawing their attention. Car doors slammed and there was a knock on the door.

Rocco peeled back the curtain and peeked out to be sure.

Charlie and Brian were kissing. She was wearing his black cowboy hat and his hand was pressed to the small of her back.

Every time he saw their public displays of affection he was surprised all over again as if witnessing it for the first time. Brian was the only man to ever soften his cousin. It was nice seeing them both happy and in love.

He opened the door. "Hey."

Charlie held up two small duffel bags. "Reinforcements are here." Stepping inside, she shoved one bag into his arms. "Grabbed the essentials for you."

Brian crossed the threshold, bringing in the smell of food with him. He set a white food sack beside the microwave. "Double cheeseburger, fries, hummus sandwich, tomato soup and two salads."

Perfect. "Thanks." Rocco turned to Mercy. "This is Brian, Charlie's significant other."

Mercy held up a shaky hand *hello*.

"You need to take a warm shower and change," Charlie said, handing Mercy the other duffel. "All the toiletries you should need. Also, there are some T-shirts, a sweater, leggings and an old pair of jeans I can't squeeze into anymore and a nightgown. You might have to roll the pants up. The only thing white in there are the T-shirts. Sorry."

"That's okay." Mercy still had that deer in the headlights look. "Thank you."

"What's the situation here?" Charlie asked. "Are you two sharing a room?"

His cousin was brusque, opinionated and ruthless when it came to protecting the vulnerable. She was particularly sensitive to battered women. It turned out that she had made it her mission to help victims of domestic violence get away from their abusers and disappear. With Mercy being embroiled in a cult, it only made sense that Charlie would seek to protect her.

"I'm not letting her out of my sight," Rocco said. Mercy

might change her mind in the middle of the night, call the compound, sneak out before he had a chance to find out what she might know. As it stood, she was his best lead. He wasn't going to let her slip away or allow anything to happen to her.

"Mercy, are you comfortable with this arrangement?" Charlie asked. "Because if you're not, I can stay with you in here and Rocco can sleep in a different room."

"If you stay, I'm staying," Brian said. "Not with you ladies, of course."

Mercy clutched the duffel to her stomach. "I'll be fine with Rocco. Really. There's no need for you to stay." Her bright blue eyes found his, and relief seeped through him that she was comfortable being alone with him.

"I don't fully understand what's going on with you two," Charlie said, glancing between them. "I thought it was one thing and then I found out it's something else." She turned to Mercy. "If you ever decide that you want to leave the Shining Light, I don't want you to feel like you have to rely on a man to help you. Even if that man is my cousin. Who happens to be a good guy. Whatever you need, a place to stay, a job, anything at all, just ask and it's yours."

Charlie was a formidable person to have on one's side. Mercy would be able to count on her, no matter what. He wanted her to have as much support as possible with whatever decision she made, but he intended to make it clear that he wanted to be there for her, too, as much as she'd allow.

"That's incredibly generous of you," Mercy said. "I'm not sure what I'm going to do yet, long-term, but thank you."

Charlie gave her a warm smile and then she turned an icy stare on him. "I need to speak with you privately." She marched outside, leaving the door open.

Rocco stepped out onto the walkway and shut it. "Don't come in hot with me. I'm not in the mood."

Rocking back on her heels and putting her hands on her hips, she swallowed the words that seemed to be burning on her tongue. She took a deep breath. "Mercy may not have been physically abused, but she's been isolated from the outside world, under the strict rule of her father, where every facet of her life has been controlled. She's in a vulnerable position right now."

"I'm aware."

"Don't take advantage of it."

"Who do you think I am?" She was treating him like he was a stranger and not the blood relative she'd grown up with.

"I think you're one of the good ones, but you're still a guy. Open your bag."

He unzipped the duffel he was holding. On top of his clothes were condoms. What in the hell? "I'm not on a date. I'm working on a mission."

"Call it whatever you want. I've seen how she looks at you. It isn't one-sided. Tell me I'm wrong and I have nothing else to say."

Irritation sliced through him. Partly because she was right. Partly because he was wet, cold and starving. "I can be a professional regardless of my personal feelings." And if for some reason he slipped, he always kept an emergency condom in his wallet. He didn't need her to meddle. "This discussion is done. Are we clear?"

"Crystal." She reached into her pocket, pulled out her keys and tossed them to him.

"Thank you for coming so quickly." He marched back inside and found Brian standing alone.

"She's in the bathroom," Brian said, keeping his voice low, and it was then that Rocco caught the sound of the shower running. "Did you learn anything concrete?"

Rocco shook his head. "But I think she might know more

than she realizes. I'll talk to her in the morning after she's gotten some rest. If I come up with nothing, I'll pursue a tip that the Devil's Warriors might have an in with the weapons supplier." He couldn't count on it going anywhere. The lead was threadbare.

Brian unhooked his holstered weapon from his hip and handed it to Rocco. "I'll leave you to it. If you don't make headway, Becca will want to give it a go."

"Yeah, I figured."

"I understand that it might be difficult, especially after whatever you two just went through," Brian said, gesturing to the bathroom, "but you can't go easy on her. You've got to push hard for answers. *Tonight.* We only have two days left."

No one needed to remind him what he was already painfully aware of—that they were almost out of time. "I got it covered."

"Nash wants to see you first thing in the morning. And so that you know, I'll be at USD all day tomorrow with Charlie. I won't let anything happen to her."

That went without saying. Rocco not only trusted Brian with his life, but Charlie's as well.

Brian clasped a hand on his shoulder and gave him a sympathetic look before leaving.

The water stopped running in the bathroom. A minute later, Mercy opened the door and steam wafted around her. She stepped out, wearing a tee and black leggings. He couldn't help but notice that she didn't have a bra on.

Get a grip. You're more than a man. You're an ATF agent.

"You should eat," he said, diverting his gaze. "I'm going to clean up." He hurried past her into the bathroom and closed the door.

Hanging from the shower rod were her bra and panties.

The sight of them was a jarring reminder that she wore nothing under her clothes.

With a firm shake of his head, he snapped himself out of it and started the water.

If he could've eaten while he showered, he would have. He zipped through cleaning up, soaking up the warmth from the hot water, and threw on a T-shirt, boxer briefs and sweatpants.

In the bedroom, Mercy had placed a spare blanket on the floor and set out the food like a picnic. She sat cross-legged, waiting for him.

"I told you to eat. I know you're hungry."

"I've always eaten with my family."

She looked so fragile, fresh-faced with pink cheeks and a gentle smile.

To call her vulnerable was an understatement. All of this was new to her, from wearing anything besides white to eating outside her commune. He would have given anything to wait until the morning to tell her the truth, but Brian was right.

He sat beside her. "Do you want half of my burger?" He wasn't sure offering it was being nice or offensive.

Frowning, she shook her head. "Just because I'm not on the compound doesn't mean I want to eat meat."

What did it mean, then? She wasn't ready to give up the ways of her commune, but she was out beyond the compound with him for a reason. "Do you want to say your blessing?"

"Yes." She took his hand. "Thank you for the gift of this meal to sustain us. May it nourish our bodies and fuel our ability to make this a better world. And thank you for keeping Rocco safe."

Not only had she included him, but she'd cut the blessing short, leaving out the bits that had secretly made him uncomfortable.

He stared down at her small hand resting on his. Soaked

in how good it felt. Too good. He looked up and met her blue eyes. Neither of them said a word. The moment stretched out, thinning until it snapped. Then it was over.

She tried the soup first and next tasted the sandwich while he dug into his burger and fries. He had to force himself not to inhale the food and slow down. Even taking his time, he finished before she'd gotten to the second half of her sandwich.

"Why did you leave with me?" he asked, needing to know what this was about for her. Whatever she needed—time, freedom, space, a new life—he wanted to make sure she got it.

Putting her sandwich down, she shrugged. "I wanted to make sure you got away safely and…" Her voice trailed off as she shifted, facing him. She cupped his cheeks in both hands, brushing his goatee with her thumbs. "I wasn't ready to say goodbye."

The scent of her—clean and sweet—tempted him to draw closer.

But she was the one to move in. She swallowed hard, then slid her hands into his damp hair. Pulled his head toward hers, taking his mouth in a tentative kiss—a ghosting of lips that sent his heart instantly throbbing.

He longed to curl his arms around her, sinking into the feel of her. To drag her against him, lie her down on the bed and plunder. He longed to touch her soft skin and find out if she smelled so good all over. Longed to see her eyes grow dark with desire and heavy with satisfaction.

He wanted her to be his.

But he held very still, absorbing her nearness, even though his body vibrated from the effort of holding back. This was more than an itch to be scratched. He'd scratched itches in the past and had been fulfilled.

This was different.

She was different.

Finally, his better sense took over. Rocco broke the kiss and lowered her hands away from him. "I'm sorry. I can't."

She closed her eyes. "Why not?" Her voice was barely a whisper. She looked confused, ashamed and it made his heart hurt.

That moment of physical connection, as slight and tender as it had been, was more than enough spark to jump-start his engines. Swearing silently, he cursed that Charlie was right.

He'd thought about being with Mercy, like this, alone and away from the USD or the compound, but in his wildest dreams he never imagined he'd be the one saying *no*.

"Mercy, look at me." He waited until she'd opened her eyes, and he saw desperation tangled with raw yearning. "There are things I need to tell you."

Soberly, she nodded. "Just tell me."

He dreaded saying the words, knowing that she was going to hate him for it. "I'm an agent with the Bureau of Alcohol, Tobacco, Firearms and Explosives. I used you to get onto the compound to investigate your father and the Shining Light."

Chapter Ten

Unable to breathe, Mercy listened to the jarring words tumbling out of Rocco's mouth. The more he said, referring to her as an *asset*—talking about ghost arms, explosives, something horrible happening on the full moon—the stronger the brutal sensation inside her, like she had walked unsuspecting into the street and a truck had slammed into her, shattering every bone and breaking her heart into a million pieces.

He stopped talking. Or had finished.

It was quiet in the room for a long time. But everything hadn't quite penetrated. She couldn't move. Couldn't speak.

He stepped forward into her space, the delicious smell of him strengthening, and her body tightened to guard against it. "Mercy, are you all right?"

She blinked once. Hot tears streaked down her face.

He reached for her. She scurried back and to her feet. Moving away from him, she kept shuffling in retreat until her spine was pressed into a corner. "None of it was real. Everything you told me was a lie."

Rocco got up. "What I feel for you is real. It has been since I first laid eyes on you." Blowing out a heavy breath, he raked a hand through his hair and paced around the room.

She cataloged the breadth of his shoulders, the damp strands at the nape of his neck, the way the tendons in his forearms shifted. She felt so much for him that she'd endangered herself to spare him any pain.

While she meant nothing to him. He'd only been using her. To betray her family.

"I omitted more than I lied, but so much of what I've told you is the truth," he said. "You have to understand why I couldn't be transparent."

"Because you think we're domestic terrorists."

She'd let him into the compound, shared their secrets, showed him they were peaceful and only interested in making the world a better place and the entire time her father had been justified in not trusting him.

"I don't think that you or most of the people in your commune are."

Horror filled her at the implication. "But my father?"

"What does he need with all those weapons?"

"To protect us. From people like you. In the event one day you decide to attack us."

"Don't lump me in with every other agent." His voice turned gentle and his eyes pleading. "There are laws preventing such a thing. The task force would never lay siege to the compound without just cause."

Oh, no. There was a whole task force? "Tell that to all the people who didn't make it out of the Waco massacre." The siege left seventy-five people dead, including women and children.

Rocco shook his head. His frustration was stamped on his face. "Agents had a legitimate search and arrest warrant that they attempted to serve," he said, and she rolled her eyes. "Mistakes were made in Waco. Agencies have studied it, learned from it. No one wants a repeat of that tragedy." He eased closer. "I would never let something like that happen on my watch. I swear it."

"What do you want from me?"

"We need to know who the Shining Light's weapons supplier is and what your father has planned in two days when there's a full moon."

All his questions about the moon and what it meant came rushing back to her. "There's nothing planned besides the shedding ceremony." When Alex would shed gray and don white. When any grievances, ill feelings or hidden transgressions would be released in exchange for the Light's favor. "I've already told you that."

"You're Empyrean's daughter. You must know something," he said so harshly that she jumped. A look crossed his face as if he regretted it. "Please, tell me what you know."

This was like a bad dream. She couldn't believe this was happening. "My father would never hurt people."

"An informant of mine died in my arms. The last thing he told me was that your father is behind whatever is about to happen. Please try and think. You must know something that can help stop it and save innocent lives."

A sickening feeling welled inside her. "Don't you think that if I knew about an attack my father was planning that I would do everything in my power to prevent it?"

His features softened. "Of course I do. But there is a plan for something big, something awful to happen that day."

She shook her head. "I don't know anything about that."

"What about the weapons?"

"My father and Alex handle all the purchases." She was kept in the dark about so much, too much, for so long. "I don't know who the supplier is."

"Where does the money come from? To pay for it all?"

Mercy wrapped her arms around her stomach. "My father started the Shining Light with his own money. From a trust fund. It's how he bought the land and had the facilities built. When people choose to become Starlights, they sign over their worldly possessions to the commune. Most of the time, people come to us with nothing."

"But there are some who come to you with quite a lot."

Lowering her head, she said, "Yes." She had questioned her father about how some novices had been recruited. Almost as though their wealthy families had been targeted for showing a weakness that the great Empyrean could exploit. Promises of saving a wayward teen, cleaning up an addict, taking someone drowning in darkness and turning them to the light was powerful. But combined with her father's charismatic personality, it was priceless.

She'd seen him at work firsthand.

The answers he'd given her had been lies. She wasn't blind or silent to the imperfections of their commune, or her father, but that didn't make them terrorists.

"There must be a money trail," Rocco said.

"I was never given access to any accounts or documentation showing how much there is or where it all goes." God, she didn't even have her own bank account. She'd had to beg her father to pay for training sessions at the USD. "What are you going to do now? Issue a warrant to go through my father's computer? Seize his bank accounts?"

"No. It doesn't work like that." He scrubbed a hand over his face. "There's no legal basis for one, and even if there was, it would take time that we don't have. Maybe if I can track down the supplier, whoever it is might know what's in the works. If they sold your father explosives, he might have mentioned what it was going to be used for."

May the Light help me...and guide Rocco.

After everything she'd told him, he still believed that her father was capable of masterminding a deadly act of terrorism.

"How are you going to find the supplier?" That might be the only way to vindicate her father and protect the compound.

"The Devil's Warriors."

The outlaw motorcycle club?

All her emotions seesawed from anger to concern. For Rocco. "They're dangerous. Violent." The commune had a former gang member, Shawn. He had been looking to escape the never-ending cycle of brutality. To this day, the horrific things he'd shared sickened and terrified her. "You can't go to them," she said, stepping out of the corner toward him.

He plunked down on one of the beds. Resting his elbows on his thighs, he dropped his head in his hands. "It's my last option."

Her heart squeezed tight in her chest. "You were almost dosed and beaten on the compound because you got caught snooping around." She sat on the other bed opposite him. "If you go to those vicious monsters asking about their supplier, they'll kill you."

"I'm not used to assimilating in places like the compound. But a deadly biker gang?" He shrugged. "I'm used to dangerous territory. That's different."

Was it?

Getting a person to lower their guard took patience and time. Months in her case for her to feel at ease sharing with him, confiding in him, trusting him. Falling for him.

He must have pushed too hard and too fast on the compound for her father to react the way he had. With time running out, only two days left, why wouldn't he take the same approach with the Devil's Warriors?

He was going to get himself hurt. Or killed. Despite her anger and disappointment with him, something inside her broke, thinking of that possibility.

"I bet you're kicking yourself for wasting too much time

on me," she said, "since I turned out to be useless." *Empyrean's daughter.* Rocco had probably thought he'd struck gold.

What a sad joke.

He raised his head, his serious eyes meeting hers. "Don't ever call yourself that. And getting to know you was *not* a waste of my time. I only wish it could've been on a more honest basis from the beginning." He scooted forward until his knees pressed against hers. "What I feel for you is real."

"What *do* you feel?"

"Way more than I should that erases any professional line."

"That doesn't tell me much."

He lowered his gaze and clenched his jaw.

"Why did you kiss me back at the tunnel? Was it so that I would go with you? Because you wanted to interrogate me?"

He shook his head. "No. I kissed you without thinking." He glanced up at her. "I asked you to come with me because…"

She wrung her hands, desperate for him to say something to mend the broken pieces of her heart. "Because of what?"

"I didn't want to let you go."

"And lose your asset?"

He slid his palm over both her hands, his warm fingers giving them a slight squeeze. "In that moment, I didn't see an asset. Only a woman I've fallen for. A woman who makes me feel things that no one else ever has. A woman I didn't want to say goodbye to." There was no filter on his expression. He looked stripped bare.

She wanted to believe him. Truly she did. But he had told her more lies than she could count. *For months!*

He had used her and maybe he wasn't done yet. It was possible there was another angle she couldn't see. How could she trust anything he said until after the full moon eclipse when he no longer suspected anyone on the commune of being a domestic terrorist? And even then, she'd always be wondering what he was hiding, what he wasn't saying.

She stood and walked around to the other side of the bed and pulled down the covers. "I'm tired." A bone-deep weariness was trickling through her, making her limbs suddenly feel heavy. She glanced at the clock on the nightstand and couldn't believe how late it was.

"I can ask Charlie to stay here with you tonight. If you'd prefer."

Mercy stiffened at the idea. Did he want to get away from her now that she had no information to offer? "Did she know that you were using me this whole time?"

"No. She found out tonight."

That made her feel a little better. About Charlie anyway. "You can call her if it would be easier for you. I don't want to make you uncomfortable by forcing you to stay." She climbed into the bed, pulling the covers up over herself and stared at him.

"I want to be with you, Mercy. I've never wanted anything more."

There was silence for a long moment that seemed to grow deeper with each pounding beat of her heart.

His chest heaved as he turned from her. She watched him clean up the food on the floor and throw away the trash. He picked up her canvas shoes that were covered in muck and went into the bathroom.

When he emerged a short while later, carrying her sneakers, they were spotless.

He set her shoes on the vent of the air-conditioning unit. Put the chain on the door. Turned out the light. Trudged to the other bed. Put the holstered gun on the nightstand and lay down on top of the covers.

She looked at Rocco, who was staring at the ceiling with

his hands tucked behind his head, and then at her shoes again. Cleaning them was a small gesture, minuscule in the great scheme of things, but for some reason it touched her deeply.

FOR WHAT SEEMED like hours, Mercy had been tossing and turning. She flopped onto her side. Her gaze slid to the clock. It actually had been hours. Three, to be exact.

She was fatigued, no doubt about that, but she wasn't sure why she couldn't fall asleep.

Maybe it was the foreign environment. The odd smell in the room. The itchy sheets. The mattress that countless others had slept on. The clothes that weren't hers.

Perhaps it was Rocco's betrayal that was like a hot knife in her chest.

Or maybe it was that he was only a couple of feet away, sprawled in a bed, and she wasn't touching him. Her opportunities to do so had been few and far between before and were dwindling with each passing hour.

She had no idea what tomorrow might hold, or even if his feelings for her were genuine. But everything she felt for him and wanted with him was real.

Mercy had spent her entire life worrying about others, their thoughts, their feelings, their expectations, their needs, their wants.

What about her desires?

Why shouldn't she be selfish for once and only think about herself?

No thoughts of the commune. Of her father. Of the ATF. Of the full moon. Of the transgression of sleeping with a nonbeliever.

She wanted to take what she needed on her own terms. This might be her last chance.

Biting her lower lip, she wondered if Rocco was awake.

He hadn't moved. He was still on his back, hands clasped behind his head.

She peeled back the covers, slipped out of the bed and climbed onto his.

Propping himself up on his elbows, he looked at her. "What are you doing?"

Slowly, she lowered her head to his, giving him time to pull away. But he didn't. He watched her intently as he leaned in, and then she kissed him. Tentatively. Testing to see if he'd reject her.

Rocco shifted, easing away, and something in her chest sank to her stomach. "What do you want, Mercy?" he asked, his voice soft, almost sweet, as he caressed her cheek.

The words rose in her throat and stuck there.

When she brought Rocco to the compound, she had hoped that he would stay there with her or that she would eventually leave with him, but that they would be together. As a couple. That she would finally feel all the passion and pleasure that she'd only experienced through reading about it in books. *The English Patient. Madame Bovary. Sula. Ulysses. Atonement.*

Although most of them didn't have happy endings. It looked as if her story with Rocco wouldn't either.

But she could make the most of the here and now. "I want you." More than she'd wanted any man she'd ever met.

"Today has been a roller coaster of emotions for you. In a few days, if you still want to, then—"

Mercy pressed her lips to his, silencing him. She didn't know if she'd be able to look at him tomorrow without feeling a rush of anger. Much less in a few days. She didn't know if she'd be in town or on the compound. All she knew for certain was that she had to do everything in her power to protect the commune. From him.

"Tonight," she said. "Unless you don't want this."

Don't want me.

"No, that's not the problem. Rest assured, I want you very much." He sighed. "I just don't want you to do anything you'll regret."

"Too late for that." She pulled her shirt over her head and slipped off the leggings, baring herself to him. "But I want this." She'd fantasized about being with him. So many times. She wondered if her fantasies outnumbered his lies. For now, one outweighed the other. She wouldn't let anger rob her of this joy, this simple pleasure—feeling good in his arms. "My turn to use you."

The words slipped out without thinking, sounding cruel, which wasn't like her.

But he sat up, his gaze raking over her, and gave her a grim smile. "I'm happy to be used by you anytime."

He took her mouth in what began as a simple kiss, but quickly heated when she wrapped her arms around his neck. He lay her down, resting her head on a pillow.

"You're insanely pretty." His words flowed like warm honey over her bruised feelings.

Coming from him, it didn't strike her as a line, but rather a sincere compliment, one that maybe he'd ordinarily be unwilling to give. Still, she reminded herself he wasn't the most honest person.

"The first time I saw you," he said, his breath brushing her lips, "I thought you looked like an angel."

Well, at the moment, she was feeling less than angelic. She spread her legs, opening to him. The solid weight of his body on her was divine. Even better was the feel of the bulge hardening between his thighs.

With one hand, she gripped the back of his neck, the other clutching his shirt. She ached to have him out of his clothes.

As if reading her mind, he pulled off his T-shirt and settled back between her parted legs, that hard bulge resting against her softness. She couldn't stop her hips from rolling against him.

"Turn on the light," she said. "I need to see you." So that she could brand this night on her mind, to warm her in the days ahead.

No matter what happened, no one would be able to take away her memory of this.

He reached over and switched on the lamp. She ran her fingertips through the hair on his chest, over his shoulder, tracing the lines of his tribal tattoo.

God, he's a beautiful one.

The most gorgeous man she'd ever known.

He sucked in a breath when her seeking fingers dipped into his sweatpants and under his boxer briefs. She closed her fingers around the thick, rigid length of him.

"Mercy," he rasped, pulling her hand back. Placing his forearms on either side of her head, he kissed her throat up to her jaw, sending sweet shivers over her skin. "Do you like that?" His voice was huskier with an edge of gravelly heat.

"Yes." Humming, she arched her body, pressing her breasts against his bare chest, exposing the line of her throat.

His hips jerked, a groan rumbling in his chest. Abruptly, he stopped and leaned over. He unzipped his bag and pulled out a box of condoms, setting them on the nightstand.

She brought his lips back to hers for a hot, steamy rush. Her entire body ached, wanting the contact, the warmth and passion he offered.

"More." Her voice was a rough whisper. "You feel so good. I want to feel you everywhere."

He brushed her mouth with tender kisses, nibbling her jaw, licking her throat, teasing her chest, rolling his tongue around her nipple. On a throaty sigh, she closed her eyes.

"What do you want?" he asked, his breath warm on her breast before closing over her mouth once more.

The deep, thunderous kiss, the roll of his hips, the graze of thick cotton against her soft skin ignited her body so quickly she feared she might burst in a flash of flame.

She spread her hands over his skin, caressing him with a slow reverence that squeezed another guttural groan from him when they came up for air. "I want you. Inside me."

His head popped up. His lips curved wryly. "Tell me what you like?"

"I—I don't know."

Realization flickered in his eyes. "Is this your first time?"

If telling him the truth meant that he'd stop, then she was willing to lie, lie, lie.

"It's important for me to know," he said.

"Yes. But I don't want you to stop."

"I won't. I just…need to slow this down."

While she was ready to rush headlong into it. Her body screaming with need that demanded to be fulfilled. "I don't want you to go slow."

"Believe me when I say that you do. We need to explore a bit. Make sure you enjoy every second. I want to give you the sweetest pleasure."

Sounded good to her. It was the least he could do. "Yes. Please, yes."

He pulled her to him, the kiss primal, absolutely raw and hot.

All her thoughts melted away. There was only him and desire and greed, tangled in her need to have his hands on her. His mouth. *Having* him…any way that she could.

He slipped his hand between her legs, his fingers caressing her, working to open her, and sent her desire soaring. She writhed helplessly, swept up in a wave of wild hunger that overwhelmed her completely, that she had no idea how to satisfy. His strokes were gentle and confident, brushing, teasing over and over at that part of her that was most sensitive.

She turned liquid, molding to the hard contours of his body. Pleasure was an ocean she wanted to drown in. Flooded with breathless sensation and something close to euphoria, she wasn't sure she'd survive it, or if she wanted to. Then he took her even higher, even deeper, at the very same time. The swell built, the pressure mounting, aching for release. With every breath, every caress, she felt herself, every responsibility, every anchor in her life slipping away. A bittersweet riptide of ecstasy inundated her, reducing her to mindlessness as she came apart in his arms—the first time.

Chapter Eleven

They were a tangle of limbs. All heat and a slow, desperate need that threatened to snap his self-control. He had touched every inch of her exposed skin and she had done likewise, with no hint of shyness. She was a woman on a mission. And he was a man seeking forgiveness with his mouth, his tongue, his fingers, every body part that brought her pleasure.

At last, when he couldn't hold on to his restraint any longer, he gave into his release. She quivered around him again, her nails digging into his back. He groaned at how incredible she felt. Tight, wet, heat. Shuddering, he dropped his face to her neck. Kissed her pulse.

His heart hammered, his breath shallow. Rolling off her, he put his head back on the pillow, drugged with satisfaction. He brought her against his side, nestling her into the crook of his shoulder.

She was perfect. Lean, soft and supple. She'd been so open. So responsive, as if drinking in his touch. Without even trying, she pulled something from him, a tenderness he'd never shown to anyone else. Being with her exceeded his wildest fantasy. Like she'd been made for him.

He'd never made love to anyone like that, feeding off the sight of her in the throes of pleasure, happy to bask in sensation and teeter on the edge. A sweet, terrible form of torture.

Every detail of her pressed close to him struck new chords of desire in him: the lithe lines of her body, the tempting curve of her breasts, the sunny blond hair that spilled over his chest, catching the light like liquid gold. And most of all, her beautiful face.

Before he'd fully caught his breath, she disentangled herself from him, slipped out of bed and padded toward the bathroom. Every movement was graceful and careful like a cat finding her way across slippery, uneven ground.

The door closed. The toilet flushed. Water ran.

He discarded the used condom in the trash bin, double-checked the chain on the door and crawled into bed.

Minutes later, she came out, but didn't meet his eyes. She climbed into the other bed, switched off the lamp and turned her back to him.

An odd pressure churned in his chest.

"Mercy…" His voice failed him, his brain staggering at his inability to come up with the right words. He thought she'd get back into bed with him. That she'd want to be held. Or talk. "Are you sore?" he asked in concern, remembering how delicate she was, how tight. He'd done his best to tamp down his urges and go slowly, gently, so as not to cause her any pain. "Mercy, are you okay?"

"Thank you for giving me what I wanted."

To be thanked felt odd. *Wrong.*

He waited for her to say more. When she didn't, he assumed it was because she was still upset with him despite what had just transpired between them. With a hot stab in the pit of his stomach, he said, "I'm sorry I didn't trust you with the truth sooner. I never meant to hurt you. If I could go back and handle it differently, I would."

But then he realized that if he had told her he was an

ATF agent that night in USD, after her panic attack, he still would've driven her away.

"I'm tired," she said. "Good night."

The knot behind his sternum tightened and spread. Tendrils of anxiety coiled through him like choking vines.

He'd never be able to separate the months of lies from all the moments of honesty.

As a consequence, he feared losing her for good.

WHEN ROCCO AWAKENED the next morning, he was unsure of the time, a rarity for him. The situation didn't look any better in the light of day. If anything, things were worse.

They got ready in silence. She wasn't being modest, not hiding her body, but they had moved around each other, with her going to great pains to avoid any physical contact. He took her cue and kept his distance.

Not knowing how long they might need the room he didn't check out. They climbed into Charlie's muscle car. He brought the engine roaring to life. "We can stop and grab breakfast," he suggested as he pulled out of the lot.

With her arms crossed, she stared out the window. "I'm not hungry."

"Then we can get some coffee at a café and talk."

"Before you hand me off to my next babysitter?"

He swallowed a sigh. At least she was talking to him. "Do you want to discuss what happened last night?"

"We had sex. What else is there to say?"

It had been more than that for him, and he'd suspected, with it being her first time, that it had been more to her as well. "How you're feeling for starters?"

"Angry. Betrayed. Confused." She shifted in her seat. "Satisfied?"

Not even close.

"Where are we going?" she asked.

"To task force headquarters. Really, it's just office space on Second Street. I have to meet with my boss, and another agent, one with the FBI, Becca Hammond, will want to speak with you."

Her eyes grew wide. "Why?"

"It's standard procedure. There's nothing for you to worry about."

Frown lines bracketed her mouth. "If I'm going to be interrogated again, this time by a stranger, I'd rather go someplace familiar. Like the Underground Self-Defense school."

He shook his head. "It would be safer and more convenient to take you to headquarters. And you won't be interrogated. Only questioned."

"Am I under arrest?"

"No, of course not."

"Then if you want me to speak with your FBI friend, we'll do it on my terms, at the USD. Or we won't do it at all."

He didn't like it, but he'd already put her through so much. Allowing her to choose the location where she'd speak with Becca was a small request. There were no windows in the office at USD. If she was in there with the door closed, then she'd be kept out of sight, mitigating any issues. "Okay. USD it is."

More uneasy silence settled between them, and he hated it. "You must have questions. About me. About my job."

Her gaze met his, those blue eyes piercing him. "Is Rocco Sharp even your real name?"

"Yes and no. It's Rocco Kekoa. Sharp is my mother's maiden name. I started using it as part of my cover when I was assigned to the task force."

"Your time in the military and special ops?"

"All true. Enlisted in the army at eighteen. Served for ten

years, including two tours in Afghanistan and a spec op mission in Syria."

"What about your childhood, growing up with Charlie on a ranch in Hawaii, wrangling longhorn cattle?"

"Those are some of my fondest memories." He came from a long line of paniolos, or Hawaiian cowboys. "When work slows down for me, I'm going to fix up my ranch here and get some horses just like I told you."

"The story about falling out of a tree and breaking your arm? The fights you got into with bullies?"

He knew he deserved her suspicion and welcomed her questions, but it didn't make it any easier.

"It really happened." He'd shared things with her that he'd never told anyone else. Had spilled the stories that made him who he was in their first few days together and he wasn't sure why. It hadn't been done as a maneuver to manipulate her. Maybe it was how she made him feel…at ease, like it was safe to be himself. She had such a generous heart. Maybe that was it.

She stilled his usually restless mind. Filled the spaces he hadn't known were empty with warmth and light.

Whatever it was, he wanted more. He wanted her. So much so that he'd do whatever was necessary to rebuild her trust. Prove how deeply he felt for her.

"I enjoyed our time together at USD. Looked forward to it. You have to believe me when I tell you that I care about you." Regardless of his job, after her panic attack, he wouldn't have let her go back to the compound alone. He recognized it as her survival instinct kicking in, a sign she needed help, even if she didn't realize it.

"How long have you been watching us?" she asked, ignoring him.

"The task force stood up a little over a year ago."

"Why *us*?"

There were multiple factors, but he'd give her the main ones. "Your numbers have grown really fast. Along with your stockpile of weapons. Your father has successfully converted over five hundred people, more than half that number in the last four years, convincing them to change their names, to hand over their possessions and to live in a secluded, heavily armed compound." The Shining Light had amassed nearly two thousand weapons, including automatic and assault rifles, shotguns, revolvers, and his task force had reports of grenades and other explosives, though Rocco hadn't seen those. Still, Marshall McCoy had a small army at his disposal. "It's a disaster waiting to happen."

She inhaled a shaky breath and shook her head. "You still think my commune is a threat?"

"I think your father is. He's a dangerous man, wielding a lot of power," he said, and she stiffened as she looked away from him. He was only sending her defenses into overdrive. He needed to tread carefully. "I have seen the good things happening on the compound. How happy everyone appears. How much they love being on the compound. How you look out for one another."

"Like any decent community should." She bit her lower lip. "If you were able to find the weapons supplier and prevent whatever tragedy is supposed to happen tomorrow, would your task force leave us alone?"

His brain stuck on her use of *your* and *us*. Neither was a good sign. "Do you know something?"

"No. I was just wondering if it's worth it for you to risk your life by messing with the Devil's Warriors."

Risking his life by infiltrating such groups was his job, but he didn't think telling her that would improve things.

He pulled into the lot behind USD and parked. "I'll do

whatever is necessary to stop the illegal shipment of weapons across state lines and save lives."

She fixed him with a stare. "Does that include telling me more lies?"

Shutting off the engine, he turned in his seat, facing her. "I will never lie to you again."

She narrowed her eyes and chewed on her lip. "You didn't answer my question. If you got what you needed, would you leave the Shining Light alone?"

"It's not my call to make," he said, and she grimaced. "But what I can tell you is that I didn't see anything to justify a warrant." If he had found explosives, or if they had assaulted him, drugged him or used ayahuasca outside of religious purposes, then that would have been a different story. "Any cooperation from the Shining Light would go a long way to establishing goodwill with law enforcement."

"I could speak to my father."

That was a horrible idea.

Mercy was a direct threat to her father's autocratic power. After she helped Rocco escape, Marshall would do anything to bring his daughter to heel.

"You're out. I don't think you should see or talk to anyone from the commune until you're sure about what you want to do."

She'd gotten a taste of true freedom. Once he and Charlie spoon-fed her more, showed Mercy the community they had forged, where they also took care of each other, she wouldn't want to go back.

He was certain of it.

Lowering her head, unease moved across her face.

"Do you believe I care about you?" he asked. "That my feelings are real?"

She shrugged.

How could he convince her? "What would it take?"

"Time. Seeing proof through your actions."

"Then, *please*, give me time. I'm begging you." And he was not the kind of man who *ever* begged. He peered closer, trying to draw her gaze to his, but she wouldn't look at him. He wanted to hug her, hold her, make love to her until she forgave him. But he didn't dare touch her. "Will you?"

ALL MERCY COULD tell him was the truth. "I don't know."

He looked out the window at the back door to USD.

He glanced over at her. "Come on." They got out of the car. "Listen to Brian. Do whatever he asks. He'll keep you safe while I'm gone."

"Don't tell me that he's a part of your task force, too," she said, half-joking.

"Actually, he is. But he's Laramie PD. It's because of the task force that we became such good friends."

For some reason, those facts made her even more uneasy.

Rocco fiddled with the keys and unlocked the back door. After they stepped inside, he turned the bolt, locking it behind them. They walked down a corridor, passing the bathroom and entered the main front space.

Charlie was in the middle of teaching a class. Brian stood off to the side with his hands clasped. An LPD cruiser was parked out front.

When Brian spotted them, he came over. "Good morning. Why don't we talk in the office?" He led the way.

They stepped inside and Rocco shut the door.

"Anything?" Brian asked.

"Afraid not. I'm going to update Nash, and I gave Mercy a heads-up about Becca."

With a grim look, Brian nodded.

"Good idea to have a couple of uniforms posted out front," Rocco said.

"The visual makes a nice deterrent."

"My father wouldn't send anyone after me," Mercy said. "It's a waste of resources."

"Would you give us a minute?" Rocco asked Brian, and his friend left them alone in the office. "You underestimate your dad. He'd do anything to keep you under his yoke."

"He wouldn't kidnap me and drag me back. I'm not an escaped prisoner." Although she felt like one.

"No, he'd only manipulate you into a courtship with a man you don't want, in front of your entire commune. And that's after years of his machinations to prevent you from claiming *penumbroyage*. But you really think he's above sending Alex or someone else to haul you back?"

"Yes." She tried to picture it. Bound and gagged and tossed into a vehicle like a hostage. Her father's methods were never so crude. He operated with far more finesse.

Over the years, whenever he'd gotten her to fall into line, he'd always managed to make her feel as if it was her own choice. She saw him clearly, for what he was. A master puppeteer, pulling everyone's strings.

Maybe the immense power of being a prophet had corrupted him.

That little voice in her head whispered to her. *The Light can illuminate. But it can also blind.*

She still believed in the commune and always would. But she was ready for a change. To choose her own path. To get out from under her father's thumb.

To be free.

"I hope you're right and those officers parked outside turn out to be a waste of resources," Rocco said.

"You don't need to worry about me. You should worry about yourself if you're still planning to go to the Devil's Warriors."

"The odds are high that they use the same weapons supplier as the Shining Light. It's our best bet at this point."

It would take time to track down the supplier and once Rocco did—if that gang hadn't hurt or killed him—it would be too late. The full moon was tomorrow.

She didn't think her father was a terrorist, but she also couldn't dismiss an informant directly linking him to whatever was going to happen.

"I may be angry enough to strangle you, but I don't want anything bad to happen to you."

"Oh, I see, you want the pleasure of doing it yourself." His mouth hitched in a sexy grin. "How about when you're in the mood to *use* me again, I let you tie me down so you can have your way with me."

She couldn't believe he was making a joke at a time like this.

His eyes trailed from her face down over her body. His gaze was like a caress, her skin igniting as if it were his fingers doing the work. Awareness sizzled between them, almost as if a fuse had been lit in the silence.

Yet, he made no move to touch her. He hadn't all morning, which she realized was because she'd given him the cold shoulder. Nonetheless, it irritated her.

As absurd as it sounded, she wanted to be so irresistible to him that he had no choice but to touch her.

"I never said there'd be a next time."

His grin fell, his eyes sobering. "I don't deserve you, Mercy McCoy. You're too good for me." He cupped her arm, his grip gentle and firm, as he leaned over and kissed her forehead. "But if you don't give me a chance to show you what you mean to me, I'll regret it until the day I die."

He enveloped her in a gentle hug. Everything about it had her struggling to ignore her bone-deep awareness of him. The feel of his powerful body against hers. The delicious, masculine scent of him. How safe and protected his embrace made her feel.

How right it felt, even though her mind screamed that it was wrong.

Then he let her go and left.

Closing her eyes, she took a steady breath, trying to push aside her complex and unsettling feelings for him. She couldn't afford to be fooled again. But despite telling herself not to believe him, she did. He'd spoken so fervently, as though the words had been from the heart.

It could've been an act. He could be playing you again.

Deep down, she wanted Rocco to be the man she'd thought he was.

Even though last night had been her first time, the depths of affection and consideration he'd showered on her exceeded lust.

He hadn't had sex with her. He'd made love to her. With every kiss, every touch, she'd felt cherished. Their bodies had reflected everything given, everything shared as they had joined as one. She'd felt his strength and gentleness, for a moment, possibly even his soul.

And that made his betrayal sting like acid, below the skin, down to her blood.

Getting close to her had been his duty. His assignment.

Which reminded her that she had a duty as well. To the commune and all the innocent people who called it home.

Brian came into the office, pulling her from her thoughts, and she knew what she had to do next with staggering clarity.

"Can I get you anything?" he asked. "Coffee? Tea? A magazine?"

"We didn't eat breakfast. Would you mind getting me something from Delgado's?"

"Sure. Do you know what you want?"

"Anything vegetarian." Not that she was hungry.

"They've got tasty breakfast burritos. Eggs, beans, avocado—"

"Sounds perfect."

He picked up the phone and placed the order. "It'll take twenty minutes. Since it's under their delivery minimum, I'll run down the block to pick it up when it's ready."

"Thank you. And you know what, I will take a magazine on second thought."

Brian grabbed a stack from the table near the entrance and set it down on the desk in the office. They all dealt with fitness.

"Is it okay if I had some time to myself, to process my thoughts? Everything that Rocco told me is still quite a shock."

"Of course. I won't disturb you until I've got your breakfast." He went to the threshold and stopped. "When you're feeling up to it, Charlie wants to talk to you about your options here in town. No pressure or anything. Rocco isn't the only one here for you. Charlie, me and others you haven't met yet will help you make a transition. We just want you to know that you're not alone."

After everything, somehow that was the thing to bring her closest to tears.

"Thank you."

He left the office, shutting the door behind him.

Mercy sat down at the desk, found a notepad and pen. She wrote a quick note to explain her decision to Rocco.

Looking it over, she knew the words wouldn't be enough, but it was the best she could do. Then she picked up the phone and dialed the number to her father's office.

The line rang and rang. She prayed she wouldn't have to call Alex to reach him.

On the sixth ring, her father answered, "Hello."

"It's me. Mercy."

Silence. Deliberate. Calculated, surely.

"I knew you'd call," he said. "I foresaw it. Are you hurt?"

"I'm fine."

"That's not true. I can hear it in your voice. Your heart is hurting."

This was what he did, each and every time. Crawled inside her head.

Had he foreseen this? Could he hear it? Her pain, her confusion, her concern.

"I need someone to pick me up." They both knew who that someone would be. She almost asked that it *not* be Alex, but he wouldn't send anyone else and that might work to her advantage.

"Certainly, my dear."

"It has to be in less than twenty minutes. The parking lot behind USD."

"As you wish."

She hung up the phone and glanced at the clock on the wall.

Heart hammering in her chest, she jumped to her feet, hurried to the door and cracked it open. She peeked out.

The hour-long self-defense class was still going on and would continue for almost another half hour. Brian stood near the front door like a sentinel, his head on a swivel as though he was scanning the street.

She moved back and sat where she could see through the slight opening in the door. Thumbing through a magazine, she kept an eye on the time and on Brian.

Sweat trickled down her spine. Her thoughts spun. Was this a mistake?

She shook off the doubt and ignored her jittering nerves.

This was the only way. If her gamble didn't work, then the commune would remain under the scrutiny of law enforcement. The Shining Light would be blamed if something horrible happened tomorrow.

And Rocco...

He could be hurt.

This was a calculated risk. The stakes were too high not to take it.

Brian grabbed his cowboy hat and placed it on his head. He gestured something to Charlie. She nodded in response. Once he pushed through the front door, Mercy was on her feet.

She sucked in a deep breath. Made sure the note was in the center of the desk, where it would be easily seen. Hustled to the door.

Crossing the main workout area, she caught Charlie's eye and mouthed *bathroom*. Through the front window she watched Brian say something to the police officers in the squad car before he headed down the street.

Mercy turned down the hall. Stealing a furtive glance over her shoulder, she passed the bathroom. No one was behind her. She ran to the back door, flipped the latch on the bolt and shoved outside.

Alex sat behind the wheel of a black SUV, waiting for her. She scurried to the rear door and grabbed the handle, but it was locked.

He lowered the window. "Sit up front with me," he said, cocking his arm on the back of the seat, staring at her. "The rules have changed."

Anger whipped through her, hot as a lash, but she pushed it aside. She needed to focus on her objective and not let anything sidetrack her from achieving it.

She hopped into the front seat. Before she closed the door,

he sped off. He turned onto the side street, Garfield. At the stop sign, he made a right on the main road, Third Street.

He glanced down at the jeans that she wore, but he didn't comment on them. Not that he needed to. The twist of his mouth and narrowing of his eyes told her plenty. He drove right past USD and the patrol car.

She gave one last look at Charlie instructing the class.

"Yesterday, Empyrean told me that you'd be back," he said. "But for the first time in my life, I doubted him."

She looked at Alex, her gaze falling to his Shining Light tattoo at the base of his throat. He had always been a true believer. Devout to the core.

"Is there something planned for tomorrow?" she asked.

"The shedding ceremony. You know that."

Out the window, she spotted Brian leaving Delgado's, holding the breakfast that she would never eat. She didn't bother ducking down. They were gone too quickly, heading out of downtown.

"No, something else that's been kept quiet," she said, hoping to learn what she needed to from him, sparing her from dealing with her father.

All he had to do was fill in the missing pieces to Rocco's puzzle for her. Then she was prepared to open the door and jump from a moving vehicle to avoid going back.

Alex raised an eyebrow. "Like what?"

"Something awful. Something violent."

He gave her a questioning glance and she saw it in his eyes. He had no clue what she was talking about. She could always read him like an open book.

"My father is grooming you to succeed him. He shares a lot with you."

"Because he trusts me."

Which in turn meant she wasn't fully trusted. It was the only explanation as to why she was kept in the dark.

She reached over and put her hand on his forearm. He glanced down at the point of contact.

"You're happy that I'm coming back, aren't you?"

"Of course." His mouth lifted in a bright smile that shone through his eyes.

"Do you want to make me happy?"

"Yes. Any good husband wants to please his wife."

Her stomach twisted at messing with his emotions. "I want you to tell me who supplies us with weapons."

"What?" He stiffened.

"Just give me a name."

He stared at her, the cloud of disbelief lifting from his face, and snatched his arm away. "You're asking me this because of *him*. Aren't you?" He barked a vicious laugh. "Even if I knew, I wouldn't tell you after the stunt you pulled yesterday." Swerving off the road onto the shoulder, he slammed on the brakes and threw the car into Park. He turned and glared at her. "You've never taken my affection for you seriously. But you need to because I'd rather see you dead than living in darkness with that man." His eyes burned with a fury she'd never seen in him before. "Do you understand me?"

She swallowed around the cold lump of fear in her throat. "I understand."

All too well. She was never going to marry Alex, so when it came to his *love* for her, it boiled down to kill or be killed.

But he was a problem that had to wait.

Pulling off with squealing tires, Alex hit the gas pedal, racing toward the compound.

Her heart sank.

If her father had trusted anyone with the name of the arms

dealer and details about any heinous event that he was either aware of or had in the works, then it would've been Alex.

That left her with no other choice.

She had to return to the compound and ask her father for help. He would give it after a performance full of melo-drama designed to saddle her with guilt. But it would come at a heavy price that she'd have to pay.

Chapter Twelve

Seated at the conference table across from Nash and Becca, Rocco was going through his debriefing when his cell phone rang. This was hard enough without interruptions. Not looking to see who it was, he silenced the phone.

He took a breath, collecting his thoughts, chiding himself for his failure. "As I was saying—"

Nash's phone rang. Sighing, he took it out of his pocket. "It's Brian."

A cold fist gripped Rocco's gut. *Mercy.* "Put him on speaker."

Nash answered, "I'm here with Rocco and Becca. We're all on the line. What's up?"

"Mercy is gone."

Shoving up out of his chair, Rocco stood and pressed his palms to the solid wood table. "What do you mean? How is that possible?"

"I went to get her something to eat," Brian said. "While I was gone, she left."

Rocco struggled to understand. "You mean she was taken?"

"No." Brian sighed. "She walked out the back door."

Rocco blinked and the room spun.

"Any idea why she would leave?" Nash asked Brian. "Did something happen?"

"She left a note."

"Read it," Rocco snapped more harshly than he'd intended.

"'Dear Rocco, my father is the only one who can give you the answers you need in time. Stay away from the Devil's Warriors. Please trust me.'"

The words hit him like a sucker punch. Her questions about whether the task force would leave the Shining Light alone if they got what they needed suddenly made sense. She'd been planning to take off for the compound before he'd even left her at USD.

"If she's on foot," Rocco said, "you can catch her."

"I drove around in a five-block radius. No sign of her. I'm sure she got a ride."

Swearing under his breath, Rocco grabbed his phone and headed for the door.

"Wait," Becca said, stopping him. "She asked you to trust her. Running off to the compound and making a scene would be doing the exact opposite. Maybe you should let this play out. We can still use the time for alternative plans."

"To hell with that."

"Becca is right," Nash said. "She's already gone. Give her a chance to work on her father. If you haven't heard from her in a couple of hours, then we'll all go together. It won't take long to get to her."

MERCY PADDED INTO her father's office.

He got up from his chair. His gaze raked over her, lingering on her jeans, but he said nothing about her clothing. He came around and greeted her with a tight hug. "Oh, my dear child. Praise the Light for your return." He ushered her to the sofa by the windows. "Alex, leave us."

"Sir, I need to tell you—"

Her father waved him off. "It can wait. Mercy's well-being must come first."

"But, Empyrean—"

"Silence." Her father's tone sharpened, but he didn't raise his voice. "Her eternal soul hangs in the balance. Nothing you have to say is more important." He tsk-tsked him away as if Alex was a dog.

But that was how he treated them both, like pets.

Alex closed the door to the office behind him.

Her father guided her down onto the sofa and sat beside her. She clasped her hands in her lap, unsure of how to proceed.

He didn't ask any questions. Didn't goad. Didn't chastise. Didn't push. He simply put a big, warm palm over her folded hands. Staring at her, he remained silent, his gaze soft, his demeanor calm.

There was no atmosphere of pressure. If anything, his approach conveyed support. Love. He was the picture of a nurturing father.

Or the perfect predator laying a trap.

The silence grew, expanding, sucking up the air in the room until she couldn't breathe.

"I need your help," she finally said.

He nodded as though he'd expected the words. "I'm listening."

There were two ways she could play this. One was to be coy, to filter details, to break down in fake tears, asking for forgiveness.

But Empyrean was much better at this game.

So she went with the second option. The unvarnished truth.

She spilled her guts about everything—Rocco using her, that he was an ATF agent, the task force investigating the

Shining Light, needing the name of the weapons supplier, the dead informant in Rocco's arms, his last words about an act of domestic terrorism planned for tomorrow, that the commune would be scapegoats, that their community would suffer, that she would give anything to protect them and Rocco.

"Rocco is going to try to get information from the Devil's Warriors, but he's going to get hurt. Please. We have to stop this. Right now. Before it's too late."

Her father wasn't quick to respond. But when he finally opened his mouth, he asked, "Did you sleep with him?"

She hesitated, but he'd know if she lied. "Yes."

Another slow nod. The look on his face was almost one of relief. "Sometimes an itch needs to be scratched. Not knowing can be more powerful than the act itself. Our imaginations are so fantastical, running wild, filling in the blanks, over and over, in such colorful, lurid ways. While memories, ah, those are designed to fade. In time."

Her stomach clenched. "Out of everything I just told you, that's what you're focused on?"

His grip on her hands tightened. "Do you want to know why I could never pick you to succeed me to lead the commune?"

A dangerous question. But one she needed answered or she'd wonder for the rest of her life, with her imagination filling in the blanks. "Yes."

"When your mother left us, it was like you had one foot planted here, and one foot always reaching for the outside world as if to follow her. You questioned everything. Questioned me. Stopped truly believing. Her last words to you were 'the light can illuminate. But it can also blind.' And after that you never looked at me the same way. With reverence in your eyes."

Mercy's heart practically stopped. For years, she'd thought

her mother had died. She didn't have memories of her anymore. There were no pictures of her anywhere. She couldn't even remember what she looked like.

The little voice in her head, warning her, was her mother's.

"My mother left? Why? Is she still alive?" A flurry of questions stormed through her mind.

"Out of everything you told me, that's what you're focused on?" he asked, regurgitating her words, making her feel sick. "I thought time was of the essence to help Rocco. Would you prefer to talk about your mother instead?"

Mercy gritted her teeth, hating this game. Because he was so much better at it than she was.

MARSHALL KNEW WHAT his daughter's response would be, what she would choose. Or rather who.

Certainly not the mother she barely remembered.

All this time he thought Rocco was the problem when really, he was the solution to one. Marshall was at his wit's end about how to get Mercy to abandon her desire to leave and accept her role in the commune. There had been times when he'd gotten close to forcing her to take her vows to shed her former self and receive the tattoo. But he never did out of fear. A cold, stark fear that she might still leave. And if she did, after taking her vows, then he could never allow her to return. She would be considered forever lost to them. One of the *fallen.*

But now she would make the sacrifice of her own free will.

Thanks to a nonbeliever.

Once this was all said and done, he'd have to send Rocco a gift basket with some of their finest goods: produce, homemade soap and a jar of their lavender honey.

"In helping Rocco, we help the Shining Light," she said, and he couldn't tell if she was trying to convince him or herself. "We have to protect the commune. They're coming for us."

Hardly breaking news. "They've been coming for a while. They planted an informant in here."

Shock spilled across her face. "Do you know who?"

He gave her a knowing smile. "Sophia."

Mercy flinched. "You've known this whole time?"

"It's the reason I started sleeping with her. As soon as I did and she saw what her life could be, she told me everything. Confessed in my bed. Her handler was Becca Hammond. I had Sophia sever all contact and she did. I'm not surprised that they would stoop so low as to seduce you next, treating you like a tawdry pawn. They would cross any line, trample on hearts, tell any lie to achieve their aims."

She looked like she was going to retch.

"Can I get you a glass of water?" he asked.

Taking a deep breath, she shook her head.

"Do you still want to protect Rocco?"

Mercy lowered her eyes.

Out of shame, no doubt. The poor girl did want to protect him. Still.

What a disappointment.

"The only way to protect the commune," she said, "is to give his task force the name of our weapons supplier and help them stop whatever is planned for tomorrow. Do you know anything about that?"

"I *am* the prophet." He didn't know what was planned, but he did know who was planning the event. It would be big. Loud. And violent. In the end, the chaos and tragedy would increase their numbers. But first he had to protect and preserve what he already had. "I can be of service to this task force. But I need something from you first."

She grew still as stone. "What?"

The flames of rebellion had burned in her for far too long. The time had come for him to extinguish that fire.

"If I do this—if I help Rocco without delay—then you must agree to take your vows to the community and seal your union with Alex on a date of my choosing."

Mercy paled, all the blood draining from her lovely face. If only she could see that this was for her own good. Once she married Alex and had a child the rest would fall into place.

"The Light has spoken through me. What say you?" he asked.

Tears welled in her bright blue eyes that were the same as her mother's.

But he would take his daughter's sorrow and turn it into joy, like water into wine.

"Okay," she said.

He reined in his impatience. "I need to hear the words, Mercy."

"So shall it be."

Chapter Thirteen

"I demand to see Mercy McCoy," Rocco said to the guard at the front gate. "I'm not leaving until I do."

Nash flashed his badge. "Special Agent Garner and this is Special Agent Hammond," he said, gesturing to her in the back seat. "None of us are leaving until we know Ms. McCoy is all right."

The guy stepped into the guardhouse, picked up the phone and made a call. He turned his back to them as he spoke on the phone. A minute later he opened the gate and came back up to Nash's car. "You're all free to go."

Nash drove up the hill to Light House, which glittered and sparkled in the sunlight. A beautiful facade hiding all of Marshall McCoy's ugly secrets.

Armed guards met them as they parked.

Getting out of the truck, Rocco noticed that his Bronco had been pulled up near the front of the house. Like they had been expecting him.

"You can go on up," Shawn said.

They ascended the steps to the front door, where Alex was waiting with a big, goading smile that made Rocco ache to punch him in the face.

"Empyrean is eager to speak with you." Alex opened the door, letting them in. "Please remove your shoes."

Rocco was already doing so in the foyer. Nash looked uncertain, but he complied as did Becca.

Alex led the way to the office with his hand on the hilt of his gun holstered on his hip.

The door was wide-open.

Mercy was inside, sitting on a sofa in the back of the office. She looked up, a grim expression on her face as she met his gaze with solemn eyes, but she didn't get up when they entered the room.

"Welcome." Marshall approached them with his arms open in greeting. "I'm Empyrean."

"Special Agent Nash Garner."

"Special Agent Becca Hammond."

Recognition flashed in Marshall's eyes. "I've been looking forward to meeting you, Agent Hammond. Your reputation precedes you."

Becca schooled her features, not giving anything away with her face, but she put a protective hand on her belly that spoke volumes.

"Please have a seat." Marshall gestured to the chairs.

"I'll stand," Rocco said, and Alex came up alongside him. He glanced at Mercy again, wondering if she was okay, but she lowered her head.

Nash and Becca took seats in the chairs that faced the desk where Marshall sat.

"My daughter has relayed troubling things to me. I'm glad you're all here so that we can clear things up. It's my understanding that you, Agent Kekoa, had an informant give you a disturbing message before dying in your arms. Is that correct?"

Had Mercy told him everything?

"Yes, that's correct."

"Would you mind repeating that exact message for all of

us?" Marshall asked. "For the sake of clarity so that we might be on the same page."

"He said that on September nineteenth something big, something horrible was going to happen and that McCoy had planned it all."

"Ah." Marshall tipped his back as though struck with a revelation. "Naturally, you assumed your informant was referring to me."

Rocco's blood turned to ice. "Yes, he was spying on you."

"May I venture to guess that your informant was Dr. Percy Tiggs? I read about his passing in the news. His son is one of my flock and Dr. Tiggs didn't exactly celebrate the fact."

Nash threw Rocco a furtive glance, but none of them responded.

"I understand if you're not permitted to confirm or deny," Marshall said. "But I believe your informant was talking about my brother, Cormac. The other *lesser* known McCoy."

Mercy's head popped up, her eyes snapping wide in shock. She stared at her father before glancing at Rocco. She shook her head, and he could tell that she didn't know.

Was it possible that Percy had been talking about Marshall's brother?

"Dr. Tiggs regularly went to his camp to tend to their horses. Mac was too radical for the Shining Light. Dangerous in the extremism that he preached—antigovernment and no laws but those of Mother Nature. He eventually left with a bunch of my people, our people, since we started this together. His faction broke away nineteen years ago, on the same day that my wife, Ayanna, left. Three paths that had been one became fractured and diverged."

Mercy stiffened and wrung her hands.

There was something more at play here, between her and her father. What sick game was he up to?

"I don't consider Mac one of the fallen, not like my former wife," Marshall said. "He calls his people the Brotherhood of the Silver Light, but they venture far too close to the sun. Whereas Ayanna wandered off in darkness. But if something big and horrible is planned for tomorrow, Mac would be the McCoy that you're looking for."

Had Percy meant that they had been wrong about Marshall? Had he been trying to tell him about Mac McCoy?

"What about your weapons supplier?" Rocco asked.

"I make all my arrangements through Mac. Like I said, he's not fallen. Contact is permitted."

"Where can we find him?" Nash asked.

"Up in the mountains. But he has a tight-knit group. Not so easily infiltrated like mine," Marshall said, sliding a glance at Becca. "You won't get access or answers without my assistance."

Becca leaned forward, crossing her legs at the ankles. "What would getting your assistance require?"

"I feel certain that my cooperation would go a long, long way in fostering goodwill with your task force." Marshall smiled at Rocco.

Those were his words verbatim. Mercy had told him everything.

"But I would like verbal assurances," Marshall added, "that we will no longer be harassed or spied on and that I can in good faith tell my people that they have nothing to fear from you."

"So long as you don't break the law," Nash said, "you'll have nothing to worry about. And yes, your unsolicited cooperation will not only be significant, but also documented. Which will carry weight."

Marshall clasped his hands on the desk. "This is how

we'll proceed. I'll send Rocco to Cormac's camp. Along with Mercy."

Alex made a guttural noise like that of a wounded animal, drawing everyone's attention. "No, you can't."

"Silence." Marshall raised his palm at Alex. "It's the only way Mac will let Rocco in. If she's there with him, pretending to be his betrothed, and explains that he's too radical for my people, there won't be questions. Then it will be up to Agent Kekoa to do his job."

"No!" Alex stormed up to the desk. "You can't do this!"

"You forget yourself, son." Marshall stood and put a hand on his shoulder. "Have faith in me. All will be well. Mercy has decided to take her vows to the Shining Light and to marry you. Isn't that right, my dear?"

Everyone turned to look at her. Rocco's heart throbbed in his chest.

Biting her lip, she held his stare. "Yes."

His lungs squeezed so hard he could barely breathe.

"See." Marshall patted Alex on the back. "This trip to the mountains will help the task force stop something heinous from happening and allow Mercy to say her goodbyes. I have things well in hand."

Alex remained silent, but he didn't look convinced.

"Won't Cormac question the timing of their arrival and think it suspicious?" Nash asked.

Nodding, Marshall sat back down. "Certainly. That's why it has to be Mercy who accompanies him. Mac never could deny her anything."

"But that was when I was five." Mercy got up, wrapping her arms around herself, and strode to the window. "I don't even remember him."

"Doesn't matter." Her father leaned back in his chair.

"He'll remember you and he will let you into his camp. I've foreseen it."

"We appreciate your cooperation." Becca shifted in her chair like she was uncomfortable. "But why would you give up your brother?"

"There is no love lost between me and Mac. He's always had a taste for violence. Giving him up to protect my people and other innocent lives is the only prudent choice. Wouldn't you agree?"

"It would appear so," Becca said.

"When would you send them?" Nash asked.

"Shortly. It's a two-hour drive. I'd want them there before it gets dark. Is this agreeable to you?"

Nash stood. "Yes, yes, it is."

"One last thing," Marshall said. "I should warn you that sending backup to the area for Rocco would not be advisable. My brother keeps men in the woods and on the mountain on constant patrol. They'll spot other agents creeping around and then there's no telling what will happen. For this to work, it has to be Mercy and Rocco on their own."

"Thank you for your cooperation." Nash shook Marshall's hand. "Rocco, a moment in the hall."

Rocco stepped out of the office along with Nash and Becca as Alex began protesting this arrangement again.

"I don't like it," Becca said, once they were out of earshot.

Nash nodded in agreement. "Neither do I."

"What choice do we have?" Rocco folded his arms, flicking a glance back at the office.

Mercy stayed near the window, her face pallid, her gaze focused on him and not Alex, who was ranting.

"You won't have any backup if something goes wrong," Nash said.

That didn't worry him. "I'm used to working on my own. It's the nature of the undercover beast."

"Her father is playing a dangerous game," Becca said. "With his daughter right at the center of it all. That's what bothers me. It doesn't fit with his profile, endangering her. I feel like we're missing something here."

Rocco felt likewise. "I've got to be honest with you, Nash. Under normal circumstances, the mission would come first. No matter what. But keeping Mercy safe will be a priority." All his concern was for her.

"What if Marshall calls his brother and lets him know what's up? This could be a setup," Becca said.

"It could be," Rocco agreed, "but we don't have much choice. Time is running out and this is our best option."

"Find out what you can," Nash said, "then get out of there with her. Don't try to be a hero by stopping whatever they have planned on your own. Just relay the information in time and we'll do the rest."

"Roger that." He couldn't afford to take the chance of heroics. Not with Mercy's life on the line. "Becca, would you mind driving my car back into town? We'll take one of McCoy's vehicles up into the mountains."

"Sure. No problem."

"The keys should be in the car. If not, one of the guards will be able to get them for you."

"Safe travels," she said.

Nash and Becca headed out.

Staring at the scene in the office, resolve hardened inside him like steel. He was going to do everything in his power to protect her, from her father, from Alex, from her uncle. From any threat.

He strode inside, and Alex's head whipped toward him, his eyes filled with hatred.

"Enough." Marshall pressed his palm to the man's chest. "You must trust me in this." He drew a deep breath. "Mercy, you're still looking quite pale. Are you well?"

"Low blood sugar. We didn't have breakfast."

"I don't think it best for you two to linger until the commune gathers for lunch, which won't be for another hour. The more time you have at Mac's camp, Rocco, the better," Marshall said, almost sounding helpful. "But it's a long drive. Let the four of us break bread together in peace before you go."

"An early lunch would be good," Mercy said in a defeated way, as if all the fight had been kicked out of her. "If that's okay with you?" She looked at Rocco.

"I'm starving." He'd prefer not to endure an awkward meal with the mighty Empyrean and jealous Alex, but he could eat. "And we still need to know where we're going and what to expect once we get there."

"Alex, go to the kitchen. See what the cooks can rustle up for us quickly." Marshall shooed him out, and Alex stalked off with clenched fists.

Rocco hoped that guy wasn't petty enough to spit in his food.

Mercy's father stepped around behind his desk, unlocked the top drawer and pulled out a map. "Here, let me show you what roads to take."

Marshall pointed out the route that ran right through the mountains, past the overlook where he was supposed to meet Percy. It was possible that the doctor might have been fleeing from Cormac's camp that night. That Mac had been the McCoy Percy had been referring to.

Her father annotated the turns to take and circled the spot where they'd find the camp.

Rocco studied the map. "How big is the camp?"

"Nowhere near our size. He's got a much smaller outfit.

About ten cabins up there. Some of his people prefer to rough it in tents when the weather permits."

"How many people?" Rocco asked.

"I don't know. I'd estimate thirty to forty."

"You buy your weapons from him?"

"I do. He has an overseas connection. Other than that, I don't know how his end of the business works. After we make a transaction, one of his guys meets Alex at a predesignated spot that routinely changes for safety purposes."

"You don't mind losing your source of weapons?" Rocco was still skeptical.

"As you've seen for yourself, we're well stocked."

Indeed, they were.

"Any suggestions on how I should handle this with my uncle?" Mercy asked.

"Just be yourself." Marshall smiled at her. "And stick to the story. The two of you are to be married. Rocco's radical views and inclination for violence made him a bad fit for my commune and I thought that Cormac's would be better."

Alex returned, carrying a tray of food. "The kitchen already had three-bean chili prepared for lunch. It's been cooking all morning," he said, setting down the tray on the desk. He handed Mercy a bowl, napkin and spoon.

She took a seat facing the desk.

Rocco chose his own bowl when Alex offered him one and sat beside Mercy.

Marshall directed the man to pull up an extra chair from the corner and to sit next to him. They said grace while Rocco listened and then dug in.

"This is outstanding," Marshall said after his third spoonful, and Rocco reluctantly agreed, not missing the meat in the dish. "Such depth of flavor. I must compliment the kitchen staff during our lunch hour. I don't do it often enough. Everyone works so hard." The rambling continued, filling in the awkward silence as Alex's gaze bounced between Rocco and Mercy. "See, we can all be mature adults and act with civility."

Coughing, Mercy put her bowl on the desk. Her face was flushed. She put a hand to her throat. Scratched her cheek with the other. The coughing turned to a wheeze.

"Mercy?" Marshall leaned forward, peering at her.

Rocco clasped her shoulder. "Are you okay?"

She shook her head and stood. "Something's wrong. Can't breathe," she uttered through a rasp.

Red bumps and welts began appearing on her face and arms, probably beneath her clothes as well.

"Oh, God." Marshall's bowl fell from his hands, clattering to the floor. He jumped to his feet. "She's having an allergic reaction."

With her hands clutching her throat, Mercy staggered backward.

"No, no, no. She's having an anaphylactic reaction." Marshall ran to her.

Rocco lurched to his feet in terrified shock.

Frozen, he could hardly believe what was happening, Mercy struggling for air, her body succumbing to the allergen in a deadly spiral of symptoms. His heart lodged in his throat, his hands growing clammy, his muscles tightening with fear. For her. He had to do something to help her.

"She's only allergic to peanuts," Marshall said, "but I don't allow them on the compound. I don't understand." His gaze flew to the bowl of chili and then to Alex.

The young man sat silent and still, staring at Mercy.

"What did you do!" Marshall howled.

Mercy gasped for breath, her wheezes shortening. Her

face started to swell. She swayed and collapsed, but Rocco lunged, catching her.

Horror punched through him like a hot blade in his gut.

Marshall dropped to his knees, taking her from him into his lap. Rocco held her hand. Her slender fingers tightened around him.

"Calm down, sweetheart," Marshall said. "Don't panic. Try to breathe."

"Where's her EpiPen? Does she carry one?" Rocco asked.

"It's in her room. At the top of the stairs. Third room on the right. She keeps it in the top drawer of her dresser."

Rocco leaped up. He raced down the hall. Flew up the stairs. Stormed into her bedroom. He yanked open the drawer and rifled through her underwear. Tossing the cotton items to the floor, he searched for the yellow and black injector. He emptied the drawer.

But it wasn't there.

In less than a minute, he scoured through the other drawers, turning her room upside down. Still, no EpiPen.

A hard knot of dread congealed in the pit of his stomach. He bolted back down the stairs and tore into the office. Marshall had Mercy cradled in his lap.

"It's not there," Rocco said, his heart hammering painfully at his rib cage. "I couldn't find it."

Her father's eyes flared wide with alarm. On his knees, he whirled toward Alex. "Where is it? What did you do with it?"

Tears leaked from the corners of Mercy's eyes. Her lips were starting to turn blue.

It was happening so very, very fast. Right in front of his eyes the woman he loved was dying.

Rocco charged over to Alex and snatched him up from the chair by his shirt. "Tell me what you did with it."

Alex's gaze stayed laser-focused on Mercy.

"Are you insane?" Marshall screamed. "She's going to be your wife."

"No, she isn't." Alex shook his head slowly, his eyes glazed, like he was in a trance. "She's going to sleep with him and never come back."

How could Alex be so low, so malicious? Only a small, weak man would do such a thing.

"She's already slept with him, you idiot." Marshall rocked back and forth with his daughter in his arms. "And she came back anyway. What does it matter if she has one or two nights with this nonbeliever, but spends the rest of her life with you. I told you to have faith, you fool!"

"If she dies, you die. Painfully. Slowly," Rocco swore, ready to follow through, but the threat didn't faze Alex. Fury and fear hit Rocco so intensely that for a second everything blurred. "Where is the damn Epi?"

"She will return from the mountains," Marshall said, clinging to Mercy. "I've foreseen it. But you must let her live." He tipped his head back and muttered something that sounded like a prayer. "There are more EpiPens in the basement. Rocco, they're in the bunker."

"I moved them." Alex's voice was low, his gaze unwavering from Mercy. "You won't find it in time."

Rocco cocked his fist back, prepared to break the man's nose. He was willing to go so far as every bone in his body. "Tell us where you put it, or I'll beat it out of you."

Alex didn't cringe, didn't even flick a glance at him. His fists were tight at his sides, his expression unyielding, his eyes dark and full of a deadly determination.

Impotent rage surged through Rocco. He could hurt this man, beat him into a bloody pulp and it wouldn't do any good.

Because this rash, bitter coward seemed unconcerned with dying himself—so long as Mercy died first.

There had to be something they could do. Rocco wasn't going to stand by and let this happen. He could run to the infirmary and see if they had any epinephrine, but as fast as Mercy's reaction was happening, he wouldn't make it there and back in time.

Think, think.

The foundation of a cult was power and control. If anyone still had an iota of influence over Alex, it was Empyrean.

Rocco turned to Mercy's father. "Make him see reason." He looked back to Alex. "What is it you want?" Rocco pressed him.

Alex nodded at Mercy. "Her. For starters."

"You *will* let her live," Marshall said, his voice ringing with authority. "Give me the EpiPen. You have it, don't you? Give it to me!" he cried. "If you don't, so help me, you will walk in darkness, forever banished, your soul lost."

Alex took a step forward, but Rocco's tight grip stopped him. "Want me to save her or not?" He knocked Rocco's hand away, knelt at Mercy's side, and leaned over her. "Do you remember what I told you in the car?" he asked her. "Blink once for yes if you do."

Gasping for air, fighting to breathe, Mercy gave one long blink, and more tears streamed down her face.

"You better come back to me," Alex said.

Mercy's eyes fluttered closed. Her hands slipped from her throat, and she went limp.

"Hurry up!" Rocco yelled.

Alex tugged up his pant leg and pulled the injector from his sock.

Marshall snatched the shot of epinephrine from his hand, yanked off the blue cap and pressed the orange tip to her thigh. He threw the used injector to the floor and rocked his daughter in his arms.

Coming up alongside her, Rocco gave Alex a fierce look that had him scuttling up and out of the way. Rocco took her hand in his. "How long does it take to work?"

"Any minute. Any minute now." Marshall looked down at his daughter, his face fraught with panic. "Come on, Mercy. Breathe. *Please*, open your eyes."

Rocco bit out a curse under his breath. He couldn't lose her. Because of some vindictive weasel. They hadn't even been given a chance.

Mercy sucked in a wheezing breath, opening her eyes. The color returned to her lips and cheeks. She squeezed his hand, her gaze finding his.

Relief pummeled him in a wave. She was going to be okay. She was going to live.

Marshall hugged her tight against his chest. He kissed her forehead and slid Mercy into Rocco's arms. Her father got up and hurried to his desk. He picked up the phone. "I need security immediately."

"Empyrean," Alex said. "I was desperate."

"I know." Marshall nodded. "You weren't yourself. You acted rashly and almost killed her."

"But I didn't," Alex said. "Her life was in my hands, and I chose not to take it."

Guards ran into the room, led by Shawn.

"Secure Alex in an unburdening room," Marshall said, "and help Mercy to one of the vehicles."

Holding her in his arms, Rocco stood. "I'll carry her."

Marshall nodded. "One of you, run to the infirmary. Tell the doctor Mercy went into anaphylactic shock. We need him to set up an IV for her in an SUV. She'll need fluids and vitamins to help her recover and an extra EpiPen for her journey just in case."

Shawn tapped one man on the shoulder, issuing orders.

The guy ran from the room. Shawn and the other guard each took one of Alex's arms.

"Get him out of my sight." Marshall waved them off with a dismissive hand.

They hauled Alex out of the office. Rocco glared at him. He'd make him pay later, but he suspected Marshall would do the job first.

Marshall grabbed the map from the desk and turned to Rocco. "I'll walk you down to a vehicle." He put a hand to Rocco's back as they left the house. "Sometimes when the medicine wears off, it's possible for the symptoms to return. You'll have an extra shot of epinephrine if they do. Watch her closely. When you get to the camp, stick to the story. Mac has always had a soft spot for Mercy. Play on that and you'll both be fine."

"If this is a setup," Rocco said, "Mercy will be hurt by it." He was now even more reluctant to involve her in her weakened state. Everything about this operation felt wrong. But there were so many lives at stake.

"I almost lost my daughter minutes ago. Trust me. I have no intention of endangering her."

As much as Marshall might have believed his own words, Rocco put no stock in them. Her father couldn't be trusted.

Chapter Fourteen

Marshall waited until after the commune had eaten lunch and his temper had subsided before going to the unburdening room.

Alex had been unhinged. There was no telling what he might do next.

Marshall nodded for Shawn to unlock the door. He stepped inside. "You may leave us," he said, and Shawn closed the door behind him. Clasping his hands, he stared at Alex.

His *son* sat handcuffed to the bed, calm and composed. Gone was the remorse in him, replaced by a steely glint in his eyes.

"The punishment for an act of violence committed against an anointed member of the commune is banishment," Marshall said.

Alex stood, the chain of his cuffs clinking against the bed rail, his head held high. "That's true. But Mercy isn't anointed. Is she?"

It was an undisputable fact. Still… "She is my daughter."

"And I am your son! You chose me. Over any other that could've been yours. You took me under your wing. Brought me into your house. Molded me in your image. It's me you're grooming to succeed you. Not *her*. She may wear white, and you may have us call her a leader, but it's one big joke. She's never proven her faith or devotion by taking her vows. Because deep down we both know she's a nonbeliever."

Marshall prowled up to him and slapped his face. "How dare you?"

Licking the blood from his split lip, Alex smiled. "How dare I speak the truth? You've given her allowances that no one else is permitted. When it comes to her there is a blatant double standard. Everyone loves Mercy—she radiates light—but they all see the truth and whisper about your hypocrisy."

"You tried to kill her!" He took a calming breath, regaining his composure. "Why would you do such a thing?"

"Because I remember," Alex said, not making any sense.

"Remember what?"

"You know." A long, slow grin spread over Alex's face. "The reason Ayanna left but Mercy stayed."

A sudden chill swept over Marshall as though someone had walked over his grave. He turned away and stared at the symbol of the Shining Light painted on the wall. Alex couldn't possibly know. Even if he did, Marshall would not speak of it. Refused to think about it.

"If I wanted to kill her," Alex said, "she would be dead. I tested her."

"You what?" Pivoting on his heel to face him, Marshall shook his head at the ravings of this madman, trying to spin his way out of this. "Others who have done far less have been banished."

"Before you can banish me, this must be brought before the council of elders. I'll argue that I haven't violated any bylaws. I will confess to putting crushed peanuts into the nonbeliever's chili. To test her faith," he said, his dark eyes glittering with unfathomable devilry. "After learning that Mercy—the woman who agreed to a courtship with me in front of everyone—ran off with an undercover ATF agent sent to spy on us and slept with him. In the end, I chose to save her, despite her transgressions. Doubt plagues your daughter like a disease. While I, your chosen son, took my vows to the commune at sixteen." He pointed to the tattoo at the base of his throat. "When will Mercy *McCoy* take hers?"

Marshall stared at Alex, bowled over that he was responsible for creating this monster.

This was a delicate situation. The issue of his daughter not taking her vows to the Shining Light had reached a tipping point. Sooner than he had hoped.

Commitment was their power. Mercy was a weak link. A liability. This problem and Marshall's hypocrisy would become the center of the discussion among the elders and the commune.

An act of violence against someone who was not anointed wasn't a punishable offence. He had designed the bylaws that way so his people need not ever fear defending themselves against someone from the outside world. For nearly three decades, he had kept peace on the compound.

As much as he hated to admit it, taking Alex in front of the council on this matter would be tricky. Everything would be questioned. Marshall's authority. His judgment. His contradictory and preferential treatment of his daughter. As well as her conduct with that agent of chaos.

The only way Marshall could ever truly protect Mercy was for her to take her vows and be anointed. He had thought his excuses for her would expire on her twenty-fifth birthday. Instead, tomorrow she'd have to choose. Become a Starlight or one of the fallen.

But he still had to deal with Alex.

My son. My monster. "You must be punished."

"I will not go quietly into the dark. I'll fight tooth and nail to stay. I'll make sure things get messy. You will not walk away spotless. I promise you that!" Alex roared, jerking at his handcuffs, the chain rattling. "Let me stay. Protect me as I've protected you…and all your secrets."

There were other things he could do to Alex that didn't require the purview of the council. "Flagellation will be your punishment. I'll do it myself."

Alex smiled. Even though flesh would be torn from his back with a whip, he smiled as though he'd been given a gift. "After I've atoned, I want to hear how you're so certain that Mercy will be back."

Oh, ye of little faith.

His daughter would return before the eclipse. Marshall was more than the prophet.

He was a man who always had a plan.

Chapter Fifteen

A warm hand rubbed Mercy's leg, rousing her.

"I think we're almost there," Rocco said.

Yawning, she looked around at the pines and snowcapped peaks. With the higher elevation the temperature would be much cooler.

It was a good thing Rocco had swung by the motel and picked up their things after he had given his boss the details of where they were headed. Charlie had packed a couple of sweaters for her, and she'd need them.

Mercy pulled out the needle for the IV from her hand.

"How are you feeling?"

"The concoction in the IV bag and the sleep made a world of difference. I'm much better now."

"You look better. No more swelling. No welts or red marks." A small smile tugged at his mouth. "Gave me quite a scare."

Alex had terrified them all. He'd watched her with a cool detachment as her airway squeezed tight, closing off all her oxygen. Her skin had turned clammy and itchy. She'd struggled for every strangled breath, her lungs burning, a scream building that she hadn't been able to release. It felt like an anvil had been on her chest. Darkness had closed in around the edges of her vision.

Rocco had been frantic, doing what he could to save her. While Alex had loomed over her, reminding her of who he was and what he was capable of.

I'd rather see you dead than living in darkness with that man.

His vicious words rang in her head, flooding her veins with ice. She might have underestimated his capacity for cruelty, but not anymore.

"I can't go back to the compound." She didn't want to flee like a traitor. To be designated as "fallen." To never again associate with the people who she called family. To not say a proper goodbye. But she didn't see any other way. "Unless I take my vows, there's no place for me in the commune." She'd put it off for as long as she could, wrestling with the hardest decision of her life. "But I can't do it."

And it was only a matter of time before Alex tried to kill her again because she would never be his. She couldn't give him that opportunity by returning to the compound.

"For what it's worth, I think you're making the right choice." He clutched her hand. "It was good of Charlie to say those things to you last night. I just want to make it clear that neither of us wants you to think that you have to depend on me to make this transition. Of course, I'm here for you. We'll both help you in any way that makes you comfortable. We have a lot of friends in town who'll support you."

"That means a lot." More than he realized. The idea of leaving the commune had seemed too big, too final. Too far out of reach. With assistance from Charlie, Brian and most especially Rocco—regardless of how deep his feelings truly ran, there was no doubt he cared about her—she could envision a different life.

One she desperately wanted.

"No pressure or anything," he said, "but I hope you won't

walk away from this. From us. The possibility of what we could be together. It's real for me. I never lied about my feelings for you. After almost losing you earlier, I'll do whatever it takes to prove to you that I'm in this for the long haul. If you want me."

She didn't answer. Didn't dare. He was offering everything she wanted. But deep down she couldn't shake the niggling fear that he was smoothing things over with her only to help sell their cover story once they got to the camp.

A man dressed in camo stepped out of the tree line into the middle of the road. He held a rifle aimed at their windshield.

Movement off to the left drew their gazes.

A second man with a full beard, also wearing head-to-toe camo, approached the driver's-side door with a rifle slung over his shoulder. "You two lost?"

Rocco rolled down the window. "We're here to see Cormac McCoy."

"I don't know who that is."

Mercy leaned over, giving him a full view of her face. "I'm Mercy. Marshall McCoy's daughter. Can you tell my uncle I'm here?"

Eyeing them, the guy stepped back and pulled out a handheld radio. A squawk resounded as he keyed it, but he was too far away for them to hear what he said.

"Tight security," Rocco said. "At least we know the directions are solid."

The man came back to the car. He held out the radio and keyed it. "Go ahead, sir, they can hear you."

"If you're really my niece," a deep male voice said over the other end, "what did you used to call me when you were little?"

Panic fogged her brain, her thoughts stumbling together.

"It was nineteen years ago. You can't expect me to remember that?"

"But I do. My little nugget wouldn't forget. Whoever you are, get gone before you get shot."

Nugget stirred up a memory. Taking her back to a time when she'd only eat chickpea nuggets and macaroni and cheese. In her head, she heard her voice, like a child, calling him something that sounded silly. "Wait, please," she said. "Uncle Mac and cheese." That wasn't right. "No, no. Uncle Macaroni."

"Let them through," Cormac said.

The guy holding the radio whistled to the other one and he moved out of the road, letting them pass.

Rocco drove down the single lane dirt path about a mile until the camp came into sight. Another armed man opened a tall wooden gate that was made from logs the size of telephone poles and waved them in.

There were seven trucks parked on one side near the entrance and some horses corralled on the other side.

Men carrying weapons, ammo and cases of something she couldn't identify were loading them in the backs of four of the larger vehicles. They were definitely in the middle of preparing for something big.

Trepidation trickled through her at the attention their presence garnered. Wary glances and narrowed eyes.

"This is the place," Rocco said, "where my informant must've been."

"How do you know?"

"The men who killed my CI and ran him off the road were driving that truck." He gestured with a subtle hike of his chin to a heavy-duty black one that had dual rear wheels.

Two stickers were plastered on the rear bumper.

Both depicted images she recognized. "Those symbols are from our teachings."

"What do they mean?"

"The iridescent silver tree represents enlightenment, but through toil and struggle. The bolt of lightning slicing through the red block signifies *vis major*. An overwhelming force that causes damage or disruption. Like an act of God."

He parked the car. "Are you ready for this?"

"Let's get it over with and get out of here." She reached into the back seat, grabbing her duffel and pulled out a sweater. Putting it on, she looked around.

The camp was in a valley encircled by peaks and trees. The surrounding mountains probably did a good job of protecting them from the icy wind in the winter.

There were small log cabins and tents set up throughout the level grassy area. The front door of the cabin at the center of the camp opened. A man with long blond hair and regal features similar to her father's, but with enough facial hair for a grizzly, made his way in their direction.

"Hey." Rocco cupped her chin, turning her face toward him.

He brought his mouth to hers. She closed her eyes for a brief moment, enjoying the electric sensation that sizzled through her body the moment their lips touched. He really kissed her. Not a quick, appropriate peck merely for show. This was hot and wet, full of such passion and desire. All of which she wanted from him. He plunged deeper, and she sank into the kiss that was oh-so-sweet.

And over far too soon when he pulled away.

"Rocco."

He brushed his thumb across her bottom lip. "The best lies are rooted in truth. Remember that."

A knock at the window had her spinning in her seat. She looked at her uncle and gave a shaky smile.

Opening her door, Cormac noticed the empty IV bag hanging from the grab handle above her head.

She climbed out. Cool air sliced through her, making her shiver. "Hi, Uncle Mac." Stepping forward, she shoved the door closed behind her.

"Well, aren't you all grown-up," he said, his face lighting up. He ran a tentative hand over her hair, taking her in as if dazed, like she wasn't real. "Come here, nugget." He opened his arms.

Mercy walked into the embrace, and he wrapped her in a bear hug, lifting her feet from the ground. She remembered this. His fondness. His hugs, warm and tight and nothing like her father's.

Setting her down, he looked her over again. Then his gaze shifted. "And who is this big fella?"

"Rocco Sharp." He proffered his hand. "Pleased to meet you."

They shook.

"He's my intended," she said, the words heating her face.

"Is that so?" Cormac gave a slow, steady nod. "What brings you two all the way up here?"

"Can we speak inside?" She zipped up the sweater. "Get something warm to drink. Maybe a bite to eat." Her appetite had returned with gusto. She had a fast metabolism and shouldn't go too long without food.

"Right this way." Her uncle roped an arm around her shoulder and led them to the cabin he'd come out of.

Inside, the furnishings were simple—most appeared handmade—and it was warm from the fire in the hearth. A savory smell permeated the area from a pot on the stove. The kitchen opened onto a small dining area and a modest living room.

"Hey, baby," her uncle called.

A door opened. A woman with black hair streaked with silver fashioned into two long braids strode into the room.

"This is my niece Mercy and her fiancé, Rocco," Mac said. "And this is my wife, Sue Ellen."

"Welcome," Sue Ellen said curtly without a smile. She was a thin woman, maybe a little older than Mac, with watery green eyes and a weathered face. "Can I get you something to drink or eat?"

"Yes, please." Mercy set her bag on the floor. "Both if it's not too much trouble."

"Will cheese sandwiches and lentil stew do for you?" Sue Ellen asked.

Mercy nodded. "That's perfect."

"Thank you, ma'am," Rocco said.

"Either of you have a cell phone on you?" Mac asked.

Rocco pulled out the phone he'd purchased at the service station.

Her uncle grabbed a gray pouch from a hook on the wall and opened it. Inside was shiny, metallic material. "Drop it in," he said, and Rocco did.

"What is that?" Mercy asked.

"Faraday pouch. Blocks all signals. RFID, FM radio, GPS, cellular, Bluetooth, 5G, Wi-Fi, you name it." He sealed it and hung it back on the hook. "Get comfortable." Mac waved them over to chairs at the dining table, and they sat. "I'll get you some hot cider," he said, picking up a clay jug and moving to the stove.

Sue Ellen took cheese from the fridge. She sliced it along with the bread and made sandwiches. Grabbing a wooden ladle, she poured soup from the pot on the stove into bowls.

Beside her was a shelf lined with labeled mason jars filled with various herbs and plants. Sassafras. Ginger. Lavender.

Catnip. Willow bark. Chamomile. All could be used for different ailments. Mercy wondered if they relied on herbal medicine.

It would make sense with them being so far from a pharmacy and hospital, but she expected that they also had supplies for a serious emergency.

Sue Ellen placed food on the table.

"Tell us, what brings you here?" Cormac asked, setting down four mugs of warm cider.

Hesitating, Mercy wasn't sure how to start. She wasn't the best liar. This was their opportunity to sell their story, and she didn't want to blow it.

"Empyrean didn't think I was the right fit for the Shining Light," Rocco said, as easily as though it was the truth, and in a way it was. "He thought I might be better suited for the Brotherhood."

"Not right for his commune, but he sanctioned this union with his daughter?" Cormac asked, suspicion heavy in his tone as well as his expression.

Mercy looked at Rocco. She pressed her palm to his cheek and ran her fingers through his hair, a smile she couldn't help spreading on her face. "My father didn't make the match, but he didn't stop it." Sliding closer to him, she glanced at her uncle. "He saw how we were drawn to each other. How kind and devoted he is to me," she said, and Rocco slid an arm around her shoulder, tucking her close to his side. "As far as I'm concerned, he's the only one for me." The line between truth and lies became even murkier.

Wiping her hands on an apron, Sue Ellen sat next to Mac, listening, watching, assessing.

"Were you banished?" her uncle asked.

"No, sir," Rocco said. "Things sort of came to a head on the compound."

Mac raised an eyebrow. "In what way?"

"The FBI planted an informant in the commune," Rocco said. "When he was discovered, I thought we should've killed him. And I didn't want to stop there. Who do they think they are? Infiltrating us, spying on us, trying to take away our civil liberties."

Mercy eyed him, mesmerized at what he was saying, at how he started taking on a whole new persona.

Cormac slapped a hand down on the table. "You are one hundred percent correct," he said, pointing a finger at him. "It's high time we took our country back. You know those Feds are conspiring to strip us of our rights, starting with the unalienable one to keep and bear arms. Once we're rendered defenseless, they plan to absorb Americans into their tyrannical new world order government."

Rocco and Sue Ellen both nodded.

Lowering her head, Mercy nibbled on her food. She figured if she kept her mouth full, then the less she'd have to say.

"The no-good ATF seized a shipment of my weapons in Colorado." Mac took a sip of his cider. "Now they're stealing money from my pocket and taking food from the mouths of my people. We're going to teach them a lesson they won't ever forget. The streets will run red with blood tomorrow."

An icy chill jolted through her veins. She didn't recall her uncle being violent or paranoid. Clearly, he was both.

Sue Ellen gripped Mac's forearm, and he stopped talking. "Which makes me wonder about the timing of your arrival. Why didn't you come last month?" his wife asked. "Why not in two days? What brings you to us specifically *today*?"

"Empyrean took the full moon and the eclipse as a sign that it was the right time," Rocco said.

Mercy tensed. That explanation would only raise more questions than it would answer. Her father would've used the full moon and the shedding ceremony to make the announcement, choosing to send them the day after. Not before.

As she suspected, Sue Ellen's eyes hardened like ice and Cormac crossed his arms as he leaned back in his chair.

Mercy set her sandwich down and slipped her hand onto Rocco's leg under the table. "Honey, I think we have to be honest about what made us expedite our plans and come today." She turned to Sue Ellen and then Cormac. "Uncle Mac, do you remember Alex?"

Scratching his beard, he nodded. "Yeah. Of course. The weird little boy who used to follow you around like a lost puppy."

Puppies were cute and cuddly. She'd always thought of Alex more as a shadow. Dark, silent, and only there when the light was blocked.

"He tried to kill me today."

"What?" Alarm tightened across his and Sue Ellen's faces.

"It's true," Rocco said. "He poisoned her. Put peanuts in her food. She went into anaphylactic shock." His grip on her shoulder tightened. "I was terrified I was going to lose her. Almost did, too. I've never felt so helpless in my entire life, watching her slip away. It was horrific."

"That's why there's an IV bag in your car?" Cormac asked.

"Yes. To help me recover. My father wanted us to get out of there as soon as possible. Alex is insane."

"He's obsessed with her," Rocco added. "He can't handle seeing her with someone else."

Her uncle leaned forward, resting his forearms on the table. "Then it's good that you came here."

His wife nodded. "Coveting anything or anyone above the Light is to make it your master. It was best to get out of that man's sight. If he wants you that badly, he would've been bound to try again."

"You're welcome to stay. We've got a spare bedroom." Cormac hiked a thumb over his shoulder at one of the doors. "Are you both okay with the one bed? It's only full-size. If not, I can have a tent and cot set up for you, Rocco."

"No, that won't be necessary," Mercy said, rubbing Rocco's thigh. "We'd prefer to sleep together. Isn't that right?"

Smiling as though he'd suddenly become bashful, Rocco lowered his head but met her eyes. "I can't keep my hands off you, so it's whatever you want, sweetheart," he said, the deep timbre of his voice sliding through her. He stroked a lock of hair back from her cheek, trailing the pads of his fingers across her skin.

Her breath caught. She tried and failed to ignore a pang of longing. So she decided to stop trying and kissed him. Soft and quick.

Rocco cleared his throat. "Provided your uncle allows us to share a bed under his roof."

Staring into his warm brown eyes was almost hypnotic. She was certainly under his spell. Even though he'd used her, lied to her and might still be manipulating her for the sake of his mission, she couldn't wait to make love with him again.

"Your father aware that you two have had relations?" her uncle asked. "I recall him being quite protective of you."

"He is," she said, a little annoyed at how her father and uncle treated her as though she was a child. "I've never hidden anything from him."

"Well, you're to be married. What happens behind closed doors, stays there." Her uncle Mac smirked. "There's only one bathroom in here. Compost toilet. All our power is solar, and we get our water from a catchment system. Not the fancy digs you're used to at the compound, but the room is yours for as long as you want it, or until we can get you two your own cabin."

"Much appreciated. We'll earn our keep," Rocco said. "I'd love to start by helping you with whatever you've got planned tomorrow. Giving those Feds payback sounds good to me."

"Happy to have an extra gunman," her uncle said. "Especially if you're a good shot."

"That I am. What exactly is the target?" Rocco asked.

Sue Ellen whispered in Cormac's ear.

"We'll get into specifics tomorrow," Mac said. "You'll have to excuse our caution. We had an informant weasel his way into our camp a few days ago. We're still a bit on edge."

"Oh, yeah, how did you deal with it?" Rocco asked.

"Same way you wanted to handle your spy." A sinister laugh rolled from Cormac. "Barry and Dennis took care of that traitor."

"Good for you." Rocco held up his mug, his body language mirroring that of her uncle's. "You sent those Feds a clear message they were messing with the wrong people."

The two of them toasted. Mercy thought she might be sick, but she kept eating.

"For now," Mac said, "I'll introduce you around and show you the camp."

They finished their food and headed outside.

"I didn't want to say anything in front of Sue Ellen." Cormac looked back at the cabin, keeping his voice low. "But I can see why Alex lost his mind over you. You're the spitting image of your mother." He gave a low whistle. "She was the prettiest woman I ever did see."

Her heart skipped a beat. "She left the compound the same day you did, right?"

"An unfortunate coincidence."

"Do you know what happened to her? Where she went?"

His brow furrowed with confusion. "You don't know?"

"Know what?"

"I gave her some money to help her get started. She eventually moved to Wayward Bluffs, but I heard she went back to Laramie every week. Hoping to see you. Run into you. Convince you to leave the Shining Light. Sometime around your twentieth birthday she assumed you had taken your vows and gave up hope."

Her father hadn't allowed her to start going into town to help recruit people until she had turned twenty-one. What if that had been by design?

What if she had missed her chance? What if she never saw her again? "Do you have her address or a phone number?"

"No. But that's how she wanted it. With as much distance from your father and the Brotherhood as possible."

A sinking feeling took hold of her. It must've shown on her face because Rocco brought her into a tight embrace.

"It's going to be okay," he whispered in her ear.

She breathed through her disappointment, hoping that was true.

With a protective arm still around her, they continued to walk.

"Now that I think of it," her uncle said, "I believe she worked as a waitress for a while. A restaurant on Third Street. Delgado's, if I'm not mistaken. It was a long time ago, but they might have a phone number or forwarding address on file."

Delgado's. She'd passed the restaurant every time she went to the USD, venturing into the same orbit her mother had once occupied. The knowledge made her chest ache.

"Why would my mom leave me like that? I was so young. I needed her." She still did.

"Your dad didn't give her any choice. She wanted out. He agreed on the condition that you stayed behind. With him. It was complicated, and not an easy decision for her. But she felt like she couldn't breathe anymore. Like your father and the movement were suffocating her." He stroked her hair. "I'm glad you're here. She'd want me to help you."

She understood that claustrophobic feeling. The sensation of the walls closing in, her world shrinking, getting smaller and smaller, while the one thing at the center of her life only got bigger, greater. Stronger. That one person.

Empyrean.

Mac scratched his beard. "Your allergic reaction, going into anaphylactic shock like that, is odd since peanuts aren't allowed on the compound anymore. Déjà vu. Alex must've had them stashed for a while."

"Déjà vu?" Rocco stopped walking. "How so?"

"Well, Ayanna was allergic, too. She went into anaphylactic shock once. I didn't see it, but I heard about it."

"When did that happen?" she asked.

Mac shrugged. "Maybe two or three months before we left. It shook her up pretty fierce. She got really quiet after that. Stopped talking about leaving and taking you with her. I would've sworn that she had decided to stay. Then the day me and my guys were rolling out, she said a hurried good-bye to you and caught a ride out the gates with us. Didn't take one thing with her but the clothes on her back. Left everything else behind."

Including me.

"Is it possible that Marshall did that to her on purpose?" Rocco asked.

"What do you mean?" Mac grew still, staring at him in horror. "Put peanuts in her food?"

"Yeah. To scare her into staying," Rocco said, his voice just audible enough to be heard over the rush of blood pounding in Mercy's head.

"No way. He loved her." Mac shook his head forcefully

in either conviction or denial. "If anything, he became more protective of her and you." He tipped his head toward her. "That's when he banned peanuts from the compound and had all those black walnut trees planted. Your dad even took you to Denver, to a fancy facility, to have you tested for allergies."

She vaguely remembered the trip. He'd called it an adventure. She'd cried when the doctor had pricked her with needles and begged for her mother, but she wasn't there. Only her father, Alex, who held her hand, and a woman whose name she couldn't remember.

It was a lot to take in. Much more than she wanted to process right now while there were bigger things going on. Lives were at stake, including theirs, if she and Rocco didn't pull this off.

Everything was a blur as her uncle showed them around the camp, making endless introductions as they shook hands or waved hello and answered questions. Thankfully, Cormac and Rocco did most of the talking.

All she could think about was her mother. What she looked like. The smell of her hair. The sound of her voice. How difficult it must've been for her, forced to decide between raising her child or having her freedom. An impossible choice.

Did her father tip the scales, threaten and poison her, coerce her into leaving without her child?

The idea was too monstrous to be the truth. But Alex had claimed to love Mercy, too, and look at what he had done.

The light shifted, sliding from twilight to dim, snapping her out of her thoughts.

Holding a lantern, her uncle led them into a cave. "Here is our weapons cache," he said. There were stacks upon stacks of crates with a lightning bolt singed onto the side and metal trunks. "You want it, we've got it. Rifles. Anything from an AR-15 to AK-47. Shotguns—double-barreled break-action to sawed off. Submachine guns to .50 caliber. Ghost pistols. Hollow point bullets to armor-piercing. Rocket-propelled grenades. High and low explosives as well as blasting agents."

A jagged bolt of fear ripped through Mercy, drawing every muscle tight. She stared at the cache of weapons, her eyes bulging in shock.

On the compound, they had a whole lot of guns, for defense only, but this…

This was the next-level. This was how wars were fought and won in small countries. This meant the death of countless innocent people. She'd never seen anything like this arsenal.

"Wow, this is seriously impressive," Rocco said, his voice filled with awe. "I can't wait to see what you have in store for tomorrow."

Cormac smiled. In the amber light from the lantern casting shadows on his face, he looked like the devil. "We're going to rain down hell on them."

A pervasive sense of dread coiled through her, and she couldn't imagine how this was all going to end.

Chapter Sixteen

Lying in bed, Rocco's thoughts churned. Cormac McCoy had a bunch of hardened survivalists riled up and ready to shed blood tomorrow. It was a wonder how the Brotherhood of Silver Light had gone under the radar for so long.

Thanks to Mercy's gutsy move, risking her life asking for her father's help, the Brotherhood could no longer hide.

But Rocco still didn't know what their intended target was or how he'd notify Nash once he did. The only thing certain was that if he failed, a lot of people were going to die.

Percy had been right. Something big and awful was in the works. Rocco wouldn't let his death be in vain. He had to stop whatever was planned and keep Mercy safe, one way or another.

In the next room, he heard the faucet shut off. A door creaked open.

"Thank you again," Mercy said.

Sue Ellen and Cormac responded from the living room, where Rocco had last seen them sitting in front of the fire.

"Good night." Ducking into their room, Mercy closed the door, and a different tension invaded his body.

She padded over to the bed, set her toiletries on the nightstand beside the burning candle and undressed. For a moment, she just stood there, watching him taking in the sight of her. He was mesmerized by her beauty and grace. Her shimmering hair captured the light, making it sparkle. He was intensely aware of everything about her, her creamy skin, soft curves, the flush creeping over her face, down to her feminine scent.

The ache inside him for the woman he would protect with his last breath flared anew. He wanted her. Under him. On top of him. Building a life with him.

Mercy peeled back the covers and slipped into the bed. "Why are you wearing so many clothes?"

She tugged at his T-shirt. He sat up, letting her pull it over his head.

"Because I didn't know if you were serious about us doing more than sleeping," he whispered. "I couldn't tell if it was part of the act."

"It wasn't." She pressed her palm to his stomach and ran her hand up his torso.

Her touch struck him like a flame to kindling. Hunger poured through him.

"Were you pretending," she said, straddling his hips and drawing her face close to his, "when you said you couldn't keep your hands off me?"

"No."

She brushed her lips across his in a slow, seductive caress. "Then why aren't you touching me?"

Good question.

He locked an arm around her waist, bringing her flush against him. Their heated bodies pressed together, skin to skin. His other hand he buried in the silky softness of her hair as he captured her mouth. All his thoughts about tomorrow dissipated in the kiss.

Rocking her hips, rubbing her core on the ridge of his erection, she made a low, desperate sound that ignited his own need instantly, sending a tremor through his muscles. He sucked tenderly at her lower lip before stroking his tongue across it and delving back into her mouth.

She grabbed his wrist, pulling his hand from her hip, and shoved it exactly where she wanted him. Down between her legs, cupping her. He found slick, wet warmth.

They groaned at the same time, the intense heat between them building higher. She twined her fingers in his hair, a shudder rolling through her, thighs trembling as she rubbed against his fingers.

He was lost in the sensation of her. All liquid fire in his arms. Primal need. Taking what she wanted. And he intended to give her everything, showing her without words how much he desired her. Cared for her. He wanted to make love to her until she was breathless and ready to come out of her skin. Make her burn the way he did for her.

"The cabin is small, and the walls are thin," he said low. "Sound will carry."

"We've got to sell our story. Engaged and hot for each other. Let's give them something worth hearing."

Happy to oblige, he flipped their bodies, putting her beneath him, and kissed her chin. Licked her throat while his hands moved over hot skin that was smooth as silk. He took his time with every warm, slow caress, refusing to be rushed. Delighting in the soft whimpering sounds she made. Enjoying her breasts one after the other until she was pleading and squirming, parting her thighs wide for him. He moved southward, kissing his way down between her legs. Glancing up at her, the molten heat in her eyes made him smile. Then he dipped his head—her fingers curling in his hair, her hand guiding his mouth to that sweet spot—and he settled his tongue on the sensitive bundle of nerves that drove her wild. She screamed his name, splintering to pieces, her cry like the crack of a whip to the desire lashing him.

He was ready to burst, but he held tight to his control since he was just getting started.

THE NEXT DAY, an unseasonably warm spell had hiked the temperature ten degrees higher. Mercy didn't need a sweater, but she wore one anyway, as part of the plan.

Rocco needed her to get his phone from the Faraday pouch without Sue Ellen noticing. Mercy looked out the window of the kitchen.

The men were huddled up outside around a table busy making Molotov cocktails.

Apparently, the RPGs were worth too much to waste in an attack on the Feds. Gasoline, bottles, fuses and bullets were cheap.

She finished washing and drying the breakfast dishes. Taking off the apron, she turned around and looked at Sue Ellen, who was wrapping up food for the men to take with them.

"I have a headache," Mercy said. "It came out of nowhere."

"Probably from a lack of sleep." Sue Ellen flashed a wry grin. "You've got yourself quite a stud there. Mac and I had to take a long walk to cool off."

Her face heated. "Sorry about that."

"No need to apologize. You're young and in love. Only natural."

Was it love?

Rocco made her feel safe. Adored. Like she could tell him anything and he'd understand. But she wasn't ready to trust her feelings or those he claimed to have for her. Not yet.

"Do you have anything for the headache?"

"Get that jar." Sue Ellen pointed to the shelf lined with mason jars. "The willow bark. Put two tablespoons in a cup of hot water. Let it steep. Sip it slowly. By the time you're done drinking it, the headache should be gone."

Mercy went to the shelf and took the jar down. Sue Ellen's gaze was fastened to her. Heading over to the pots and pans, Mercy waited for the older woman's attention to shift. The second it did, she let the jar slip from her hand, shattering on the floor.

"Oh, no." Mercy stared at the mess. "I'm so clumsy and with this headache pounding—"

"It's all right." Sighing, Sue Ellen stood. "Clean it up and then take these sacks of food out to the trucks that they're going to use. I'll run over to Barb's cabin. See if she has any."

"Thank you." Mercy grabbed the broom and dustpan. "Sorry about the hassle."

Sue Ellen trudged outside, and Mercy quickly swept up the debris, tossing it in the trash bin.

She looked out the window. The woman marched passed the group of men without a glance behind her. Cormac was completely engaged, chatting and laughing with Rocco.

Mercy made a beeline to the Faraday pouch. Velcro buzzed as she opened the bag. She took out the phone and shoved it into the pocket of her sweater. Quickly, she closed it and returned the pouch to the hook the same way she'd found it.

Scooping up the sacks of food, she scurried outside. The four loaded trucks were parked in a row, all facing the gate, ready to leave.

She caught Rocco's eye and gave a curt nod, letting him know that she'd gotten it. Now she just had to slip him the phone without anyone seeing. She hurried to the trucks and set a sack on the console. As she put the last one down, the front gate swung open.

A black SUV pulled in. Shawn was driving.

Worry flooded her nervous system. Why was he there?

Soon enough she'd find out, but whatever the reason, it wasn't good.

Making a U-turn and pulling up beside her, he stopped the vehicle. Cormac and Rocco set down glass bottles and both headed in her direction. She went around to the driver's side.

Shawn hopped out, leaving the car running. "I'm here to bring you back, Mercy."

A jolt shot through her, spurring her to step away from him. "I'm afraid you're wasting your time. I'm not going back to the compound."

He reached into his back pocket, pulled out two envelopes, and handed her one with her name scrawled on the front. Her uncle's name was on the other.

"Read it," Shawn said.

Hurriedly, she tore it open, pulled the handwritten note out and glanced at it.

My dear Mercy,
Come home.
    Or you leave me no choice but to tell your uncle the truth about Rocco.
Empyrean

Her heart twisted, her eyes stinging at the words. Anger built like a pressure wave behind her sternum.

There was no end to his manipulation. To his schemes.

Shawn opened the rear door. "What's it going to be?"

Her breath stalled in her lungs. She wanted to run. She wanted to fight. She wanted to rip the second note to shreds. She wanted to strangle Shawn with her bare hands, preventing him from uttering a word since she wasn't sure how much he knew.

But her father always had a fail-safe.

"Decide. Now." Shawn held up the other envelope, waving it in her face.

Crumbling her note in her hand, she climbed into the car before she lost the nerve to do so. The only thing stronger than her rage was her fear for Rocco.

Precisely what her father had been counting on. As much as she wanted to deny her feelings for Rocco, there was no escaping how much she cared for him.

Shawn closed the door and stuffed the other envelope back in his pocket.

Cormac and Rocco approached them.

She rolled down the window. "I've decided to go back to the compound."

Looking as blindsided as she felt, Rocco shook his head. "What? No."

"Marshall radioed earlier saying he was sending someone up and to keep it a surprise," her uncle said, "but he didn't mention who or for what purpose."

"Empyrean fears for the safety of his daughter," Shawn said. "He got a bad feeling during morning meditation and decided to bring her back for tonight's ceremony."

"Is it safe for her there?" her uncle asked. "I heard about what Alex did to her."

"My father locked him up." But that didn't mean she'd be safe.

"It's for one night. She'll be well protected." Shawn got back inside the SUV. "Rocco, you're welcome to get her tomorrow. Empyrean believed you'd be inclined to stay behind."

He had no choice but to. Her uncle still hadn't told him what the planned target was for the attack. Cormac had decided to wait until they were on the road.

The thought occurred to her that the only reason her father would extend the invitation to Rocco was because he didn't expect him to be able to act on it. Her father didn't think he'd survive.

"Mercy, get out of the car." Rocco grabbed the door handle as Shawn engaged the locks with a *click*.

"I have to go," she said.

"Sure this is what you want, nugget?"

She glanced at her uncle. "I'm positive."

"What's happening?" Rocco reached inside, taking her hand. "What did your father do? Get out and let's speak privately."

His frantic eyes bore into her, their gazes fused.

"She's not leaving the vehicle," Shawn said.

She slipped the crumpled note into his palm, closing his fingers around it. "This is for the best. There's no way around it."

A sick, helpless feeling welled in the pit of her stomach. She was stuck. Staying meant Rocco would be exposed and surely killed. But by leaving, he'd have no one to watch his back.

Had her father foreseen something? Were his visions even real? Or was it all one big con—the puppet master pulling more strings?

A true headache began to pulse in her temples.

"Say goodbye," Shawn said.

Cormac patted Rocco on the back. "I'll give you a minute."

"Whatever the problem is, we can solve it together," Rocco said. "Just get out of the car. You don't have to do this."

"Yes, I do. Believe me." She wouldn't let anything happen to him. Not because of her. "You have to let me go. *Please*."

Shawn revved the engine.

Rocco leaned in through the window for a slow, thorough

kiss that left her tingling all over, and her heart about to split in two. "I'll come for you," he said.

"I know you will." And that was what worried her because her father would assume the same and take steps to prevent it.

He kissed her forehead, his lips lingering and the warmth of his exhalation caressing her skin.

In that moment, with her uncle not watching and Shawn averting his gaze, she took the cell phone from her sweater, reached over, and slipped it into the front pocket of his jeans. "Be safe. Stay alive."

"I love you, Mercy."

Shawn hit the gas, speeding off, tearing them apart before she could respond. Not that she was sure what to say. He rolled up her window and raced through the gate.

She turned around and looked through the rear windshield. Rocco stood there, looking achingly gorgeous. Formidable.

A heavy, burning weight settled in her chest.

He wasn't even out of sight yet, and she missed him already. Being in his arms, with her head on his shoulder, her face pressed to the crook of his neck felt right.

Meant to be.

As if all the times she'd gone into town, looking for something to change, for something that was uniquely hers, for something to spark in her heart, she'd been searching for him.

Not simply a man. Not someone like him, but Rocco.

She hated her father for wanting to take this away from her.

Shawn keyed a radio. "Empyrean. Come in."

A strange fear crept over her.

"Do you have Mercy?" her father asked, making her temples throb and her breath grow shallow.

"I do."

A tingling sensation spread through her arms down to her fingers. Her heart raced, each beat pounding through her.

"Good. Hurry home."

Facing forward, she tried to swallow the bitter dread rising in her throat at what her father had planned for her at the compound.

The sense of impending doom wormed through her veins, tightening in her chest, blurring her vision.

What was happening to her? Was it another anxiety attack? It was nothing like her allergic reaction, but she still felt like she was dying.

Panic washed over her in a cold, blistering wave, and all she could do was roll down the window, letting the fresh air rush over her, close her eyes and pray.

Chapter Seventeen

Two hours.

Mercy had been gone only two hours, and it felt like a lifetime.

Rocco was split down the middle, a war raging inside his heart as he rode in one of the trucks. He would've done anything to stop her from leaving…if he didn't have a job to do. If lives weren't hanging in the balance.

After reading the note, he understood. Her father's trap. Her choice to save him.

Fury was a noose strangling him.

Any minute, she'd be back at the compound, if she wasn't there already. What was going to happen to her then?

The uncertainty had unease slithering through his veins.

At least Alex would be locked up, unable to hurt her again.

He tightened his grip on the AK-47 in his hands. He'd been given the weapon along with a bulletproof vest that would protect the Brotherhood from shots fired by law enforcement. But it wouldn't protect Rocco from their armor-piercing rounds.

Their vehicle hit a pothole, jostling them. They'd left about thirty minutes after Mercy and were almost out of the mountains. He was in the back seat of the lead truck—the black dually that had run Dr. Percy Tiggs off the road. Rocco was sitting beside Barry—a man who smelled like he'd been sleeping outdoors for one too many nights without a shower. Mac was in the passenger's seat and behind the wheel, in front of Rocco, was Dennis.

Although Rocco had an assault rifle, the two up front also carried backup 9 mms while Barry had a Calico M950 sub-machine gun slung over his right shoulder and a bowie knife holstered on his left hip.

Rocco gave a furtive glance down at the knife on Barry's hip beside him. "I heard about how you two took care of a federal informant."

"Sure did," Dennis said with a nod. "Barry shot him, and I ran him off the road."

"That's what I'm talking about." Rocco patted Barry's shoulder. "Wish I had been given the chance to do the same to the ATF agent who wormed his way into the compound."

"Don't worry. That one might've gotten away, but you're about to have a much sweeter opportunity."

"So, where are we headed?" Rocco asked. "The not know-ing is driving me nuts."

"All right. You've earned the right to know." Mac drummed his fingers on the dashboard. "We are going to hit the main headquarters for the ATF," he said, and Barry howled. "Fed-eral building in the capital. If we're lucky we might take out some secret service, too."

Rocco's gut clenched.

Not only was the ATF and secret service in that federal building, but the US district court as well. The building was made of reinforced concrete, spanned almost two acres, and had guards. It wasn't a quick and simple target, but it was teeming with people. More than two hundred federal employ-ees worked inside, and countless civilians passed by there every day.

"That's a big, fortified site, isn't it?" Rocco asked. "Maybe we should pick a smaller target. Easy pickings, you know. Molotov cocktails won't do much there."

"Don't get your panties in a bunch." The horse guy gave his arm a playful punch, and Dennis laughed.

"I've got an inside person working in the building," Mac said. "Security guard who has been there about a year. We've worked it out. He's going to pull the fire alarm once I give him the signal. As everybody pours out of the building, milling around, we'll strike. The site is large, taking up an entire square block. That's why we've got four vehicles to cover all the exits. I promised you blood in the streets and I always keep my word."

MARSHALL STOOD IN the foyer as Shawn hauled his daughter inside the house. Mercy glared at him, seething and silent. They both removed their shoes, and Shawn brought her up to him.

Clasping his hands behind his back, Marshall gave her a sympathetic smile.

She looked ready to spit in his face, but then schooled her features. Standing with a sense of grace and decorum that belied her anger, she now appeared so composed, so poised that he might have believed this was any other day.

Except that her hands trembled ever so slightly.

"We will speak later, my dear, and all will be made clear," he said to her. Marshall looked at Shawn. "Take her up to her room. Lock her inside." He handed him the padlock and key.

She thought she hated him, but his work wasn't finished yet. After this was all said and done, what she was feeling now would only scratch the surface.

Marshall watched them ascend the stairs and returned to

his office. He'd broken her heart, wounded her deeply in his actions. This did not please him. He found no joy in her pain.

Now that Mercy was safe under his roof and locked away in her room, Marshall picked up the radio. Once Rocco was dead and she had no one else to turn to on the outside, she would finally fall into line. Take her vows.

The commune, this family, would help her heal. The memory of Rocco would fade in time.

And she would find true happiness in the Light.

If she never forgave Marshall for what he was about to do, so be it. Defining relationships and responding to them with exactly what was needed was one of his greatest skills. He would make the same choice again, sacrificing her love for him, to save her soul from darkness.

But Rocco had to die for this to work.

Everything Marshall was doing was necessary. This was his responsibility as father. As prophet. As Empyrean.

Heavy is the head that wears the crown.

STARING OUT THE window at the trees rushing by, Rocco struggled to come up with a way out of this. To his left was an escarpment, a slope falling at least two hundred feet. No guardrail, only a precipitous drop with trees along this stretch of road. To his right was the rocky, equally steep mountainside.

A bad place to ask them to pull over so he could answer nature's call.

In a few more minutes, they'd pass Wayward Bluffs and clear the mountains. Just before they hit the interstate, he'd get them to make a pit stop. Blame it on nerves or a weak bladder. Anything to give him a chance to get a message to Nash so he could warn the folks at the federal building.

The radio up front squawked. "Mac. Are you there?" Marshall's anxious voice crackled over the static.

Rocco's heart squeezed, a flurry of worries whirling in his head.

Was Mercy okay? Had something happened to her?

He met Mac's gaze in the rearview mirror, a thought suddenly niggling his mind. What if Marshall wasn't calling about Mercy?

What if it was about him?

Only a blind fool would think her father incapable of a double cross. But if things kicked off in the cabin of the truck it would not bode well for Rocco. All he had was a long assault rifle. Trying to fire it in a confined space that required close-quarters combat would prove disastrous.

Not to mention there were three more trucks of heavily armed men right behind them.

Mercy's uncle grabbed the radio from the dash and hit the button on the side. "I'm here, Marsh. Go ahead."

"I just found out. I'm in shock, ashamed, at having been fooled," Marshall said in a rush. "But we've all been deceived."

A prickle of warning crawled up Rocco's neck. He tensed, his muscles coiling with readiness.

"What on earth?" Mac leaned forward, hunching over the radio. "Deceived about what?"

"Not what, my brother, but by *who*. Rocco is an undercover ATF agent. I trust you to handle it as you see fit."

Rocco's chest constricted, his adrenaline kicking into high gear.

Nanoseconds bled together. Everything happened in slow motion. Barry turned for him. At the same time, Rocco raised the AK-47 and slammed the butt of the rifle into the man's face.

Bone crunched. Blood gushed.

Mac was in motion, shifting in his seat.

Rocco swung the buttstock ninety degrees. Smashed it forward between the front seats against the side of Mac's head, sending his skull crashing into the window.

The truck swerved as Dennis reached for a weapon. Rocco ignored him. Only the other two men mattered at the moment.

With his right hand, Rocco snatched the bowie knife from Barry's holster. He rotated his elbow up and jammed the blade back into the man's throat.

A wet gurgling came from Barry.

Rocco yanked the knife free. Barry's hand, now gripping the wound, was so coated in blood it seemed as though he had slipped on a crimson glove.

Almost too late, he caught sight of Mac grabbing a 9 mm. *Almost.* Rocco pounced forward. A bullet rifled by him—close enough that he felt the heat at the side of his neck—shattering the rear windshield. He thrust the bowie knife into flesh, sinking the sharp blade into Mac's wrist.

The 9 mm clattered to the footwell.

Rocco grabbed the strap of his seat belt, wrapping the webbing around his left arm. Lunging up, he pressed the button on the buckle for Dennis, releasing the driver's safety belt. He punched Dennis in the temple with a hammer fist, using the fleshy side part of his clenched hand.

Then he grabbed the steering wheel and yanked it hard, pitching them off the road and down the steep hillside.

His heart whipped up into his throat. His stomach dropped. The saliva dried in his mouth. Bracing, he tightened his grip on the seat belt webbing that locked in place.

A string of curses flew from Mac's mouth. The man tried to wrangle the steering wheel with his one good hand, but it was no use. The truck was out of control.

The heavy dually whooshed down the slope. Angry metal chewed through brush, barreling over shrubs. Nausea welled in Rocco. A burst of fear slicing through him was razor sharp.

Fear that he would fail to stop the other men from launching the attack. That he wouldn't keep his promise to get Mercy out of the compound.

The groan of steel crunching and rending filled his ears when the passenger's side of the truck wrapped around a tree, bringing them to a bone-jarring halt. The sudden impact had him lurching forward, but the safety belt he clung to jerked tight, snapping him back against the seat.

His brain felt like it had been caught in a blender. His stomach in a knot. His left shoulder ached from the force of the impact.

Clearing his head, he gained his bearings.

Barry was dead, bled out beside him. Mac was unconscious with a deployed airbag in his face.

But Dennis was gone. His body had been thrown from the vehicle, out through the windshield.

Rocco looked around. Found the Calico submachine gun and the 9 mm Mac had dropped in the footwell. He grabbed both.

He pulled on the handle of his door. It stuck. He had to kick it open.

Glancing back at Mac, he ached to put a bullet in him, sending his soul straight to hell. He had to remind himself that he wasn't a vigilante doling out his own brand of justice.

Self-defense was one thing, but taking the life of an unconscious man wasn't how he operated. Not now. Not ever.

He shoved out of the truck. The air was dank and thick with the smell of gasoline from the shattered Molotov cocktails that had been in the back. But there were plenty more in the other trucks.

Shouts and hollering came from the hillside above. Voices and footfalls were moving downhill. Mac's men were racing to help him. They were drawing nearer. Getting close. Too darned close, way too fast.

On a surge of adrenaline, he cut through the trees, moving laterally, away from the crash. He stuffed the 9 mm in the back of his waistband and kept hold of the submachine gun.

His heart hammered. With each frantic, hurried step he took, he cursed Marshall McCoy and the depth of his betrayal.

Once he made it several yards west, he veered north. Going uphill. Circling back toward the vehicles that had stopped to help.

Branches slapped his face. He climbed upward. Shoving off trees for leverage. He licked his lips in desperation. *Faster.* He needed to move faster. Sweat ran down his spine. His shoulder hurt like hell. The air was thin, and his lungs were on fire.

Hurry, hurry!

He scrabbled up the hillside. Running. Trying to stay low in the trees, to keep his footsteps stealthy as he hurried. Determination propelled him forward.

Drawing close to the road above him, he stopped and strained to listen. At first there was only the pounding of his heartbeat like a drum in his ears. He swiped at the moisture in his eyes and drew in a long, calming breath.

There.

The scuffle of boots on asphalt. Two voices.

Concentrate. Focus. He needed to be sure.

A third person coughed. There were three men. One had probably stayed behind with each truck.

He crept up higher to a tree just off the road and rolled

across the back of the trunk, taking a position where he could see them. Standing at an angle, his bladed body presenting a narrower target, he peeked out.

They were farther back on the road. All three men were peering over the edge, their focus on the wreckage down the hill.

Rocco had gauged correctly and was only a few feet from the front bumper of the first truck. But he'd never make it to the door, much less inside the vehicle before they spotted him.

A bullet bit into the tree trunk near his head, forcing him to duck. The gunfire had come from downhill. Some of the guys must have tracked him.

He rolled out from behind the tree, taking aim at the men on the road as he rose onto a knee.

A quick squeeze on the hairpin trigger. Four bullets popped off with a *rat-a-tat-tat*.

Two men dropped, screaming and clutching their thighs. The third one managed to sidestep out of sight.

Rocco aimed for the tires of the second truck. Fired a shot, flattening the front tire. He did the same with the third vehicle. Squeezing off more rounds to force the third guy to stay concealed, he bolted for the driver's side door and hopped in the truck.

In their haste to help Cormac, they'd left the keys in the ignition with the engine running. He threw the gear in Drive and sped off.

Gunshots rang out behind him. He prayed none would hit any of the explosives in the back.

Pop! Pop!

The rear windshield exploded. Rocco flinched, lowering his head. Flooring the gas, he took the bend in the road as fast as he dared.

He flicked a glance in the rearview mirror. All clear. But

he didn't ease off the accelerator. He pulled the cell phone from his pocket, turned it on, and waited for it to power up.

As soon as he got a signal, he called Nash Garner and told him everything.

Chapter Eighteen

The padlock outside her bedroom door rattled. The shackle clicked, unhinging and metal clanged as the lock was removed from the hasp.

Wearing the same clothes that she'd arrived in, blue jeans, a T-shirt and gray sweater, Mercy stood. She steeled herself to face her father.

No matter what he said, she was done with the Shining Light. She was leaving after Rocco's mission. Today. As one of the fallen.

She'd deal with the implications to her soul once she was free of Empyrean.

The door swung open, and Alex stepped inside.

Her heart clutched.

He shut it behind him, bent down and shoved a door stop tight under the lip.

Mercy's blood turned to ice. In the time it would take for her to remove the wedge and open the door to get out, she would be at a distinct disadvantage, and he would be on top of her. "Why aren't you locked up?"

Alex pressed a palm to the door and leaned against it. His eyes had a weird, glassy look to them. "I atoned and father released me," he said, his words slurring. Like he was drunk. Or high.

Which was odd. Alex didn't drink and he didn't do drugs. He only did ayahuasca once for his shedding ceremony.

"How did you get the key to get in here?"

He grinned. "I have my ways."

Alex must have coerced Shawn to give him the key.

Biting her lip, she forced herself not to panic. "What's wrong with you?"

He chuckled. "There are so many things, I don't know where to start."

Alex was on something. But why?

"When you look at me, what do you see?" he asked. "Be honest."

A pathetic, petty, green-eyed... "A monster."

He gave a sad laugh that tugged at her heartstrings, despite telling herself not to care about him. "You'll never marry me, will you? Not after the chili."

Trying to kill her was the point of no return. Not what put her off as a potential partner. He was delusional. Deranged.

Squeezing her eyes shut for the span of a breath, she hoped he didn't have a gun tucked at the small of his back with plans to put a bullet in her head.

"Why would you want to marry me when you know I don't love you?" she asked.

"Because I love you enough for both of us. I'd do anything for you."

She looked at him. "Even let me go?"

Smirking, he wagged a finger. "True love requires conviction." He shoved off the door and stalked toward her.

"True love requires compassion. Kindness. Neither of which you showed me when you tried to kill me." She stood her ground, clenching her hands into fists.

He grasped a handful of her hair, gently, and put the strands to his nose. Inhaled deeply. "I always thought we'd save ourselves for our wedding night. But then you gave away your purity to that man. I feel cheated."

Her skin crawled.

"How about you give me a taste of what you gave him, huh?" He leaned in to kiss her.

She wasn't a violent person. She wasn't even a fighter. But Rocco had taught her that raw, desperate fury in a strong body should never be discounted.

Because it was powerful.

Mercy rammed her knee up into his unprotected groin. She felt the softness there and knew she'd made contact when he cried out and hunched over. But she didn't stop. She shoved him away.

He staggered back, trying to recover. As soon as he straightened, she punched his chest, striking the spot Rocco called the solar plexus. He'd told her when you got the blow right it caused momentary paralysis of the diaphragm, making it difficult to breathe.

The force of the punch, or more likely the shock, knocked Alex off his feet. His back hit the floor and he flailed like he was being electrocuted. Gasping and thrashing, he rolled onto his side. His face was wrenched in agony.

She never wanted anyone to suffer. Her instinct was to help him. But she ran to the door. Pulled out the wedge and tossed it to the side.

"Wait," he wheezed, gasping for breath, looking weak and pained. "Help. Me."

Mercy stared at him. Frozen. Unsure what to do.

He rolled onto his hands and knees. Bloody spots bloomed on the back of his gray shirt.

Her feet were moving before she thought to act. She grabbed his outstretched hand and got him up onto her bed. Helping him was a force of habit.

He lay down on his side, curling up in a ball.

"What happened to you?" she asked.

He unbuttoned his shirt and showed her his back that was covered in gauze soaked with blood. "Flagellation."

"You took something strong for the pain?"

With those glazed eyes, he nodded.

"Alex, I have to leave. I can't stay here any longer."

Tears fell from his eyes. "I know. Because of me."

This was so much bigger than him. "I was never meant to be a Starlight." She let his hand go and inched away to the door.

"Do you remember my favorite book?" he asked, stopping her. "When we were younger."

How could she ever forget. "*Frankenstein* by Mary Shelley. You read it ten times."

"Everyone thinks the Creature is the monster. He was just misunderstood. And lonely. But Victor Frankenstein, the one who made the Creature—he was the real monster. Why doesn't anyone see it?" A sob broke through him, and he cried. "I've become a monster, too. But I'm what our father made me. I only did to you what he did to Ayanna. And yet, his princess still loves him."

"What?" She went to his side and lowered to her knees.

"The allergic reaction."

"He put peanuts in my mother's food?"

Alex nodded. "I watched him do it. He didn't know I was there in the kitchen. He even made sure the doctor was close by to save her. That's how I got the idea."

A hot flash of rage tangled with the sorrow rising in her chest. "How could I be so blind to who he is?"

"He worked very hard to blind you. And I helped him do it."

She was on her feet, headed for the door.

"Mercy. Please," he begged, "don't leave me. I need you!"

With hot tears welling in her eyes, she flew out the door. Ran down the steps. Grabbed her shoes. Reached for the handle of the front door.

A squawk from a radio made her still.

"Marsh, pick up." Her uncle Cormac's voice carried through the house.

She spun around and crept down the hall toward her father's office.

"Pick. Up," Cormac demanded.

Passing the mural of the Shining Light's symbol on the wall, she looked around for any guards. There were none lurking.

"I know you can hear me, Marsh. Pick up, you son of a—"

Static cut through the line. "I'm here, Mac," her father said. "Did you take care of our little problem?"

She stopped outside his office and peered in through the open door.

Her father strode to a window with the radio in his hand.

"You didn't tell me everything," Mac said.

"What do you mean? Of course, I did."

"Rocco is more than an ATF agent."

Her heart seized. Mac knew the truth. Rocco was in danger.

"Was he Special Forces?" Cormac asked "SWAT? What the hell is he? A former assassin?"

"I have no idea." Her father sounded confused, overwhelmed, two things he never was. "I told you everything I know as soon as I learned it," he said, and she tipped her head back against the onslaught of pain at yet another of her father's betrayals. "Does this mean he got away?"

"Yeah, he got away. He's more slippery than a prairie rattlesnake. Deadlier, too. He killed two of my guys. Wounded me and two others before he escaped."

Praise be. Relief flooded her. She thanked the Light.

"It was a mistake to hesitate," her father said. "You should've dealt with him immediately."

"The mistake was yours, sending an undercover agent into my camp." Her uncle's anger radiated over the wireless.

"I'm sure there are things you'd like to further *discuss* with him. His task force has an office here in town." Her father gave him an address on Second Street. "Ground floor. Perhaps this time more preparedness is required."

How did he know where their office was located? Did he have Nash and Becca followed after they left?

"We'll take care of Rocco," Cormac promised. "Then we're coming to the compound for you and Mercy."

She tensed, thinking about the hundreds of innocent Starlights that had nothing to do with this.

"As I've stated, I only just learned the truth. Mercy was devastated to hear her intended was a deceitful Fed." The radio chirped. "Mac?" Her father pressed the button on the radio several times. "Cormac?"

"What have you done?" Mercy asked, storming into his office.

Her father spun on his heels. "My dear, what are you doing out of your room, scurrying around the halls, like a rat?"

"You disgust me. How could you betray Rocco after I came back like you wanted?"

He set the radio down. "If that man lives, you will leave again. But if he dies—"

"I would hate you forever."

"A price I'm willing to pay, so long as you stay where you belong."

Mercy shook her head in disbelief. "You made an agreement in good faith with Agents Garner and Hammond and Rocco."

"I signed no papers. Gave no oaths. My only obligation is to this commune and the Shining Light."

"To the Light?" Mercy barked a harsh laugh. "All you know is darkness. You knew what Cormac was planning all along. Didn't you?"

"Not the specifics. That would make me culpable. My hands are clean regarding anything the Brotherhood does."

Her stomach pulled into a tight, hard knot. "Naturally, you'd want plausible deniability, but you were aware that people were going to die today as a result of whatever he was going to do and you had no intention of stopping it."

"I am not my brother's keeper." Sighing, he half sat, half leaned on the edge of his desk. "Besides, why would I stop it? Every time there is chaos and death in the streets our numbers increase. Your uncle has gotten far more active in the last five years and the number of my followers have grown tremendously as a result. I welcome his actions. He is doing me a service."

Everything her father was saying made her furious and queasy at the same time. "I once believed in you and what you preached. Then you tried to kill my mother and forced her to leave me behind. That's when it all changed for me." She studied his face, looking for a drop of remorse. Waited for him to explain, even though it would only be more lies.

Clasping his hands, he nodded, slowly, soberly. "Alex let you out and told you. If he can't have your love, I suppose he doesn't want me to either."

"Aren't you even going to deny it?"

"Would you believe me if I tried?" He stood and moved toward her, but she backed away. "This reminds me of that part in the *Wizard of Oz* when Dorothy sees behind the curtain."

The Great Empyrean was smoke and mirrors. A fraud.

"How could you do that my mother?" she asked. "To me? Separate us like that."

"I did what was necessary. Even though it was hard. To protect you."

"You've never protected me. All you've ever done is manipulate and coerce me to follow your will. Now you want to kill Rocco. Why? Because you think he's going to take me away? Because he loves me?" Saying the words, she felt them to be true.

Rocco did love her. He'd been nothing but compassionate, kind and caring. And she loved him, too. She'd sacrifice anything to keep him safe. Even her own happiness. In her heart, she believed he'd do the same for her.

Mercy stared at her father. A mix of anger and anguish filled her heaving chest. "You're *evil*."

"Evil? No, no, my dear." The great Empyrean threw his arms out to his sides with flourish. He approached her with an air of dignity and grace as though he were more than a man walking on water, but she stayed out of his reach because she now saw the truth. "I am no more evil than a hurricane, an earthquake, fire or flood. All serve a purpose that is not easily understood. Underwriters classify those as acts of God."

She reared back. "You are not *vis major*. To even insinuate such a thing only goes to show how polluted your soul has become. He was right about you," she said, thinking of Alex. "You're the real monster. I was just too naive to see it."

"Mercy, everything I've done has been to keep you safe."

"Stop saying that. Everything you've done has been to protect your power and your status. Not me." She wrapped her fingers around the Shining Light necklace that she wore and yanked it off. "I'm done. With you. And this place." She tossed the pendant at his feet.

"Rocco might not survive. If he doesn't, you'll need us."

His tone was gentle and coaxing, sickening her. "You'll need me. Stay the night, my dear. Wait to see what happens before you decide."

She steeled her spine. "My mother left this place with nothing but the clothes on her back and she made it without you. So will I."

"I put you on a pedestal, ensured you were revered above all but me. And the thanks you give me is to throw it away because you want to roll around in the muck and mire with that pig." He narrowed his eyes, his composure slipping away like a discarded mask. "If you leave like this, you will be considered one of the fallen. Banished from the Light. Shunned for the rest of your days."

Her throat closed. She was leaving the only home she'd ever known. People she loved. Everything that was familiar. A movement she had once had complete faith in.

But she had to get far away from Alex. And from the suffocating hold of Marshall McCoy.

"Just like my mother," she said and headed to the door. At the threshold, a whisper of warning made her look back at him. "If you do anything to prevent me from leaving, pull some stunt, I will tell any acolyte willing to listen who you really are. The devil. And they'll believe every word from my mouth. Let me go and I wash my hands of you and the commune in every way."

He was quiet for a moment, thinking, plotting, ever scheming. "You'll say nothing of the things you've overheard?"

Disappointment seared through her. They were talking about her life, her safety, and he was bargaining for his reputation. "No. Not a word."

Even if she did, her father had a remarkable knack for wiggling out of trouble. None of Cormac's despicable deeds would stick to him.

"You may doubt me, but I love you and have only worked for your highest good. If you're certain you wish to leave… so shall it be." He picked up the phone and pressed a button. "Mercy is on her way down to the gate. She is not to be given a ride, but you are to let her out. Then we're going on lockdown. No one else in or out of the compound. Security is to be tripled. A credible threat has been made against us." He pressed down on the receiver and then dialed a number, three digits. After a moment, he said, "I'd like to report a potential attack on the office of a federal task force on Second Street."

That was just like her father. Covering his bases. Protecting himself above everyone else.

Mercy rushed to the front door and put on her shoes. She ran down the steps and the hill. Her lungs opened and it was as if a massive weight had lifted from her, but Rocco and the task force were still in danger.

The guard spotted her. He waved. The front gate swung open.

"I need to use the phone," she said, breathless, and pointed to the one in the guardhouse.

"I was only told to let you out."

"My father said I wasn't to be given a ride. He said nothing about me using the phone."

Uncertainty crossed his face, but he stepped aside. "Hit nine for an outside line."

She moved past him and picked up the phone. After she pressed nine, she realized she knew just one phone number and dialed it.

"Hello, this is the Underground Self-Defense school. How can I help you?"

"Charlie," Mercy said, her pulse pounding. "Rocco, Brian, the entire task force is in danger." She hoped her father had called the police, but she knew better than to trust him.

"Slow down. Where are you?"

"Outside the gates of the compound. I'm heading to town. On foot."

"I'll come get you."

"First, you have to help them. They need to evacuate the office on Second Street. Call the police. And the sheriff." Was there time to mobilize the national guard? "The state police, too. Let them know that the Brotherhood of the Silver Light is on the way. They're radical, dangerous and heavily armed with guns and explosives."

Chapter Nineteen

Finally, back in town, Rocco sped down the road up to the meeting spot. Nash had called him back with an update. The FBI's CIRG—Critical Incident Response Group—were mobilizing to raid Cormac's camp and seize the cache of weapons. SWAT had secured the federal building in Cheyenne and authorities were searching for Cormac's insider. But their target had changed. The Brotherhood planned to launch an attack in town.

Now the Laramie PD, sheriff's department and state highway patrol were gathered at Cottonwood Park, conferring on how to handle the Brotherhood. Rocco had expected Cormac to alter his plan, but he hadn't counted on him waging war in town.

He pulled up to the park. Wearing a bulletproof vest, Brian waved him past two officers standing by police cruisers.

Rocco stopped near a long row of law-enforcement vehicles and got out.

Brian was looking through the arsenal loaded in the back. "Two more trucks like this are coming?"

"Yeah, and they won't be far behind. Fifteen, maybe twenty minutes."

"They're finalizing the plan now," Brian said, hiking his chin at the huddle of law-enforcement officers. "All the businesses in our section of Second Street have been evacuated. Thanks to Mercy, we had a good idea of what to expect."

"Where is she?" The words grated painfully against his throat. If she was still trapped on that compound and had only managed to get out a message, he was going to lose it. There'd be no way for him to focus on the task at hand—putting a stop to the Brotherhood.

"Rocco!"

The sound of Mercy's voice had him spinning around. The sight of her running to him burrowed into an empty place in his heart, filling it with warmth.

She flew into his outstretched arms or he into hers. All he knew was that he was holding her tight.

"Don't ever leave me like that." He kissed the crown of her head and squeezed her tighter. "Don't leave me at all."

"Think you're stuck with me," she said between quick, shallow breaths.

That was fine by him. "I love you so much."

"Love you, too."

He put her down and stared into those blue, blue eyes. "Say that again."

She pressed a palm to his cheek. "I love you, Rocco. I was afraid of how I felt, of whether to trust your feelings for me, but not anymore. I'm out of the movement. Done with my father."

With his fingers, he brushed the hollow of her throat where the Shining Light pendant used to rest. He was pleased she'd taken it off and relieved she'd finally gotten free of her father.

"Sorry to break up this reunion," Nash said, standing with several others who had been watching them. "But we've got domestic terrorists to stop."

Rocco looked over the group: Sheriff Daniel Clark, Chief of Police Willa Nelson, Becca, Charlie, Chief Deputy Holden

Powell and his brother, state trooper Monty Powell. They had quite the audience.

"I flattened a couple of their tires," Rocco said, "but it won't take them long to change them."

"We've got highway patrol on the lookout for them. The plan is to trap Cormac McCoy and his men on Second Street, where it's clear of civilians," Nash said. "We've put out the warning for folks to get inside, stay off the streets, and we're positioning some plainclothes officers. We'll funnel them in, helping them get to where they think they want to go. Then we'll block off Second Street with LPD on one end and the sheriff's department on the other."

A solid plan. They had to be smart about this. No room for mistakes. With the Brotherhood using armor-piercing bullets they couldn't approach this situation as they might under normal circumstances.

"What about us?" Rocco asked.

"You, me, Brian and the state troopers will take positions on the rooftops. Everyone is aware that they're using armor-piercing ammo. If they open fire, we shoot to kill."

IN A DPO—discontinued post office—the task force had previously requisitioned as a backup headquarters, Mercy stood beside the chair Charlie sat in. She was too nervous to sit. Becca was seated across the table along with an LPD officer.

The DPO was located on a side street that intersected Second, right around the corner from the task force's primary office. Mercy stared at the three law-enforcement vehicles, including an armored tank, parked outside, positioned at the ready to block off Second Street once the Brotherhood had entered the trap.

"They're here, just got off Highway 130," a patrol officer said over the radio that was on the table. "Four men inside each vehicle along with four more sitting in the truck beds, holding assault rifles. Sixteen gunmen total. Both vehicles are now turning onto Snowy Range Road."

"So far, they're taking the route we expected," Becca said, her gaze bouncing between Mercy and Charlie. "We've also closed off certain streets to prevent a detour."

Mercy wrung her hands, trying not to worry, but it was impossible.

"It's going to be okay," Charlie said low to her. "They've got this. None of the good guys out there will let any civilians get hurt."

But what about the good guys getting hurt?

"They just turned onto Second," the trooper said. "Ten blocks away. Looks like a ghost town with no one on the street. So far they don't seem suspicious. Still headed in your direction. Going the speed limit. Nine blocks."

Fear coursed through Mercy, her mind racing. Rocco had to be all right. Brian, Nash, all the officers who were putting their lives on the line to protect the town needed to be safe.

They just had to be.

"Seven blocks," the patrol officer said. "Six. They're stopping at a red light. I'm hanging back."

The authorities were armed and well-trained, but their tactical gear wouldn't protect them. Not from armor-piercing rounds that would tear through their vests like a hot knife through butter. At least officers on the ground had a tank to hide behind.

But those positioned on the rooftops would be partially exposed.

"Five." The tension in the patrol officer's voice vibrated through her. "Four."

"We've got a visual," Nash said. "Got them in our sights."

Seconds crawled by. With each one, Mercy forced herself to take deep, steady breaths and not panic. It wouldn't do anyone any good, least of all Rocco.

"Three blocks…two…you're a go."

The vehicles outside, with the armored tank leading the way, sped into position.

Mercy ran to the window and looked down the street. She could see where the officers stopped, blocking off that end of Second Street. But then her stress skyrocketed with the next sound.

The assault kicked off without warning.

A single shot became a raging torrent of gunfire faster than the ear could comprehend. Automatic weapons spit out a barrage of bullets.

She hated not knowing what was happening. The only thing certain was that this was risky. Dangerous for anyone going up against her uncle and his people.

"Officer down," someone said over the radio.

Terror rushed over Mercy now in a hot, stifling wave. It took every ounce of willpower for her to stay put. Who had been shot?

"Would they use the term 'officer' to refer to any law-enforcement person?" Mercy asked.

With a grim expression, Becca nodded. "Yes, they would."

Her first thought was Rocco. Lying in a prone position on the roof, if he got hit, it would be to the head. Was he okay?

Pacing in front of the window, she interlaced her fingers and prayed. To the Light. To the universe. To any higher power that would hear and answer, to let everyone make it through.

"Another officer down," a female voice said. "Officer down."

Ka-BOOM!

An explosion thundered, making Mercy jump as she

looked outside. It was deafening. A tower of flames, smoke and debris shot up into the air past the clearance of the two-story building.

"Oh, no." The words slipped from her lips as every muscle tensed.

There were two more gunshots. Then nothing.

Mercy released the breath she'd been holding and opened her eyes when the gunfire stopped.

It was quiet.

With guns raised, the officers she could see down the street moved from behind their vehicles and rushed down the street out of view.

Was it over?

Who was hurt? Or worse, who had been killed?

The fear and adrenaline rubbed her nerves raw.

"We need an ambulance," someone said over the radio. "Deputy Holden Powell was shot in the shoulder. He's going to be okay. But Officer Tyson…he didn't make it."

No, no, no.

Mercy covered her mouth with her hand. She'd never met Officer Tyson, but he was someone's son, possibly a brother or husband. There were people who loved him, who'd miss him. Who would grieve his death.

"We've got Cormac McCoy and two of his men in custody," Nash said. "The rest are dead."

So many senseless deaths. And for what?

In the distance, Mercy heard the wail of the ambulance that had been on standby. Since it was coming from just three blocks over, it wouldn't take long to get there.

Rocco rounded the corner. Alive and unharmed. Headed her way, taking those long, powerful strides. Relief thrust her breath from her lungs in a long sigh even though she already knew he hadn't been injured. Seeing him made it real.

He'd done it—he and this team made sure that the Brotherhood wouldn't hurt anyone else ever again.

Four days later

ROCCO COULDN'T BELIEVE his good fortune. He had one month of use or lose vacation days that Nash had ordered him to take after they wrapped up the case with the Brotherhood of the Silver Light.

During the FBI's CIRG raid on Cormac's camp, all members of the Brotherhood were arrested and taken into custody without any injury to law enforcement. The weapons were seized.

Unfortunately, the task force couldn't make any charges stick to Marshall McCoy. His lawyer used the call he'd made to 911 reporting Cormac's intention to help his client slither out of trouble. Rocco wanted Alex arrested for the attempted murder of Mercy, but the district attorney was only willing to go with aggravated assault. When the task force went to arrest Alex, he'd conveniently disappeared.

Rocco suspected it had been through the tunnel in the basement. As long as Alex was on the run, out of town, Rocco would take it as a win.

"I'm glad you're on vacation," Mercy said with a smile as they put away equipment inside the Underground Self-Defense school. She wore simple workout clothes, but looked like a knockout in the pink tank top and navy leggings that clung to her sensational curves.

"Me, too." He had decided to spend the time with the woman who'd captured his heart. They were going to fix up his ranch and create a business plan for Mercy to open a holistic wellness shop, selling candles, soap, bath oils, crystals, legal medicinal herbs and honey. Buying a bee apiary was a feasible and affordable way to start. Bees first. Horses down the line. Putting the idea of opening a shop into action would probably take a year, after scrimping and saving, but he thought it was essential for her to have an actionable plan she was excited about to focus on during her transition. "But somehow working at USD doesn't feel like a vacation."

Mercy chuckled as she bopped to the beat of the music playing—a pop song on the radio. "You're a good cousin. Charlie works too much. She needs this down time with Brian."

Yes, she did. The woman didn't understand what a lazy day was, but Brian would show her.

"And you're a good girlfriend for helping me."

"I need something constructive to do until my job at Delgado's as a waitress starts," she said. "Besides, spending the time with you is no hardship."

Even though she had the keys to Charlie's place, where she could stay whenever she wanted time to herself since Brian and Charlie were officially cohabitating, so far, Mercy had been spending the nights at his ranch.

He was grateful for every second he got to be with her and couldn't wait for his parents to meet her. They were flying in for Mercy's surprise birthday party next month.

Rocco had the works planned. A live DJ booked, a custom cake and a special guest of honor. Mercy's mother, Ayanna.

The two had connected thanks to Becca tracking down her mom. Reuniting had been healing, transformative for both women. But they hadn't seen each other yet in an environment that was carefree and all about having fun.

He desperately wanted to give Mercy that gift if it was in his power.

Along with his coworkers, the sheriff's department, the LPD and local state troopers were invited to the party. Pretty much half of the town was coming. Mercy might not have the commune, but Rocco was doing everything he could to give her a family. Not one based on vows to the Shining Light, but stronger and more reliable because it was rooted in goodness, basic values and it was comprised of people who all believed in service and self-sacrifice.

He ached to share the details with her, and this was the toughest good secret he'd ever kept.

"I'll dump the trash and load these dirty towels into the car for us to drop off at the cleaners, then we'll lock up and go," he said.

"Okay, I'll shut down the computer."

He grabbed the trash with one hand and the laundry with the other and headed for the back door.

BITING HER LOWER LIP, Mercy watched Rocco walk away and thought about all the things she wanted to do to him later in bed. And what she wanted him to do to her. Experimenting and exploring had been fun. But last night, he'd held her, with no clothes between them, their gazes locked, and time seemed to halt. They stared into each other's eyes, connecting on a level of intimacy that made her heart expand, swelling impossibly big as a balloon in her chest. It was the way he looked at her. Like he wanted her to see his soul, what she meant to him, how much that physical moment affected him.

She wanted lots more of that, too.

A shiver of anticipation ran through her. She shut off the lights in the private training rooms and danced her way to the office, happy to help out. Escaping the jaws of her father's lies and machinations had required more grit and determination than she could have ever imagined. No way could she have done it without Rocco and Charlie. Their support had been unwavering.

She owed them both more than she could ever repay.

Grabbing her purse, she slung it over her head across her body. It was strange having a handbag. But a good kind of strange like everything else she'd tried.

The cherry-red purse and small matching wallet were thoughtful gifts from Charlie, sustainable and vegan. She'd never had one before since there hadn't been a need. But now she had things to carry around. A state-issued ID. Soon a license, since she was learning how to drive. Money—though it was given and not yet earned. In time a bank card. Lip gloss. A cell phone. And Rocco's gift, a SIG Sauer P220 pistol.

She turned off the computer and the radio. Stepping around the desk to hit the lights, she froze.

Alex stood inside USD in front of the office. Her gaze fell to the gun in his hand. Her heart nosedived. His eyes burned with a white-hot rage that sent a different kind of shiver up her spine.

Then a calmness stole over her. Mercy had never been afraid to die. She believed in an afterlife and a paradise for good souls. Even if it wasn't as her father had described, deep down a part of her was still invested in that idea.

But she wasn't ready. Not yet.

She'd barely had Rocco, a chance at this new life. She was just getting started. "Alex—"

The back door to USD slammed closed.

Rocco.

Alex lifted a finger and pressed it to his lips.

Heavy footfalls came down the hall, Rocco's boots thudding with each step. That was when a bolt of fear flashed through. Fear for him.

Tears burned at the back of her eyes. She loved Rocco. *Loved* him. And she couldn't let Alex hurt him.

Rocco came around the corner, the smile slipping from his mouth, and stopped cold.

"I want you to watch her die," Alex said, with his back to Rocco, staring at her. "I want you to feel the pain that I feel."

Rocco crept forward, heel to toe, slow and silent.

"Take another step and I'll shoot her in the face." Alex slid his finger to the trigger. "No open casket."

Rocco halted. "But you don't want to kill her. You want her to suffer. You want her to be alone. So, shoot me instead. In front of her. Make her watch me die, slowly, bleeding out and she'll never forget that agony. She'll never dare to fall in love again."

His words gutted her. Because they were true.

To lose Rocco was unimaginable. But in such a horrific way would be unbearable.

Something in her chest cracked and tears welled in her eyes. Alex saw it. That Rocco was right.

He pivoted on his heel, pointing the gun at Rocco.

Adrenaline surged in Mercy. She opened the flap of her handbag.

"Do you want to know why she doesn't love you?" Rocco asked, stalling.

She shoved her hand inside the purse, closing her fingers around the cool grip of steel.

"Why?" Alex asked.

Pulling the SIG out, she flicked off the safety and took aim at Alex's chest, the way he'd taught her, center mass.

"Because," Rocco said, and she put her finger on the trigger, "you're a weak, simpering coward."

She fired. Blood splattered. She pulled the trigger, again and again until Alex collapsed to the floor.

Rocco ran to her, kicking the gun from Alex's hand along the way. He gripped her shoulders and steered her backward, around the desk and down into the chair. She didn't realize she was shaking until he pried the gun from her hand and put it on the desk.

He picked up the phone, dialed 911 and reported it. As soon as he was done, he knelt in front of her. "It's going to be okay." He took her hands in his and kissed her fingers. "It's over. He's dead. He'll never hurt you again."

She looked down at him. "I'm sorry."

"No, honey. Alex had it coming. There is nothing for you to be sorry for."

Alex had shown her that it was kill or be killed. "I don't regret shooting him to protect you. I'm sorry for endangering you."

"What?" He wrapped his arms around her and held her.

The hug lasted, seconds, minutes, she couldn't tell. But she soaked in his warmth until she stopped shivering.

Rocco pulled back and cupped her face in his hands. "Alex endangered me because he was insane and obsessed with you."

"Exactly. If you had never met me—"

"You've got it all wrong, honey." He kissed the words from her lips. Her heart beat faster. Not in fear, but at the sheer beauty of how his touch made her feel like being with him was where she belonged. The tears that had been brimming in her eyes fell. But they were tears of relief and love.

She loved him. He loved her. And they'd do anything for each other.

"Meeting you was the best thing to ever happen to me," he said, caressing her cheek and wiping away her tears. "You saved me. Not just by shooting him. But by forgiving me. By loving me." He brought his face to hers until their foreheads touched, and she was lost in the warmth in his eyes. "You saved me in more ways than one."

She thought about her father, the years of his insidious

control, and the movement—the cult she'd finally escaped because of Rocco. "I guess we saved each other."

"We did and every day I get to spend with you is worth any danger." He pulled her into another tight hug as a siren wailed, drawing closer.

She sank against him, grateful to be with him, free from her past. They had been through so many trials and had both come so close to dying to get to this point, but she truly didn't have any regrets. She wanted this life, building a future, in love, and safe in his arms, where she belonged.

* * * * *

COMING SOON!

We really hope you enjoyed reading this book. If you're looking for more romance be sure to head to the shops when new books are available on

Thursday 14th September

To see which titles are coming soon, please visit

millsandboon.co.uk/nextmonth

MILLS & BOON

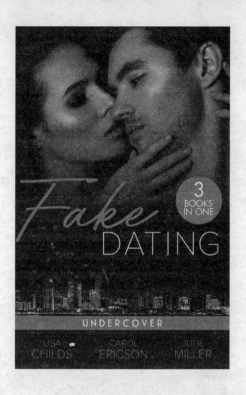

LET'S TALK
Romance

For exclusive extracts, competitions and special offers, find us online:

f MillsandBoon

🐦 @MillsandBoon

📷 @MillsandBoonUK

♪ @MillsandBoonUK

Get in touch on 01413 063 232